SALT OF THE KING

MUSIC, MADNESS, AND ENERGY LINES IN A SMALL TEXAS TOWN

HENRY D. TERRELL

This book is a work of fiction. Names, characters, businesses, organizations, places, events, and incidents are either a product of the author's imagination or are used fictitiously. Any resemblance to actual persons, living or dead, events, or locales is entirely coincidental.

Published by River Grove Books
Austin, TX
www.rivergrovebooks.com

Distributed by River Grove Books

Design and composition by Henry D. Terrell
Chapter heading art: © www.gograph.com / Floss
Cover design by Greenleaf Book Group
Cover images used under license from
©Shutterstock.com/Inspiring; ©Shutterstock.com/Harvepino;
©Shutterstock.com/kovalto1; ©Shutterstock.com/Pierre Leclerc
Author photo: Sarah S. Terrell

Publisher's Cataloging-in-Publication data is available.

Print ISBN: 978-1-63299-508-7

eBook ISBN: 978-1-63299-509-4

First Edition

For my sons Edwin and Sean, musicians

PROLOGUE

November 1907, Ferris County, Texas

"Errors, Mr. Finn," said Malloch. "Errors do not fade away or correct themselves. Even the least of them can persist, unseen, and compound with other errors, until the numbers we depend upon are useless."

"Colonel, if the chains are true, then the survey will be true," said Finn. "The men are good—the very best, I think—as are the instruments."

Old Malloch raised his field glasses, tipped back his hat, scanned the desert horizon, then turned southwest to spot the rodmen, six chain lengths distant on a low rise near the dry wash, nearly 400 feet. This was the best survey crew that could be hired in this lost world. He was lucky to have found them, especially the master surveyor, Abraham Finn.

"I trust you and your men," said Malloch, "but chains can stretch. An error of one link—just eight inches—could put us off by fifty feet, and then a hundred. We must be *methodical.*" He gazed through the glasses, watching the rodmen raise the flag. "Errors . . . errors . . ." he muttered under his breath. Though Hamish Malloch had lived in this country for over fifty of his seventy-two years, there was still a trace of Scotland in the way he said his Rs.

Despite Malloch's insistence on perfect accuracy, the survey team had to work quickly. They were already two days beyond their planned schedule, and the crew and mule team were costing money. They had established the target latitude some days ago, and remeasured and reverified the figures until the colonel had confidence in the numbers. But the meridian was trickier. A slight anomaly in the magnetic compass could prove critical, so Malloch insisted that they use three of them and average their readings. In the end, everything would be compared against sextant and chronometer, as if they were at sea.

Finn turned his attention back to the transit mounted on its heavy tripod, lining up the distant rod through the scope, taking measurements, then scribbling numbers in his field notebook. The colonel left the surveyor alone so he could concentrate on his task.

Malloch walked back to the camp, half a dozen canvas tents and four wagons parked beside the salt lake a quarter mile distant. The West Texas sun was warm. despite the late-fall season. For the first time in years, his old war wound bothered him. He wondered if it were a sign that he was nearing his goal. In the past, when his wound troubled him, he took it to mean he was approaching some important crossroads in his life. He'd felt it the day he had met his wife, decades ago, and also the night she died, ten years past. He reached beneath his shirt and rubbed the scar on the front of his shoulder where the feeling had never quite returned.

Though he had served in the Union Army during the great struggle, Malloch had never held the rank of colonel—that was a term commonly used these days for older men of status. Forty years earlier, Corporal Hamish Malloch had ridden with the Seventh Ohio Cavalry during the bloody Knoxville campaign. One evening, his patrol got into a skirmish with a small band of rebel pickets. One of them had fired a retreating shot that dropped Hamish off his horse. The pistol ball struck him under the pit of his arm and tore through the flesh, lodging beneath his shoulder blade.

An army surgeon had extracted the bullet as two orderlies restrained Malloch, moaning and biting hard on a leather harness. If the bullet had struck his shoulder, they would have taken his whole arm. But since it was deep in his back, all the surgeon could do was remove the bullet, clean and bandage the wound, ply him with a bitter opium tincture, and wait for him to grow feverish and die.

However, Malloch did not die, and after his close brush with the next world, he vowed to use his extra years to accomplish worthwhile things. Such as what he was doing today.

When he reached the wagons, Malloch asked a mule tender to tack up one of the saddle mules. He wanted to explore this flat, arid country, ride and clear his head, and stay out of the way of the surveyors. Today, he hoped, they would find their mark.

The colonel mounted and rode west. As the day grew warmer, he covered many miles, crossing the white flat bed of a dry part of the lake. The salt let nothing grow out here, even right beside the water's edge, but the far side of the lake was hillier and less barren, and a few scrubby plants—mainly soaptree and skunkbush—struggled to survive in the saline soil.

He found a dry wash, one of a braid of streams that fed the lake irregularly during wetter years. He rode down into the sandy gulley and followed the wash for a few miles, riding between its steep banks. In time, he found a way out and rode northeast, circling around the lake. Even from this great distance, he spotted many of the flags the surveyors had left in their slow progress across the sections of land. The lake attracted a few flocks of birds that fed on the hardy crustaceans in the shallow, salty water, but there were no other animals visible. Coyote, deer, and wild cattle would not drink from the lake.

Early in the afternoon, Malloch stopped beside a rocky outcrop and sat in its shade while he ate a few hard biscuits and drank some brandy water. (He always spiked his water with brandy, which he believed strengthened the blood.) This lost land could not be more unlike the Scotland of his childhood, the misty hills of Perthshire, but the gray, weathered rocks seemed familiar, hard and flinty, some of them poking from the earth with their strata vertical, as if they had been upended and placed there for a purpose. Near his hometown of Crieff, there were many such rocky cairns, some of them twice the height of a man. These had been studied closely by antiquities scholars, but no one knew who, if anyone, had placed them. The older locals believed the cairns held great significance and built their farmhouses, churches, and graveyards in alignment with the mysterious trackways that often seemed to connect the stones.

Refreshed, Malloch remounted and rode north again in the direction of the survey camp. It was five o'clock by his pocket watch when he came upon a wide, low outcropping of smooth gray stone, weathered like a mountaintop, sixty feet across and rising only a few feet above the desert floor. He dismounted from the mule and climbed the rock. The air seemed unusually clear, and Malloch spotted Finn and the crew five hundred yards away. They had wound the chains and pitched the tents. Nearby fluttered a red flag on a twenty-foot pole. This was the central marker. Finn apparently believed he had found the intersection.

Malloch's pulse quickened, and an odd tingling bothered his neck. He reached under his jacket to rub the scar again. Nearby, the mule twitched and stamped, restless. Despite the long shadows of the approaching evening, the landscape was bright and distinct.

Malloch climbed down off the rocky prominence, remounted, and rode down to meet the crew. As he approached the camp, Finn spotted him and waved.

"Colonel, I think we have accomplished our job," he called. "We're awaiting your approval. If you agree with my calculations, then we can declare the job finished."

"I shall have a look at your numbers," said Malloch.

In the largest tent, which served as the survey office, Finn had set out his field books on the folding table, along with the Thacher calculator, a delicate and costly device. The Thacher was a large cylindrical instrument three feet long, with numbered wheels on each side connected by fifteen parallel rules etched with finely engraved lines and numbers. It functioned like a slide rule, but the multiple rods gave it an effective length of 360 inches and an accuracy of 1 in 10,000. It was an extremely precise machine and difficult to master. Malloch had the practice and skill to use it, as did Finn and his assistant, Taylor. To everyone else on the crew, it was mysterious as a crystal ball.

Malloch removed his hat and jacket and stood over the table, studying Finn's calculations. He rotated the Thacher slowly, moving the markers and jotting a few notes in the margins of the field book as he checked and rechecked Finn's numbers. Outside the tent, the sixteen members of the crew—chainmen, flagmen, runners, and mule tenders—all waited in anticipation. No one spoke.

After a few minutes, Malloch said simply, "Mr. Finn, I believe your numbers are true." The two men emerged into the bright sunlight and shook hands, and Malloch then shook each man's hand in turn. "Thank you, gentlemen," he said. "You have done a great thing."

"Colonel, may we serve the men whisky, then?" asked Finn.

"Indeed, and I will be the first to offer a toast," said Malloch.

Bottles were opened and drinks poured all round. When he had his glass of rye in hand, the colonel raised it to the crew and then to the red marker flag that fluttered in the evening breeze. He recited a ditty his father had taught him sixty years ago:

"And now we're met upon the square, may love and friendship jointly reign. May peace and harmony be our care, and ne'er be broke the adamantine chain."

"Here, here!" shouted Finn.

"Here, here!" echoed several of the men and lifted their glasses, though among the crew, only Finn knew the meaning of the toast.

The cook prepared the evening fire for dinner, while the men worked at packing away the surveying equipment. The Thacher instrument was carefully returned to its velvet-lined and padded box and placed in a wagon.

Later, in the long Autumn twilight and after the dinner of johnnycake, beans, and beef, a north wind rose. The red flag flapped sharply. The men built the fire high, since they no longer had to conserve fuel, and huddled in their heavy coats, glad the job was done. In the morning, they'd be starting back to Duro, where they'd return the dray mules and saddle mules to the livery, crate up the surveying gear, collect their pay, and return to Huntsville on the eastbound train.

One of the crew had a four-string banjo and strummed a popular song, "You Been a Good Ol' Wagon, but You Done Broke Down." Several men joined in, and when that song was done, they sang others, old and new. Later, some of the Mexican crewmen sang in Spanish, and the other men tried to sing along on the choruses. Everyone was in very fine spirits.

Malloch retired to his tent, exhausted. Despite his weariness, he lay awake a long time. In the back of his mind, he was uncomfortable with the day's result. He was not satisfied with where they had placed their marker flag, but he couldn't say why. He went over the numbers again and again in his head. Finn's calculations were as right as they could possibly be, but Malloch's gut told him something was amiss. Eventually, after the men turned in and the camp quieted down, he slept.

In his dream, Hamish Malloch was back in the fields of his childhood. He stood on the slope of a hill, which he recognized as one near Crieff. He knew he was dreaming, but the gray stones and dark green hills looked real. A wet mist lay in the vales between the hills, and above him shone a feeble white sun, which he could look straight at without discomfort.

A little way below the summit of the round hill was a pair of tall weathered stones, each one higher than a man, set a few paces apart. He had seen the stones many times in his wanderings as a youth. But in this dream, there was something different: A stone lintel lay across their tops, connecting them, and on the lintel, a beam of dim light shone straight down from the clouds. On one side of the lintel, letters were carved.

Hamish climbed the hill so he could read the words:

AND THE DEAD SHALL BE RAISED

Far away, on another hill, miles distant, a second shaft of light appeared. And far, far away in a straight line, there was a still more distant hill, upon which a third shaft of light fell.

Malloch woke. The wind was still, the camp silent except for muffled snores from a few men. He sat up and put on his boots, then pulled on his overcoat without buttoning it. He retrieved the brass carbide lamp from the small table, dropped a couple of lucifer matches into his pocket, and stepped outside the tent.

The air was cold and clear, and the moon very bright, high in the sky, and near full. The landscape was stark and colorless but clearly illuminated. The carbide lamp was not needed, so he returned it to the tent.

He could see the landscape around him for miles. He walked up to the marker flag, now hanging motionless. Looking all around him, he thought, *This is not the right place.*

Malloch walked, careful not to catch his foot on stones or cactus. He wasn't worried about rattlesnakes, because it was so cool the vipers would be curled under rocks and in burrows. When he had walked a few dozen yards beyond the camp, something caught his eye. In the distance, he saw the rocky prominence he had ridden over in the afternoon, appearing dark against the desert sand, and the clumps of cactus and thistle. Something that had not been apparent in the bright sunlight now showed clearly in the ghostly white light of the moon: a line, or trackway, emerged from the base of the rock and came toward him straight as a rifle shot. He stepped aside a few yards, and the line disappeared, and the land once again became moonlit desert. He returned to the trackway, turning this way and that. It was not his imagination or an accidental desert feature. Behind him, the track stretched off into the distance to the northwest, over a low rise of land, but before him, it went straight for several hundred yards to the flat rock, as if it were the trace of an old, abandoned road. Why had he not seen this before?

He walked and walked along the track, stepping carefully around short, thorny plants, until he reached the rock. He climbed up and stood on its broad top. From this vantage in the moonlight, he could see another trackway, at an angle of perhaps thirty degrees, which crossed the first from southwest to northeast. He stood a long time, gazing at the unreal landscape.

This is the place, he thought.

Though he had been trained as an engineer, Malloch wished his father could be here with his copper dowsing rods. Old Kinnon Malloch had been a practitioner of the divining arts, using the rods to find the best locations for houses and water wells and the proper sites for burials. And though Hamish Malloch had always rejected dowsing as superstitious nonsense, at this moment, in this wasted country, he sensed that the rods would tell him he was standing at a powerful, important crossing, regardless of what the survey instruments indicated.

In the near distance, a coyote, roused by moonlight, howled a long, mournful, rising note, and Malloch shivered. He buttoned his overcoat. A second howl, from the opposite direction and farther away, rose to answer the first, and then a third, even farther. They sounded to him like souls crying in purgatory. He became aware once more of his old wound—a steady, dull throb—and thought of his own mortality.

He stepped off the rock and started back to camp, his body casting a sharp shadow on the rocks and sand. The coyotes kept up their competing howls for several minutes, then abruptly stopped.

He had come to a decision. No matter what his chief surveyor might say, in the morning, Malloch would insist on a change. They would move the flag.

CHAPTER 1

JJ and Harold Need Space

They drove slowly down Sherman Boulevard, watching for those rare buildings that might have street numbers printed on them somewhere, above the doors or on a side wall. In this dilapidated part of Duro, Texas, most property owners didn't bother with addresses. If people needed anything out here, they probably knew where they were going.

Harold was driving a Vega notchback, the cheapest thing he could rent. The car was stodgy and underpowered, with the smallest, least-useful trunk he had ever seen. Fortunately, he and JJ hadn't brought musical instruments, just two overnight bags and a quarter-inch reel of recording tape with a demo of the new song.

As they drove south, the address numbers became more sporadic as they descended to zero. After the road dipped under the interstate highway, the numbers rose again until they eventually reached five digits—11200, 12000, 15100—the buildings farther and farther between, without a trace of Best Studios.

They passed a cheerful but faded billboard with a cactus, an oil derrick, and a cartoon cowboy:

LEAVING DURO

Y'all Come Back Soon!

They were outside the city limit, and the town had dwindled to nothing. No more street signs, only a road sign. State Highway 341.

"Okay, I give up," said Harold. "We definitely missed it." Harold pulled over to the shoulder and looked both ways. Not a vehicle to be seen in either direction. He U-turned, heading back to Duro.

"He said it was 18500 South Sherman," said JJ. "The last address we saw was that warehouse—13200. It's got to be after that, but there's nothing. Maybe the guy was crazy, or he doesn't remember his own address."

They drove back by a closed and decrepit convenience store that sat on the edge of civilization. Mesquite bushes on both sides of the wide road were decorated with decaying fragments of plastic bags. When they reached the interstate, Harold turned on the access road into a Pride filling station.

"I'm going to try calling him," said Harold. He shut off the engine and fished into his pocket for a dime.

"This whole thing is pissing me off," said JJ. "We can't even find the place. And we still have to get to a motel and check in."

JJ Johns and Harold Prensky were both originally from Colorado, and neither one had the least affinity for a place as flat and dry and hopeless as Duro. But World Famous Best Studios was here somewhere, and they had driven all the way down from Tulsa, Oklahoma, in search of an affordable studio to record their new project on sixteen tracks.

Harold got out of the car and walked over to a payphone on the side of the building. He pulled out his wallet, found a piece of paper with the phone number, dropped in a coin, and dialed.

JJ sat in the passenger seat and brooded. He hated this town already and had been here all of forty-five minutes. But this is where the studio was, a legendary place with a reputation for breakout records. A minor star named Rockin' Rick Watson had recorded his first chart single, "Bettie Said She Loves Me," at Best Studios back in 1962. A singer named Marla Robbins had scored that same year with a hit on the Gospel charts. The Cap Rockers had made their first album here in 1964. Roy Orbison supposedly recorded some demos around that time, though nobody knew what they were.

If the ad in *Wax Trax* magazine was telling the truth, recording costs were half what a professional sixteen-track studio in Tulsa would charge—and a freefall from the ridiculous rates in Nashville or Memphis.

It was a warm September day in 1972. The summer had been unrelentingly hot and dry, and the grass in the front yards was brown. Streaks of dust lay in the streets, and the occasional tumbleweed that found its way into town would roll across the wide, empty streets before catching on a fence or a stand of mesquite.

By this point in his career, JJ should have been living and playing and recording in LA or San Francisco, somewhere on the West Coast. In less than a year, he would be thirty, and then he might as well join the ranks of middle-grade journeymen musicians, thousands of them on both coasts and more in Nashville, chasing sessions, giving music lessons, working weekends in cover bands, hiding from creditors. His current situation was his own damn fault. It had been his decision to leave a successful band and go solo. If his luck was going to change, JJ needed to get a tune back on the charts and soon. He was counting on his old friend and producer Harold, a catchy new song, and a budget recording studio in a forgotten part of Texas to make it happen.

Harold returned to the car. "Believe it or not, we didn't go far enough. It's five-point-six miles after you cross the freeway. I heard it from the mouth of Allen Wallace himself. Let's go."

They headed south again. Harold watched the odometer, and beyond the city-limit sign, he took it up to seventy miles per hour, a real strain for the little rented Vega. At five miles on the ticker, he slowed down. They bumped over a railroad track and entered what appeared to be some sort of hamlet or maybe just a little more Duro. There was a gas station and a few other buildings, cars and trucks parked here and there, a highway intersection with a stop light. A small grocery store with a sun-bleached sign and unpaved parking lot appeared to be a neighborhood gathering spot. Women emerged from the store carrying groceries, while a few men lingered outside, talking and smoking. Three or four children pedaled around on bicycles. Harold and JJ didn't know it, but on state maps, the place was known, without irony, as Shady Farms.

One block farther, they came to a steel building with rusty double steel doors and the number 18500 painted on the side but no other signage.

Harold and JJ looked at each other. *Really?*

They pulled the car into the rough, unpaved parking lot in front of the building. From here, they could see a small paper note taped to the right-hand door: "BEST."

As they hesitated, the door opened, and a middle-aged white man emerged, squinting in the sunlight. He was skinny and wore suspenders over an open-collared white dress shirt. A porkpie hat sat on his boney, buzzcut head, and he squinted through thick horn-rim glasses. This was the famous—some say notorious—music producer Allen Wallace. He grinned broadly as he walked over to the car.

"Are you Mr. Prensky?" he asked.

"I am. Harold Prensky. You must be Mr. Wallace," said Harold. "And this is JJ Johns."

"Hi, JJ. I know you by reputation," said the producer. "Call me Allen. It's great to meet you guys at last. Before you get settled, could you do me a favor? Pull your car around behind the building. I like to keep everything on that side, away from the main street. I'll meet you at the back door." He turned and disappeared through the double doors.

At the back of the building, the parking lot was in better shape and appeared to have been recently leveled. A white mid-1960s Ford Galaxie was parked there. Beyond the parking lot, the desert stretched out into the distance, flat and barren, beige sand with white patches shimmering in the bright sunlight. Many miles away, low mesas rose from the horizon.

Behind the building, two large air conditioning units hummed away inside a rusty chain-link security cage. Concrete steps led up to a wide landing and a metal security door next to a large steel rollup. Harold shut off the car, and they both got out and waited. In a few moments, the security door opened, and Allen Wallace came out.

"Be sure and lock your car," said Wallace. "I'm glad you found me. I should have been more clear about the distance. You're not the first one to think they must have missed it and turned back."

"You are in the middle of nowhere," said Harold.

"Well, this place is far from town, but it's definitely somewhere. Come on up."

They had nothing with them but a recording tape and a change of clothes, but Harold locked the car. Against what threat, he wasn't sure. They climbed the steps into the square, utilitarian building. Wallace shut the security door hard behind them and locked it. It was dim inside this outer room and so cold it was bracing. Cardboard boxes were stacked against the walls, and there was a beat-up wooden desk missing one leg propped up by pieces of scrap lumber wedged beneath. On top of the desk was an old dusty reel-to-reel tape recorder with *Concertone* printed on the top, the brand name that TEAC once used for recorders sold in the United States. The machine was missing a couple of knobs.

"That's a classic," Harold remarked.

"The best 1952 had to offer," said Wallace. "Can't bring myself to get rid of it. Come on, I'll show you the studio." At the back of the outer room was another heavy door with a deadbolt lock. This led to a narrow, dim hallway and another door with a lock. As they passed through that one, Harold and JJ entered another world. Where the outer room had been dirty, dark, cluttered, and unkempt, the control room was orderly, scrubbed, and gleaming. The air inside the studio was even colder than the outer room.

"I know what you're probably thinking," said Allen. "The whole point of that first room is that if somebody breaks in and gets that far, they'll think they're in a nasty old warehouse and are wasting their time. I keep a low profile. I have thirty thousand dollars' worth of equipment in here. It's not like I get walk-in customers."

On a table of polished cherrywood, there was an enormous mixing board, with two large horizontal recording units positioned on either side.

Harold checked out the shiny new recorder on the left. "This is your main deck?"

"Yep," said Wallace. "Sixteen-track MM 1000. I've had it a few months. It still has a new-car smell and is almost a virgin. The other machine, the eight-track, is my workhorse. I've recorded a couple of radio commercials with the sixteen to break it in, but otherwise, it's waiting for somebody like *you.*"

Along one wall were shelves with dozens of boxes containing reels of one- and two-inch magnetic tape. Along the other wall were a couple dozen large hooks where coiled electronic cables of varying lengths and thicknesses were hung. Everything was neatly labeled.

Above the soundboard, there was a sloping glass window, but the room beyond was dark. On the left side of the room, there was another plate glass window, not sloped. It was dark on the other side of that one too.

"Here's where the hits get made," said Wallace, chuckling, and flipped a switch beside the desk. On the other side of the sloped glass, the recording studio lit up.

JJ and Harold exchanged glances. The room was tiny, even for a small studio. It was filled with microphone stands, moveable sound baffles, and, against one wall, an upright baby grand piano, turned so that the back faced the center of the room. Beyond the main recording area, there was another window and what appeared to be a small isolation booth.

"It's . . . really compact," said Harold. "How do you get a whole band in there?"

"We just put everybody tight and close," said Wallace. "I find that musicians play better when they're packed together like they're onstage at a small club. The microphones are good, so there's not much bleed-over. Anyway, these days, we do a lot of multitracking. Let's go in."

He opened the studio door and led them inside. Heavy industrial carpet was on the floor, and the walls and ceiling were covered with corrugated sound panels. On one wall, there was a door, barely four feet high, also covered in panels.

"Here, let me show you something," said Wallace. He shut the door to the control room, then walked over to an oversize switch on the wall labeled *FAN.* "Now, be as quiet as you can."

He threw the switch. The air conditioner, which had barely been noticeable anyway, went completely silent.

"I keep the air conditioner running day and night, except in really cold weather. It's for the equipment and the tapes. Now, listen." He put his fingers to his lips.

JJ breathed as quietly as he could. In a few seconds, he could hear his own heartbeat. Half a minute later, his ears began to ring faintly.

Wallace broke the silence. "If you sit in here long enough, it's amazing the sounds you hear. If you get a little high-pitched tone, that's air molecules bouncing off your eardrums. When we record, we turn off the fan and the fluorescent lights so we don't get a sixty-cycle hum."

"That *is* quiet," said JJ.

"I think it's the quietest recording studio in the US, if not the world," said Wallace. "Even when a train goes by, you can't hear it. Now, check this out." He walked over to the wall with the short door and opened it. Inside was pitch black and even colder than the studio. He stooped, reached around, and found another switch, and the room lit up. He stooped low and went through the door, and the two men followed. It had a smooth concrete floor, with walls and ceiling coated entirely with stucco. One wall had two rows of shelves with some more tape boxes, but otherwise, the room was bare. Wallace clapped, and the sharp sound reverberated for several seconds.

"Whoa," said JJ. "It's a real echo chamber. I didn't know these existed anymore."

"I probably have one of the last usable ones. Norman Petty's got one at his studio in Clovis, but he just uses it for storing old tapes these days. I have to confess I do the same thing with my most important recordings, but the echo is still authentic. Nowadays, everybody's using spring reverb or solid state, but I like natural echo. It sounds sweeter, and you get just as much control if you know what you're doing. Which I do."

Harold looked around. "So, if the door's shut, how does the singer even *see* the control room?"

"Oh, you don't put a singer in here," said Wallace. "Just speakers and microphones. It's a little cold for a singer anyway. That's just how the air vents are. The singers stand out in the recording room with everyone else. Nothing happens in here but music and echo." They stooped through the door back into the main studio.

"Do you guys want something to drink? I have Dr Pepper, and there may be a Tab," said Wallace. "I can also make a pot of coffee if you need to shake off the chill."

They both shook their heads.

"Then let's go in my office." He switched the air conditioner back on and led them out to the little hallway and through another door into a cramped room with a couple of chairs, a wide wooden desk, and a typewriter. A small refrigerator stood against one wall. On one side of the room was a threadbare cloth sofa with mismatched pillows and a red knitted kaftan. Running along the top of each wall, there was a row of signed publicity photos, mostly of people JJ and Harold had never heard of. Stars that had faded, or never really shined.

"I run a one-man shop," said Wallace. "I do all my own engineering, plus keep the books and pay the tax man. I've hired an assistant from time to time, but not in a couple of years. I can manage by myself."

Harold and JJ sat in chairs facing the main desk. They looked at each other, then Harold spoke. "I think we need to clear up something, Mr. Wallace."

"Please, call me Allen."

"Yes, well, Allen, when I talked to you on the phone, I said what we needed the most was space. Frankly, there are lots of little studios around Oklahoma that are too small for what we have planned. Some of them are bigger than this one."

"Bigger doesn't mean better," said Wallace.

"I get you," said Harold. "But we are thinking about ten, twelve musicians with all their gear. This is a project that needs room to spread out."

"I understand what you're saying," said Wallace. "My fault. I didn't show you Studio B."

"You have another studio?"

"Yeah, come on." Wallace led them back into the hallway and through a pair of double doors at one end.

They stepped into a large, dark space. Wallace flipped three switches inside the doors, revealing a bare warehouse area about forty feet wide by seventy-five feet long. The ceiling was at least twenty feet high, and the walls were cinder block, the metal ceiling beams exposed. Water pipes and electrical conduit ran overhead. Aside from a few cardboard boxes and a dozen standing sound baffles bunched together in a corner, it was mostly empty. On one wall, the lit-up control room showed through the window.

"You record in here?" said JJ.

"We do. Very successfully."

"What about the . . . sound? There's a lot of flat surface in here."

"We bring in sound baffles," said Wallace. "We move mics around to our hearts' content. This is opposite of the small studio. In this room, you don't want dead air. You want a big sound. You want a concert hall. Out here, I think of the room as one of the instruments."

Harold tried to imagine a really big setup, with singers, amplifiers, and stringed instruments.

"I don't know," he said. "We were thinking a couple of drum kits, timpani, violins, and double basses. I'm just not sure . . ."

"Let me tell you something," said Wallace. "Last summer I had over forty musicians in this room, plus tech people. We recorded a Christmas record. Fifteen members of the Duro Symphony, plus about twenty-five or thirty singers. You want timpani? We had two of them on that side of the room and other drums as well. It was beautiful. If you want to listen to it, I can play you the master. *Christmas at Broadmore Church.* It just went on sale in the record stores."

Harold and JJ were silent. Then Harold spoke. "Twenty dollars an hour?"

"Twenty dollars an hour," said Wallace. "No surprise expenses. I provide all mics, tape within reason, and engineering services, and I won't ever waste your time. You're not going to find a better deal."

"Well, we don't have another idea at the moment," said JJ.

Legendary music producer Allen Wallace led the two men back to his office. Just as Wallace turned off the lights and was closing the door to the big studio, JJ caught a glimpse of a small rodent skittering across the oil-stained floor. What had they themselves gotten into? He didn't mention it to Harold.

CHAPTER 2

In Grover's House, the Walls Are Strong

Holly Paulson wondered why they couldn't, just once in a while, take a Saturday off. Education was a very serious matter. It was true that regular schools in the world taught for longer hours in a typical day, but Holly's teaching methods were more efficient, she thought. Three hours of academic subjects in the morning, an hour for lunch, rest, and reflection, then three hours of religious study in the afternoon. There might be fewer hours in the school day, but Holly wasted no time on nonsense.

Still, why did Grover insist on Saturday school? By the end of the week, the kids—her own two plus Mary Lynne Costello's daughter Rachel—were worn out and grumpy, and Holly was exhausted. Sunday was a day of rest, but Holly still rose at 6:30 a.m. to prepare the family's breakfast and get the kids ready for worship, the first of three services they attended every week at Sacred Truth Pentecostal Holiness church. A day when she could sleep in, just one day a week, sounded like heaven.

Recently, Holly had thought up a good line of reasoning and had worked up the courage to approach her husband about it.

He was sitting in his favorite armchair reading one of his World War II books. Aside from building Christ's kingdom on Earth and hunting whitetail deer in the fall, the great war was one of the few subjects that interested him. Grover had served in the army from 1944 to 1947 as a truck mechanic, but he never left stateside, and he soothed his regret by studying the conflict in intimate detail.

It was 8:45 Tuesday evening, and the kids were in bed. Grover seemed in an agreeable mood, so she broached the subject. She knew better than to just interrupt his reading. She came into the den quietly and sat in the chair across from him. Rather than picking up her knitting or a book of her own, Holly simply sat facing him. This was the signal that she needed his attention. It sometimes took a few minutes.

After an interval, Grover spoke without looking up.

"Yes, Dear?"

"Darling, I had an idea about school I'd like to toss around, if you have a few moments," she said. "It's about Saturdays."

"What about Saturdays?" he asked.

"Well, you know the children work so hard every day, even little Rachel, and by Saturday, they all need a bit of a break."

"That's why God commanded us to rest on His day," said Grover. "I don't remember anywhere in the Bible where it says we should take any day off but the Sabbath. Two-day weekends were an invention of the world."

Holly had anticipated this line of argument and had a response. "Well, it's just that maybe we, I mean the kids, could sometimes do some other things on Saturdays besides just hit the books. They're children, and they need some other wholesome activities."

"Like what?"

"Like go see a family movie," said Holly. "Or go play in the park. A few weeks ago, Peter was invited to a birthday party. It was a good Christian family, but we wouldn't let him go. He was crushed. I think we need to lighten up a little bit."

Now Grover looked up. He placed his thumb in the book he was reading—*Beachhead at Okinawa*—and closed it partially. He sighed.

"You know very well why I said no to the party. I felt bad having to do that. It's not that the family isn't good and Christian. They may be. It's that I don't personally know them, and they don't attend our fellowship."

"Ben and Rita are good Christians," said Holly. "I've known them both for a couple of years."

"That may be true, but I still need to meet them first. That is a simple fact. I'm the head of the household, and it's my job to be this family's shield against the world. Do you understand my point?"

"Dear, it's just that . . ."

"Holly, listen to me please. It was a question. *Do* you understand my point?"

"Yes, sir," said Holly. "I do understand. I'm sorry." She knew how to talk to her husband and felt stupid to have forgotten a very simple rule: Always, *always*, answer Grover when he asks a question, no matter how rhetorical.

"Very good. Next time, give me some notice in advance, and I'll do what I need to do to make sure a household is acceptable before we send our children to visit." He picked up his book again, then put it back down. "And also . . . about movies. That's fine with me, but I need to know about it ahead of time so I can read a review in *Christian Family Magazine*—or at least *Reader's Digest*—so we can avoid the filth."

"We only go see the ones rated G. Like cartoons or Christian stories. There are wholesome movies that come out every year . . ."

"Well, yes," said Grover. "But even with so-called Christian films, I need to read something about them. So we won't have a repeat of that fiasco we had last spring."

The fiasco Grover referred to was a movie they had all gone to see as a family at the drive-in, taking along both of the younger kids, Peter and Martha, and even their oldest girl, Rebekah, who was home from college that weekend. The movie was called *The Emperor and the Cross,* the story of how Rome became the first Christian nation. It sounded completely safe. The theme was biblical, but the movie was pure Hollywood, with lots of swordplay and epic battles. Grover thought it was pretty good. At least until about halfway through the film.

In one unfortunate scene, the emperor Constantine soaked in his enormous gilded bath, attended by a half-dozen scantily-clad female servants whose wet garments clung to their nubile bodies. As the actor playing the emperor bathed his tanned and sculpted weight-lifter body, he brooded his way through a monolog:

"Why do these people, who say they follow the son of the Hebrew God, refuse to give up their heresy . . . even as my soldiers imprison their priests, burn their houses of worship, smash their crosses into splinters?"

Then the actor rose up in the bath and was revealed to be wearing only a tiny wet cloth across his obviously prominent manhood as water dripped down his chiseled legs. Two barely clothed women attendants toweled him off.

That was too much for Grover. If they had been in a regular theater, he would have made a very loud exit with his entire family, then sought out the manager to abuse him for his poor judgment at screening inappropriate filth. But since they were at the drive-in, all he could do was hang the speaker back on its hook, start the car, and drive away as the children protested, especially eleven-year-old Peter, who not only liked the battles but was enjoying the salacious bath scene. That must never happen again.

Holly knew she could press her case only so far. "I'd just like you to think about it," she said. "Children need time to play. And . . ." She hesitated. "I need a break from the books once in a while, too."

Grover looked up at her over his reading glasses and gave her a bemused look but didn't say anything. After a few moments, he returned to his book. It was a dismissal. Holly stood up to leave.

As she walked toward the door, Grover spoke again.

"Hey, come here," he said. She turned, and he was smiling softly at her. He put aside his book and patted his thigh, so she walked over and sat in his lap. Holly was a small person, and this was Grover's favorite affectionate gesture. He put his arm around her waist and leaned up to kiss her on the cheek.

"I will think about it," he said. "Maybe you're right. They're kids, and they do need to run in the sun. Just remember that outside these walls, the world is waiting in all its wickedness. But we'll discuss it later. Now, let me get back to my book. I need my breaks, too."

That was the best Holly could do for now. She thanked her husband and left to plan tomorrow night's supper. On Wednesdays, the evening meal was served early so the family had plenty of time to get ready for church.

But, just for a moment, she needed to rest. She sat in a chair at the kitchen table. She did not put her head down—that would be too much—but she closed her eyes and breathed slowly. How hard it all is. Supposedly, God never gives you more than you can bear, but Holly often felt this idea being tested. Being both a teacher and a housewife meant she could never leave work. She lived and ate and slept and taught in the same house, all the time. There were small breaks for shopping and church, but, otherwise, there was no escape. Grover had no idea how hard it was.

She let herself sit for a couple of minutes, then stood. There were still chores to do, but, first, she had to check on Peter. He'd been sleeping poorly since an accident one week ago, but he finally seemed to be turning the corner.

It had started with a simple head cold. The little boy was so stopped up he couldn't rest, and Holly, who didn't usually accept what the world called medicine, soaked some chopped-up wildflowers in water and poured the herbal concoction into a popcorn popper to serve as a vaporizer. It wasn't a great solution, but it did fill his bedroom with mild sinus-clearing vapors. Unfortunately, when Peter tried to pull himself up in bed, he had inadvertently grabbed the electrical cord, pulling the near-boiling liquid onto the bed and soaking his left foot in its thick sock.

As Peter screamed, Holly quickly picked him up and carried him to the bathtub, where she ran a stream of cold water over the sock and over his foot. After a couple of minutes, she peeled off the sock, taking a big swath of skin with it, as Peter shrieked in pain.

Holly figured this would qualify for an exception to the no-worldly-doctors rule, but Grover forbade it, so she did her best with herbal poultices, soft bandages, and ice. It was a bad night, when no one in the house slept, Peter alternatively dozing off for a few minutes and waking up to cry. The next day, when Grover was at the dealership, Holly went next door to a neighbor she barely knew, and the woman had given her a pain-relieving cream. It helped somewhat. She never told Grover.

Tonight, Holly quietly opened the door to Peter's bedroom and was reassured to hear his soft breathing. That was a relief.

She returned to the kitchen and checked the pantry. They had several number three cans of corned beef hash, number two cans of mixed vegetables, and instant rice. It would make a presentable dinner, not especially creative but on time. It was more important to get to church before seven o'clock and get a good seat up front. Grover never complained about canned food on Wednesdays. There was plenty of it in the pantry.

Grover had once known a Mormon man at the local Chevrolet dealership, a fellow sales manager. He couldn't help liking the guy. His Mormon friend was funny and smart and easy to work with. They had many spirited but civil discussions on their coffee breaks (other salesmen learned to avoid the coffee room whenever the subject drifted to religious doctrine). The fact that such an upright and moral family was doomed to eternity in Hell unless they found the True Christ caused Grover much private distress.

The two men agreed on very few spiritual matters, but Grover was impressed by the way the Mormons stockpiled food to prepare for the coming apocalypse. He told Holly to purchase cases and cases of canned meat and fish, as well as corn, peas, spinach, and green beans. The latter, especially, were vile—waxy and yellow, with an aftertaste of formaldehyde—but they could sustain life in a pinch.

If the world consumed itself in nuclear Armageddon, the Christians—both true and apostate—would still eat.

Holly cleaned the kitchen, the last chore of the day. As she scrubbed the side of the old stove, she caught a whiff of gas. She sighed. The pilot light in the cranky old oven had gone out again. Holly feared that someday she wouldn't notice the gas smell until it was too late, and then the whole family would go to meet Jesus in a natural gas holocaust.

That would be your fault, wouldn't it?

"Be quiet," she said. As she opened the oven door, a strong odor of gas wafted out. She picked up a couple of sections of newspaper from the kitchen table and fanned the oven to clear it out, then retrieved a kitchen match from the box on the shelf, knelt down, and struck the match against the inside of the oven. Relighting the pilot light took practice and nerve. You had to hold the burning match just the right distance from the lighting hole and keep holding it as the flame got closer and closer to your fingers.

Ouch! Pain seared through her thumb, and she dropped the match, which went out.

Try again. You can do this.

Holly lit a second match and held it close to the hole, watching the yellow flame creep close to her fingers. As she was about to give up and try a third time, there was a WHOOMP, and blue flame spouted from the hole and from the open seams around the side. The pilot was lit and would burn until the next time a gust from the back door snuffed it out again.

She rarely used the oven anyway. The thermostat was so inaccurate that the temperature could be off by fifty degrees one way or the other. Just like her mother and grandmother before her, Holly was a frying-pan cook.

The kitchen cleaned and ready for another day, Holly wondered if she should just go to bed. She was behind on lesson plans, but tonight, she was particularly tired. Sleep was never certain. Her mind was too busy with thoughts she couldn't control, and she could no longer pray in privacy. No, tonight it would be pajamas and bed and a book. Perhaps sleep would come. Grover would follow in his own time.

The sound of a car slowing down outside caught her attention. The Paulson house was right on the curve of a cul-de-sac, so they didn't get much traffic. Holly went into the living room and lifted the slat of a blind. A dark-colored Ford Fairlane was idling on the street just outside their driveway. Someone got out of the passenger side, and Holly heard talking. A suitcase was retrieved from the back seat.

"Thanks! See you in a few days!" said a girl's voice, and the car pulled away. The voice sounded like . . . could it be?

The girl walked into the light of the driveway vapor lamp. It was Rebekah, their oldest daughter. She was called Becky by everyone outside the family, but her parents would never allow even such an obvious nickname.

"Grover!" called Holly. "Rebekah's here! Oh, my goodness! I wonder what's going on. I hope everything's okay at school."

"I'm sorry," Grover yelled from the den. "I forgot to tell you. She called yesterday while you were at the grocery store. She said she was coming home for a few days." Grover came into the living room.

"I don't have her room ready!" said Holly. "I wish I had known."

"It slipped my mind," said Grover. "But Rebekah's a big girl and can make her own bed. She says she has some news for us but didn't say what. I don't think it's a bad thing."

There was a tiny tap at the door, and their daughter came in. She was at that transitional phase in leaving home where her instinct was to simply barge in, but she thought a little heads-up knock would be the right thing to do. Becky was twenty-two, ten years older than the next-oldest child, and had just begun her senior year at Central Texas Christian College.

"Hi, Mother!" said Becky. She set down her small suitcase and gave Holly a big hug. "I don't suppose y'all have some leftovers? We didn't have time to stop. I'm famished. Danfour has to get on home to McCauly tonight. He was really sweet to give me a ride, and it was out of his way. Poor guy still has another fifty miles to go."

"Oh, Baby!" said Holly. "I didn't know you were coming or I'd have saved you a plate. Just give me a minute. I'll whip something up."

"Please don't," said Becky. "I'll make a sandwich. Are Pete and Martha still up? How's Peter's foot?"

"The children are in bed like children should be at this hour," Grover said. "Peter's foot is healing nicely. But how about me? Do I get a kiss?"

"Of course, Father!" said Becky, and bounced over to him. Grover embraced her and picked her up off her feet, laughing. In just a few seconds, just like that, the house was more alive. Grover missed his little girl—his grown-up little girl—more than he admitted. There had been a lot of stress and raised voices during Becky's teenage years, but all that was behind them now.

"Let me put my stuff away," said Becky. "I have some news." She picked up her suitcase and headed for her old bedroom.

"I'll make the bed!" called Holly.

"Mother, really! I can take care of it later," Becky yelled from the bedroom. "Do y'all have some tuna fish? Or just some peanut butter and jelly?"

"I'll whip up some tuna spread," said Holly, and opened the refrigerator to retrieve the mayonnaise and pickle relish.

"Mother, please!" called Becky, but Holly could not be deterred. Whipping things up was something she did.

Becky put her suitcase on the chest of drawers and quickly unpacked her few things. She always unpacked wherever she went, even for a short stay. It was a family trait.

She heard a child's whisper behind her. "Bekah!" She turned to find little Martha standing in the doorway in her night gown. The nine-year-old beamed and hopped. "Bekah!"

Becky swept her little sister up and gave her a kiss on the forehead. "Hey, Pie," she said. "I know a little girl who's gonna get a whuppin' if she gets caught out of her room. Now, hurry back to bed. I'll see you tomorrow." Becky set her back down. Martha hugged her big sister around her thighs, then scurried back to her bedroom as quickly as she'd come, shutting the door quietly.

Becky found fresh sheets and a pillowcase to make the bed. By the time she emerged, a fat tuna fish sandwich and glass of iced tea were waiting on the kitchen table.

Grover and Holly sat with their daughter, while Becky ate and bubbled about college. Grover was pleased that his big girl seemed so happy—the subject of college had rent the family terribly for a solid year, back when Becky was getting her high school equivalency and applying to various institutions around the state. College was her first and greatest moment of defiance, but now, all was forgiven. Grover had to admit to himself she was probably right in choosing CenTex.

Their first big collision had come over the very idea of college. Grover thought that a degree was inappropriate and unnecessary for a female who wasn't formally schooled. Becky had only the barest acquaintance with public education before her parents pulled her out of school in the second grade. Her math and science skills were admittedly weak, and she had just squeaked through a practice SAT test. Then Becky had shocked them by seeking out and hiring a tutor to help with her deficiencies and paid for the tutor herself from her weekend job. She had nailed the real SAT that fall and applied to several colleges.

If she was going to go to college, Grover insisted that it had to be a strict religious institution, like Warner Bible College in South Carolina or Robert Brown University in Ohio, and then, only if they could secure a good scholarship.

To their horror, Becky showed no interest in the insular religious schools but sent applications to liberal arts universities across the South, even some that Grover considered completely off limits, like the University of Texas, which was awash in drugs and radicalism. Becky stood her ground, and sometimes, loud voices shook the house while the small children hid in their rooms. Holly mostly stayed out of it.

Before father and daughter reached a final breaking point, Becky received a full-ride scholarship to Central Texas Christian, and that settled it. The daughter apologized for being so hard-headed, her father worked really hard to be forgiving, and the two reconciled. CenTex was a Methodist college, which was a bit disturbing, but what could he do? It was fully paid for. Becky left Duro for Fort Worth in the fall of 1970. She studied communications, with a focus on film. She made the dean's list every semester. She made friends in the world.

As Becky ate her sandwich and rambled about life at the university, Grover wondered what she had up her sleeve. Something was afoot, and he feared a dramatic revelation was coming.

Not a boyfriend, thought Grover. *Please, not that. Not yet. Was it that boy in the car? Dan Something?*

Becky finished eating, dabbed her mouth with a napkin, and grinned.

"And now," she said. "I have something to . . . share. I'll be right back. Stay seated please." She got up and whisked into the bedroom. Grover and Holly exchanged concerned looks. In a moment, she returned with a brown envelope.

"Look at this," she said, removing an eight-by-ten photograph.

It was a picture of Becky, standing on a stage wearing a cute but conservative dress (and, to Grover's disgust, lipstick). With her was a bearded young man in a suit and ill-matching tie. They were holding a trophy between them and beaming to the photographer, while a few older men and women stood onstage with them and applauded. The gilded trophy was of a stylized, old-fashioned movie camera.

Holly examined the picture. "What?" she said. "When was this?"

"A week ago," said Becky. "That's me and my friend Danfour."

"Danforth?" asked Grover. "You've never mentioned him."

"Dan-*four*. It's what a lot of people call him. He's Dan the fourth in his family. And, yes, I have mentioned him. Y'all are just not famous for listening. He's the boy who worked on the film with me last semester. You remember the film, don't you?"

"That movie you were making about old people?" asked Holly.

Becky rolled her eyes and laughed. "Well, sure, if you want to put it that way. It was about the Seacrest Home in Benbrook. The state was going to shut it down, but the families of the old people got together and found some rich folks to invest in saving it and fixing it up. Is this ringing any bells? I told y'all the whole story. We went out to the place four times and got two hours of film interviews and somehow got it edited down to ten minutes."

"You said you weren't happy with the film," said Holly.

"Well, yeah, I wasn't, but Professor Bourne said we should submit it for a Dwight Award. So we did. And, get this, we . . . *won*."

"You won?"

"Yeah, Best Documentary Short Subject. I found out the first day of Film Writing class. They loved it."

"What is a Dwight Award?" asked Grover.

"It's a college film contest," said Becky. "Any college student in the country can submit a film for the Dwights. There were forty-some-odd entries for short subject. *Saving Seacrest* won first place. It's a really big deal."

"Oh, honey, we're so proud of you," said Holly. "That's wonderful! Can we see the film?"

"Sure you can," said Becky, "but you'll have to wait. Right now, they're taking all the winning entries from campus to campus and showcasing them. But, really, I'm still not that happy with it. We had to leave out some of the best interviews. That's not the main thing. There's something else, and it's big. Huge."

"Okay," said Grover. "Please, tell."

"Get this. The first-place winner in each category gets a grant to make another film. And guess how much? Just guess."

"Really, honey, I have no idea," said Holly.

Becky paused for drama and held up both hands as if she were conducting an orchestra. "The grant total for Short Subject is . . . one . . . thousand . . . dollars."

Grover whistled. "My goodness. That's . . . a lot. Seems like you could make ten films for that kind of money."

"Really, father, you have no idea how much these things cost. *Seacrest* would have cost that much just for film, except that the university has tons of leftover sixteen-millimeter from the government. If we shoot this on better film—maybe not color but better grain—and with good sound, it's going to take every penny."

"Wow," said Grover. "I'm just . . . wow."

"What's the new film going to be about?" asked Holly.

"I don't know . . . yet," said Becky. "But I do know I want to make it with Danfour, and I don't want it to be about old people. It should be something my friends would like. We're just going crazy with ideas. We talked about it for three hours in the car, the whole way here. I'm pretty sure I know what I'd like to do, but first, I have to talk Danfour into it. But I think it's a great idea. And it has to do with Duro."

Becky got up and rinsed off her plate, then put it in the dish drainer.

Grover chuckled. "I'm not sure there's anything in this town that would interest the youth of today. What would it be about?"

"Murder," said Becky.

"Murder?" said Grover. "You mean . . . a real—"

"Murder. Right here in Duro. At least everybody thinks it was a murder. They never found a body, and the crime was never solved," said Becky. "It's a story that's begging to be told."

She gave a little diabolical laugh, then disappeared into her childhood bedroom.

CHAPTER 3

The Ring of Power

Even though he was a year younger at thirteen, Ken outweighed his friend Carlo by twenty-five pounds, so when he sat on the back of the bike and they tried to climb a steep hill, the front of the little Honda Trail 50 kept flipping up so that the rear wheel would ride out from under them. The first time it happened, Carlo was really pissed off. They had ridden down one side of Two Fork Wash without trouble, and Carlo gunned the little engine hard to make it up the other bank.

"Lean forward!" Carlo yelled, and Ken did, but it didn't help. As they started to climb, their center of gravity was hopelessly high and far back, and the little motorcycle rose and pointed at the sky. Carlo had to let go to keep the bike from landing on top of him, and both boys fell on their butts in the soft sand. The bike flipped up and came down on its handlebars, then fell over and slid down the bank, engine still putt-putting away.

"Jesus Toad, Ken!"

Carlo had landed almost in Ken's lap. The bigger boy pushed him off, and they both got up brushing away the sand.

"It wasn't my fault, man!" said Ken.

"It was. It's 'cause you're so fat. You didn't lean forward."

"I did. You just gunned the engine too fast."

The boys climbed back on the Honda and tried again. Carlo putted down the wash about fifty feet to where the far bank was a little less steep.

"This time, *lean forward!*" yelled Carlo. He accelerated and turned the bike up the slope as Ken pushed his body forward as far as he could so he was practically digging his face into Carlo's back. The bike started up the bank and made it about half way before the wheel popped up once again.

"CRAP!" Carlo screamed, hitting the brakes and putting both feet down. But it was too late. The overladen trail bike spun out from under them, and they both jumped off to avoid getting run over as it slid back down the embankment.

If they were getting out of the wash, it wasn't going to be this way. Carlo picked up the bike and walked it to a flat, hard place in the middle of the wash. He pointed the wheel at the slope and turned to his friend.

"I'm doing this by myself," he said. "You can climb out."

"Eat cow farts," Ken said, but Carlo was already buzzing toward the bank. He didn't make it any farther than the two of them had managed before, but he tried to stay on out of shear cussedness, leaning forward and holding on for dear life as the wheel flipped up and back. Carlo and his Honda came back down the bank in a confused tangle, and he ended up eating a mouthful of desert dust. He sat up and spat, wiping sand out of his eyes.

"Ha! . . . Ha!" said Ken.

Carlo used half the water from his canteen to rinse the sand from his mouth, eyes, and nostrils. Then the boys climbed back on the bike and motored down the wash, dodging mesquite bushes as they went. They had to get back to the overpass on Highway 652 by six-thirty so that Carlo's Uncle Jeff could pick them up in his truck. That had been the agreed-upon rendezvous point when he dropped them off just before noon Saturday, along with the small motorcycle, two peanut-butter sandwiches, two quarts of water, and a bag of Fritos. It said a lot about small-town Texas that nobody worried about them.

Carlo and Ken were stuck in Two Fork Wash unless they either abandoned the Honda and walked the three miles back, or found a place they could drive it or haul it up the steep bank.

A couple of miles down the wash, the sandy banks were farther apart and not as tall. Carlo spotted a likely escape point.

"Lean FORWARD!" he yelled, and they zoomed for the embankment. They skidded and slid, but this time they mastered the laws of momentum and gravity, and the little bike reached the top and popped up on the other side onto flat desert.

"WOO!" they both yelled.

They stopped so they could get their bearings. There was less here than almost anywhere. Off to their left, a few miles distant, were some low, beige sand hills. Straight ahead, a few hundred feet distant, they could see the brilliant white of the salt flat. People said that long ago it had been a lake, but nowadays, there was only standing water after a hard rain, which is to say, almost never.

The boys lived in the tiny town of Autry, where, during the school year, they had to endure a fifty-minute bus ride twice a day to and from Duro High School in the next county. During the summer, Carlo and Ken worked at Pepper Ranch, a 50,000-acre cattle ranch owned by a retired Pecos dentist. They were both experienced on horseback, but ever since Carlo got the little off-road motorcycle, they had discovered a new thrill: exploring the mysteries of the open desert with an 89 cc four-stroke air-cooled engine. Ken was saving up for his own bike, but in the meantime, he endured the indignity of riding behind his friend as they motored around the empty county.

They took off again, maneuvering around the stands of mesquite, prickly pear, and Russian thistle. After a mile or so, they rolled down a gentle sandy slope and found themselves on hard-packed, featureless flatland. Carlo pointed the bike west and rotated the throttle to full power. The boys whooped and yelled as they zipped across the salt pan at fifty miles an hour, their hair and T-shirts whipping in the blast.

A quarter mile farther, they came to what had once been an ancient shoreline. The land rose again, rocks and thorny plants returned, and Carlo had to slow back down to a crawl. Unexpectedly, they found themselves popping out onto a narrow hardtop highway. Carlo stopped the bike. They looked up and down the road.

"You think this is the same highway we came in on?" asked Ken.

"I don't know," said Carlo. "What else could it be? If this is the highway, then the overpass is that way." He pointed to the right.

"Let's see what's the other way, then. We still have a couple of hours."

"Okay." Carlo revved the little engine and they zoomed off down the highway to the southwest. Now that they were on hard, smooth road, he was able to take the bike back up to full speed. They weren't worried about getting stuck again, and there was an extra quart of gas in the compartment. This little beast got about a hundred miles to the gallon anyway.

Ten minutes later, they spotted a historical marker on the left side of the road, and Carlo pulled over to read it.

Under the symbol of the lone star, there was a worn and pitted metal sign.

FREEMASON ENERGY LINE MONUMENT

The structure you see 175 yards to the east is a step pyramid built in 1937 by the members of Duro Freemasons Lodge 886 A.F.&A.M. Designed by the architect Frederick Pyle, the pyramid marks the point where ley lines intersect. These are believed by some to be lines of magnetic and spiritual energy that crisscross the Earth. Along with one such point near Sedona, Arizona, and another in Baja California, the site is reputed to be among the most significant in North America.

Originally, a smaller monument—based on a 1907 survey—was placed 450 yards farther southwest. Later calculations determined that the earlier survey had been in error, and a new monument was built in this current location.

Before 1960, Freemasons from across Texas and the West used the site frequently for sacred rituals and inductions of new members. Area Masonic lodges still utilize the structure occasionally.

Carlo and Ken looked to see what the plaque was talking about and saw, way off to their left, a gray blocky thing made of three successively smaller levels stacked, with a central post.

"Let's check it out!" said Carlo, and they zipped off the road headed for the strange ziggurat.

Up close, it proved to be a neglected mess. There was a lot of painted graffiti, numerous scars in the gray concrete, and plastic trash strewn about the ground and on the lowest level. Rocks, dirt, and tumbleweeds were mounded up against the sides. The first level was low to the ground, but the next two were each about four feet high, and the boys had no trouble hoisting themselves up.

On the highest of the three platforms, there was a rusted metal plate set into the concrete. The message was corroded but still legible:

Dedicated to the First Freemasons of the Republic of Texas:
Steven F. Austin • Anson Jones • John M. Allen
"To Daily Live the Masonic Life
& to Serve Intelligently the Needs of the Great Architect"

In the very center was a pillar one foot square and seven feet high. The boys walked around it. Embedded on one side was a strange symbol with a big letter V and a smaller upside-down V on top of it. On the other three sides were odd words cast into the concrete: *ORDO* and *AB* and *CHAO.*

"Weird," said Ken. "I bet they had human sacrifices up here."

"I'm gonna stand up on the top!" said Carlo. He could just reach the top edge of the obelisk. He grasped with both hands and tried to hoist himself up, scrambling and seeking purchase with his tennis shoes, but the surface was too slick.

"Give me a boost," he said. Ken bent over and interlaced his fingers to make a stirrup, and Carlo stepped up. He managed to get one elbow on top and pull himself part way up, while Ken pushed from below.

"Hey, cool!" Carlo said. "Look what I found." He picked something up, then hopped down again. He held it out for Ken to see. It was a gold ring. He turned it over in his hand. It had a small setting that appeared to be a diamond.

"Holy moly!" said Ken. "Is it real?"

"Of course, it's real," said Carlo. "I bet it's worth a lot of money."

"Who would put an expensive ring right there?" asked Ken. "I bet it's fake."

"Bet it's not," Carlo said. "And I found it. It's mine now."

"We both found it."

"Dream on. I found it." Carlo stepped back and looked at the shaft again. "Weird. Somebody put it up there on purpose. I wonder if it's been there a long time."

"It looks new," said Ken.

"Yeah, but gold never rusts and neither does diamond. I bet it's been there a long time. Maybe since they built this thing. I wonder who it belonged to. And why would they leave it here?" He turned the ring back and forth so the stone glinted in the afternoon sun. "Well, it's mine now. Finders keepers."

"We both found it," said Ken.

"Dream on," said Carlo.

CHAPTER 4

Two Years Ago Tonight

As the long Autumn dusk settled in, Duro High School was still lit up like a cruise ship. Beverly, Chase, and Perry sat across the street in Beverly's Comet, watching and waiting.

"Let's go get cokes or something," said Chase. She shifted her position in the front passenger seat. "He's going to take all night. We can come back later and see if he's gone."

"It's past eight o'clock," said Beverly. "Mr. Wiggins will be leaving any time now. He just works a little late on Friday nights."

"We could just come back tomorrow night," said Chase. "Let's roll down the windows. I'm hot."

The girls rolled down the car windows, and a cool desert breeze blew through.

"It has to be tonight," said Perry from the back seat. "It's the two-year anniversary." Of the three drama students, he was the most determined to come here, and the one who insisted it had to be Friday night, September 15.

"Well, I wish he would hurry up," said Chase. "And I don't know why you think this is the anniversary. My mom said it's just the day they discovered that she was missing."

"And they found her car in some little town—clean," said Perry. He enjoyed the sound of the word, so he said it again, with more drama. "Clean, clean as a whistle. Not a drop of blood. Not a hair. It's the day she officially disappeared. And the day weird stuff started happening . . . in the theater. They found the car on September 16, which means she was probably murdered the night before. That was two years ago tonight."

Just as he finished speaking, the lights on the second floor began going out one by one.

"See? He's leaving," said Beverly. The three waited. After several minutes, the downstairs lights went out, too. The three teenagers watched the side door and waited. Finally, it opened, and Mr. Wiggins, the night custodian, came out.

For as dismal a job as high school janitor must be, Wiggins was in no hurry to wrap it up. He took a long time locking the side door, even longer walking to his car, and then spent a full three minutes sitting in his car with the engine running.

"What is he *doing?*" moaned Chase.

"He's leaving. He's leaving," said Perry. Another minute went by. "He's just taking a while picking his nose."

Beverly snorted with laughter. "Or pulling the hairs out of his butt."

"Come *on,* old man," said Chase.

Finally, Wiggins's car pulled away, and the school parking lot was empty.

"Okay, drive over behind the gym," said Perry. At fifteen and only a sophomore, he still felt he could assert male dominance over the two seventeen-year-old girls.

It was time to do this, the plan they had talked about for a couple of weeks. Beverly started her car, and they pulled into the huge parking lot and around the back of the school, parking in the shadows beside a stand of elm trees at the edge of the lot. They rolled up the car windows and got out.

Perry pulled from his pocket their most precious possession—a copy of the janitor's master key. The key was the biggest secret among the students in the Duro High drama department. During the Spring semester, one of the boys had managed to get ahold of the custodian's keys one day and took them to a hardware store during lunch. He took the master key off its ring, placed a small piece of masking tape over the engraved words *FCISD PROPERTY—DO NOT DUPLICATE,* and then had the key copied. The man at the key-grinding machine never did more than glance at it. By the end of the day, the custodian, who thought he had lost his keys and was dreading telling the school administration, found them on the floor of one of the mop closets.

Phew, he thought. *Got to be more careful.*

Andrew Waylan, one of the rising seniors, had claimed the right to hold the key and doled it out judiciously to various school marauders after extracting a promise they wouldn't leave a trace—and wouldn't rat on him if they were caught. So, a few times during the semester, some copies of upcoming tests were spirited from classrooms, a handful of snacks were pilfered from the cafeteria, and, in one case, a trio of fat gerbils was set loose in the library. But any plans for obvious theft or vandalism were vetoed by Andrew, who took his master-key responsibilities seriously. Too many kids knew about it already, and they must not make the school staff suspicious.

Tonight, Andrew had allowed young Perry to borrow it for a secret mission to contact the Other Side.

As the two girls stood in the shadows, Perry unlocked the door and peeked inside.

"The coast is clear," he said. "Come on," and they all went in.

The hallway was lit only by *EXIT* signs and a small red light on the fire alarm.

"Just go all the way down the hall to the theater," said Perry.

"God, this is creepy!" said Chase. The two senior girls and one sophomore boy walked as quietly as they could down the small hallway, then turned right on the main hall with its trophy cases and motivational posters.

When they got to the auditorium, Perry unlocked the main door. The dark theater was even creepier than the hallway. With its high, dark ceiling, every tiny sound they made echoed in the cavernous space. The air vents sounded like supernatural whispering. They walked up the left side aisle, feeling their way along the wall.

"Let's go up on stage," said Perry. They went up the side stairs onto the main stage, where the curtains were all pulled back and up out of the way. Along the edge of the stage, glow tape had been placed to prevent accidents during scene changes.

"Why didn't we bring a flashlight?" whined Beverly.

"Because people might see the light through the windows and think we're burglars."

He looked at his watch, and he could just make out the time from the glowing green tips of the minute and hour hands. "We shouldn't really try this 'til later. It's not even nine o'clock yet."

"I don't want to wait," said Chase.

"Me neither," said Beverly. "I'm weirded out. Let's hurry this up."

"You can't hurry something like this," said Perry. "That's not how it works. We have to just sit quietly and wait. Clear your mind, so you're receptive to the spirit world."

"Oh, come on," said Chase. "That's such bullshit."

"Be a doubter if you want, but I've heard the more you are open to the idea, the more she's likely to reveal herself. Some people saw her last year."

"Y'all, I really don't like this," said Beverly. "I think I'm going to go back and wait in the car."

"No," said Perry. "We have to have at least three people. That's what I read. To make a circle." He sat down on the stage next to the glow tape. "Now, Bev, you sit over here to my right. You're righthanded, aren't you?"

"Yes."

"Then sit on my right," said Perry. "Chase, you're left-handed, so sit on my left."

"What difference does it make?" asked Chase.

"That's just what I *read*," said Perry. "It's supposed to make a complete spirit circle."

"What*ever*."

The three students sat on the stage.

"Now, hold hands," said Perry, "and be quiet. Clear your mind."

For several minutes, they sat, trying not to fidget.

Suddenly, Chase breathed in sharply. "I heard something!" she whispered. "I think it was somebody walking!"

"It's probably just the air conditioner," whispered Perry. "There's nobody here but us. Nobody from *this* world. Now, be quiet, and in a few minutes, we'll call to her."

"I don't like that part," said Beverly.

"We just have to let her know it's okay to reveal herself."

"Oh, God, this is such bullshit," said Chase, but she gripped their hands.

They sat still. They heard various small sounds, the clicks and thumps of an old building, idling and cooling in the night air. A couple of times, the girls thought they might have heard quiet footsteps. After a couple of minutes, Perry spoke in a low voice.

"Helen . . . Helen . . . We are open to your presence."

"Such bullshit," whispered Chase.

"This is how you do it," whispered Perry. "Now speak along with me." He gripped both girls' hands tightly and began again, louder. "Helen . . . Helen . . . We are open to your presence. If you are here, make yourself known."

"I don't like it, either," whispered Beverly.

"Shut up, both of you," whispered Perry. "This is serious." He raised his voice more, so that it echoed a little bit in the auditorium. "Helen . . . We are your friends. We are not those who hurt you. Helen, make yourself known to us." Perry shifted his sitting position on the floor. "Now, come on, guys, let's speak together. Just call her. Say, 'Helen.' Come on. Say it with me. 'Helen . . . Helen . . . Helen.'"

The girls reluctantly joined in the incantation.

"Helen . . . Helen . . . Helen . . ."

Chase squirmed. "Perry, I think—"

Suddenly, there was a crash, as if something had been kicked over, coming from somewhere back in the wings. Both girls screamed involuntarily.

"My God!" said Beverly. "What was that?"

"Listen!" said Perry. "I think we're making contact. Now do this with me. Helen . . . Helen . . . Helen . . ."

From someplace deep backstage came the voice of a young girl.

"I'm so cold . . . so cold. Help me . . . I'm so cold . . ."

Chase screamed sharply, and Beverly shouted, "Oh God!"

"That's it, I'm out of here!" yelled Chase. She got up and headed for the side of the stage, stumbling down the stairs and running up the center aisle. Beverly jumped up and followed. Chase got to the main auditorium door and blew through it, with Beverly rapidly closing in. Perry heard the clack-clack-clack of their footsteps as the girls ran down the hall. He climbed down off the stage and hurried after them.

When Perry got outside the building, both girls were in Beverly's car. The engine was running.

"Wait!" Perry yelled. He ran up to the car, out of breath, and opened the door. "I have to go back in! Wait for me!"

"Oh my God, WHY!?" screamed Chase.

"I didn't lock the auditorium," said Perry. "I have to do it, or they'll know we were there."

He trotted back to the door and went inside, then hurried down the hall to the auditorium door. He pulled it open and leaned inside.

"Andrew!" he called.

There was a burst of laughter from the front of the room. Andrew Waylan appeared out of the dark, along with his friend Randall and Randall's little sister, who was in ninth grade.

"That was GREAT!" said Andrew. "They practically peed their pants! You did really good with that séance shit. I loved it! I thought I screwed up when I knocked over that ladder, but it just added to the effect. Amy, you were fantastic! 'I'm so coooold.' That was perfect. Just perfect."

"Can we go now?" asked Amy. "I'm hungry."

"We have to wait for them to leave," said Andrew. "Perry, you go outside and tell them you saw Helen. Act like you're locking the door, but give me the key right now."

Perry handed over the master key. He could still hear the two boys laughing and talking as he ran down the hall and through the outside door. He pushed the door shut and faked a locking motion. He sprinted to Beverly's car and dived past Chase into the back seat.

"I saw her!" he said. "Oh, my *God!* I don't know why I did it, but I opened the auditorium door before I locked it," he panted. "There was a girl standing in the middle of the stage, I swear to God. She was all in white! I just locked the damn door and got out of there! Oh, God! Drive! Let's get away from here!"

Beverly revved up the Comet, and they tore across the school parking lot. As the car entered the street, the spinning tires bounced against the curb. When they came to the first intersection, Beverly paused only long enough to make sure nobody was coming, then gunned through the red light.

CHAPTER 5

The Hits Keep Coming

Allen Wallace stared at the tape machine on his desk, sipping his drink, rubbing his wrist. He should listen to that demo one more time, but he was afraid it would bring him down even more. The TEAC four-track hummed. The quarter-inch reel of tape JJ Johns had given him was treaded onto the machine. Wallace took another sip and shuddered.

He was drinking scotch that somebody had given him last Christmas. He kept it deep in a desk drawer and indulged in it only once in a while. Allen didn't particularly like scotch, unless it was really dry and not very smoky, and this one was too strong by fifty yards. But he wanted a drink and had nothing better, so he diluted the dark scotch with water from the bathroom sink and sipped. Maybe he should have another Equanil, which his doctor told him to take for anxiety, morning and evening, on an empty stomach. He'd already taken his second pill for the day, but he was allowed as many as four a day if he needed them. He thought a moment, then fished the pill bottle out of his desk and flicked one of the bitter white pills into his mouth and washed it down with a shot of scotch. He was running a little low on pills, but there was another bottle at home.

When he found himself in this sort of mood, brooding about all the things that had never worked in his life—his two marriages, his daughter who wouldn't speak to him—Allen turned to his tapes. The studio shelves held at least a hundred and fifty reels of tape in different sizes, including twenty-five completed demos and many more masters. Some of them were so old they had been produced by Roger Best, the studio's original owner, back when Allen was an assistant engineer. The very best of them, the ones most intimate to him, were stored in the echo chamber, where the temperature stayed cave-like.

The studio may have been named for its original owner, but the name was appropriate, because something about this far-from-everywhere location brought out the best work in musicians, in Allen's view. "Must be something in the water out here," Roger Best liked to say. It was more likely that this dreary industrial warehouse sitting on the east side of a huge salt flat simply took away all other distractions, let the artists stay focused. Allen had a few opportunities over the years to move the studio closer to town, but he turned them all down. Out here was where he did his best work, and others did, too.

Over the years, a few recordings had found their way onto vinyl, pressed and shipped off to radio stations and music promoters around the country. Almost none of them had ever seen the light of day—consigned to studio round files as soon as they were received. Only a few had ever been played on the air, and only a tiny fraction—fewer than a dozen—had been released by a major record label.

Well, one, mostly. The other eight were minor efforts that slightly cracked the Billboard, Country, or Gospel charts, then fell off quickly. "Bettie Said She Loves Me" was Allen's only bona fide hit as producer. For a while, the song had paid the bills and, very briefly, made Rick Watson a star. Watson wasn't the most talented musician Allen had ever recorded, not by a long shot, but he was easygoing, professional in the studio, and willing to take guidance.

After the GoldTone label signed Watson, and the song climbed into the top ten for a couple of weeks, Allen never expected to see the young rockabilly singer again. But six months later, Watson was back in Duro asking Allen for help with a follow-up. The two had ground out many late nights at Best Studios, first hashing together the tune, then recording it. This time, the arrangement was better, and the session musicians were sharper. Allen had written most of the music but didn't ask for cowriting credit.

"Bettie's Coming Home" was pretty good—certainly better than its predecessor. It debuted at number eighty-eight in the spring of 1963, then dropped off the charts a week later. Undeterred, Rockin' Rick Watson had returned to Allen twice more that year, and together, they had written and built a couple of very decent tunes, searching for the secret ingredients that got a song noticed. Demos were mailed out by the score, but the label declined to promote the records, and they dropped Rick at the end of his contract, just as the Beatles were dealing a death blow to rockabilly. The last Allen had heard from him, Rick was playing

Nashville lounges on weekends, working in his father's furniture factory, and hoping for a comeback.

Except for a couple of modest regional successes and a few gospel recordings, that was the story of Allen Wallace. He was a more-than-decent record producer, with a good sense of what made a pop song work, but what Allen excelled at was *creating* legend. Through some sneaky self-promotion and the judicious planting of rumors, he had managed to prevent his name from being forgotten—not easy in this business.

If the truth were to be told, Roy Orbison had never set foot in World Famous Best Studios. There were no mysterious lost demos, though Allen never explicitly denied their existence. Buddy Holly had never stopped by for late-night sessions with Sonny Curtis. The great Freddie Fender had never come out to Duro after his release from Angola Prison Farm to record a follow-up to "Wasted Days and Wasted Nights." But, if people thought he had . . . Well, who was Allen Wallace to disagree?

Many, many artists—good, fair, and awful—had come through these doors over the years. And now, more and more, feeling the approach of twilight, Allen sat alone, listening to tapes of so many sessions that should have been hits.

And then there was Mabel.

She was a brilliant, dynamic singer. And it could have worked. Back when they were both younger and Allen was happy . . . It really could have worked.

Allen shook his head to clear the thoughts. He took another sip of scotch, then reached down into the desk drawer, fished out the bottle of Cutty, and splashed a couple of dollops into his glass. He hated the sight of an empty glass. He considered adding more tap water, but his taste buds were now sufficiently numb. The smoky flavor wouldn't bother him.

Okay, he had to listen to JJ Johns's demo again but dreaded it. The working title of the song was "Earth Is Crying," and it was the sort of overblown, heavy-handed, relevant-message drivel that made Allen cringe. The demo was a full six minutes, way too long for a pop single. JJ's mournful, pleading voice gave him goosebumps for the wrong reason: It sounded both angry and constipated.

Besides JJ's guitar, there was Prensky's Rhodes electric piano, much too sharp and intrusive, a bored session drummer going through the motions, and two female backup singers who didn't seem to be listening to each other. And these guys wanted to record the song with a *symphony orchestra*? Jesus, what ever happened to subtlety?

Allen rewound the tape on the old machine, then hesitated. Maybe it would sound better played through the main console in the control room. He usually played the quarter-inch tape machine through a little practice amp attached to a small RCA speaker salvaged from an old radio. It wasn't a great set-up, and the sound was flat, but the equipment fit on his desk. After thinking it over a few seconds, Allen unplugged the reel-to-reel. Though it wasn't easy—since the accident, Allen's right hand had been very weak—he picked up the bulky machine and lugged it into the main control room. He plugged it into the forty-watt amp driving two Altec nearfield monitors.

It took some huffing and crawling around on his old knees, but Allen managed to get the system set up. He returned to his office to retrieve his drink, closed the control room door, turned on the big amplifier, punched the *PLAY* button, and scooted back a couple of feet to put himself in the center of the sound field. He massaged his wrist and listened.

At least JJ's guitar sounded a lot better, and the piano wasn't as piercing. He listened to the earnest lyrics:

The Earth will turn, with or without us
She will never hate or ever doubt us
We don't respect her, we're not even trying
But listen to her, friends, the Earth . . . the Earth is crying

Don't think about the dumb words. Just try and visualize the song. Allen turned up the volume and closed his eyes. *Okay, it's not awful. Maybe a little slow. The tune is pretty good, actually, just not great. What can I do to make it great?* Allen listened to imaginary tracks in his head. *What we need after the first chorus is a bass with a lot of bottom, plus another guitar for support.* Then, well, maybe Prensky was right—some violins and violas right on top and some kind of deep drums—not timpani, surely, not a full orchestra, but definitely a bigger sound. It was time to outfit the large room.

Allen picked up a pad of paper and jotted notes.

Get the sound big. Focus on chorus. (Maybe chorus first?) Tweak lyrics. Drop the first verse or rewrite. Drum intro?

He was glad he'd taken the trouble to play the demo through the big speakers. So what if ninety-nine percent of their target audience would hear "Earth Is Crying" through rattly four-inch speakers in their Ford Pintos? You make a song from the top down. Worry about the kids and their little transistor radios later. Get a good-sounding mix first.

He got himself another drink, rewound the tape, and listened to "Earth Is Crying" for the third time.

CHAPTER 6

The Spirit Finds the Chosen

Dandridge Cavendish Park IV arrived early Sunday afternoon at the Paulsons' house on Bluebonnet Lane and parked in front. He left his cowboy hat in the back seat of the Ford and retrieved his small leather suitcase. Apparently, he was spending the night on the Paulsons' couch, though he had offered to stay in a motel. Once Rebekah had assured her father that Dan was just a friend and no hanky-panky was in the cards, Grover had insisted he stay with them. Besides, for his own reasons, Dan wanted to attend church with them for Sunday evening worship, and that was certainly fine with Grover. The two students would drive back to college on Monday.

Dan could easily pay for his own lodging, because he had more money than he wanted or needed. He wore jeans and scuffed cowboy boots and drove a modestly dented four-year-old sedan, but the Parks were a rich family by West Texas standards. His father, Dandridge Park III, was part owner and president of South Plains Pipeline in McCauly, Texas. His family lacked nothing and would have gladly sent their only son out of state to an Ivy League school if Dan had wished. Instead, Dan picked Central Texas Christian, less than a day away from home. He wanted to ween himself from the old homestead, his old life, and his old friends, at his own pace.

Originally, he'd pursued Becky Paulson as a romantic possibility. She was pretty in a country-girl way, with conservative clothes and no makeup, sharp, funny, and fun to be with. But their personal chemistry led to friendship rather than romance, which took the pressure off and allowed them to work well together when they teamed up in film school. They could argue about how to shoot a scene without being hurtful or personal. Lately, they'd been arguing quite a bit, amicably. They had a thousand-dollar grant and a golden opportunity to make a meaningful film—but about what? The partnership of Becky and Dan was trying to hash that out.

Dan knocked, and Grover answered.

"Mr. Paulson? I'm Becky's friend Dan." He extended his hand. Grover hesitated just a bit longer than necessary, then took it.

"Very good to meet you," he said. "Please, come in." If Dan had been expecting a *Please, call me Grover*, he would have been disappointed. "My wife has made lemonade," said Grover, "if you'd like some."

"That would be great," Dan said. He walked in, looking around for Becky. Grover gestured that he should follow, and led him into the family den, with its short couch, several cushioned chairs, and one small TV. When Grover was not personally watching television—and aside from news, he watched very little—the TV stayed unplugged.

"Please sit," said Grover, gesturing toward one of the chairs. Dan put down his suitcase and sat. Grover pulled his favorite chair close, facing Dan. "So, you and Rebekah have been making movies together. I hear congratulations are in order."

"Thanks," said Dan. "Winning the Dwight Award was a big surprise. We thought the film was good, but there were so many other great ones, I didn't think we had a chance. But I'm not going to complain." He looked around. "Is Becky here?"

"She'll be along pretty soon," said Grover. "She and her mother are taking a walk around the park. We don't drive on Sundays, except to services. We'd walk there if we could, but it's too far for the kids. Besides, we sometimes take a covered dish for potluck supper."

"I see," Dan said.

"So, Dan," said Grover. "Is your full name Daniel?"

"No, sir. It's Dandridge."

"Dandridge. That's a bit unusual. And Rebekah says you're a fourth. Is that right?"

"Yes, sir. Dandridge Park the fourth. I know it sounds pretty silly, especially out here in this part of the state. I just tell everybody I'm Dan. My family calls me Danfour. Becky calls me that, too."

"Hmmm," said Grover. "It sounds like you have a name to be proud of. What does your father do?"

"My dad runs a pipeline company. He was born in Connecticut but came out here to get into the oil business. My grandfather was part owner of a shipping company back east. He liked to say, 'We Parks don't make 'em; we just move 'em.'"

Grover chuckled. "Well, you should take pleasure in your family but avoid pride, which is the devil's way of making us think we're better than other people."

Dan nodded, looking around, wishing Becky would appear. And hadn't lemonade been promised?

"By the way," said Grover. "Are you happy with how you look?"

"Excuse me?"

"Your face. I don't mean to be too personal. Are you satisfied with your appearance? You're not ashamed of your face, are you?"

"Uh . . . no, sir," said Dan. He shifted in his chair.

"I was just wondering," said Grover, "because you hide your face. None of my business, of course. Just thought you might be unhappy with the way you look."

"No, I'm . . ."

"It's just that we used to say 'You can judge a man's character by his face.' But for some reason, you decided to cover up your face. It looks like maybe you're trying to hide something."

My beard, thought Dan. *He's objecting to my beard.* "No, sir. It's just a beard. I'm blessed with a pretty thick one, I guess. It's easiest just to let it grow, so I do."

"Does your father have a beard?" Grover said, leaning forward.

"Uh . . . no, sir."

"How about your grandfather . . . Dandridge Park Junior, I assume?"

"I don't think so," said Dan. "I just barely remember him. But I know my great-grandfather did. I've seen pictures. Big thick beard right down to the middle of his chest."

"It was a different time," said Grover. "Let me ask you something personal, if that's all right."

"Sure."

"You and Rebekah are friends—just friends—am I right? Or is there something more?"

"No, nothing more," said Dan. "She's a very good friend and easy to get along with. She's so . . . cheerful. I like working with her."

"Well, then I'll put something straight to you," said Grover. "Man to man. Watch out for her. Our duty as men is to protect women. Rebekah is very smart, but she's not . . . wise about everything."

"Uh . . . she is very smart."

"But she's not always . . . sensible. I want you, as her man-friend, to be the one with common sense, to keep her from going off and following every crazy idea that pops into her head. Can you do that?"

"Of course," said Dan. "But Becky's really level-headed. I'm not worried."

"Okay," said Grover. "But I want you to always keep your eyes open. Especially, I want you to watch out for questionable people. She's not always smart about the company she keeps."

"I can do that," said Dan, "but, really . . ."

To Dan's great relief, he heard the front door open and Becky's chatty voice.

"Oh, Mother," she was saying, "Nobody wears dresses in college, except at dances."

"Well, I hope you don't attend any of those," said a woman's voice.

A little girl's voice: "Mother won't let me wear jeans, even when it's freezing cold."

"Danfour! Where are you?" called Becky.

"He's here with me, in the den!" said Grover.

Holly and Becky and little sister Martha came in. Dan stood up.

"This is my mom, Mrs. Paulson," said Becky.

"Mr. Park," said Holly, and offered her hand. Dan was glad she did, because he didn't know the custom among Pentecostals. He took her small hand for a moment but didn't grip.

"It's a pleasure," he said. "Please, call me Dan. And thank you for letting me stay here."

"Are you going to church with us tonight?" asked Martha.

"I believe I am. You must be Martha."

"You'll like our church," said Martha. "It's fun."

"Now, young one," said Grover, "We'll let Dan decide what he thinks of our little country fellowship. Dan, where does your family church?"

It took Dan a second to realized Grover was using *church* as a verb.

"Uh . . . we go to All Saints in McCauly. When I was little, we used to drive all the way up to Odessa every Sunday, because there wasn't an Episcopal church in our town. But fortunately, they built All Saints, and we didn't have to drive so far."

"Hmmm," said Grover. "All the saints, huh? Every one of them. That's a lot of saints. Seem like they should just pick one."

"Oh, Father, be quiet," laughed Becky.

"I'm not here to judge," said Grover. "Dear, will you bring us some of your lemonade?"

"Yes, sir," said Holly, and slipped away quickly.

BECKY RODE WITH DAN to the little wood-shingled church on the west side of town. Grover and the rest of the Paulsons went ahead, though it was still thirty minutes until evening services. Sacred Truth, like a lot of Pentecostal churches, held three full services a week; Sunday morning at nine, Sunday evening at seven, and Wednesday Bible Study at 6:30 p.m. Most members of the fellowship attended at least one service a week. The Paulsons made it to all three—always, without exception, save possibly when severe illness was involved. Peter, even with his injured foot, was attending this evening, hobbling with a borrowed cane. His foot still bothered him, but he was glad to get out of the house.

"Okay," said Becky, "now that I've got you alone, why are you so eager to go to church with us? Is Episcopal getting too boring for you?"

Dan grinned. "Oh, I just thought I could use some Holy Spirit."

"Yeah . . . right," laughed Becky. "You just thought it would be fun to watch holy rollers in action."

"Well, I am intrigued by the idea of speaking in tongues. I've always wanted to see that."

"Really, you want to hear speaking in tongues? That's why you wanted to come? It doesn't happen every time, you know."

"But you said it happens most often Sunday nights, and I want to witness that for myself."

"Ah hah!" said Becky. "You're just being an anthropologist. Observe the natives in their habitat. I know how you think."

"I'm not quite that bad," said Dan. "But I do want to see it."

"Okay," said Becky, "but remember, if you feel yourself getting the spirit, don't fight it. Just go with it."

Dan looked alarmed. "Really? Does that . . . ever *happen* to people? People who just walk in?"

Becky laughed. "Danfour, I was kidding!"

"Well, *phew*."

"According to Father, it's happened, though," said Becky. "Skeptics, nonbelievers, even Catholics. People get the spirit, and suddenly, they're up front in front of everybody, speaking away. I've never seen it, but he has."

"Wow. Okay. So . . . Becky . . . did you ever, uh, personally . . ."

"Sort of. Just once. It was a long, long time ago," laughed Becky.

"Double phew. I guess."

As Dan and Becky got out of the car, the other Paulsons walked slowly toward the front door of the church, Holly and Grover on either side of Peter, supporting him. Grover made him leave the cane in the car.

Dan was surprised to hear the thump of a kick drum coming from inside and the twangy crunch of amplified guitar. Then a loud, fat bass guitar followed, running a short scale. It sounded like a rock band setting up, but it was just the volunteer musicians at Sacred Truth doing sound check. It was still twenty minutes until services began.

Dan had been brought up in a church of incense, robes, pipe organ, and a well-rehearsed choir. But here was a five-piece band, complete with rock drum kit, two guitars, bass, and a B3 electric organ on a stand, all plugged in through heavy, battle-scarred tube amps.

Dan wore a button-down shirt, having been assured by Grover that no one would be wearing a tie, but he was still surprised by how casual it all was. The band milled around, tweaking their instruments, while early arrivals stood about, chatting. A couple of men smoked outside the main door.

The Paulsons sat in the front row. Pastor Davies, a thin middle-aged man in a short-sleeved double-knit shirt and polyester slacks, spotted them and immediately came over to talk to Grover. Then the pastor bent over and said something to young Peter, who looked up attentively and nodded.

One of the guitarists played a few licks of a screaming lead so loud that Dan was startled.

This was the best-attended service of the week, and Pentecostals were arriving by twos and threes, filling up the little church as the hour approached. The conversation level was cacophonous.

A few minutes before seven, the band took their positions on the low stage and strapped on their instruments. The drummer sat down and picked up his sticks. Dan expected the pastor to call everyone to attention, give some sort of greeting or opening remarks, but he just picked up a microphone and pointed at the drummer, who kicked off a fast, loud intro, and the band roared to life. They were good—and together. In a few moments, the whole congregation was clapping and swaying. The Pastor sang at the top of his lungs:

Got a home prepared . . . where the saints abide!

The congregation responded:

Just over in the Glory Land!

The windows rattled, and the floors shook. *How did they know what hymn they were going to sing?* Dan looked around for a little wooden sign on the wall, like the Anglicans used—*PROCESSIONAL: HYMN 239.* Nope. The Pentecostals just knew.

And I long to be . . . by my Savior's side!

Just over in the Glory Land . . .

Dan had never seen anything like it. He looked at Becky and mouthed the word *WOW.* She laughed and kept smiling, rocking, and clapping. Young Martha jumped up and down gleefully. She turned to Dan and shouted, "I told you our church was fun!"

That was how it went. A lot of songs were played, all at a rollicking clip and chest-thumping volume. There was no sermon per se, but between hymns, the pastor shouted an earnest, rambling message, working himself into a copious sweat. The message was mostly what Dan had expected: Have faith in Jesus, and you can move mountains. Watch out for the Devil, who is lurking everywhere. There was also a lot of "We're us, and we're not *them.* We are *not* the whiskey drinkers, the liars, the fornicators, the sinners, the hypocrites. Above all, we're not the world." He also railed against "papists" and "Masons," though more as an afterthought. In particular, the preacher had it in for the city of Las Vegas, which he brought up repeatedly and compared to Gomorrah. Dan doubted that many of these folks had visited Las Vegas.

The service was free-form, with young men going in and out of the church to talk and smoke. Even Grover left at one point, apparently to talk to somebody outside.

The highlight of the evening was young Peter Paulson and his bandaged foot. The pastor knelt down right in front of the young boy sitting in the front row and gently lifted the wounded foot with one hand while praying into the microphone.

"The Bible says Jesus *called* to his twelve apostles and gave them *authority* over unclean spirits, to cast them *out,* and to heal every *affliction*!"

Other members of the congregation crowded around Peter and touched him. The ones who couldn't reach him touched the backs of the people in front of them, a mob that, strangely, did not include any member of the Paulson family. Grover stood off to one side with his eyes closed, nodding his head. The only one who didn't seem engaged was Holly, who sat unmoving in the front row. *Maybe she's embarrassed,* thought Dan.

"I cast you OUT, demon!" the pastor shouted. "We have *authority* over you! Leave this young boy! LEAVE him NOW! Get BEHIND me, demon!"

Geez, the kid's not possessed, thought Dan. *He's got second-degree burns.* He wondered what young Peter thought about all this, but the boy seemed to enjoy being the center of attention.

The unction ended quickly and simply. "Praise Jesus," said the preacher, and the healing scrum dispersed. There was one more hymn, a slower one, and the service was over. The musicians turned off their amplifiers and wound the cables, put the electric instruments back in their cases.

Nobody had spoken in tongues, but Dan was still fascinated. Most of the congregation remained behind for a potluck supper—dominated by varieties of potato salad—but the Paulsons didn't stay.

Back in the car with Becky, Dan said, "Now *that* would make a great film."

Becky gave him a contemptuous look. "I knew that's what you were up to. It's not going to happen, Buster."

"But, really . . . just look at it objectively," said Dan. "This is part of America most people don't know even exists. We wouldn't make fun of it. It's just . . . interesting. They're real people."

"Maybe it would be interesting to some," said Becky. "I can't really say. I was raised with it. But admit it: Unsolved murders—they're a lot *more* interesting."

CHAPTER 7

Nicky Can Go Home Again

The idea of Nicky Pomeroy returning to Duro was so crazy it hadn't occurred to anyone. Especially not Nicky. But it did make some sense. There were more jobs for pipeliners in Duro and in the basin than anywhere else.

It would take only modest courage to come back. Though many people knew his name, few would recognize Nicky on the street or in a grocery store or a bank. He would not have to endure stares or whispers, at least not often. But, given the circumstances of his leaving, coming home was nearly unthinkable.

The job offer from Dooley Pipeline Services came the first time he talked to them in person, after driving down on a whim one Wednesday morning from Cline, Oklahoma, where he'd lived in self-imposed exile the past eighteen months. There was such demand for skilled labor in the oilfields that Dooley and other companies had begun leasing temporary signs, the street-legal kind with wheels and tail reflectors, and placing them at strategic highway intersections.

WELDERS, PIPELINERS NEEDED
IMMEDIATE PLACEMENT

As he approached the city limits, Nicky spotted one of those signs. He drove to a grocery store and called the phone number. That afternoon, he sat down for an interview with a Dooly VP and had a good offer on the table half an hour later. Eighteen dollars an hour to start, raised to twenty dollars after two weeks if he worked out. The VP didn't blink when Nicky gave his name. He was Nicholas Pomeroy. He was a graduate of Duro High class of 1969 and had worked for a couple of Oklahoma service companies the past year and a half. The company man looked over his scant resume while Nicky sat bouncing his right knee. He wondered if the man would show a flash of recognition. *Hey, I know you. We don't want your kind. Take a hike.* But, no, he was all business and wanted to conclude things quickly.

"Alright, I can offer you the job," said the VP. "You'd report to Glen Moore out at our West Duro office at 8800 West First Street. Day crews meet at six in the morning to go over assignments. Trucks roll by seven and not a minute later. Standard shift is twelve hours. You'll work six days a week, but your day off will vary, depending on the work. When we run night crews, you'd be expected to rotate every three weeks. Does that sound okay?"

Nicky said yes, and the two men shook hands.

"When can you start?"

"I can move down by the end of next week, and I guess I could start the following Monday."

The VP looked a little disappointed.

He was hoping I could start tomorrow, thought Nicky.

At first, he didn't tell his parents he was moving back. He didn't know what they'd say. They probably both wished he'd stay away a little longer, let the rumors cool down. Maybe a lot longer, maybe for good.

Ten days later, Nicky returned to Texas, his Javelin loaded up with clothes and shoes, a portable record player, some books, and a twelve-inch black-and-white TV. He checked into a motel and called his dad. Tony Pomeroy sounded thrilled and immediately suggested they meet for lunch at the lodge, which hosted a fish fry every Friday.

When Nicky arrived at Caprock Masonic Lodge 886, his dad's black Eldorado was already in the parking lot. Businessmen of all strata were arriving and heading inside. The fish fry was popular and free to Masons. Guests and wives could get in for a nominal fee. Though few women ever came to the lodge, they were allowed in for the Friday lunch.

Tony Pomeroy was sitting by himself just inside the door. Nicky hadn't seen him in almost a year. Dad had sprouted more gray hair and gained weight. His golf shirt fit tightly, over which he wore suspenders to support his white slacks.

Dad wasn't the hugging type, but he smiled broadly and gave his son a firm, manly handshake. Tony paid the three dollars to get Nicky in, and they lined up with trays for food.

"I'm happy you decided to give the old town another chance," said Tony. "I was intending to call you. The market for skilled men is really hot right now, and I knew you could get a job anywhere you applied, just for asking. Have you talked to your mom?"

"No," said Nicky. "I'll call her later."

"Yeah, you should do that. She's been kind of a wreck lately, worrying about you and about everything else. She's even been calling *me*, and I'm pretty low on her buddy list." Tony chuckled.

"I'll call this evening."

"Good," said Tony. "Let's grab a table over by the window."

They carried their trays of catfish, slaw, and hushpuppies to the small table, where they unloaded their dishes and set the empty trays aside to be whooshed away by the dining room staff.

"You have a place to live?" asked Tony.

"Not yet," said Nicky. "I'm looking at a couple of apartments this afternoon. I think prices have gone up since I was here last. I'm surprised how hard it is to find something."

"I hear what you're saying," said Tony. "That's what happens in a boom-or-bust town. In a couple of years, they'll have apartments they can't *give* away, but right now, housing is scarce." Tony spread his roll generously with three butter pats, served between squares of wax paper. "I'd let you stay with me if I had room. Since your mom got everything but my cars, I've been living in that little place on Poplar."

"I'm okay at the motel. It's just costing me eighteen bucks a night."

Tony whistled. "That's robbery. Well, like I said, I'd let you stay on my couch if I could. Things are a little . . . close at the moment." He leaned over and lowered his voice, glancing around. "The truth is, I have some company staying over right now, if you know what I mean." He attempted a comical wink.

"I understand," said Nicky. He didn't want to think about his dad having a girlfriend. He scanned the dining room. Across the aisle, two men in business suits were looking at him. Or maybe not. No, they were definitely looking. One of them gestured in Nicky's direction, and they talked with their heads close together. He looked down at the fried fish and the glob of ketchup on his plate. Father and son ate in silence. Tony finished his iced tea and looked around for somebody to fill him up again.

"Well, how was Oklahoma?" asked Tony.

"It was okay. I didn't know anybody. Never went anywhere. The companies couldn't give me very many hours. At the last one, I had to stay on twenty-four-hour call and couldn't really go anywhere. And then they didn't call much. I wasn't getting thirty hours a week."

"I know how that works," said Tony. "Now that you're back, you need to start breaking out of this pit you got yourself into. Pick yourself up, and move on. It's time."

"I know," said Nicky. "But everywhere I go in this town, everybody is the same as they were before I left. All my old friends are still here. Some of them got married, had babies, and all that, but they're still the same. But I'm *not* the same."

"Of course, you're not," said Tony. "Nobody would be. But, it's like Dr. Hain said, 'You have to go through the motions of being normal, and your life will come back to normal.' It just takes time. I know it's been hard. But it's also been two years, son." He paused as a small woman with a pink apron refilled his iced tea. "Here's an idea: Come out to movie night at the church next Monday. No pressure, but you could see all your old church friends. You know, they never blamed you for anything. Also . . . just an idea . . . there are a couple of young ladies who've moved to town with their families recently. I noticed one of them at movie night two weeks ago. Cute girl. You can introduce yourself. Get back in step."

Nicky glanced sideways. The two businessmen across the aisle were no longer looking his way. "I'm not quite ready for that, Dad. Thanks, though."

"What are you not ready for?" said Tony. "Having a life? I think that getting a girlfriend might be what the doctor ordered. It doesn't have to be serious. Just find a young lady to have some fun with. Get around. Go to dinner."

"I know. It's just that I'd feel like I'm being . . . disloyal to Helen."

"Oh, Nicky." Tony leaned back. "I know how you feel. But you should have accepted it by now. She's not coming back."

"I suppose not. But I wish I could talk to her, fix things between us, one way or another."

"Son, that's not going to happen."

"She needed to make it right, Dad. I can't do it. It's been really hard, especially with everybody thinking I'm the one who's responsible."

"Please, son, you worry me. Forget what other people think! It wasn't your fault."

"Yeah, but it was, in a way. Some people even think . . ."

"I know, I know. Please don't say it," said Tony. "We agreed not to talk about it."

"I have to say it. Because everybody's thinking it. I can hear almost them. They think I killed her."

CHAPTER 8

Test Run

Night security guard Albert Puga was supposed to get home around eight in the morning, have a bite to eat, watch a couple of morning shows with his girlfriend Victoria after she got her kids off to school, then be in bed by 11:00 a.m. for a long day's sleep with the blinds pulled. It was the life of a night-shifter.

This morning, he was going to vary his routine.

That's what they used to tell him when he was in the service in the Philippines. *Vary your routine.* It was even printed on a sign over the door of the mess hall at Clark Air Base.

GOING ON LEAVE? BE SMART
PAY ATTENTION
VARY YOUR ROUTINE

The precaution was understandable, because there had been some assassinations of US air and navy personnel in Angeles City. Political tensions were running high, and the naval and air bases on Luzon were a focus of local ire, and their personnel was a target for radicals. The typical scenario was that two guys on one of those ubiquitous little motorcycles that buzzed through the crowded streets would pull up right by the sidewalk where one or two servicemen were walking, pull out a .45, and BAM! BAM! Then disappear into the traffic before anybody could react. Four men had been killed in as many months and two more wounded. A few weeks after the third murder, the local police made a very high-profile arrest followed by the rapid and public trial of two young men they said were responsible.

Well, that's a relief, some of the men thought. But then, five days after the alleged sidewalk assassins were put away for life, a Navy man was shot as he came out of a small café in a tourist area. Same MO: Little motorcycle pulls up, shots are fired, buzzes away. After that incident, some servicemen just stayed on base on their days off or tried to bum a flight out to Tokyo, but Corporal Puga didn't want to go completely bonkers, so he took his chances in Angeles City. Just don't make it easy for them. Vary your routine.

Now, Albert was settled down with a steady if not lucrative job in Duro, Texas. He worked for a security company, guarding four warehouses on the west side of town where drill bits, pipe, and sundry oilfield equipment was stored. Since the start of the oil boom, thieves had gotten more brazen.

Albert first noticed the light blue Mercury Capri four evenings ago as he was leaving his house for work. It was unmarked, but everything about it said *cop car*. The trim was the super-charged 2.8-liter V6, a powerful beast for its size, with a collision bumper for forcing other vehicles off the road. Nobody drove cars like that but young men with doubts about their own manhood and cops. It was parked three houses down. He had never seen it before on Brayburne Circle, a working-class street that reflected a more prosperous past. Nobody in this sad neighborhood owned a car that nice. Albert wasn't sure, but he thought there was a guy sitting in it.

Who the hell is that? I know everybody on this street. Nobody parks here by accident.

The next morning, after Albert clocked out, changed out of his guard's uniform, and secured his gun in the locker, there was the blue Mercury again, parked catty-corner to the first warehouse. It had followed him all the way to his job on the east side. This time, as he drove past, Albert got a good look at the guy in the front seat. It was a fortyish man in a functional gray suit, curling gray hair trimmed short, and with horizontal age lines that crossed his tanned neck. He wore wraparound sunglasses. The man didn't move his head as Albert passed.

That is definitely a cop. Who the hell is he watching? Not me. They said they were done with me six months ago.

This became the pattern. The man never bothered him or tried to make contact. But every evening at his home and every morning at the warehouse, he was there, presumably watching Albert. After three days of this, there could be little doubt.

So, on day four, he varied his routine. Instead of getting straight into his car, he walked the other direction past the warehouses to Fifth Street and crossed the street to a shabby little diner called the Bluebird to have breakfast. He took his time, ordering eggs with tabasco sauce and toast and three cups of coffee, which he drank slowly. He sat by the window but didn't see the blue car. When he was finished, he paid, left a fifty-cent tip, then walked back outside.

There it was again, parked just down the street, the same guy sitting in the front seat.

It had been half a year since the cops last talked to Albert. He'd sat through four, no, five interviews. Variations of the same questions every time:

Where is Paul Zapeda?

"I have no idea."

When's the last time you saw him?

"August first. I told you."

That was at your girlfriend's house?

"That's right. At Victoria's house. It was his house, too. They were still married at the time."

What did you guys talk about?

"I've said this fifty times, man. I told him if he ever hit her again, I'd turn him in to the police."

And what did Mr. Zapeda say?

"He told me he and Victoria were finished, they were getting a divorce, and he was gonna move out. That was the last time I saw him."

So, what happened? Did he move out?

"I guess so. He left."

Why didn't he take his clothes?

"I don't know."

Albert, where is Paul Zapeda?

"I DON'T FUCKING KNOW!"

Mr. Puga, do not use disrespectful language in this station.

"Sorry."

The cops had tried to wear him down. They asked him to take a polygraph test. His lawyer said he didn't have to, that those things are unreliable, inadmissible in court, and wouldn't help him anyway, so he said no. They found Zapeda's car in Pecos, parked at the high school stadium. They told Albert to stick around town but never contacted him again.

Months went by. Victoria was granted a divorce based on abandonment. Albert moved in. The kids, especially the five-year-old boy, were upset that a new man was in the house, but they'd get used to him. Maybe someday, they'd even start calling him Daddy. They just needed time for things to settle down and move on. The cops had stopped bothering Albert.

Until that blue Mercury showed up. What should he do? Ignore it? Walk over and knock on the window? *Hey, man, why are you following me around?*

On the day he varied his routine, to his great relief, the car wasn't waiting on the street that evening as he got ready for work. It was not there the next morning when he clocked out from his shift. He started to relax. Maybe it was his imagination, or they had decided Albert wasn't worth it after all.

He had Saturday night off, but when he arrived home from work Monday morning, there was the car again and the man, this time parked on the street right in front of Victoria's house.

Albert was having no more of this crap. After he got out of his car, he walked right up to the obvious undercover car. He wasn't sure what he would say, but the obvious undercover cop saved him the trouble. The window rolled down as he approached the driver's side. The man with curly gray hair was there, and he smiled as he took off his sunglasses.

"Hello, Albert," he said.

The first name again. It seems like the more the cops had it in for you, the more they tried to make it personal. He didn't know this guy from Sergeant Friday. That pissed him off.

"Who are you?" demanded Albert.

"Name's Lamborn," said the obvious cop, still smiling.

"You a policeman?"

"I'm doing some work with the Duro police," said Lamborn.

What the hell does that mean? Is he a cop or not? Albert wanted to get the upper hand, let this guy know he wasn't taking any crap.

"What do you want? I already told the cops everything I know. Or is this about something else?"

"I have no idea what you think I want," said Lamborn. "But it's not complicated. I just was hoping you could help me."

"Help you do *what*?"

"Albert . . . come on," said Lamborn. "You know what we want. We need your help finding Paul Zapeda."

"I told you . . . I mean, I told the other policemen . . . I don't know where he is. He walked out on his wife and kids, and she divorced him. That's all there is to it. Where he is now, I have no idea. I can't help you guys."

"I think you could, Albert. In fact, I was hoping you could make some time for me today . . . so we could talk."

Albert stepped back from the car window. "I got nothing to say to you guys anymore. You can call my lawyer if you want. But I'm done."

The smile had melted away so slowly that Albert hadn't seen it go. Lamborn looked straight at him, serious. "Albert, your lawyer dropped you as a client three months ago. I don't care about him. We need to talk to *you*."

Okay, it was true that the attorney had told Albert that he couldn't represent him anymore, but it shouldn't have mattered. The cops were done with him anyway. That's what the lawyer had said.

"That's it," said Albert. "I'm not talking to you guys. I've said all I'm gonna say. I'm finished. Now, I'm a little bit tired, because I *work* for a living. I gotta sleep." He turned and walked away, defiant. Lamborn said nothing, and didn't attempt to follow. Once he was inside the house, Albert watched the Mercury through the kitchen widow. After a few minutes, Lamborn started the engine and drove away.

Victoria came in, drying her hair with a towel. "What were you looking at?"

"Nothing," said Albert. "Just a guy I know from work. He wanted me to trade shifts with him. I told him I couldn't do it. He's gone now. Hey, what you got to eat around here?" He started for the living room, hesitated, then went back to the kitchen window and looked out once more.

Sergeant Correa wanted to talk to Captain Lewis first thing this morning, to get his requested vacation dates confirmed, hopefully in writing. He needed to put down a deposit on the Wyoming cabin and wanted it to be the last week of October, opening week of deer-hunting season. After he hung up his jacket and headed down the hall, he saw that guy from Austin, Rob Lamborn, coming out of the captain's office, with Lewis beside him.

Correa knew little about Lamborn, other than he was a detective from the state capital and was spending the latter part of his career free-floating between precincts, supposedly teaching amazing policing techniques to the small-town yahoos. It was a mystery why he'd been brought to Duro PD, though the men enjoyed guessing.

Some said it was for the Zapeda case, which made little sense. The case was a piece of shit. Experts not needed.

"I'll talk to you this Friday, most likely," Lamborn was saying. "We'll get back to it Monday. Keep up the loud surveillance. Use the same car, but don't talk to him."

"Sounds good," said the captain. Lamborn left, and Lewis returned to his office.

Correa tapped on the captain's open door.

"Got a minute?"

"Sure. Come on in, Cory," said Lewis. "I got your request. I've been looking over our calendar for the next three months, and, really, the second or third week of November would work better for me. We have a busy fall ahead of us."

Correa didn't try to hide his disappointment. "Captain, it's the first week of hunting season. Snow comes early up there. I'd like to get ahead of it this time."

"You manage to bring home a large buck every year, Cory. Somehow you always make a late start work for you. I'm sorry. We need to finish the Zapeda case, and then we have some other cases coming up, including our old favorite. Plus we need to work around Detective Lamborn's schedule."

"I don't see why you think we need a mercenary like Lamborn," said Correa.

Lewis sat at his desk and took a stack of papers out of his inbox. "The man is a pro. It's that simple. I was against bringing him in, too, at first. But I've watched him work, and we could learn a thing or three from this guy. His methods are effective. He has a helluva track record."

"But for the Zapeda case? Really, captain, if you guys would just give me two hours with Albert Puga, I'd have him singing like a yellow bird. He's a lightweight. We don't need an expert to make him crack."

"Of course," said Lewis. "That's not the point. Yes, we could crack Puga. We just need to refine some techniques for the important cases. The Zapeda case just seemed like a good opportunity for a test run."

"Hah!" said Correa. "I wonder what the poor bastard would think if he knew we were just using him for practice?"

"Just as scared," said Lewis.

CHAPTER 9

Chase Gets the Part

"Duet acting," said David Bellamy. He sat on the edge of his desk, one leg up, casual. He paused. "I said . . . ah-*HEM* . . . *duet acting.*" He looked up at his class of eleventh and twelfth graders. "Come on, people! Duet acting. Not one taker?"

A girl raised her hand.

"Yes, Miss McFall?"

"So . . . in duet acting . . . how much of the play do you do?"

Bellamy chuckled. "Well, considering that the average play is an hour and a half to two hours long, and there are five to ten teams that compete . . . hmmm . . . I think it would be better to do a single *scene* from a play, unless you want to tackle *Macbeth* and just recite the whole thing real fast."

Nobody laughed. Then Russell, a lanky boy sitting in back, let out a snorting guffaw, and then the whole class laughed—at Russell, of course, not at Bellamy's joke. *What a stiff bunch of kids*, he thought. *Well, it's early in the school year.*

Bellamy stood up and walked to the chalkboard. He wrote:

DUET ACTING

Time limit, 10 min.

Two actors

Dramatic material

No props allowed

Again, Chase McFall's hand went up.

"Yes, Miss McFall?"

"Dramatic material? Does that mean we can't do a comedy?"

Bellamy walked to the front of the class and leaned forward on a front-row desk with the knuckles of his right hand. The boy whose desk it was leaned back.

"That's a good question. The simple answer is, no, there is no rule against performing from a comedy, per se. You could, for instance, find a serious scene in an otherwise comic play. Two years ago, two of our students won first place at the state level with a scene from a Shakespeare comedy. *Much Ado About Nothing.* But they did a dramatic love scene."

"But we can't be funny?" asked Chase.

"Again, there is no UIL rule against performing a funny scene. There's just one problem . . ." He paused, looking around the room. He wanted these kids to pipe up on their own. This was upper-level speech class, and Bellamy was one of the "cool" teachers.

"Come on, *somebody*," he said. "What do you think is the big danger you face when you do a comic scene in acting competition?"

Silence. Then one of the boys in front answered. "You have to be funny?"

"Bingo!" said Bellamy. "You have to be funny. This is a *competition.* You have a total of ten minutes. There will be three judges, all of them drama teachers or theater directors. Serious, serious people. If they laugh—fine, wonderful. Go for it. But if they don't . . ." Bellamy squinched up his face and held his nose. The whole class burst into laughter. *Finally, they lighten up*, he thought.

He looked up at the clock. Five minutes until the bell. Since this was the last class of the day, he knew he couldn't keep many of them down on the farm for long. He held up a clipboard with a legal-sized sheet attached.

"Sign-up sheet," he announced. "If you haven't signed up for an event, do so today. It's just four weeks 'til the first meet. If you don't sign up, then I'll sign you up. We still have openings for persuasive speaking, short story reading, poetry reading, debate, and . . . please, people . . . duet acting. I need two brave souls, and four if we can get them. If we get three, well, I guess I'll just have to force one of you hooligans to act at gunpoint."

Again, the class laughed tepidly. Then they all rose at once, and the room filled with loud bumps, chair squeaks, and talk as they shuffled into a messy queue in the center aisle to sign up for speech events. Voluntary compliance was the only way to get out of being assigned to one of the two dreaded ones—duet acting and—*shudder*—debate. The Speech Club president (and Drama Club vice president), Andrew Waylon, grinned at Mr. Bellamy, then wrote his name next to *Duet Acting*.

Well, that's one, thought Bellamy.

The piercing bell clanged. 4:00 p.m.—school's out. The kids thumped through the door, talking, laughing. Bellamy was pleased that there was no great escape from his classes when the bell rang, no crush for the exits. One or two of the kids usually stayed behind to ask questions or discuss some problem. Chase McFall almost always stayed. *Today? Yep, there she is, waiting her turn.*

Chase was a pretty, medium-height girl with a round face and high forehead, light brown hair flicked into shoulder-length wings, and a toothpaste-commercial smile. She usually had a request for clarification or an anecdote she wanted to share. Sometimes, she even asked for help with math (earlier in his teaching career, Bellamy had taught junior-high geometry). She spoke with an uptick at the end of her sentences, whether they were questions or not.

However, first to his desk for after-school time was Dale, a junior with more talent than confidence (Bellamy had plenty of the other kind, too). Dale picked up the clipboard and thumped it with his index finger.

"Mr. Bellamy, is there a way I can get signed up for short story reading?" he asked.

"Mr. Collard, it appears to be full up," Bellamy said. "How about poetry? We need two more participants."

Dale made a tastes-bad face. "I'm . . . Well, I just think I'm . . . better suited for short story. Russell signed up, and he's terrible."

"He's also quicker at signing up than you are. Look, poetry is great. There are fewer restrictions on expression. You can shout. You can cry. Plus, we have a great collection of poems edited down to the perfect length."

"But . . . poetry? It's just not a thing guys . . . do."

"Not true," Bellamy said. "But even if it were, that would mean you'd stand out from the crowd. I think you'll be great at it." He took the clipboard from Dale and scanned it. "Well, if you really hate the thought of reading poetry, you could go for duet acting. We only have one signed up, so far."

Dale's face fell. "Okay . . . I'll do poetry, I guess."

"Great! I'll write your name in. You won't regret it."

Dale slunk away. Chase stepped up. Beaming face, eye contact.

"Mr. Bellamy," she said, "You know how I asked you about comedy? There's a reason. I really want to sign up for duet acting."

"Excellent!" said Bellamy. "Good girl! You'll be working with Andrew, and he's fairly good, if you can keep him from hogging the stage. There are a lot of fine boy-and-girl scenes we could choose from."

"What I was thinking, though . . ." Chase squeezed her lips together. "I don't know if you heard, but I got the lead part for the all-school musical next spring, *My Fair Lady*. I'm going to be Eliza Dolittle."

"Well, that's wonderful!" said Bellamy. "I'm proud of you."

"Here's what I was thinking," said Chase. "Since I have to learn the part anyway . . . why not use a scene from that play? I know it's a musical comedy, but there's some great scenes . . . like this one scene where Eliza meets Henry Higgens. He's a language professor."

"I know," said Bellamy.

"Eliza and the professor have this back-and-forth that would be perfect for duet." Chase stood straight with her shoulders back and, as Bellamy feared, attempted Cockney. "'Oh, what 'arm is there my leaving Lisson Grove?'" she recited. "'It weren't fit for a pig to live in, and I 'ad to pay four and six a week!'"

Bellamy kept a straight face. "Good start," he said. "But, really, just taking a scene from another play you're already in kind of blows the point. Forget what I said about doing comedy. You're in school to learn and stretch your wings. Duet is different from drama. You have to convey the meaning and the emotion in a short scene, voice and gestures only, no props or costumes. I love *My Fair Lady*, but it's all about the costumes and the songs."

"Are you sure we couldn't make it work . . . somehow?" Chase asked. Sad eyes.

When she does that, she looks like Helen.

Bellamy picked up the clipboard and wrote in Chase's name beside *Duet Acting*. "You're going to be great, Miss McFall. I know you'll make us proud. We'll start looking at scenes tomorrow."

More sad eyes. "Okay." She turned and started away.

"Miss McFall," Bellamy said. She turned back to him. "You're one of my best students, and I count on you to lead by example. When you step up and take on a challenge that's a little harder, the others think they can, too."

The soft smile returned. "Okay . . . tomorrow."

"Tomorrow." Bellamy returned to his clipboard as Chase left the room. He watched her go.

Strike the set. Another school day is done.

David Bellamy was accustomed to crushes from high school girls. There was at least one every year. It had never happened when he taught math, but in the six years as the speech teacher and during the year and a half when he was interim theater teacher, several of the more artistically inclined girls (and, undoubtedly, some of the boys) had adored him, perhaps a little too much. A few times, he had to have *the conversation*:

"[Name], I am your teacher. I'm here to help you learn. I can also be your friend, but I can't be more than that. If you have any personal things you need to talk to somebody about, there's the school counselor."

In the Duro, Texas, school system, there was no formal plan for dealing with the possibility—or even the appearance—of an inappropriate student–teacher relationship. If there had been, then what happened at Richard Dowling Junior High in the fall of 1968 might have been dealt with more . . . effectively. At least before it became a major scandal, a criminal plea, and a civil suit.

After that unbelievable morning when the social studies teacher, Joe Weiser, had bolted across the state with a fifteen-year-old ninth grader named Brenda Whitlock—whom he had convinced himself was his one true love—everybody in town looked at all the male teachers in a different way. Especially the young, popular ones. That may or may not have been the reason Bellamy was booted from his job teaching theater. He wasn't fired, but they had declined to give him the job permanently and had moved him back to speech when they found a replacement. You couldn't blame them for hypersensitivity, but Bellamy had been doing well with the theater classes. Everybody said so.

It's true that Joe Weiser and he had been good friends—of course they were. They were about the same age, had both been long-distance runners in college, and kept up the good habit well into their thirties. They ran together most weekends. But it wasn't like they confided their innermost secrets. When Joe absconded with the Whitlock girl, the first person the police talked to was Joe's ex-wife, but the second one was David Bellamy. The Duro police had grilled him for two hours. They assumed that, because he was Joe's friend, Bellamy must know something. But he didn't. He was as shocked as everyone else.

Fortunately for all concerned, the fleeing May–November pair made it only as far as the Louisiana border before being caught and hauled back (in November's case, in handcuffs). It was ugly, ugly, ugly and appalling. Not just for the school but for every male teacher in the district. They all knew that, in the future, closer scrutiny was coming.

Bellamy had been assigned as interim theater teacher after the unexpected resignation of Mrs. Bullock just before the school year began. Bellamy had stepped into the gap, learning theater on the job and then directing a crackerjack production of *Guys and Dolls* for the all-school musical. The choir teacher directed the vocals, the dance teacher choreographed, but it was Bellamy who had managed the big, ungainly show and pulled it off. They got raves from the parents and standing ovations on all three nights.

That was where he'd first noticed Helen Orlena. She was just a sophomore, but she had a good stage presence, and her singing voice gave him chills. She didn't get a major part, but she had shined in the chorus. Bellamy continued to teach speech class, which Helen signed up for the next fall. Most of the kids had to be cajoled into giving it their best, but Helen tried hard from the first day. It was Helen who'd volunteered for duet acting and suggested they try one of the Beatrice and Benedick scenes from *Much Ado*. Bellamy had been reluctant, but Helen and her partner excelled at the performance, practiced it, and got even better, then landed first place in UIL Regionals.

The school coughed up the money to send them to the state competition in Austin, where they won easily. For a time, Helen, strange girl in so many ways, was a Duro High School star.

Nobody blamed Bellamy for what happened later. At least not to his face.

CHAPTER 10

Hitting Up the Local Talent

JJ picked up both his guitars in their road-worn cases and carried them up the steps into World Famous Best Studios. Harold opened the hatch of the station wagon and slid an enormous flat case out a couple of feet. The two aspiring hitmakers were back in Duro. They had made the trip in Harold's Ford Country Squire station wagon, a long, butt-crushing drive from Tulsa, with large suitcases and sufficient clothes for at least two weeks, along with two guitars and Harold's Fender Rhodes electric piano.

"I'd help if I could," said Allen Wallace. "My right hand is bad. Can't take any weight."

"That's okay. We got this," said Harold. JJ came back down the steps, and the two of them began the familiar chore of lugging the brutally heavy Rhodes piano out of the car and into the building.

"They sure make 'em like they used to," grunted Harold as they hoisted the ungainly case up onto the landing and into the building.

"Come on in and have a Dr Pepper," said Wallace. "I'll bet you guys are wiped out. I've made that drive myself a few times."

JJ took him up on the offer, but Harold had to leave right away. He had an appointment with the doctor.

HAROLD HAD BRUSHED his longish hair back over his ears, but now, as he sat in the symphony conductor's office, one little lock of hair kept dropping down over his right ear and tickling his cheek, driving him mad. Actually, it was Dr. Frederick Dietz who was driving him mad, but the errant hair was punctuation. Every few minutes, Harold pushed the hair back up over his ear, trying to not be obvious.

"Mr. Prensky, do you know what the AFM is?" asked Dietz.

"Uh . . . the American Federation of Musicians," said Harold. "I'm not a member, but I know about the organization."

"Good. Are you aware that the Duro Symphony Orchestra is an affiliate of the federation?"

"I didn't, but that shouldn't be an issue. I can pay union scale."

"I see. That's good," said Dietz. He leaned back in his high-back leather seat. "So, you are then prepared to pay all sixty-two members of the orchestra, including myself, full scale for all the time involved, including rehearsal."

"I don't *need* the whole orchestra," said Prensky. He had explained this already. "I just need four violins, two violas, two cellos, and a timpani. Nine musicians. I would do all the rehearsing and conducting."

"Ah, I see," said Dietz. "You're looking to hire nine professional musicians from our orchestra for a specific period of time—"

"Four days, at least six hours a day," said Harold. "Two days for rehearsal, two days for recording. If we have to go longer, I'd pay for it."

Dietz was not smiling. He had not smiled since the two first shook hands. He leaned forward and put elbows on the desk and his hands together. "Nine musicians, nine instruments. By the way, it's not *a* timpani. The word *timpani* is plural. And you say you'll pay union scale, plus overtime."

"There shouldn't be any overtime."

"Of course," said Dietz. "Well, I'm afraid I can't be of service."

"You mean . . . you can't tell your musicians about the gig? I'm sure some of them would jump at the chance to make a little extra money."

"You may be right," said Dietz. "But that's not how the orchestra functions. We are not a bevy of freelancers, ready to jump into the studio to help record a bebop tune."

"It's a serious recording project," said Harold. "I'd call it *art rock*."

"Whatever you call it, the Duro Symphony Orchestra is a unit. The individuals are not for hire."

Harold had not expected a slammed door. "But . . . Mr. Dietz . . . *Doctor* Dietz . . . it's not a union project. I just need some musicians who want to work."

"Then run an ad in the newspaper," said Dietz. "My musicians are not available."

"Can't you just let them know?" asked Harold. "Tell them there's this chance for a little extra work on the side?"

Dietz looked down over his glasses. "I'm afraid not. In fact, if any of my artists decided to try and sneak around behind my back for a little extra cash at your . . . ahem . . . gig . . . they would be booted out of the orchestra and out of the union."

"Wow . . . that's harsh," said Harold.

"Firm, I believe, is the word you're looking for. The rules are clear and were established to protect the musicians and the integrity of the business."

A big, fat monkey wrench, tossed right into the gears. Harold knew there was always unexpected turbulence at various points in a project. It always happens. But hiring local classical musicians was not something he had worried about. By going straight to the conductor, he was keeping everything aboveboard and clear, avoiding threats to anybody's territory. What he got was a complete roadblock. Not only could he not hire union musicians, he'd be putting their careers in jeopardy if he talked a few into helping him. *What a fatuous ass.*

The phone rang, and the conductor took the call, nodding toward his guest to let him know the conversation was over.

Harold drove back to Best Studios, where JJ Johns was working with Allen Wallace on test recordings. Harold was glad to be away from the studio, because Allen Wallace had a reputation for tweaking lyrics and arrangements, and JJ did not take well to somebody messing with his words. Tension between engineer and artist was likely, and Harold thought it best to stay out the way. Still, he had to break the bad news.

Harold had written a two-hundred-dollar "we're serious" check, and Wallace, in turn, had given Harold a key to the studio. This showed a lot of trust on the part of the studio owner. He told Harold and JJ they could let themselves in anytime as long as they followed the cardinal rules: Park in back, leave nothing in the car, and lock every lock both coming in and going out. Also, keep the thermostat at sixty degrees.

Harold pulled up behind the studio. He hoped it was going well. Rather than banging on the metal door, Harold used his key to let himself in through the double layers of security.

Wallace and JJ were both in the little studio. JJ sat in a folding chair with his Telecaster, which was plugged into a small tube amplifier. Wallace waved to Harold when he walked into the control room.

"Let's try it my way now, just one time," said Wallace.

"Start from the second verse?" said JJ. "Man, that makes no sense. If I do that, start right in the grim part—the poison river and the polluted air and everything—it's too fast. Plus, the audience isn't going to know what I'm talking about. It's a weird place to start the song."

"You're right," said Wallace. "But it will hook them right away, make them sit up and say 'What's this guy talking about?' And then they're going to say 'I wonder where this is going. I better keep listening.'"

"Or just get mad and turn off the radio," said JJ.

"Just try it, for me."

"Okay," sighed JJ. "Second verse, chorus, *then* first verse?"

"No, second verse, first verse, then chorus. The chorus is your payoff."

"Alright. I'll try it."

"Fantastic! Now, this time I want you to lean a little back from the vocal mic. Especially during the chorus."

Wallace stepped in to the control room, where Harold waited. "You want to play piano on this? It's just a test run to get a feel for the song."

"No," said Harold. "That's fine. Go ahead."

Wallace shut the studio door, then sat down at the soundboard and switched on the engineer's microphone.

"You with me?" he said.

On the other side of the glass, JJ gave a thumbs up. Wallace was using the older eight-track recorder. He punched the forward button, and the reels turned.

"Okay, we're rolling. Take it from the top."

JJ shut his eyes and leaned back a little, then began strumming the rhythm part. As instructed, he began with the second verse. JJ crunched a hard chord on the telecaster and sang loud.

"The roiling deathly waters here
Roll towards a poisoned sea.
Beneath these clouds of smoke and soot,
And I wonder why nobody else can see
What's going on . . . what's going on . . ."

JJ paused. "You want me to go straight into the first verse right there."

"Exactly," said Wallace. "Except . . . wait a second. Let's work on that line 'Wonder why nobody else can see.'"

"What's *wrong* with it?"

"You're rhyming *sea* with *see*."

"They're *different words*," said JJ. "It's a perfectly good rhyme."

"It's off-putting," said Wallace. "Let's go with something stronger. How about 'Sometimes I think nobody cares but me'? Doesn't that sound good? Makes it more personal. And it's a better rhyme."

"Maybe . . . whatever," sighed JJ. He scribbled notes on his tablet, adding to the tangle of previous notes.

"Take it from the top," said Wallace. "We're still rolling."

"All right."

"I see the deathly waters here . . ."

The session was under control, if tense, so Harold left the room to get a soda out of the refrigerator and to think. What a glitch! In Tulsa, he would have had no trouble collecting nine classical musicians, easygoing, professional, and willing to make a few bucks on the side cutting a pop record. Not here. Could he find anyone else to drive out to the Texas desert for four days of low-paid work? Possibly, but not likely. What other options were there? Well, there were other orchestras in West Texas. Also, he knew there was a local college here in Duro. It might have a music department, and he could round up some acceptable student talent. It was worth checking out.

Harold retrieved a Dr Pepper from the refrigerator and popped off the cap with a bottle opener attached to the door by a piece of kite string. He sat down at Wallace's desk and took a sip. The expansive desktop was mostly bare. There were a couple of stacks of notes and some sheet music. The only decoration was a framed picture of an attractive Black woman with tall, girl-group hair. It was a five-by-seven publicity photo. Harold picked it up for a closer look. There was a notation on the bottom, in a looping, flowing script.

Love to Allen,

my Heart and Soul

your Mabel

Harold didn't know the singer, though her wide face and hairstyle reminded him of Eartha Kitt or maybe one of the Ronettes. Of all the artist photos in the office, this was the only one that had earned a place on Allen Wallace's desk. Harold was fascinated by the woman's face, sepia toned with soft focus. Striking dark eyes, just a hint of smile . . .

"That's my second wife," Allen said from the doorway. Harold hadn't seen him come in.

"I'm sorry," said Harold. "I was messing around with your desk. I just saw the picture. She's a beautiful woman. I love these old-style fan photos." He set the picture back in its place.

"She was a beautiful girl," said Allen. "She still is. And I miss her every day. Hey, could I get into that desk for a second? I need a pen that works." Harold scooted out of the way. Allen chucked an old Bic pen into the trash can, slid the center drawer open, and found a replacement. He made a couple of quick doodles on a scrap of paper to make sure the pen worked, then returned to the control room.

"Okay," Harold heard him say from the other room. "Strum one bar, then go into the chorus."

Allen Wallace was married to a Black soul singer? Here in this roughneck part of the world? People are interesting....

CHAPTER 11

A Chance to Make It Right

Unlike almost every other Freemason lodge in the South, Local 886 was growing. This could be explained in part by what was happening in Duro, which was bathing in its fourth major oil boom since the town was incorporated in 1895. The population had swelled by 5,000 in just the past three years.

Typical Masons were grayheads, with an average age in their mid-fifties. Young men showed little interest these days in their fathers' fraternal organizations. The Shriners, Elks, Jaycees, and Odd Fellows were all experiencing a similar decline. The Duro chapter of the Loyal Order of Moose had closed its doors for good in 1969.

In contrast, the Duro Masons had inducted six new members in the past year, all of them young professionals in their twenties and thirties. This was a notable accomplishment, and many in Lodge 886 credited the past master, Tony Pomeroy, with the turnaround. In his two years as worshipful master, Tony had emphasized both recruitment and a high public profile for the lodge. When they sponsored a fundraising drive to help Duro residents whose homes were damaged in the flash flood of 1970, Tony had coordinated the effort and made sure everyone knew the lodge was behind it. He curried friendships among local newsmen and TV reporters and kept them apprised of Masonic activities, both major and routine. Food, clothing, and toy drives were all reported and touted, and every parade had a Mason float.

In January, Tony had stepped down from the master role and was elected senior warden. The new master, Eddie Hudson, was perfectly happy to let Tony continue as the public face of Craft Freemasonry on the Caprock.

Lately, Tony had been occupied with a new assignment: planning, and paying for, a restoration of the old monument out on Highway 652. The October general meeting of the lodge was held the second Tuesday of the month. For October, Tony had located, befriended, and invited a special guest speaker: Alex Dunbar, historian of Grand Lodge 460 of northwest Texas, based in Lubbock. It was said that he knew everything there was to know about Texas Freemasonry, all the way back to 1835, when that first group of Tennessee Masons had ferried across the Sabine. Tony hoped that Dunbar could give the members of 886 a sense of the rich history surrounding the monument and perhaps impart a little more excitement about the restoration and a willingness to cough up money. Tony was almost alone in his interest in the monument. He had visited it many times as a kid and a young man and had found the place wonderfully mysterious and beautiful, even in decay.

These days, its condition was, in a word, disgraceful. There had been no attempt to repair, clean, or even mow the grounds around the structure in many years. Few Masons even bothered to drive out and see it. Some of the newer members didn't know it existed, much less that it once held special significance for Masons the world over. As late as 1965, the lodge had held an induction at the site, and even then, it was an embarrassing mess. The facing stone was chipped in numerous places, the iron plaque had rusted, trash had piled up around the base, and graffiti marred the central obelisk. The small parking area and footpath to the site were overgrown with hackberry, prickly pear, and other shoe-piercers.

The old monument's greatest flaw, Tony knew, was its location. It may have been only a dozen miles from Duro as the crow flies, but there was no easy or obvious way to get there. Its position by the big salt flat was a major impediment, because the state never built a highway across it; hard desert rains every few years would briefly turn it back into a real lake. From Duro, it was a twenty-mile drive involving several meanders and two ninety-degree turns. The closest human dwelling was five miles away, in Autry, a tiny village on its way to becoming a ghost town. However, the location was the one thing they couldn't do anything about.

Master Hudson couldn't make the Tuesday night meeting, so Tony served as chairman. There were nineteen members present. Respectable, though Tony had hoped for more, especially since he had personally invited an out-of-town guest. There were also two visitors, a young engineer recently moved up from the Rio Grande valley, and Tony's own son Nicky.

Now that Nicky was twenty-one and had returned to Duro, Tony hoped he would consider joining the lodge. He hadn't shown much enthusiasm so far, but he did agree to attend tonight's meeting. At the very least, Tony could count on Nicky to pay attention during the guest lecture. The boy had loved the monument when he was growing up, loved it when the family drove out to see it, loved hearing stories about it and making up his own. If the site's restoration were up to Nicky, it would be a surety.

The lodge meeting began, as usual, gradually. There was the casual half hour of hobnobbing, shoulder rubbing, and social networking by the members before Tony brought the regular meeting to order. After the invocation, he hurried the group through the minutes, old business and new business, as efficiently as possible, for which everyone was grateful. He then introduced Alex Dunbar.

Dunbar was a short, bald, and owlish man who talked confidently in a high, raspy voice. He had asked Tony to provide a slide projector and screen. This got everyone's attention. Whatever this guy was planning to say, it involved visual aids and might be interesting. Tony gave a short introduction and turned the meeting over to the historian.

"Good evening, gentlemen," Dunbar said. "And thank you, Master Pomeroy. I really appreciate these opportunities to talk to fellow Masons in some of the smaller, out-of-the-way lodges around the state."

The remark irritated Tony. *We're not that small, friend.* But he kept his mouth shut, smiled, and nodded.

Dunbar continued. "I was especially excited when I heard about your plans to restore the energy-line monument out in the western part of this county. The Pyle Monument, it's usually called. The structure has a fascinating history, and I'm hoping that, tonight, I can put its importance into some context. I also have a suggestion that I hope is not too radical. But I get ahead of myself."

Dunbar switched on the slide projector, with its noisy fan.

"If someone could get the lights, please."

Tony complied.

As the projector fan rattled, the first slide chunked into place, and Dunbar adjusted the focus. It was a black-and-white outline drawing of the United States, with the state borders rendered as simple lines. In addition to latitude and longitude, the map was crisscrossed with diagonal lines, forming thin diamond patterns on the map. Some of the lines were thicker than others.

"Many of you have seen this famous map before, I'm sure. It shows the major and minor ley lines that cross North America. From this photo, we can't appreciate the extreme detail of this map, which is enormous—four feet by six feet. The original, which is stored in the Masonic Temple in Washington, DC, is in very delicate condition, but fortunately, there are excellent copies. As you can probably see, two major ley lines cross through West Texas and intersect a few miles southwest of town. Now, here's a detail."

He switched to the next slide, which showed the western part of Texas where the southeast corner of New Mexico juts in. The ley lines were prominent, and at their crossing point in West Texas there was a small printed notation:

31°31'31"N

103°10'3"W

"Please note the significance of that latitude and longitude. We'll come back to it in a bit. Meanwhile, it's important to remember that the map predates any attempt to describe and survey this part of West Texas. In other words, our forefathers, the ones who studied these azimuthal alignments, knew nothing whatever about Texas geology. They just calculated locations on an inaccurate map. However, they knew the importance of numbers. The latitude thirty-one degrees thirty-one minutes north is of particular importance. If you follow that line around the globe, you find yourself crossing some of the most studied temples and burial sites in Egypt." He flipped through a series of slides of Egyptian tombs, probably photographed from travel books. "Keep going east, and you pass through some truly ancient burial sites in northern India." A slide of several eroded statues. "And eventually, you find yourself at Longhua temple in Shanghai, China." Another slide, this time of a vine-covered ruin. "Not as famous as the Jade temple, but older and more historically important."

Dunbar looked up from his notes. The Masonic faces in the room, lit by projector, were mostly blank, as if they were watching slides of somebody's vacation. He kept going.

"Now, the longitude one hundred three degrees ten minutes west is special for a different reason. There are some very powerful magnetic anomalies along the parallel but little in the way of human historical sites. In Texas, it passes through the edge of the salt lake that's near the Pyle Monument—La Sal Del Rey, it's called. Most of you have at least driven past it, though I've heard there's not much water left. Did you know it's one of only two natural lakes in Texas?"

He looked up. No response.

"Like I said, nothing very special in the US, but when you get to Mexico . . ." He went to the next slide, which was of a series of enormous round earthen structures. "The longitude passes through a very significant pre-Aztec ruin, the temple called Tzintzuntzan. Let's say it together—*tzin . . . tzun . . . tzan*." He chuckled. Not a laugh out of anyone.

Tough crowd, he thought.

"So, what I'm trying to show is that the lines are important, but there are many such lines around the globe, and the ancient Egyptians and Greeks and Chinese knew them well. What makes the Pyle site meaningful? I'll show you."

He went to the next slide. It was a distorted straight-down view of the northern hemisphere, with the north pole at its center.

"Here's why it matters. Pretend this is a globe, and we stick a pin on this side, at the ancient Cambodian city of Ankar. Most of you know why that's special. Now, take some imaginary string and run it across the top of the globe to the Nazca Desert, in Peru, on the opposite side of the world. The site is famous for its petroglyphs, giant figures carved into the desert floor. Monkeys, panthers, birds . . . Some of them are over a thousand feet across and can only be appreciated from an airplane. If we stick another pin in the Nazca plateau, what do you suppose is at almost the exact halfway point? Way up here in Alaska. Anybody?"

Dunbar wasn't budging until he had an answer. The Masons looked at each other. Fortunately, Past Master Tony knew. (Dunbar had planted the answer, just in case.)

"Mount McKinley," said Tony.

"Exactly!" said Dunbar. "Mount McKinley. Called *Denali* by the Athabaskan people. McKinley is the central vortex of the Northern Hemisphere. The ley line from that mountain to the largest vortex in South America passes through . . ." The West Texas slide came up again, but this time with a thick red line running northwest to southeast. "That's right. It passes right through the intersection of thirty-one degrees thirty-one minutes and one hundred eight degrees ten minutes. Only a few places on the globe are more significant, and this one sits right in your back yard. Here's one more slide." It was a photograph of the Pyle Monument, in color, but it looked hand tinted. The structure was clean and beautiful, and the copper trim reflected brightly. It was the Pyle from decades ago, before it fell victim to neglect.

"This picture," said Dunbar, "is from a book in the archives at the Grand Lodge of Scotland, in Edinburgh. It was considered important enough to merit its own page. Okay, if someone could get the lights, please." Tony turned on the bluish fluorescents. Dunbar looked around the room at the blinking men, hoping he had made an impression.

"I'll be happy to take any questions in a moment," he said. "But first, I mentioned a radical proposal. Most of you know, I hope, that the first monument, which was a simple concrete structure with a bronze plaque, was not where the Pyle is today. It was originally placed some thirteen hundred feet farther southeast—along the major ley line. That was based on the first private survey from 1907, which was bankrolled by five Mason businessmen from Huntsville, who bought that section of land and some others nearby, sight unseen. It was called the Malloch Survey.

"When the location was resurveyed in 1930, everybody assumed that the Malloch team must have gotten it wrong because their instruments were less accurate. How else could they have missed their mark by a quarter of a mile? Well, gentlemen, after studying these old documents, I've come to believe those boys at the turn of the century knew exactly what they were doing. I think they got it right. And, moreover, I think you should consider moving it back to the old location, since you're renovating it anyway."

Dunbar raised himself as tall as he could manage with his truncated frame. "I realize it sounds crazy, but some more recent studies have lent credibility to the original location. What's changed is our knowledge of the geology beneath our feet. Thanks to the good old Texas oil industry, there have been many seismic surveys out there in recent years. The original monument sat on a rocky dome about five feet high and fifty feet across. The size is deceptive. The dome is actually just the tip of a pluton. If we have any geologists in the audience, you'll know what I'm talking about. It's a plug of solid igneous rock that formed about six million years ago. In this case, it's mostly granite. Only a tiny fraction of it protrudes above ground, but it goes down into the Earth for miles.

"That's where you should locate your monument. It's a powerful energy center. Ley lines don't run strictly according to mathematics. They wiggle and turn at various points depending on shape and density of the rock. This is true all over the world. If you want the Pyle Monument to be sitting on the intersection of three powerful energy lines, it belongs a thousand feet southeast."

There was a long pause. Finally, Dunbar said, "I'd be happy to take questions." Tony wanted to ask a quick question to save his guest from embarrassment but couldn't come up with anything on the spot. To his relief, Nicky raised his hand high.

"What do you mean when you say *ley line*?" asked Nick. "I hope that's not a dumb question."

"No, it's a great question. The term refers to the lines of magnetic energy—some say spiritual energy—that crisscross the planet. They were well-known by ancient civilizations but were mostly forgotten for hundreds of years. Then scholars in the British Isles about two hundred years ago noticed that all the really important Druid and Celtic monuments were in an orderly alignment with each other and with natural rock formations. The ancients build their structures along these lines, and the same patterns were discovered around the globe, where they form grids. The knowledge spread from the British Isles to the rest of the world, including North America. The term *ley line* was coined by a Mason named Watkins back in the 1920s. It comes from an old word for 'path,' because many of these energy lines had actual footpaths on them. Thank you. That was a very good question."

Dunbar looked around the room. He feared he wasn't reaching anyone. This happened a lot when he gave these talks, even to Masons, who, at one time, were at the vanguard of the geomancer studies.

"Any others?" He waited.

Nicky raised his hand again. "So, when you say the ley lines cross where that . . . rock—"

"The pluton."

"—where the pluton is, are you saying that's where the most energy is."

"That's right," said Dunbar. "That's right. I'm not saying it could be measured by seismic instruments, but I do believe the energy is there. And the monument should be there, too. Excellent comment. Are there any more questions?"

Before the silence had a chance to become awkward, Tony stood up. "Thank you, Alex. That was a very interesting and informative presentation. I know I learned a lot. As Masons, we have an obligation to keep in touch with our history and pass it on to the next generation. Excellent job." He clapped, and the rest of the Masons joined him, half-heartedly.

After some final lodge business, the chaplain led the group in prayer recitation, then Tony gaveled the formal meeting to a close, and the collation open. In some lodges, collation meant punch and cookies. At Duro 886, it was an open bar. That was what most of them came for anyway: the business contacts, the camaraderie, and liquor.

As he sipped his rum and coke, Tony was relieved that some of the men were making conversation with Dunbar, though he doubted they were discussing topography or energy lines. He was especially pleased that his own son had made a point of speaking to their guest. *I guess I raised him a little bit right.*

Tony's friend Caleb Hays sidled up. "Well, he had me until he started talking about moving a fifty-ton structure. That was kind of a deal killer. Interesting talk, though. A bit on the fruitcake side."

"Yeah," Tony agreed. "Not practical but fun to discuss, I suppose. We forget how much our ancestors cared about things like energy lines. And some of us still do. It's a little bit embarrassing, like the crazy uncle nobody talks about. But it is our history. Personally, I find it fascinating."

Caleb laughed. "It is interesting. The one question I could have asked—but didn't—is 'Who cares, really?' Even if we raised the cash and moved the damn thing, what would we *do* with it? How exactly would that help our lodge and Freemasonry in general? And so what if it's not sitting on the exact perfect spot? It's pretty darn close. Why go to all the expense and trouble to move it? Especially since that puts it even farther from the highway. And a minor highway at that."

"Why? I don't know. Maybe it would give us more . . . *energy*," said Tony. They both guffawed, and Caleb almost choked on his Dewar's.

"I could use some of that extra energy," said Caleb. "You ready for another one?"

Tony nodded, and the two walked toward the bar, where Nicky was standing with a can of beer.

"You remember my son, Nicky?" said Tony.

"Good to see you again," said Caleb, and they shook hands. "What did you think of the meeting tonight? The subject was a little unusual, I know."

"I liked it," said Nicky. "In fact . . . I like this group. I've been thinking it over, and I believe I want to join. You guys do good things, and I'd like to be part of it."

Tony beamed. "That's wonderful!" he said. "Nobody ever said they regretted the day they became a Mason."

"Good decision, son," said Caleb.

"You can tell me what I need to do next," said Nicky. "Anyway, I want to talk to Mr. Dunbar a little more before he gets away. It was great to see you, Mr. Hays."

Nicky excused himself. He had more questions for the geomancer.

CHAPTER 12

Holly Checks the Stove

Holly woke to the smell of gas. She sat up in the dark. Grover slept beside her, breathing deeply. The glowing dial on the bedside clock read a few minutes until three. Holly sniffed the air. She swung her feet off the bed, found her house shoes on the floor, and slipped them on.

Now that she was fully awake, she no longer smelled gas. She breathed slowly through her nose. Did she dream it? Someone had said once that if you are exposed to a strong odor long enough, you won't smell it anymore. She had to check the stove. It was something she did many nights.

Holly went into the dark kitchen and sniffed again. Nothing out of the ordinary. There was a faint whiff of last night's dinner; canned cowboy stew, carrots, and peas. No gas, however.

Check the stove.

Holly felt the stovetop in the middle between the burners. The white enameled metal was warm from the burning pilot light. She opened the oven door. The faint yellow light shining through the hole at the bottom told her the oven pilot was burning, too. Outside, the trees swished as an October wind blew over the Caprock. She stood by the kitchen door, looking out the window into the back yard, shadowed from the streetlights and completely dark. She wanted to look at the stars.

Get your robe.

She slipped back into the bedroom and took her robe from its hook outside the closet door. Grover was still breathing evenly, sound asleep. She could barely see the outline of his face in the dim window light. She watched his profile for a couple of minutes.

Aren't you going outside?

Holly returned to the kitchen, opened the back door as quietly as she could, and slipped out into the yard. It was a cool, breezy night and felt like Autumn. A feeble quarter moon showed just above the roofline of the house next door. The city lights of Duro gave the trees and rooftops a soft yellow cast, but the stars were bright. So many stars! And the imagined patterns they called constellations. Beautiful, beautiful.

When she was a young girl, Holly had sometimes heard the voice of God when she looked up at the stars for a very long time. She had loved to lie on her back in the grass, on a hill just outside their farm near Ranger, Texas. If she lay with her head just right, the surrounding trees and buildings would be out of her peripheral vision, and she could imagine herself floating among the stars, and each light was a soul who had lived a good life and had now gone to live with Him. She had hoped that someday when it was her time, her flawed soul would rise and burst into light, and she would become a star herself, and her own wickedness would vaporize.

Now that she was grown, it would be undignified to lie on her back, but Holly gazed upward. Everything was different now. She would never be up there. Perhaps her children would, but not Holly.

That's enough. Go back inside now.

She stood a moment longer. A particularly bright star, almost exactly overhead, caught her attention. She wondered what its name was. All the big stars had names.

It's called Arcturus. Now, be a good girl, and go back inside and check the children.

Holly slipped back inside the house and shut the door carefully. Stepping quietly, she visited her children's bedrooms, stood over each of them looking down at their innocent shapes. The two young ones were deeply asleep, even Peter. Last, she went into Becky's empty bedroom.

With each passing year, there was less and less of Becky in this house. The old teenage motivational posters had come down long ago. The bookshelf still held her childhood books, the youth novels Grover disapproved of. Becky would probably never live in this room again. She was already talking about going to Europe for a few years after college. Or perhaps she would find a good boy, marry, live a moral life, have children, and raise them before the world ended. Holly could imagine that Becky might become a star when she died. Despite her independent ways, Becky resisted the world's wickedness. But the younger children? Now, at this time in their lives, they were pure and untouched by Satan and the world. How much longer would they stay untouched?

The wickedness was out there, growing stronger every day, sniffing and scratching at the gates and burrowing under them to get at the children. Holly couldn't protect them much longer.

Hanging over her head was a problem Holly hadn't even mentioned to Grover: The school district was giving her trouble again. Some states had laws where any small group of people could get together, declare themselves a private school, and educate their children at home, with minimal interference. Texas had no such regulations. The tiny number of families who opted to teach outside the world and outside the formal religious schools existed in a legal limbo. For years—the whole time they were raising and educating Becky—the Paulsons had gotten away with it by simply sending a letter and a form to the Ferris County Independent School District, checking the box that said *Attends private school*, and no one had batted an eye. She knew that, around the neighborhood, they were known as the people who didn't send their kids to school, but little Becky was so bright, outgoing, and obviously smart that no one complained or reported them to the authorities.

Holly had finally collided with the world two years ago. A man from the school district arrived at her door and informed her that she was risking a charge of "abetting truancy" unless she wrote and submitted a detailed monthly report outlining her curriculum for teaching the required subjects of math, English, history, and good citizenship and exactly what books and materials she used, along with a full list of students. Holly smiled and agreed, then did nothing.

Letters came, some trying to be persuasive, some threatening, all tossed into the trash as soon as they were received. She didn't bother Grover with it. He was their breadwinner and didn't need the extra worries. She also feared that he would fight for their educational choice so aggressively that they would draw serious legal trouble.

Would the world take their children away? Put either Grover or Holly—or both—in jail? That was her nightmare: the world removing the children and raising them in the world.

Go back to bed now. The men from the world are coming tomorrow, and you need to rest.

Holly complied, but first, she checked the stove one more time.

CHAPTER 13

Too Many Good Ideas

Dan parked on the street next to Becky's off-campus apartment in Fort Worth and gave the car horn a short bap. That was all it took to get Becky moving.

It was late Thursday afternoon. This semester, neither he nor Becky had classes after noon on Thursdays, so there was a long weekend every week. Also, they didn't have to be back in class until Monday afternoon, so a predawn departure from the Caprock would return them to Fort Worth on time. How the rest of their coursework would get done, they weren't sure, but they were going to need several of these long weekends this semester if they were really going to shoot a film in Duro.

The film. The film about *what*? They still hadn't settled on a project. They had to work this out soon, so they could plan equipment checkout, and shooting schedules. Dan was having serious reservations about Becky's favorite idea. He had an alternative up his sleeve, but he needed to use tact. Let her talk it out.

Becky came out of the apartment with her small weekend suitcase and tossed it into the back seat of the car.

"So, did you talk to the Duro police?" asked Dan.

"Yes," said Becky. She sighed. "Some detective named Correa. At least I think he was a detective. Anyway, it was useless. Absolute waste of time."

"What, he wouldn't give you any information?"

"None. Goose eggs. I even asked him some questions about things that have already been reported in the paper, just to see if I could loosen him up. No dice. Not only would he not talk to me, but he wouldn't give me a name of anyone I *could* talk to. 'It's an *ongoing investigation*.'" Becky made quotes with her fingers.

"Really?" said Dan. "No progress has been made on Duro's number one murder case in two years? Assuming it *was* murder. No body, no suspects. I don't think *anything* is ongoing." Dan started the car and pulled out onto the wide parkway that led to Highway 80.

"I think they're just covering for their own failures," said Becky. "They can't solve a case even with a drawer full of clues. I mean, what have they got? First, there's the ex-boyfriend." Becky held up one finger. "They supposedly talked to him about six times, but he never gave them anything, played dumb, never cracked. Is he just that tough, or is he really innocent? Did he and Helen have an argument? Did he try and get her back? Nobody's saying. The cops never charged him with anything, but they never cleared him, either. But if it wasn't him, then who?"

"Really, it didn't have to be somebody she knew well," said Dan. "Just someone who knew her. Maybe somebody at her school."

"Well, they said she was having problems in school," said Becky. Second finger. "She was an A student, won some kind of big award at the state level. Great at everything. Then, she started getting in trouble, got suspended. Why? Again, nobody's saying. Did she get in with a bad crowd?"

Becky held up three fingers at arm's length so Dan could see them even while driving. "Finally, there's the car. Whoever killed her went to a lot of trouble. Cleaned that car inside and out. They found it parked at a flea market in some little town fifty miles from Duro."

"Then how do we know she's dead?" said Dan. "Maybe she abandoned her own car, cleaned it, and left it, just so she could make a break with Duro and high school and everything. Have you thought about that?"

Becky sat back and shrugged.

"Maybe," she said. But my theory is the cops have absolutely no idea what happened to her. If they admit the investigation is going nowhere, everybody will know how incompetent they are."

"That *is* possible," said Dan. "But maybe they just don't want a couple of college film-makers messing up their case and tipping off the suspects."

"I suppose," said Becky. "But that's not the point. We're not trying to investigate the murder itself."

"Disappearance."

"Disappearance. Whatever. I just thought we could interview a bunch of people who knew her. Not her family, of course. That would be cruel. But friends, teachers, actors at the theater. The film could be about how everybody was affected when a girl disappeared—a girl they thought they knew but didn't really know."

Dan was silent. As they pulled on to the highway and picked up speed, he looked over at his friend.

"Becky, I have to be honest with you. You have great ideas, but I don't think this one can happen. Not in the time we have to do it." Dan never talked down to Becky, but they couldn't waste time and resources running down blind alleys. He had to be the voice of practicality. "We have to put our energy where it will do the most good."

Becky looked away, and Dan let the subject drop. He knew he was right, but he had to give his partner space. Becky watched out the side window as they left the sprawling Fort Worth suburbs behind. Gradually, wooden fences gave way to barbed wire and open, treeless prairie.

"All right," Becky said at last. "We have to make the film about *something*. We can just go find another smelly retirement home somewhere and interview a bunch of old farts."

"Don't be discouraged," said Dan. "I really like the idea of a film about West Texas. We both grew up out there, and it's not like the rest of the state. Duro is in its own strange little time warp but with odd bits of the modern world mixed in."

"I guess so," said Becky. "But if you're thinking about making a film about the crazy holy rollers . . . that's just too close to home for me. I wouldn't do that to my family."

"I understand, but actually, I had another idea," said Dan. "Something I read a couple of days ago."

"I'm listening."

"Have you ever heard of Allen Wallace? He's a music producer."

"Can't say I have," said Becky.

"He used to be pretty famous," said Dan. "He has a music studio just outside of Duro. It's been there since the fifties. Nobody remembers it anymore."

"All right. I'm interested."

"I saw a classified ad in the *Fort Worth Star-Telegram*. It said something like 'World Famous Best Studios in Duro, Texas, seeking classical musicians for a project featuring recording artist JJ Johns.'"

He waited to let that sink in. Becky looked at him blankly.

"*JJ Johns*," said Dan.

"Who's that?"

"Who? You're kidding me! He was the lead singer and guitarist for the Blue Zephyrs."

"Who?"

"The Blue Zephyrs. Geez, Becky. You know . . . 'Step Outside Our Love'?"

"Never heard of it."

"Oh my God," said Dan. "It was a huge. It was all over the radio a few years back." He sang in a scratchy falsetto:

"Step outside our love, girl
My heart needs room to grow"

He looked at Becky hopefully. She laughed and shook her head. "Danfour, please. I was *educated at home*. We just barely had a radio."

"Well, trust me, it was big. If you lived on Earth, you heard it. JJ Johns wrote it and sang it. It was the Zephyrs' biggest hit, though they have a bunch of good songs."

"I trust you," said Becky.

"Now JJ Johns is coming to Duro, Texas, from wherever he lives—Tulsa, I think—to record his newest single at a tiny little studio nobody in Texas remembers with an engineer who made a bunch of hit records back in the early sixties."

"Good for him," said Becky.

Dan shook his head. "Well, I think it's a great idea for a film. There are all these great questions: Why? And why Duro, of all places? Is he trying to resurrect his career? And why is he advertising far and wide for classical musicians? I don't know about you, but I'm intrigued. Something interesting is going on, right under everybody's nose. It's a story begging to be told. And best of all . . ." Dan paused for drama. "We could probably shoot it in three days."

Becky watched out the car window as the low, rolling farm country gradually gave way to arid prairie. Dan knew Becky pretty well and also knew that she didn't let go of ideas easily. At least he had planted the seed.

After a couple of minutes, Becky looked over. "Okay. I'll think about it. But tomorrow, I'm supposed to have lunch with a newspaper reporter, Nolan Batts. You can come, too, if you want. They say he knows more about the Helen Orlena case than anybody else in town. At least anyone who'll talk. Depending on what he tells me, I'll consider putting the subject aside . . . for now."

"Save it for when you go to work for *Sixty Minutes*."

"Right."

They drove on. On the other side of Abilene, the sun fell low in the sky, setting right over Highway 80, casting a brutal glare. Dan squinted through his sunglasses and pulled the car visor down as low as it would go.

"I wish we could make this drive in the morning," he said. "This is going to happen every single time. And we always catch the rising sun full blast on the way back. By the time this film project is over, I'll be blind."

Becky didn't respond. She had pulled her floppy hat down over her face and scooted down low in the front seat. Dan wondered if they could stop somewhere to break up the four-hour monotonous drive.

"You want to get something to eat or just punch straight through?" he asked.

"Straight through," Becky said from beneath her hat.

CHAPTER 14

A Small Detour

Unlike most of his friends, Nicky liked getting up early. He always had, even as a teenager. He loved the dark and quiet and the idea that he was the only one awake.

The job with Dooley Pipeline was going pretty well. The days were long, but the work was interesting. They were laying a gas pipeline in one of the counties west of Duro, which called for long drives to and from the field. Nick performed all the usual pipeline roustabout duties, but his specialty was epoxy coating the pipe joints behind the welders. Nick was put in charge of a small crew of men, all younger than he was. They got along well, but he didn't try to make friends. During the drives out and back, Nicky didn't kid around or crack jokes like the other guys. He preferred to watch the prairie out of the van window as the light slowly rose and as it gradually grew dark in the evening.

Nicky set an alarm clock when he went to bed every night, but it was almost never needed. Most mornings, he woke a few minutes before it went off, showered and shaved, ate a bowl of cereal, then was out the door of his apartment before there was any traffic on the street or a hint of light in the sky. He was often the first one at the shop, even beating the field engineers most mornings. Sometimes, he was so early he would drive around town for fifteen or twenty minutes to kill time.

This morning, he made a strange mistake. He woke in the dark as usual, glanced over at the green glow of the clock, and saw it was five minutes until the alarm would clang. He clicked it off and got up, dressed, and prepared for his day. As he drove down Fifth Street on his way to work, he passed a little café that was popular with the early morning oilfield workers and with men coming off their night shifts. Usually, it was bustling by 6:45 a.m., but Nicky noticed there were only a couple of cars parked in front this morning, with three or four men sitting in the booths. Strange.

When he arrived at the office, the parking lot was empty. Then another thought struck him: *It's too dark.* Usually the streets were gray with predawn light by now.

What time is it? Nicky didn't wear a watch when he went into the field. That was a company rule, for safety reasons—no watches or rings. So Nicky drove back up the street to Farm & Ranch Savings, which had a large outdoor clock.

5:51. He had misread his alarm clock and gotten up an hour early. *Damn, that was stupid.* Well, nobody would ever know except Nicky. But still, how incredibly dumb!

Oh, well. What now? Go back to the apartment for half an hour? Drive to the café and get a plate of hash browns?

Nicky headed north through town. When he reached East County Road, he turned right and drove up the wide street that hugged the northwest side. At Twenty-Fourth Street, he turned right again, driving past his old junior high and the park where he and his friends had played Pop Warner football. He hadn't been to this neighborhood in a very long time. He'd lived in Duro his whole life, but being away for two years had made everything seem so odd and unreal when he returned. Everything looked smaller, and the colors he thought he remembered had faded.

He turned left on Stonewall Lane and drove slowly, looking at the large houses that lined these comparatively well-off blocks. It suddenly occurred to him: He was driving to Helen's house. Nicky hadn't been there since . . . when? Then he remembered, and a blanket of sadness came draped over him. Two years ago. More than two years. It had been the middle of summer, and Helen was planning to leave town for a drama workshop. That was the last time he had been really happy.

Nicky sat with Helen at the breakfast table in her parents' kitchen. Helen read the letter through a couple of times, to make sure she wasn't missing anything. It read:

Congratulations on your acceptance into the Central Texas Christian University Summer Theater Workshop, June 29 through August 24. Your previous status as an alternate gives you first rights to any openings in our program. We are pleased to inform you that an opening has become available. If you still want to participate in the program, you must sign and return the enclosed acceptance letter by June 19.

She signed her name at the bottom of the letter and dated it.

Helen Angelica Orlena – June 16, 1970

She looked up at Nicky, who sat across from her, silent. "This is it. I'm doing it," she said.

"Okay," said Nicky. His eyes were moist.

Helen folded the letter and inserted it into the return envelope. "Let's go to the post office."

"You can just put it on top of your mailbox," said Nicky. "The mailman will get it."

"The *post office*," repeated Helen. "Do you want to drive? We can go get burgers at Sambo's later."

"Let's go in my car," said Nicky. Despite the fact that Nicky drove a shiny blue 1969 Javelin, his graduation present from a year ago, they usually went everywhere in Helen's old car. Nicky usually drove.

There was a clenched fist in the middle of Nicky's chest. Helen would be gone for over a month. But at least he and Helen were back together. He didn't know how he would survive if they broke up again. The week before, they'd fought about something dumb and didn't speak for two days. Nicky couldn't eat, could barely sleep. He had called her house a dozen times over the weekend, and when she finally took his call, he was relieved beyond words. He'd been so close to losing her, much too close.

Nicky started the car and backed out of the driveway.

"I know I've been acting ridiculous," he said. "I'm sorry. I really am. I'm gonna try to be good." He gave her a sheepish smile.

Helen chucked him on the shoulder, "You better, Moose."

"When you get back from the workshop, let's spend a few days out at my dad's lake house. Before school starts. It will help us renew our relationship."

Helen gave him a sideways glance but didn't say anything.

After a few blocks, Nicky turned left onto Twelfth Street to get to the main post office. He pulled into the parking lot, then around the loop to the outdoor postal box, and rolled down his window. He held his hand out for the letter.

"Wait," Helen said. "Let's park. I want to hand it to somebody inside. I'm not taking any chances."

Nicky parked beside the flagpole in front of the post office, leaving the engine running.

"I'll be right back," said Helen and hopped out. Nicky waited, watching her as she went inside. He loved the way she swished her hair and bounced as she walked.

She never wore her hair high and stiff like so many other girls he knew. Normally, this little thing would have made him happy. Not today. Today there was the fist in his chest.

When Helen returned to the car, she was grinning.

"I gave the letter to the postal guy and said 'Post this for me, please, my good man.'" Helen used her upper-crust British RP accent. "He said 'Oh, this must be im*por*tant,' and I said, 'Yes, 'tis! 'Tis!'"

Nicky drove out of the post office lot and west on Twelfth. He leaned over and spoke in a hushed tone. "You know, it's only eleven-thirty. It's a little early for lunch. My mom goes to the office at nine-thirty. My dad moved out a month ago. It's the housekeeper's day off . . . hint hint."

Helen laughed. "It's morning! Aren't *we* impetuous!"

"Uh-huh." He nodded, smiled, and moved his eyebrows up and down. "But I have to work tonight. We're doing inventory."

"Okay," Helen said. "Two important questions. First, are you prepared?"

Nicky nodded vigorously. "Two in my wallet," he said.

"Secondly, and most important, who is in charge?"

"You."

"Who calls the shots?"

"You."

"Who says what we do and what we do not do?"

"You, you, baby. Nobody but *you*."

"All right," said Helen. "Carry on then, my good man. To the boudoir!"

Nicky accelerated the Javelin, pushing it faster when a traffic light turned yellow. It was red before he got through the intersection. The cops call that *running an orange*, but Nicky got away with it. He looked forward to a close and happy morning.

That day now seemed so long ago it must have happened in a previous life. Back when Nicky the shy lug had a girlfriend and a life that felt full. Now, having returned home a stranger, he was growing used to being alone.

The sky was turning a predawn gray when Nicky found Helen's old house. He wondered if her mom still lived there. The place was dark, and the morning newspaper lay in the yard. He stopped across the street. The low-roofed, beige-brick ranch style house looked less colorful than he remembered. A broken lawn chair leaned against the fence, which had several missing slats. The grass was brown, typical of Duro after a dry summer. But the whole time Nicky had known Helen, her father always kept the yard watered, trimmed, and neat. Her parents divorced six months after she went away. She was their only child. The strain of losing her must have broken them.

Nicky knew he shouldn't just sit here, parked in front of a stranger's house, watching, at six-fifteen in the morning, but he waited several minutes. He imagined Helen coming out the front door, grinning devilishly when she saw him, and bouncing over to the car. He would give anything—anything—to go back and do it all over.

Nicky put the Javelin in gear and pulled away, heading back south toward the pipeline office. As he passed a convenience store on Sixteenth Street, there was a sign that said *Try Our Four New Slurpee Flavors!*

Helen liked blue Slurpees, whatever flavor blue was.

Nicky started to cry.

CHAPTER 15

Light a Morning Cigar

In the moonless dark under a dusty canopy of stars, they waited for the Loving County JP. The Duro police chief, Mike Lewis, was there, along with the special investigator, Bob Lamborn, and a couple of sleepy Duro cops. Two deputies from the Ferris County sheriff's office were there, too, one of them dozing in the front seat of his cruiser. In the first car, the emergency lights were on, slashing the prairie in harsh red and blue. It was standard protocol for a crime scene, but there was no traffic to be warned, no other souls within miles.

Except for a low voice now and then and the scritch of desert crickets, it was dead quiet.

In the back seat of Lewis's unmarked car sat Albert Puga. He was the reason they were here, five miles off the paved ranch road, half a mile down a gravel section road, fifty feet off an unmarked oilfield road. He had managed to locate the place, despite the absence of landmarks. He'd remembered turning by a dilapidated pump jack that had *Yellowjackets '67* spray-painted on the side. A couple hundred feet beyond the pump jack was a dry stock tank, and inside the tank was a weathered and torn yellow mattress. One of the cops had tied a large red ribbon to a rusty post beside the tank.

Body location, not yet removed.

Morgan Matano had been justice of the peace in Loving since 1958, and nobody could hurry him. He hated working in the middle of the night and made sure everybody knew it. There was no county business that couldn't wait until morning. They had no choice but to bide their time.

Albert Puga stared straight ahead. He was under arrest, but they had not cuffed him. Chief Lewis asked a young female deputy named Karyn Crowsie to sit in the backseat with him, to try to get him talking. Deputy Crowsie wasn't having much luck with Puga, but she tried. He'd been read his Miranda rights, so anything he told them was fair game.

"Were you born in Duro?" asked Crowsie.

"No," said Puga. "I'm from San Rafael, California."

"I've never heard of that place. Is it nice?"

"It's okay. It's a small city north of San Francisco."

Puga stared straight ahead. Sad but resigned.

To the west was a gray hint of dawn, and the stars were dimming out in the dusty sky. The wind had fallen to a soft breeze, but the past three days of whirling gusts had lifted ultrafine dust high into the atmosphere.

Deputy Crowsie yawned and put her hand over her mouth. "Excuse me," she said. "This is a bit early for me. I'm not used to it."

"I've always worked the night shift," said Puga. "I *am* used to it."

It had been a long night for Albert Puga. The police had been waiting outside his girlfriend's house when he went out to get the mail at 3:30 in the afternoon, shortly after he rose from a day of fitful sleep. Victoria was at work, and the kids were at her sister's house. They didn't arrest him then, but they gave him a choice: Come downtown and talk to Detective Lamborn, or they would detain him for questioning, which would involve a very public handcuffing in front of neighbors. He briefly considered calling his old lawyer but went with them voluntarily.

The police hadn't threatened or used any special interrogation techniques. He sat in a cushioned chair in a well-lit office, talking and listening. Detective Lamborn had found his weakness, and he knew it. Puga's Achilles' heel was the certain fact that he wasn't a murderer. Not by nature. Not in his heart.

They talked about family, about wives and girlfriends and kids, about the bewildering pain of loss and never seeing someone again. And about Paul Zapeda, who would never see his two children grow up, go to school, graduate, and marry. He would never know grandchildren.

About two in the morning, Albert Puga broke. It wasn't the kind of emotional, blurted confession you saw on *Dragnet*. He and the two cops were just making small talk. Puga told them about his first fiancée, who was Filipina. They had met and fallen in love overseas, and she had been excited about coming with him to live in the States. But she could never adapt to a new life in a strange country, find work, or make friends, and after two miserable months, she had left him and returned to Manila. He might have gone with her, if she had asked, but she didn't. He still missed her sometimes, though it had been ten years. Until he moved to Duro and met Vicky, he had been deeply lonely.

"How did you get to know Victoria Zapeda?" asked Detective Lamborn.

"We met at the old VA Hall. The one they tore down last year. It was at the Cinco de Mayo Dance."

"Did she invite you?"

"Yes . . . Well, Paul invited me. They both came."

"Her husband, Paul? Were you two friends?"

"Yeah," said Puga. "He was the first guy I hung out with at work."

"Did you like him?"

"Oh, yeah. We were good friends. I just didn't like how he acted toward Vicky."

"How did he treat her?" asked Sergeant Correa. "Was he abusive?"

"He didn't hit her, but he yelled. He was always worried about where she was, checking up on her, and getting after her about her friends. He thought they acted like a bunch of dumb high school girls. And of course, he didn't want her to have guy friends, either. He wouldn't let her go out anywhere unless he went along. He was jealous a lot."

"Was he good to his kids?" asked Lamborn.

"Oh, yeah," said Puga. "He was a good dad. The little girl, Annie, thought he was the best. And Roland, too, the boy. The kids loved him."

They let that thought hang in the air. No one spoke. Finally, Puga took a deep breath and exhaled slowly. He put his head down, covering his face with his hands. The sergeant started to speak, but Lamborn held up his hand. This was the moment he had waited for, that sigh. Puga had to take the next step by himself. The detective offered Puga a tissue, which he took, blew his nose, then raised his head. His eyes glistened.

"Albert, you're ready to put this whole thing to rest, aren't you?" said Lamborn.

Puga started to speak, then shut his mouth again. He nodded his head.

Sergeant Correa spoke: "Albert, we know you're not a bad guy. Believe me, we get some bad characters in here, guys who'd hit their own mother over the head for her welfare check. Guys who murder just to stay in practice. You're not one of those. You're a decent man, and you know how to do what's right. You're not a killer."

"No," said Puga. "No, I'm not."

"Albert," said Lamborn, "will you take us to him now?"

"Okay. Right now? It's pretty far away. We can wait 'til it gets light."

"There's no point in waiting."

"I guess not," said Puga. "I need to look at a road map."

Albert had left the body of his friend and rival in an adjacent county, which made things a little more complicated, legally. Eventually, the Loving County JP showed up. Matano got out of his car, lit a cigar to cover the smell of death, and stood watching beside the dry stock tank as two county employees lifted the mattress. The police photographer snapped pictures, the flash bulbs lighting up the inside of the stock tank in bursts of brilliant white light.

They let Albert Puga out of the car and showed him the desiccated body, lit by four crisscrossing police flashlights.

"Is this Paul Zapeda?" asked Lamborn.

"Yes, sir," said Puga. He turned away and started back to the car. Suddenly, he stopped, bent over, covered his mouth with one hand, and coughed hard.

"Are you all right?" asked Deputy Crowsie. "Are you gonna be sick?"

Puga stood up straight and took a breath. "I'm okay," he said. She opened the back door of the car, and he climbed back in.

Inside the stock tank, two county medical workers used long-handled shovels to roll Zapeda's body onto a canvas sheet. When the body was face down, Mike Lewis removed a wallet from the back pocket. They had to have a backup on the witness ID. There wasn't enough left of the face to rely on a visual.

Puga sat in the back seat, facing away from the grisly goings-on, toward the gray half-dawn. The deputy thought it best to leave him alone for the time being. But after a few minutes, he spoke.

"I wish it hadn't gone the way it did."

"I know," said Crowsie.

He turned away again and watched the horizon, which stood out long and sharp against the gradually lightening sky.

CHAPTER 16

Broken Glass

At World Famous Best Studios, Allen Wallace used window cleaner and crumpled newsprint to clean the inside of the glass window that faced the big room. He hadn't used the big studio in a couple of months. On the other side of the glass, JJ and Harold were with Garrett Miller, a cellist with the Lubbock Symphony Orchestra. Miller was a large and genial man with a Marine Corps haircut. He looked more like a gas-station attendant than a classical musician. Allen couldn't hear what they said, but he watched the three men walk around the room, gesturing to various empty spaces on the floor and up to the ceiling. They were discussing microphone placement and sound baffles. They didn't know the room's acoustics like Allen did, but he'd let them do the initial setup. Allen would come in later and tweak the room as necessary.

Miller had driven 160 miles to Duro, was expected back this evening, and had no time to waste. Miller claimed he could deliver himself and seven other members of the Lubbock Symphony—four violins, two violas, two cellos—for union scale plus expenses, which included gas money, food, and three nights at a not-crappy hotel. Harold didn't have a final figure on that, but it was a bit more than they had budgeted for. Gas was cheap, but he knew nothing about the local hotels. Harold suggested the Golden Sunset in downtown Duro, where he and JJ were staying. It was a six-story hostelry from the '50s boom days whose best years were long past. The restaurant on the second floor was okay, he said, and there was a heated pool on the roof.

Allen stood in the control room and examined the thick glass. There was a previously unseen constellation of fingerprints in the lower left corner. He crumbled up another piece of newspaper, spritzed on a little Ammonia D, whatever that was, and rubbed in a circle. He hated spots on glass.

Allen had a poor history with glass. He found himself flashing back to that afternoon twelve years ago, sitting on the floor in the family room at the old house in north Duro, looking down at his right wrist as blood streamed off his fingertips, dripping in a puddle among large, jagged shards of glass from the patio door. His five-year-old daughter screamed while his wife shouted at him.

What did you DO, Allen? Oh my God! What did you do?

Allen shook his head to dislodge the memory and turned back to the soundboard. Mentally, he checked off everything that needed doing. He had finished testing all sixteen channels on the MM-1000. This would be the machine's first real challenge, and he knew from experience that nothing sapped the energy out of a recording session like technical problems. He also put every cable through its paces and turned all the control knobs on the console back and forth and moved the sliders up and down, listening for static. They were smooth and quiet.

He had tested all the microphones and forced himself to set aside a beautiful, classic Neumann U-87 because of a slight but audible buzz. In a studio, especially with professional musicians, you could get away with using these more delicate ribbon microphones, which produced a sweeter sound than the tougher stage mikes. Fortunately, he owned two more Neumanns, which he counted on to record the string instruments.

Allen decided to join the producer and musicians in the studio.

"I can get everybody here on the seventeenth," Garrett Miller was saying. "I haven't talked to one of the violists, because he's down in Galveston. I'm pretty sure he'll do it, but I can get somebody else if he won't. I'm sure the rest are game. Sorry I can't help you with the timps."

"That's all right," said Harold. "I'm still working on it." He might have to let the idea of the large timpani go and think of something else.

"Remember, we just have to have it all done and wrapped up by the twenty-first," said Miller. "We start rehearsal for our new season in two weeks."

"Once we get them all in here, it should go smoothly," said Harold. "Rehearsal, recording, tracking. Bing, bang, boom. Four days, and you're out of here."

"What about the pay?" Miller asked. "Half up front?"

"Half the performance fee up front," said Harold. "The rest when the tracks are in the can. Expenses will be worked out separately, with receipts and such."

"Okay," said Miller. "I can let you know by day after tomorrow."

"Can it possibly be sooner?" asked Harold. "If you guys fall through, we need time to get a backup."

"We won't fall through," said Miller. "But I'll try to let you know for sure by tomorrow. It's just that we're talking about seven guys—or, rather, six guys and a girl violinist."

"All right." The four men went back into the control room. Allen spent a few minutes showing off his sixteen-track machine.

"You want me to demonstrate something for you?" asked Allen. "I've got a great recording of a choir you should hear. You'll be amazed at the clarity."

"Actually, what I'd like to hear is a demo of your new song, if you've got it," said Miller.

"We have a demo," said JJ. "Allen, why don't you play him what we were working on yesterday?"

The tape was already on the deck, so Allen just ran it back to the double-zero mark. It wasn't a finished track, but it would demonstrate the richness and depth of the guitar sound. They all stood and listened. Allen watched Miller's face, but the cellist listened without expression, nodding slowly as the song played. Miller betrayed a slight wince when JJ's voice came in, but he didn't say anything. JJ had a style and timbre that took getting used to, but his pitch was spot on.

After listening a couple of minutes, Miller turned to Allen. "We can work with you," he said. "If the charts are ready and make sense, our people should be able to give you a nice orchestra track. I doubt any of them have ever worked on a pop song before, but they're professionals. I don't suppose there's some sheet music I can take with me today."

"Not yet, but I'll have all the charts done by the end of the week," said Harold.

"Excellent. I'll call you."

Miller, Harold, and JJ moved toward the outer office, while Allen stayed in the control room to recue the tape.

As Harold opened the back door for Miller, they were surprised to see a bearded young man walking up the steps.

He smiled at Miller. "Hi, I was just coming up to knock. Nobody answered the front door. Are you Allen Wallace?"

"No, I'm just a poor traveling musician," said Miller. "Mr. Wallace is right inside. Come on in."

Before they could question the protocol of inviting a stranger into the fortress that was World Famous Best Studios, the young man was up the steps and into the outer office. He glanced from one man to the other, then his face lit up.

"You're JJ Johns!" he said.

"I am," said JJ. He loved the rare moments when he was recognized.

Allen Wallace came out of the control room.

"Hello," he said. "Are you the guy I talked to on the phone yesterday?"

"Dan Park," the young man said, extending his hand.

"Good to meet you, Mr. Park," said Allen. "Gentlemen, this is that award-winning filmmaker I told you about."

JJ and Harold exchanged baffled looks. *Filmmaker?*

"I'm a documentarist," Dan explained.

Documentarist?

JJ shook Dan's hand while Harold walked Garrett Miller out to his car.

"I told you there was a filmmaker coming by today," said Allen.

Uh, no you didn't, thought JJ, smiling congenially. "Okay."

"Dan and I were talking on the phone about the possibility of a documentary about the studio," said Allen.

"And it would include the project you're doing right now," said Dan. "I think telling the story about making a record—while it's happening—would make a great film that people would want to see. My partner thinks so, too."

Harold came back into the studio.

"I'm Harold Prensky," he said. "I'm the producer."

"Wonderful," said Dan.

"Come on, let me show this spaceship," said Allen, and led the young man away.

Harold and JJ waited in the hall while Allen gave Dan the tour.

"Wait," whispered JJ. "What's going on? This is the first I've heard about a film."

"Allen never said a word to me," said Harold. "I'm not sure this will work. We can't have this kid underfoot while we're trying to herd a dozen musicians."

"Plus, he said he has a partner," said JJ. "That's two guys underfoot. And how do we know it's even a real thing. That guy is too young to have made many films."

"I better talk to them right now," said Harold, "before this scheme goes too far."

Harold followed Allen and the young filmmaker out into the little studio. JJ decided to let the producer handle it and turned back to the control room. He was starting to get the presession jitters. The last thing JJ needed was a camera pointing at him while he tried to focus on resurrecting his career.

He sat at the control board and studied it, then practiced working several volume sliders at once with both hands, a tricky maneuver that Allen Wallace could handle with great dexterity. JJ wanted to learn the skills himself, both to protect his own interests and because someday he might end up permanently on this side of the glass. Allen had lent him the machine's thick instruction book, and JJ read it carefully. He slid the headphones over his ears, ran the tape back to zero, switched off the room monitors, and hit *PLAY*.

He had never liked the sound of his own voice, but others had convinced JJ long ago that he should be himself when he sang and not try to sound like a typical pop star. Maybe a little reverb would help. The guitar sounded beautiful and rich. He imagined violins and cellos and deep, booming kettles during the last chorus. The song would come together. The project *had* to work. You only get so many last chances.

Harold and Allen came out of the studio with Dan Park.

"I promise you won't even notice us," said Dan. "We will stay out of the way. If you're ask us to take the camera out, we'll do it instantly, without question. We will work with you."

"That would be very important," said Harold. "I don't want to feel like we're being watched all the time."

"I've done this a lot," said Dan, "and what happens every time is that, after a day or two, cameramen are like the furniture. You just won't notice us anymore."

JJ exchanged glances with Harold. *What the hell?* Harold shrugged. "Allen really wants to do it."

"Give me a call in a couple of days," said Wallace. "I'll let you know when you can come by with your partner—take light readings and do test shots, that sort of thing."

"Wonderful!" said Dan. "You won't regret it." He and Wallace walked toward the back door. Dan suddenly turned back. "Oh, Mr. Johns, one more thing. Could you do me a huge favor? I have a copy of the Zephyrs album *Hard Wind* in the car. It's my favorite album of all time, and it's in beautiful condition. Could you maybe autograph it for me, if it's not too much trouble?"

"Sure," said JJ. "Of course! Happy to do it."

"I'll be right back," said Dan, and bounded down the steps to his car.

"I like that kid," said JJ.

"I just hope it goes like he says and doesn't slow us down," said Harold. "If they start to drag the session, then those guys will have to leave."

"I think it will be all right," said JJ. He searched the office for a pen.

CHAPTER 17

Tunes from the Tonewheel

Reporter Nolan Batts got to Fonde's Cafeteria a few minutes after one o'clock. He liked to make himself late for appointments, unless it was with some bigwig with a low patience threshold. That way he could get right to work the moment he sat down. There was nothing he hated more than waiting around for some clown who might or might not show up and who might or might not have something interesting to say. Better to let the other guy get there first, make your entrance in a big swoop, cut through all the introductory horseshit, get straight to the meat, let them know who's in charge, escape if necessary.

Today was different. He had agreed to meet with a young woman for no good reason at all except to do her a favor—very uncharacteristic of Nolan Batts. The girl on the phone wanted to pump information out of *him*, not provide a good political tidbit or even a sticky crumb of gossip. She had called him three times in three days and was very sweet on the phone, even a little flirtatious, but relentless with the questions. She wanted information about the Helen Orlena case for some kind of college film project. Nolan didn't have much information to give and thought a documentary film was a bad idea. What little he did know about the case he couldn't reveal if he wanted to keep his reciprocal relationship with the Duro cops.

But she sounded cute, if it was possible to sound cute over the phone. It was Nolan who'd asked her to meet him for lunch on Saturday, and it was he who suggested Fonde's, which was not only cheap, but also the location least like a "date." If this Becky Paulson turned out to be annoying or fat, then he could just talk politely to her for a little while, finish his Salisbury steak and whipped potatoes with gravy *au jus*, and escape for some invented reason. If she was cute, however . . . got to keep your options open. Nolan was thirty-two, unmarried, a little too short, pudgy in the middle, and his tastefully longish hair was thinning on top. For a couple of months, he'd been casually dating a girl who worked in a real estate office. That relationship might turn out to be something, but still . . .

He was halfway between his office at the *Duro American-Post* and the cafeteria downtown when it suddenly occurred to him: *It's Saturday. Ah, shit! That ignoramus will be playing the damned organ. Why didn't I remember that?* Nolan hated cafeteria music. Whoever decided that diners needed digestive entertainment from a double-row Hammond tonewheel organ should be skinned alive. Bennie the organist, a perpetually grinning sixty-year-old with a light-blue suit and a preposterous toupee, knew every bubblegum hit there was, learned new ones as they came out, and played them in a cheerful cadence at a volume designed to penetrate skulls. Children frequently made requests, and Bennie accommodated.

Nolan hoped the organist might have wrapped it up by one o'clock when the lunch crowd began to disperse. But as soon as he opened the glass door at Fonde's, the rollicking sounds of "Gypsys, Tramps, and Thieves" came pouring out. *Ah, man.*

He scanned the room, filled with Saturday diners. He didn't know what the girl looked like, and they hadn't arranged any sort of recognition signal. He briefly made eye contact with a fortyish woman in a pantsuit, dining alone by the dessert table, but he was relieved when a ten-year-old boy came out of the restroom and plopped down at the table across from her. The rest of the patrons were mostly older couples, some with their much older relatives.

He spotted a nice-looking sandhill blonde sitting at a booth along the far wall, blessedly distant from the torturous organ. She saw him, too, and waved. *Must be her. Well, okay. I can do this. She's not glamorous, but she is young and fresh.* She probably recognized him because his picture ran in the paper every Sunday in the "What's Happening in City Hall" column.

"Are you Mr. Batts?" she asked.

He extended his hand. "Call me Nolan. And you must be Becky."

Nolan was perfectly happy to spend time chatting up a pretty girl and watching her cheerful face and naturally pink cheeks, but today, the shoe was on the other foot. She pulled out a pencil and notebook and got straight to the questions.

"Nolan, did you know Helen Orlena?" Becky asked.

"No," said Nolan. "I did see her at the Duro Playhouse a couple of weeks before she disappeared. She was in a local play. She stood out enough that when we got word she had vanished, I knew who she was."

Becky wrote in her notebook, with a handwriting tight and impeccable.

"Second question," said Becky. "Do you consider this case to be a disappearance? Or do you think it might have been murder."

Nolan laughed. "My, my! Going straight to the heart, aren't we? Well, they never found a body, so no one can say."

"What do you think?"

"Really, I . . ." Nolan was caught off guard, a condition he wasn't accustomed to. "Hey, Miss . . . um . . . Becky. Are we here for lunch? I was thinking we could talk while we eat. I do have to get back to the office in a while." He left it ambiguous, in case he wanted to stay longer.

"Sure," said Becky. "Let's eat." Beautiful, wide smile. Big, white teeth.

As they pushed their trays along the stainless-steel rails, Becky loaded up on mac and cheese and selected several mushy servings of vegetables.

"Are you vegetarian?" asked Nolan.

"No. Not really. I don't eat a lot of meat. I like corned beef, and fish sticks, too. The food at the university café is pretty bland. My friends and I get chicken-fried steaks at a little steakhouse every couple of weeks, just to get our grease."

Nolan chose Salisbury steak and brown gravy, pale green beans, and exhausted French fries. He hesitated over the lemon custard pie, shining bright and yellow under a four-inch layer of meringue, but forced himself to pass. That was a shame, because that pie was one of the few things Fonde's did really well.

As they returned to the booth balancing their trays, the organist struck up a peppy rendition of "We're So Sorry, Uncle Albert," with lots of bouncy bass notes played on the pedals.

"You know, there's only so much information I can give you," said Nolan. "The case is still very much active, and I have to respect confidentiality."

"I understand," said Becky. "It's just that she disappeared two years ago, and the case doesn't look any closer to being cracked."

"Why do you think *that* would make a good film?" asked Nolan. "You really couldn't have any kind of ending to your story, unless you solve the case yourself."

"I understand your point," said Becky. "But, the way I see it, the story is not about Helen but about how a small town deals with the disappearance of one of its own kids. And a rising star, if you could call her that. I'm sure lots of people knew her. She's cruising along in high school, smart girl who's a talented actress, great future, then WHOOSH, she's gone. What does that do to people? And what do they think? Is she dead? Or maybe she just couldn't stand it anymore, and she's living under an assumed name somewhere."

"What's your opinion?" asked Nolan. "Dead or just disappeared?"

"I . . . really don't know," said Becky, taking a bite of wilted brown cauliflower. "I'd like to think she's alive, living in some other town. Is there anything you can tell me about it, one way or another? I know you can't name names."

Nolan buttered half of his soft dinner roll, then dipped it in brown gravy. "I can't tell you much, but let me put it this way: Helen Orlena is not really considered a missing person."

"But she is missing."

"Of course, but at the moment, nobody is looking for her, and they're not looking for a body, either."

"So . . . have the police given up?"

"No," said Nolan. "Like I said, it's an active case." He grinned.

"Really? Then what are they waiting for? Somebody must know where she is."

"Somebody probably does. Almost certainly."

"And they just expect him to spill the beans someday."

"Him or her," said Nolan. "Don't assume."

Becky pretended to drop her head into her plate of cheesy noodles. Nolan laughed.

"I *know* you know something," said Becky. "I wish you could give me a hint."

"No hints," said Nolan. "Sorry. I keep my promises. That's why I've had good luck. That's why I have two awards for statewide reporting, if I do say so myself."

"Okay," said Becky. "I just don't have anything to work with. It's just such a great mystery."

Nolan finished his steak and wished he'd gotten the lemon meringue. He looked back across the room to the desserts. *Willpower, man. Willpower.* He picked up a limp fry.

They talked a while longer, but the reporter wasn't giving up any secrets. Becky ended up telling him about how she wanted to be taken seriously as a woman in the documentary film business, a career held almost exclusively by men since the days of the Lumière brothers.

"Well, I may be a member of the old boys' club, but I'm sympathetic," said Nolan. "And the world is changing. I don't know about the film business, but when I started in newspapers right out of college, there were *zero* women reporters or news writers. There were maybe three in the whole state. Now we have four at the *American-Post.*"

"It's not just the business," said Becky. "It's the culture I grew up in. I had a Christian raising, as my father likes to say. Men work and have the interesting careers. Girls get married and raise kids. Neither one of my grandmothers even finished high school, though they were both smart as whips."

Nolan let her talk as he chewed the last of his French fries, then scooted his chair back. As dull as his work was today, putting together the Sunday edition, he had to get to it. "Miss Becky, I think I know how you feel. I hope you have success as a filmmaker. I think you will, if you stick to it. There's just not a lot to go on with this particular case. Not yet. The story of Helen Orlena would make a great film, someday. It will also make a great article, which I will be happy to write. You just can't tell the story now, because there are events in motion. One of these days, we're all going to know a lot more, I think."

"That you can't talk about yet . . ."

"Bingo," said Nolan. "Hey, let's go outside."

They left the cafeteria, as Bennie pumped away at "I Feel the Earth Move."

"I'll walk you to your car," said Nolan.

Becky laughed. "Car? You mean walk me to my bicycle." Becky had arrived on the same Schwinn she had pedaled in high school. The only car in her life was Dan's, and he was across town chasing a story about a former pop star's comeback.

"I'm impressed with your determination," said Nolan. "If you ever decide filmmaking is not for you, consider being a writer. You could write for the *Post.* They need new blood. They've already used up a lot of mine."

Becky climbed on her bike, which she hadn't bothered to lock. "I like to write. I particularly love writing for film. It's my camera skills that are weak. I'm trying to get better at those."

Nolan liked this girl and wanted her to like him. He could give her *something* . . . just toss her a juicy fact. Be titillating. He knew he shouldn't, but . . .

"You know, there is one thing about the Helen Orlena case that is not public knowledge," said Nolan, "but you have to promise to keep it to yourself. It's not for general consumption, but you might find it intriguing."

"You have my attention," said Becky.

"Okay," said Nolan. "Helen's car. The one they found in Stanton, Texas. It had been sitting in a store parking lot for a few weeks before somebody noticed it. What do you know about it?"

"Just that it was cleaned and empty. No fingerprints or blood or anything."

"That's almost right," said Nolan. "They said nothing was found in the car. Except . . . one thing that didn't make it into the paper. Something was found under the back seat. A small brochure."

"What kind of brochure?"

"It was just a little four-page tract. I can almost remember the exact title," said Nolan. "It was 'For Your Baby's Sake, Stop Smoking.' Or something close to that."

Becky looked at the reporter blankly. "What? Did she have a baby?"

"No."

"You mean . . . she was pregnant?"

"I don't know," said Nolan. "But it was an interesting choice of reading material, don't you think? Now, I must take off. Miss Becky, have a good day. I enjoyed talking to you. If I can help you with anything else, call me."

As Nolan walked away, he remembered to keep his back straight and suck in his gut.

I think she likes me.

CHAPTER 18

Somebody Wants to Speak to Holly

Lucille was nineteen. On most days, she helped homeschool the Paulson kids and Rachel Costello. She'd never been to college but graduated top-ten in her high school class. She was patient, engaging, and funny when she taught them English and penmanship.

Normally, Lucille came to the Paulsons' about nine in the morning, but today, Holly asked her to be there by eight o'clock sharp. She was expecting visitors. Two people from the world were coming—people she must engage and deal with, who had the power to make real trouble for Holly's little Christian home school. In a phone call, a man who said he represented FCISD, the school district, hinted strongly that if she continued withholding her children from public school, the law could get involved. He said they'd be there at eight. He didn't explain who *they* were besides himself.

Holly had fudged it a little bit with Grover, telling him some county officials were coming to make sure her house and teaching space complied with safety regulations, and it was no big problem. Grover was willing to be late to work so he could help deal with the strangers himself, but Holly insisted she could handle the situation.

The white FCISD Chevrolet arrived at 7:55. Holly watched out the living room window. There were two men, both in dark suits and ties, apparently waiting for the precise minute of eight o'clock before getting out of their car. She wished they'd just come and knock on the door so she could talk to them before Mary Lynne came with Rachel and before Lucille arrived.

As it happened, Lucille did show up a minute later and reached the front door just as the two men were getting out of their car and coming up the walkway. She turned around, perplexed. One of the men wished her good morning and gestured for her to go ahead of them.

Holly opened the door and spoke quickly.

"Hi, Lucy," she said. "Peter and Martha are all fed and ready to go. They're in the classroom already." She was referring to the converted garage with a half bath that she used for teaching. It had been built for Grover's late mother, who had lived with them a couple of years before she passed on, and was now utilized for Christian education. "Let's start with arithmetic today. Martha is starting to catch on with subtraction. I'll be dealing with school business in the den. Rachel should be here in a few minutes."

"Yes, Mrs. Paulson," said Lucille. She came inside, leaving the two men standing on the front porch.

"Well," said Holly. "You must be the gentlemen who think I don't know how to teach children."

"I'm Jim Fellows," said the first man, a heavy-set man with salt-and-pepper hair. "I'm deputy superintendent for the Ferris County Independent School District. This is Claud Vanderberg. He's our truancy officer." The second man nodded. He was thinner and younger, with a shiny bald crown, unsmiling.

"Hello," said Holly. Nobody tried to shake hands.

"If we can just have a few minutes of your time," said Fellows.

"Of course," said Holly. She stood aside and gestured for them to come in.

Early that morning, when Grover was in the shower, Holly had told James about the impending intrusion. She usually didn't speak with him about real problems. Mostly, they made small talk, some of it meaningless, most of it quickly forgotten. But this morning, she'd had no one else to confide in. Sometimes he had advice for her, sometimes not. This morning, he had listened without comment.

James had first come to her when she was almost sixteen, him and the others. At first, the soft, deep voice frightened her, though it never threatened. Usually, the voices came in the morning, early, before she'd had her breakfast and tea. The first few times she heard them, she had searched through the other rooms in the house, looking for the source. Her family didn't own a television, but she thought perhaps she was hearing a radio somewhere.

She'd told her mother that she heard a man's voice nearby and sometimes other voices, too, but her mother just looked at her strangely and said, "I'm quite sure there are no voices, Holly. You're dreaming." When Holly tried to broach the subject again, her mother rebuked her. "Stop talking nonsense, Holly. They're not real."

So she stopped mentioning them. But the voices continued. Usually, the things they said were trivial.

It's damp today. Your hair will curl. Wear a scarf. That was a female voice that sounded like her fifth-grade teacher.

Other times—and these annoyed her—they were critical. Not in a cruel way but more intimately than anyone but a close friend should be.

A teen-age voice: *Do you really think Doreen and Patty like you?* Or *Everybody's gonna notice you didn't wash your hair.* Or *That color doesn't go with your complexion. You look better in light blue.*

After she realized that no one else could hear them, Holly didn't respond to the voices unless she was alone or out of earshot from the rest of the family. When her sister married and left home to start her own life, Holly had the small bathroom to herself, and there she let herself have conversations with the deep male voice, because he was never critical. She told him she didn't like the way the other voices talked about her and her friends, that these things they mentioned were too personal. He must have told the others, because after that, the criticisms mostly stopped. Eventually, his was the only voice she heard.

For a time, Holly's maternal grandmother had lived with them. One day, she overheard Holly talking to her voice and asked who she was speaking to. Holly hated lying, so she told grandmother about the deep voice she heard on most days, especially early in the morning or sometimes if she was unable to sleep at night. She asked if maybe she was going crazy or if the voice was bad, like the devil. It didn't seem bad.

Surprisingly, Grandmother took her seriously. She also had advice.

"You can let yourself talk to him for a little while each day, but you have to draw boundaries," her grandmother said. "When you don't want to talk to him anymore, tell him so. You have the right to be left alone."

So, after that, Holly talked to her voice in the morning as she washed up before breakfast. But when she was ready to emerge from the bathroom to eat breakfast and begin her day, then she would tell him she couldn't talk to him anymore today, and he should just be quiet. That usually worked. If she heard the voice later in the day, she ignored it.

It was about that time she started thinking of him as James.

Holly sat upright in a straight-back chair, knees together. The two school board men sat on the small couch in front of her. They both spoke firmly.

"We were hoping your husband would be here," said Jim Fellows. "This problem concerns him, too. They're also his children."

"I'm head of the school," said Holly. "My husband does not participate. It's just me and my assistant, so any questions about my children's education should be addressed to me."

"Let me elaborate on what I told you in our last letter," said Fellows. "No one in the school district has any problem with how people choose to raise and educate their children, as long as they are in no physical danger. But the laws of the state of Texas are very clear—every child between the ages of six and sixteen is required to attend a bona fide school full time unless there are extraordinary circumstances, such as special disabilities."

"My children are being educated as we speak," said Holly. "I'd be in there helping, if you gentlemen didn't insist on taking up their school time."

"I appreciate that we're interrupting your day," said Fellows. "We are sorry for that, but you and your husband need to understand this is not something the state can be flexible on. The law is clear. Every child in the state must be educated in a way that meets the standards of the Texas Compulsory Education Code. Do you know what *compulsory* means?"

Don't let him make you mad.

Holly took a deep breath. "I know what it means. And I've read the education code, too. If I'm remembering right, it says that children must be taught reading, writing, arithmetic, and good citizenship. It does not say it has to be done in one of your official public schools, which are just factories to make them into nice little citizens who don't need God. My children are taught all the required subjects, plus something all those other children are not taught: how to live as real Christians. And we *pray* in our school."

Claud Vanderberg, who hadn't said much, leaned forward. "Mrs. Paulson, just because someone claims to be running a school doesn't mean it qualifies as an educational institution."

"There are private schools all over the state," said Holly. "The Catholics teach their kids their own way. So do the Lutherans and the Baptists . . ."

"All those private schools you mention comply with state requirements, including safety, fire codes, everything," said Fellows. "They also give tests to their students that show us they are learning. Their books are open to inspection."

"Mrs. Paulson, have you ever heard of the Murphy school?" asked Vanderberg.

It was a private school. They shut it down.

"It was a private school, and the world—I mean, the state—shut it down," said Holly.

"I'm surprised you knew that," said Fellows. "It was several years ago. But you're correct. The state forced the school to close. It's not that they weren't teaching. They may have even been doing it well. But they would not allow the state to observe the classrooms in action or see tests the kids took. It took a year, but, yes, the state put them out of business. After repeated warnings, I might add."

"I don't see how you can shut us down," said Holly. "The children are in their own home. We are not a business. We are a Christian school. The standards we answer to are higher than yours."

"You have an employee, I see," said Fellows. "We met her coming in."

"Lucille is a volunteer," said Holly. She was stretching the truth. Grover provided fifty dollars cash every week for Lucy.

Fellows and Vanderberg exchanged looks. Holly sat expressionless. Vanderberg tried another tack.

"Have you thought about what your kids are going to do later in life?" he asked. "What about when they get out into the work world, try to get jobs that require a good education. What if one of them wants to go to college? They wouldn't be prepared."

Tell them about Rebekah.

"I'll have you know my oldest daughter was educated by me right here in this house, from the second grade on. And today—at this moment—she is an honor student at Central Texas Christian University. She just won a big award for a film project she did."

"That's impressive," said Fellows. "But . . ."

"Educating our children the way we think they should be taught is *our business*," said Holly. "The bible makes it clear: 'The fear of the Lord is the beginning of knowledge; fools despise wisdom and instruction.' What we're doing isn't a crime. And I'd appreciate if you could leave now and let me get back to what I know is right."

The two school district men were silent, then both of them stood up.

"Mrs. Paulson, please think about what we said today," said Fellows. "And talk to your husband."

"I might point out that you are mistaken about one thing," said Vanderberg. "It *is* a crime. Truancy is a crime. The state and the school district take it very seriously."

"So what are you going to do?" asked Holly. "Take my children away? I'd like to see you try. The truth is on our side."

"We don't take children away," said Vanderberg. "Only the state can do that. But if they think the children are in a bad situation, yes, they can—and will—take them out of your home."

The two men showed themselves out. When they were gone and the front door was shut, Holly took a quick, deep breath, collected herself, and headed for the classroom.

Don't tell Grover.

Holly had already told James she couldn't talk anymore today, but she stopped in the hallway.

"I have to. He's my husband."

Don't tell him yet. He'll only make things worse.

"Maybe so, but he's still my husband. I'll need to talk to him about it sooner or later. And, please, don't speak to me anymore today."

She pushed open the door to the garage room, where the three kids and Lucille sat around the small table with open books, and strode into the room.

"I hope everybody's in a learning mood this morning!" she said.

CHAPTER 19

You Have Ten Minutes

Andrew Waylon sat on the stage in the auditorium, dangling his feet over the edge, studying his lines. He'd taken the script home several days ago, with the understanding he would be well on the way to memorizing his part by now. Mr. Bellamy was counting on him to be the easy half of the duet acting equation. But Andrew hadn't quite gotten to the memorization yet. Actually, this was only the second time he'd cracked open the book, *Short Scenes for High School Players.* The first time was during their only read-through. The play was called *The Sand Man Wakes*. Andrew thought it was okay. He had a lot of lines, more than his partner, Chase. But Andrew believed in himself and that he could fake his way through anything. It was the key to his high school success.

The side door of the theater banged open, and Mr. Bellamy came in.

"Good. You're here," said Bellamy. "I only have about twenty-five minutes, but we can at least get through the scene once. We'll talk about blocking as we go. Andrew, you stand in the center to start. Chase . . . Wait. Where's Chase? I thought she was already here."

"I thought she was, too," said Andrew. "I saw her in the hall, and she said she was on her way to the auditorium."

"Damn," muttered Bellamy. "Okay, start reading your opening monolog. I'll try and find Chase." He started up the center aisle to see if she was out in the foyer.

Andrew stood tall and cleared his throat, put his shoulders back, and read in his stage voice, with an accent he imagined to be sophisticated.

"They say even the brightest-lit buildings have their dark secrets. This old museum is no exception. Oh, who am I? I'm Floyd, the caretaker."

Mr. Bellamy turned and yelled from the back of the auditorium. "Stop a second. It's not 'Oh, who am I?' It's like this: 'Oh,' then pause because you notice the audience. 'Who am I?' Pause again. 'I'm Floyd . . . the caretaker.' You're introducing yourself. Now start again."

Andrew swallowed some spit and started over. Bellamy reached the main double doors in the back, opened them, and stuck his head out. "Miss McFall!" he called.

She was standing in the foyer, next to the little box office.

"Oh, hi," said Chase. "I was just waiting for you guys."

"We're waiting on *you*, Miss McFall," said Bellamy. "Get up on stage with Andrew. I don't have much time. I thought you were already there."

"I was . . . but I came back out," said Chase. "I don't like the stage."

Bellamy laughed. "Well, no actor in the history of the world ever said that."

Chase went in and took her place stage left from Andrew and opened her script. Bellamy sat in the center of the front row.

"All right, let's start. Chase, take it from your first line," said Bellamy.

Chase turned toward Andrew, quickly glanced back over her shoulder, and began. "There you are, Floyd. I've been meaning to speak with you. Some of us on the museum staff are concerned about the quality of your work lately."

"Stop," said Bellamy. "Chase, you should be walking as you talk. Go to the back of the stage, and walk forward briskly, like you're all business."

Chase walked back a few paces, looked left and right, then stood waiting.

"Andrew, give the last line of your monolog again."

Andrew took a few moments finding the line, then began. "When you've worked in a palace as long as I have . . ."

"A *place*," said Bellamy. "Worked in a *place* as long as I have."

"Sorry, I'll start again. Ahem! . . . When you've worked in a place as long as I have, you get to know it well. Better than your wife, better than your own children, perhaps." He paused, then turned around. Chase was looking back over her shoulder. "Your line."

"I'm sorry," said Chase. She walked downstage. "There you are, Floyd—"

"Hold it," said the teacher. "Miss McFall, you need to pay attention. You should be moving by the time he says 'your own children.' Do it again. Same place."

She took her place at the back of the stage, glancing back over her shoulder.

"Miss McFall, what is so darned interesting backstage?"

"Sorry. I'm ready," said Chase.

"She thinks the stage is haunted," said Andrew. He grinned at Chase, who shot him a fierce look.

Bellamy laughed. "Ah, yes, the ghosts of the Duro High theater. I've heard about them. Well, I'm quite sure none of them are going to bother us while we're rehearsing."

"There's only one ghost," said Chase.

"Oh, really?" said Bellamy. "I suppose you've met him."

"It's a her," said Chase. "I've never seen her, but I heard her voice. Her name is Helen."

"Helen," repeated Andrew. "I'm pretty sure I saw her one time."

Bellamy said nothing. After few seconds, he spoke curtly. "This ghost business is pure horsepucky, and I don't want to hear any more about it. Helen Orlena was a real girl, and she shouldn't be treated as a joke. Now, Chase, please give your first line, and walk quickly, like you've just breezed in from another room."

"I wasn't making a joke," said Chase.

"I apologize," said Bellamy. "I didn't mean to suggest you thought it was funny. It's just that I . . . a lot of us knew her, and it still hurts that something bad may have happened to her. It's hard to hear students treat the event like it's just an amusing school legend. I realize you never actually met her."

"She's here, Mr. Bellamy," said Chase. "Her spirit is on this stage. If you stand still, you can feel her presence sometimes. You probably think I'm crazy, but it's true. There are places on the stage that are cold. It's weird."

"That's because they have the air conditioning vents pointed at the stage," said Bellamy. "Because it gets so hot with the lights and all."

"It's not that kind of cold."

Bellamy knew he wasn't going to win this argument. "Let's move on, okay? We have two weeks to get this scene perfect, and neither one of you knows your lines yet."

"I know most of them," said Chase.

"Good. Okay. Then let's start. We only have a few minutes, and I'd like to get through the whole thing at least once today."

Chase moved back upstage, and Andrew began.

"They say even the brightest-lit buildings have their dark secrets . . ."

After the 1:20 bell rang, and the two students departed, David Bellamy stayed behind, sitting in the cushioned seat, front row center.

Helen wouldn't haunt this stage, thought Bellamy. She never did perform on the big stage, except as part of the chorus in the all-school musical, her sophomore year. No, if anything, her spirit would be back in the wardrobe closet, looking through the costumes for interesting things to wear. She loved costumes and loved trying them on in funny combinations. Like a queen's crown and a ragged peasant dress. Or plastic faux-metal armor used for *Richard III* over a country-girl gingham dress made for a production of *Our Town*. In fact, so many pieces of costume had wandered out of the storeroom with Helen that Bellamy had to take her aside and lay down the law—no more borrowing of costumes or props without explicit permission. Even then, odds and ends from the prop room still wandered away from time to time.

One of the boys in photography class had turned in a series of stunning black-and-white photos of Helen for his senior project. He was never her boyfriend—Helen dated one of the football players exclusively—but the pictures he'd made of her wearing a large range of costumes and a variety of creative poses were so well done, with such obvious affection, that Leslie Ross, the new theater teacher, had taped them up in the main theater classroom for inspiration. And there they stayed, even after Helen vanished in the summer of 1970. Ms. Ross had never really known Helen, so it wasn't painful to see those pictures every day, not the way they hurt David Bellamy. If the school had let him stay on teaching theater, he would have taken them down, out of respect.

Bellamy had responsibilities, but he stayed in the front-row seat. He looked up at the clock, with its official school time (consistently four minutes behind real-world time). He had no class until 2:50, but there was a stack of sophomore papers to grade and the upcoming speech competition to plan. But he stayed in the quiet auditorium, listening to the chaotic bustle of kids out in the halls heading to class, sounds echoing, muffled by thick concrete walls. Voices by the hundreds, footsteps, banging lockers. After a few minutes, the sounds faded, and the 1:30 bell clanged.

What if she had gotten the part? Bellamy mused. *Would things have been different?*

When they were casting for *The Music Man*, that spring two years ago, what if Helen had gotten her wish and landed the lead female role of Marian the librarian, the only part she'd been willing to read for?

Bellamy regretted not giving her the part. It had been a close call. Debbie Bishop was a better dancer, but Helen had a finer voice. Yes, Helen could have learned the dance parts, which weren't difficult. She would have been great as Marian, but she would have been wonderful at any one of several other parts. But she had refused to consider anything but the lead. If she hadn't gotten so mad . . . so mad and disappointed that she'd stormed out of the room, left school, missed the rest of her classes for the day, and been suspended for two days, she could have been talked into another part. But once she had been suspended, she wasn't allowed to be in the musical.

It was harsh, but rules were rules.

When she returned to school, Helen had not been the same. No more high-pitched laughter, no funny costumes. She sat in drama class and took notes, did the assignments, passed the tests, but she didn't participate unless called on directly, and then only in a perfunctory manner. Bellamy assumed—hoped—that she would bounce back after a week or two. But Helen stayed withdrawn.

It was the same in Bellamy's intermediate speech class. Helen was present but disengaged. When rehearsals started for all-school musical, the other students knew not to mention it in front of her. At the end of every school day, Helen waited outside the west entrance, where her boyfriend, a former student named Nicky Pomeroy, appeared with his car like a chauffeur to whisk her away.

Other than Nicky, she didn't seem to have many friends. She was likable and easy to talk to but an outsider. The other kids mocked her mercilessly when she wasn't there. A phrase Helen had shouted angrily in class one day became a school cliché.

"I have no response to you!"

Bellamy heard that a lot throughout the school year. A gaggle of girls would be gossiping in the hallway, an incomprehensible babel of voices, and then one girl would throw her head back with a hand across her forehead and shout, "I have no response to you!" and they'd all laugh. If Helen heard it, was hurt by it, she didn't let it show.

The musical was performed the first week of April. The work was exhausting, but *Music Man: High School Edition* was a hit with the parents and the administration, and Bellamy assumed he was a shoo-in for the permanent job of theater teacher. Which he should have been. But after the incident in El Paso, he was removed from the short list. He had been lucky to keep his job.

Bellamy decided he needed to go for a run after school. The weather was still nice, if windy, and there would be fewer temperate days in the coming weeks and months, so he should run while he could. When the weather wasn't amenable, he swam laps in the YMCA pool. He was a strong swimmer and enjoyed it. But it was long-distance running that brought him peace. Usually.

CHAPTER 20

From the Top, on Three

Of the eight classical musicians who were supposed to start work in exactly three days, one of them was definitely a no-go, and three more were expressing serious doubts, according to Garrett Miller. Harold Prensky was losing his gig, and they were miles from being ready. The studio was booked and paid for from Wednesday at noon through the following Saturday at midnight, when the gig officially ended. What would they have to show for it by Sunday morning? Not much, if they couldn't get the musical talent to show up.

That damned weasel Miller had promised—sworn upside down and backward—that he could produce the musicians on time and on budget, and then had the audacity to say it was no big deal when it turned out fully half of them might not come after all.

When Harold called his answering service Sunday morning, there was a message from Miller saying he had some bad news to relate. Harold called him back immediately.

"What can I say, Mr. Prensky? They're artists. I thought most of them would jump at the chance for a little extra scratch. But it's a long drive, and most of them have day jobs. I am sorry."

"You promised me they could all work out their schedules for a paying gig," Harold said. "It *is* a damn day job."

"Yes, of course," said Miller, "but—please don't take this the wrong way. It's not your fault or mine, but several of the guys said they'd just rather not participate in this sort of project."

"You mean an art-rock project."

"Well, whatever you want to call it. Pop music. Rock and roll. What can I say? *De gustibus non disputandum est.* It's not everybody's sauce. I really am sorry."

Harold had hung up the phone without saying goodbye.

Now, he was in a pickle. There was no way in bloody hell they could get the sound they wanted with only a few instruments, even with bouncing and multi-tracking. And one of the holdouts was the only other cello besides Miller himself. The deep resonance of the cello was central to the sort of rich sound Harold was going for during the bridge and final chorus, when the song would go from catchy to thrilling. He hoped.

And so, less than a week before rehearsals were scheduled to begin, Harold sat in his room at the Golden Sunset returning phone calls, paying absurd long-distance rates, hoping for a miracle.

JJ had walked to a café four blocks away. They had both grown tired of the overcooked, unimaginative fare at the Golden Sunset's restaurant. The other café wasn't special, either, but it was different. If it had a name, they didn't know what it was. The big painted sign over the doorway read simply *EAT*.

All of Harold's phone messages turned out to be insignificant business matters, no help in the current situation. Harold checked his watch. 9:30 a.m. JJ should be finishing breakfast by now. The plan was for Harold to pick up his star musician at the café, and then go to Best Studios to start laying down guide tracks. He hadn't told JJ about the fuckup with the string players.

JJ had been in a particularly good mood since last night, when they both went to unwind and drink beers at a little club on the northeast side of town. There was a passable cover band playing, and the bandleader had recognized JJ Johns and asked him to come up and sing a song. That might have annoyed most pop stars, but JJ happily bounced up on stage. The band knew one of the Zephyrs' old songs, and JJ sang it with nuance and gusto. The medium-sized bar crowd was enthusiastic, so JJ sang another song, a cover of an old R&B standard, before sitting back down to lusty applause.

Three starstruck local ladies had come over to socialize, and they all ended up staying at the club longer than intended. Late in the evening, Harold had to take JJ aside and talk him out of his idea to take the girls to see the studio in the middle of the night. There was a lot of work to do the next day, and Harold was not entirely convinced they were all over twenty-one, as they claimed.

As Harold pulled up in front of EAT, JJ was just coming outside. He hopped into the station wagon, toothpick dangling from his lips.

"Let's go make a hit record," he said.

Harold couldn't bear to puncture JJ's confidence.

"I'm up for it!" he said.

They didn't expect Allen Wallace to be there, but it didn't matter, since Harold had a key. However, when they got to World Famous Best Studios, Wallace's car was parked behind. When they'd left yesterday, Harold had noticed a windblown grocery-store flyer wedged under one of the rear tires, and it was still there this morning, flapping in the morning breeze. Wallace wasn't in early. He had never gone home.

They found him in the control room, asleep with his head resting on one arm next to the soundboard. The older eight-channel recorder was lit up, and the tube amp glowed. When Harold shook Wallace gently, he moaned but did not rouse. In the trash can next to his chair was an empty bottle of scotch. Also, in the trash can was what appeared to be vomit, some of which had splashed over the side of the container.

"Gross," said JJ.

"Drunk as a boiled owl," said Harold. "Help me get him onto the sofa."

They each took a side and stood Wallace up. This brought him back to consciousness, somewhat, and he looked around.

"Ah, shit," he said. "I think I better go home."

"You just need to get some more sleep first," said Harold. "I'll take you home after a while."

"Okay," said Wallace. He took a couple of steps and staggered, and the two sober men caught him. "I'll just take a little nap," he said.

With some awkward struggling to get him through the door, they deposited the inebriated studio owner on his cloth couch. JJ lifted Wallace's head and put a pillow under it.

"Thanks, friend," said Wallace.

Within ten seconds, he was snoring. Harold took the knitted kaftan that was draped over back of the couch and covered him. It was even colder than usual in the building, but that didn't bother Allen Wallace. JJ and Harold left him alone and shut the door behind them.

Next to the console were several tapes, one of which had been threaded onto the eight-channel machine. Harold switched it on. The soft, breathy voice of a female R&B singer came through the speakers, doing a simple arrangement of an old Buddy Johnson song, "Just Your Fool." The handwritten label on the empty tape box read *MABEL WHITE & RON JORDAN 6-2-61*. The woman's vocals sounded good, with only a piano accompaniment. Bumps and clicks in the tape, as well as an audible cough from the pianist, suggested it was just a demo.

"Who do you suppose that is?" asked JJ.

"His ex-wife," said Harold.

"Really. She's good. I never heard of her."

On the desk was a bottle of prescription medicine. JJ picked it up and shook it. There were half a dozen pills remaining.

"Downs," said JJ. "Booze and pills. Listening to old tapes all night . . . passing out. The man is a wreck, Harold. What are we gonna do if this happens on Thursday?"

"I have no idea," said Harold. "We don't absolutely have to have him. I'm getting to know this equipment, and so are you, but we really could use his experience." He leaned over the console, hit *REWIND*, and the reel spun until the leader cleared the heads. *Fap fap fap.* Harold removed the tape carefully and returned it to its box. "Let's get busy. If the whole project falls apart and we have to find somewhere else to record, we'll still need the guide tracks."

JJ moved the soiled trash can to the other side of the room.

All the positive energy had been sucked out of the studio, but there was no other plan. Harold got to work wiring up the microphones while JJ moved some of the baffles around. Harold powered up the sixteen-track machine, where their practice tape was already cued up. He put on the headphones, then ran the tape forward.

"We'll start the guide tracks in the second verse," said Harold. "Violin parts first."

Guide tracks for strings were usually recorded with organ or piano, but the easiest thing to do in this case was for JJ to sing the parts. They recorded three guide tracks in succession—second verse, chorus, third verse, then the all-important bridge where they were going for the full orchestra sound. JJ sat in the studio, monitoring the guitar, vocal, and click track and la-la-laing through a nylon pop screen into the ribbon mic. He sang "boom-boom ba-boom" where the kettle drums would be, if they ever found any.

JJ sang the first violin part, then second violin, then cello—they could only pray there would be cellos. He did the first violin part three times before he was happy. It was a little out of his range, but he got it on the third try. When all the tracks were recorded, Harold rewound the tape and gestured for JJ to come into the control room.

They sat back away from the monitors, in the sweet spot where the sound from the two speakers converged. Harold balanced the sliders, then hit the *PLAY* button. For the first time, "Earth Is Crying" came through with all its parts. JJ's voice was clean and clear, Harold's B3 sounded sweet, even JJ's la-la-las and hums on the guide tracks came together in a good harmonic mix. For the first time, even without drums, it sounded like a real song.

"All right," said Harold, when the tape ended. "What do you think so far?"

"I think . . . I think I want to work on the harmony vocals now. Let's get as much done as possible. In case we have to take the tape and get out of town."

"Very good," said Harold. "I can sing the baritone on the chorus, and . . ." He paused. "What was that?"

"What?" said JJ, but then he heard it, too. A metallic tap. Someone was outside, knocking at the metal door.

"I'll check it out," said Harold. He walked out of the control room and opened the outside door. It was the young filmmaker, Dan Park, big Bolex camera under one arm and a girl—a cute blonde girl with pink cheeks—carrying a portable tape machine.

JJ called from back in the control room. "Who is it?"

"It's the film guy," called Harold. "And a girl."

"Becky Paulson," said the girl, extending her hand. "We're here to do some test shots. We talked to Mr. Wallace yesterday."

"Pleasure to meet you," said Harold. "I'm not sure this is the best time . . ."

"Mr. Wallace said Sunday morning would work best, so here we are," said Dan. "Is he here?"

"Uh . . . no. Well, yeah. But he's asleep."

"Asleep?"

"In his office," said Harold. "He's really tired. Poor old guy was up all night working and mixing tracks." He looked around. "I guess you can do your test shots, but please stay out of the office. It's the door at the end of the hall."

"We'll be quiet," said Becky, smiling sweetly. She and Dan came in and headed for the studio.

"Pay no attention to us," said Dan. "Remember, we're invisible."

By noon, all the guide tracks had been recorded and rerecorded. Dan and Becky stayed out of the way the best they could, considering the size of the working area.

At one point, Dan sat in the corner of the small studio with the bulky Bolex 16mm camera on his shoulder while Becky held the boom microphone with its fuzzy dead-cat wind screen, as JJ recorded harmony guides. He said he wasn't nervous, but the closeness of the camera unsettled him, and he had to rerecord several tracks. Harold suggested he hold his guitar while he sang, so he did, and that settled him down. When they were finished, Dan took shots of the control room from various angles.

While Becky packed away the portable recorder, the office door opened, and Allen Wallace emerged, rubbing the back of his neck and rolling his shoulders.

"Hello, Mr. Wallace," said Dan.

The studio owner grunted a reply and nodded, then disappeared into the small washroom. Bumping and splashing sounds came from behind the door for several minutes and the toilet flushed twice before Wallace came out, drying his face on a hand towel.

"Sorry. I was asleep when you came," he said. "I was organizing tapes until the sun came up. It's the life of a recording engineer."

"It's alright," said Dan. "These gentlemen have been very cooperative."

"That's good," said Wallace. "Now I'm going to go home for a while and take care of a few things around the house. I guess I'll see you this Thursday."

"We probably won't be in until Friday," said Dan. "We plan on driving from Fort Worth Thursday evening and setting up the next morning before you fellows get started."

"Very good," said Wallace. He went back into the office for his hat and left by the back door.

Harold went into the office to call his phone service one more time, hoping for good news.

"Well, Danfour," said Becky, "did you get everything you need?"

"Pretty much," said Dan. "I think I've got about two more minutes of film on this roll. I'll do a few establishing shots outside." He hoisted the Bolex and followed Wallace out the steel door.

JJ watched Becky as she wound up the microphone cable and closed the recorder case. She reminded him of someone he'd known when he was young, maybe a girl he'd liked in junior high. Round, naturally flush cheeks, not a trace of makeup, a high, round forehead with blonde hair pulled back into a simple pony tail.

Becky saw JJ watching her. She smiled. "I really hope we don't get in your way," she said. "This wasn't my idea, but Dan thinks we can get a good film."

"You're not bothering me," said JJ. "You say you're from Fort Worth?"

"Born and raised in Duro," said Becky. "We just go to college in Fort Worth. CenTex Christian. Dan and I made a film last year that won a cash prize, so now we have the money for a follow-up."

"Was your other film about music?" asked JJ.

"No," Becky laughed. "It was about something completely unrelated, an old-folks home that the state was going to close down. It was fun, but I wanted to make a film about something more . . . exciting. I had a really great idea, but it didn't pan out. Dan just heard that you and your friend were making a record here, and we needed a new subject, so I said okay."

"Ah, I see," said JJ. "I was not your first choice. Tell me, miss . . . uh . . . It's Becky, right? Becky, what did *you* want your film to be about?"

"A local murder."

"Wow," said JJ. "Big difference."

"Oh, yes," said Becky. "But we ran into nothing but obstacles. It's a murder that hasn't been solved, and supposedly—supposedly—the detectives are making progress on the investigation. I guess they're afraid we'll mess up their case."

"Who was murdered?"

"A high school girl. It was a couple of years ago. Actually, they never found a body, so it's not officially a murder. But everybody thinks it was. It could have made a great film, but . . . here we are." Becky shrugged.

JJ laughed. "I understand your dilemma," he said. "On one hand, a local, unsolved murder mystery. On the other, a washed-up singer trying to make a record the public will actually buy. What do we do?" He held up both hands and looked from one to the other. "Unsolved murder . . . JJ Johns . . . unsolved murder . . . JJ . . . murder . . . JJ . . ."

Becky giggled. "I think maybe we made the best choice. And Dan says if your record goes . . . on the charts or whatever you call it . . . maybe people will like our movie too."

"Well, we most definitely want to get JJ on the charts again," said JJ. "It's an exciting place to be. A big rush and a short high. Very addictive."

"Dan said you had a hit."

"With the Zephyrs," said JJ. "Four songs in the top forty *and* a number one hit."

"I've heard you were good," said Becky.

"You've *heard* we were good," said JJ. He put his head down with both hands over his face, pretending to weep.

"Oh, don't feel bad," said Becky. "I've never heard of anything. I was raised in a highly religious family, and we weren't allowed to listen to rock and roll."

"That's so sad," said JJ. "A life without rock. Well, frankly I don't think you're any worse off. But for me . . . it's strange to meet somebody who's never heard of me. A bit of a thrill, actually. You have no preconceived notions. Well, I hope you like my new song. I guess if I can reach you, a person from a different world, I can reach anybody."

Harold stuck his head in the room. "Hey, JJ. Why don't we all get some lunch? The film crew can come, if they want. I'll just lock up the studio."

"Let me pack up my guitar," said JJ.

Becky watched him place the shiny Martin carefully into its case.

"What does JJ stand for?" she asked.

He grinned at her. "Now, that's a secret between me and my mama."

"So, did they call you JJ when you were growing up?"

"Nope. That's just what people started calling me when I got into the music business. Truthfully, I sort of picked out the name myself."

"You got to pick your own nickname?" said Becky. "That's hilarious. I'm just Becky to my friends. My parents call me Rebekah and always will."

"You can't choose what your mom calls you," said JJ. He stashed the guitar back in the recording studio. Harold locked the door.

"Are you coming to lunch with us?" asked JJ.

"I suppose we could," said Becky. "If Dan wants to."

"If you come with us, I'll tell you a secret," said JJ.

"Oh?" Becky stood in front of him looking up with her healthy, scrubbed face, cheeks accenting a wide smile.

JJ leaned close and spoke in a hushed voice. "It's Jerome," he said. "Jerome Johnson."

"Jerome Johnson?" said Becky. "That's a perfectly nice name."

"And my middle name is Kelsey," said JJ. "You are now one of only a dozen in the world who knows this fact. You must solemnly swear never to tell."

"Still a fine name, but I promise to call you JJ."

They all walked out to the car, and Harold locked the outside door. Unfortunately, Dan couldn't go to lunch with them.

"I promised my dad I'd spend the rest of the day with the family in McCauly," said Dan. "I was going to take Becky to her house and pick her up on my way back to Fort Worth in the morning."

"We can get you home after lunch," said JJ. "I really hope you'll come."

"Okay," said Becky.

Dandridge Park locked the university's 16mm camera and portable recorder in the trunk of his car along with their one exposed roll of test footage, then drove away south down Sherman Street. Ten blocks farther, Sherman became Highway 281, which led out of town, off the Caprock, and down to McCauly, forty miles distant. He'd be back in the morning before dawn.

JJ climbed into the station wagon and scooted over to allow room for Becky. Harold had been wondering if the back seat could even be raised anymore. It had been folded away so long, but he stopped worrying. Becky got into the front passenger seat and shut the door.

"Do you like barbecue?" asked Harold.

"You bet!" said Becky.

As they drove north, JJ put his arm across the seat back behind Becky's head. After a few moments, he changed his mind and put his hand back in his lap.

Don't rush it, man.

CHAPTER 21

Early and Loud

"Just how early does this guy get up?" asked Sergeant Correa.

"He leaves his house before seven, so you need somebody waiting there by six," said Detective Lamborn.

"But no contact?"

"Not unless he initiates it," said Lamborn. "Keep your distance, but be there."

"Okay. Sounds boring." Correa sipped at his coffee, steaming in a paper cup.

"It is," said Lamborn. "Surveillance is boring. Just like ninety percent of police work. That's why they invented coffee and cigarettes."

It was still quite dark, and a brisk, dry wind had come up in the night. Correa turned the unmarked Mercury onto Thirty-Second Street, where the Crown apartments sat mid-block, one of many tidy but unremarkable buildings that had appeared during the last big oil boom in the 1950s.

They parked across the street from the apartment parking lot.

"Which one is his car?" asked Correa.

"Right there in the corner, under the streetlight," said Lamborn.

"Okay." They waited. After a few minutes, Lamborn rolled down the passenger-side window and lit a cigarette.

As the gray predawn slowly illuminated this dreary part of town, they watched several men and the occasional woman emerge one by one from the apartments and drive away to their various jobs. Some were working class, wearing overalls with nametags, while others wore shirts and ties. They didn't see any children.

Correa finished his coffee and crumpled the cup, tossing it onto the backseat floorboard.

"So, should we follow him when he leaves?" he asked.

"No. At this point, you should just be here. The same thing when he gets back this afternoon from . . . Wait. That's him, I think."

A man had emerged from a first-floor apartment, climbed into the car sitting under the streetlight, started it, and let the engine idle.

"Yep, that's our boy," said Lamborn. "Don't look at him when he goes past, but don't turn away, either. Just let him see that somebody is in the car."

Correa complied. After a minute, the green Chevy's headlights came on. It pulled out of the parking lot, turned left, and passed the two officers. As it went by, the driver leaned over, trying to see who was sitting in the blue Mercury. Correa kept his eyes straight ahead. When the Chevy had passed and turned at the intersection, the police sergeant started the car.

"He saw us, for sure," said Correa.

"That's the point of a loud surveillance," said Lamborn. "In a couple of days, he'll start thinking he's being watched. And he'll be right."

That morning, Nicky got a late start, uncharacteristic for him, then he ran into a trouble that slowed him down further. As he drove south on Sixteenth Street, he could see, two blocks ahead, the flashing lights of an emergency vehicle. Even though it was just 6:45 in the morning, a dozen cars were lined up waiting to get through, as if it were rush hour. The lights were from a fire truck, parked at an oblique angle. A policeman stood in the middle of the street, directing traffic.

As he reached the intersection, Nicky saw an old sedan sitting at a crazy angle to the street, front end mangled and front wheel up against a bent-over parking meter. Just beyond that, a pickup truck was parked in the street with its passenger-side door caved in dramatically. Clouds of steam rose from beneath the hood of the car. The fire truck was hovering there as a precaution, blocking the southbound traffic.

The police officer waved his arm and pointed, and the first car in the line made a U-turn while the northbound traffic waited. Nicky turned right to find another way through.

Fifteenth Street was smaller, with a four-way stop sign at each cross street, but it was clear of traffic. On both sides of the street, smaller, older storefronts squatted side by side. This was the Duro of the 1950s, before the better stores moved north and east into the large, modern strip centers. Many of the properties were empty.

There was an army surplus store, a wig shop, a used-book store, a couple of other small shops, but not much else.

One little store on the left side caught his attention. A hand-made sign on the window read *FINAL CLOSE-OUT SALE! EVERYTHING MUST GO.* It was a place he knew well, Bissett Jewelers. He felt a tight squeeze in his chest and memories intruded, insistent. He thought of the last time he had been in the store, back when old man Bissett was still alive and worked behind the counter.

Back then, Nicky had worked at an auto-parts store. On one particular Friday in the middle of that terrible, hot summer two years ago, Nicky got paid when he got off work at 3:30 p.m. He had just enough time to make it to the bank before the lobby closed. He drove fast and, with ten minutes to spare, dashed inside. A guard was standing by the door, ready to lock up at the stroke of four o'clock.

Nicky cashed his $120 paycheck. He now had $840 in twenties. Bissett Jewelers closed at 5:00 p.m., so there was plenty of time. Anyway, unlike the bank, a jeweler would stay open for a serious customer. Nicky was serious. It was time to buy the ring.

He didn't absolutely *have* to have cash. The store owners knew him and his father, so they would have taken a personal check. However, his father told him that when you wave a fistful of cash, deals can be made faster, and bargains can be had.

Bob Bissett himself was behind the counter. He often worked at the store, though he was well into his seventies and had passed the management responsibilities to his son. He had started Bissett Jewelers at this location in 1946 and would continue to work until he could no longer walk in the door.

Bissett knew exactly which ring Nicky wanted, though he pretended he didn't. He liked getting customers to try alternatives, especially pricier alternatives.

The ring was a twisted gold band set with a half-carat diamond. Helen would love it, Nicky was sure. She had to.

"It is a lovely piece," said Mr. Bissett. "I think your young lady will appreciate it. But have you thought about going to a full carat?"

"I think I like this one the best," said Nicky. They had been through this conversation before. The last time, Bissett had steered him up to the half-carat diamond from the quarter-carat. Now he was trying to upsell him again. There was no way Nicky could afford a one-carat diamond. And, anyway, today was the day. He had the money in his pocket and would leave with that ring.

"A full carat will cost you twelve hundred seventy-five," said Bissett. "I know that sounds like a lot, but this is a one-time gesture on your part. It will last forever, and she will always remember the day you gave it to her. We can help you with the financing."

"I really think she'll love this one," said Nicky. "And, honestly, I want to pay for it now, all at once." Why was Bissett playing with him? This was the biggest expenditure he'd ever made.

"I'm sure she'll love it," said Bissett. He checked the tag, as if he didn't have every price memorized. "That's eight hundred seventy-five, plus tax."

Okay, here we go.

"I was really hoping you could do a little better," said Nicky.

"I'm afraid the price is pretty firm, son. The margins on fine jewelry are just not very high."

Yes, they are. Dad said you mark up the rings at least fifty percent.

"I know you have to make a profit," said Nicky. "I just thought you might consider giving me a bit of a break. Since you know my family, and my parents have bought stuff from you." *Dad said bring family into it early.*

"I appreciate repeat business. I really do," said Bissett. "But I can't go lower. I already give the best deals in town. Here, let me show you something not quite as nice." He reached into the case and took out a simpler gold band with no setting.

Be persistent. That's what Dad said.

"I really prefer the half-carat diamond," said Nicky. "This is for somebody really special. I'm going to ask her to be with me the rest of her life. I just think maybe you could do a little better."

"I couldn't go a dime below eight fifty," said Bissett. "I'll bet this lovely lady will jump right into your arms. This will show her how serious you are, if you're willing to spend the money."

Show him you've got cash. Take your time.

Nicky pulled out his wallet and counted out some bills, holding it at an angle so that Bissett couldn't see how much he had. He laid sixteen fifty-dollar bills on the counter.

"Will you take eight hundred even? It took me four months to save it."

"Well, you know you *can* wait another month. Then you'd have the full amount. If she's really the one, she will be patient."

"I can't!" Nicky had not meant the outburst. Mr. Bissett was startled.

"Really, I think . . ."

"I just *can't.* I have to give it to her!"

Bissett looked at him, puzzled. There was a long pause. Nicky knew he had blown any advantage.

"All right," Bissett said, finally. "How about eight hundred dollars plus tax? Can you at least pay the sales tax?"

"Yes!" said Nicky, almost shouting.

"Let's do it, then," said Bissett, and used a pencil and a scrap of paper to calculate 3.25%. He took forever. Nicky could barely breathe and didn't take his eyes off the ring, lest it change into something less beautiful if he glanced away. In a few moments, he would own it, and everything would be all right again.

"Eight hundred twenty-six," said Bissett.

Nicky handed over his two remaining twenties. The old man rang up the amount on an ancient National cash register with wood veneer and handed back the change.

"Let me get you a box."

"That's okay."

"You need a box," said Bissett. "It's a very expensive ring. She's going to want you to give it to her in a box. Trust me. Girls love the moment when they open it up in the restaurant." He produced a black ring box with a white plush interior. He held out his hand for the ring, but Nicky clutched it tightly, unwilling to give it up even for a moment. Finally, the old jeweler just closed the box and handed it to him. "She'll love it."

"I know she will. She has to."

She should have loved it.

CHAPTER 22

The Company One Keeps

Typically, Mondays were slow days at Rochester Chevrolet. In the past year, however, business had been brisk even at times you'd think people wouldn't be car shopping, such as a weekday morning. Currently, Duro was riding the crest of a prosperity cycle, and car dealers across the city were deliriously busy. The petroleum business was prospering, despite the notorious oil-price ceiling, and gasoline was still cheap. Good times let them survive the bad times, when cars sat unsold on the lot for weeks.

Grover had a personal goal, which he eagerly shared with his fellow salesmen: Sell at least one car every day. He wasn't too hard on himself if this benchmark wasn't met on any given day, but it only made him more fiercely determined to make up the difference the next.

He hadn't sold a single car on Saturday, usually his best day, though he'd dealt with customers from dawn to dark and had gone for many test drives. Young men with decent paychecks for the first time in their lives were especially drawn to the new generation of Camaros, with their crazy-high horsepower and four-barrel Holley carburetors. Grover loved taking them on test drives and encouraging the prospectives, if the highway was clear, to punch the accelerator to the floor and feel the raw power. The cars practically sold themselves.

Unfortunately, with particularly bad timing, a drawn-out autoworkers' strike in Detroit had put a sharp crimp on the supply of the popular muscle cars, and a recall for defective bumpers had pulled thousands more off the market. It forced the salesmen to explain to an eager customer—standing there with a checkbook in his teeth—that he'd have to wait up to six months for his new Camaro to be delivered. Sometimes they waited. More often, they just went down the street to Murphy Ford, where the big-block Mustangs beckoned.

Grover began every workday with a stroll around the lot, checking the inventory and making sure the signs and stickers were straight and in order. On Saturdays, the sales manager selected a few cars to be festooned with helium balloons, as if they were discounted. They weren't, of course. The balloons adorned the cars that had been on the lot too long, in the manager's view. If they didn't sell on Saturday, the cars would be moved to a different location on the lot, and more balloons would be added.

The dealership opened to the public at 10:00 a.m. Grover and the other two salesmen on duty chatted outside for a few minutes, ready to pounce on any potential marks, but there were no early birds today. The youngest salesman, Rob, agreed to take the first outdoor shift. Grover and the other Rochester salesman, Harry, went back inside the showroom.

Grover had little to do in the way of paperwork this morning, so he puttered about his office, setting random stacks of paper and car brochures here and there around his desk, as if it were the middle of a busy but manageable day. Then he drew a cup of coffee from the big percolator, stirred in two packs of sugar, and took a few moments to catch up on the college football games in the local newspaper. The front part of the paper was all Vietnam and politics, which Grover ignored. The world would do what the world would do, but it had no relevance for a true Christian. Sports, however, was interesting.

He'd been in his office fifteen minutes when Harry stuck his head in.

"Grover, there's a customer who wants to talk to you," he said.

"Who is he?" asked Grover.

"A lady," said Harry. "She said she only wants to talk to you. I tried my sweetest soft-shoe dance, but no dice."

"Oh, okay," said Grover. "Let me have her."

The customer turned out to be a woman he knew. It was Leslie Redford, a young woman of about thirty, a Pentecostal who attended Sacred Truth with her husband, Martin, and their kids. The Redfords only went to church once a week, on Sunday mornings, but who was Grover to judge? They did have four small children. Could they really afford a new car?

"Good morning, Mrs. Redford!" he called.

She smiled nervously, and offered her hand. "Mr. Paulson."

"How can I help you today?" asked Grover. "Would you like to test drive one of our new station wagons? I can make you a great deal on a '72, because the '73s will be coming on the lot any day now. The manager said pull out all the stops to sell 'em. We have to make room."

"Actually . . ." she said, glancing around. "Actually, I'm really sorry, Mr. Paulson, but I'm not here for a car. I don't want to waste your time. I just needed to speak with you." She bit her lower lip.

"It's all right," said Grover. "What can I do for you?"

"I was just speaking with my husband."

"About what?" asked Grover.

"It's just about . . . uh, Mr. Paulson, can we talk privately?"

"Sure," said Grover. "Let's go into my office."

He led the way and gestured for her to sit in one of the plush leather chairs for customers getting the hard sell. He started to shut the door but changed his mind. It didn't seem appropriate.

"I really don't want to take up your time," said Mrs. Redford. "Anyway, my husband and I were talking about something yesterday. We should have spoken to you at church, but we didn't get a chance to go last night. So Martin asked me to come see you at your car place. He'd be here himself if he didn't have to work."

Grover sat up straight in his chair. "I understand," he said. "Please, tell me what I can do."

Mrs. Redford looked down, then raised her gaze, not quite high enough to meet his, but close.

"This is something that we know is not our business," she said, "but we all worship with the same fellowship, and we're sort of like family, so we thought we needed to let you know about something that happened yesterday."

"My goodness, what?" said Grover. "Is everything okay with your family?"

"Oh, we're fine," she said. "It has to do with your daughter."

"My daughter? Martha?"

"No, no. The big girl, Rebekah. We . . . uh . . . saw her yesterday."

"She was in town for the weekend," said Grover. "She left to go back to college early this morning."

"We've known her since she was ten," said Mrs. Redford. "Really sweet girl and a good Christian."

"Yes, she's a good girl," said Grover. "She's gotten kind of headstrong since she grew up, but what can a father do? Where did you see her?"

"After church yesterday. Martin said we could go to Fonde's for lunch. Just a special treat; we don't go every week. Anyway, after we ate, we were getting the kids out the front door, and we saw this big station wagon go by. An old Ford, a little bit banged up. We saw that Rebekah was sitting in the front seat . . . with two men."

"Wait," said Grover. "She does have a young male friend from college. His name is Dan. He's not a boyfriend. He has a beard, which I don't care for, but he is a Christian. And we trust our daughter."

"These men did not look very young," said Mrs. Redford. "I'd say they were in their thirties or close to it."

"You're sure it was her?"

"Yes, I'm afraid so. The car was going by pretty slowly, and she saw me. She even waved. It was definitely Rebekah."

"Well . . ." Grover sat back. "She certainly didn't mention that yesterday, except to say she met a musician from out of town. Dan and she were going to start making a film about him next weekend. I don't approve, of course, but I try to give her a long leash. Maybe too long."

"That must have been the musician," said Mrs. Redford, "and this is really none of my business, but he was not the sort of man you'd expect a girl like Rebekah to know. His hair was really long—at least a foot, down over his shoulders. And he had sideburns that came all the way down his jaw. Very rough character."

"Wow . . . I . . ." Grover focused on his breath, a technique he used when a customer got irate about something. *Stay calm.*

"The other man was older," said Mrs. Redford. "His hair was not as long, but he was a hippie, too. At least it seemed so to me and Martin. The man was wearing a hippie jacket and those round hippie glasses. He was the driver."

"I honestly don't know what to say," said Grover. He was telling the truth. Grover the fast-talking salesman was at a loss for words.

"We just thought you should know," said Mrs. Redford. "I'm really sorry. It's not our business. We weren't sure we should even tell you."

"No, no. You did the right thing," said Grover. "This is . . . something I need to know about and deal with. I really had no idea. Thank you for telling me. I'll talk to Rebekah. There is probably some innocent explanation."

"I'm sure there is," said Mrs. Redford. "I won't use up any more of your time. I'm sure we'll see you in church. Please give my best to Holly and the children." She rose, collected herself, and left.

Innocent explanation? Really? What might that be, exactly? Grover needed to talk to his daughter. Riding around in a car with low men of the world! He wished he could call right now, get her on the phone long distance at the university. But that wasn't feasible, and he knew it.

Grover wondered if his ears were red, which sometimes happened when he got excited. He left the office and paced the showroom.

"Are you all right?" asked Harry.

"Yes, of course," said Grover. "Just a lady I know from church. It's nothing really serious."

He went outside for air. Grover thought back to yesterday morning. Rebekah had told them she couldn't go to morning fellowship because she and Dan were meeting a man at some recording studio. That should have been a warning sign. What kind of place or business was more important than God? Paulsons did not skip worship services, ever, not if they could rise from their bed. Grover had been upset with his daughter but didn't feel it was his place to insist. He should have. Rebekah might be legally an adult, but Grover was the head of the household. The Bible says, "Children, obey your parents in everything, for this pleases the Lord." Why hadn't he said something?

Grover had quit smoking years ago, but he craved a cigarette. He needed to find out what was going on. Who could he talk to about this? Should he tell Holly? She was Rebekah's mother, after all, but she had not said a word in protest when her daughter skipped church. Holly should know the consequences of her inaction, of not backing up the husband she had promised to obey.

But Holly had not been herself lately. For weeks, really. She'd been oddly removed, and the only subject she wanted to talk about was her little Christian school. Other than that, there were few words. Grover sometimes overheard her talking to herself in the morning. She'd been doing that for years—carrying on what sounded like one side of a conversation—but it had been happening more frequently. When he asked her about it, she just laughed it off. *I've always talked to myself,* she'd say.

The thought of his eldest girl consorting with hippies made the acid in Grover's stomach churn. He paced some more, twice around the lot, concentrating on his own breathing. Rebekah had been raised right. Maybe that boy Dan was behind it in some way, leading her down the wrong path.

"Sir, could you help me?"

Grover was startled. He turned to see a young man in his early twenties. He was not a hippie, but his longish light-brown hair and leather jacket rubbed Grover the wrong way. He wasn't sure he could handle this, not right now.

"Yes, what can I do for you this morning?" Grover asked. He forced a smile.

"I'd like to take a look at your Novas," the young man said.

"You came to the right place," said Grover. "We have about twenty on the lot. The new Nova models are the best yet—more room in the car, more horses under the hood. Let me show you."

As they walked across the lot, Grover's head swam. He spotted Rob, the young salesman, and waved him over.

"Rob, this young man wants to check out the new Nova line," said Grover. "Can you help him?"

"Sure," said Rob, bewildered. Did the senior salesman at Rochester Chevrolet really just hand off a customer to him? What was that about? He wondered briefly if Grover wanted to double-team the guy, but the older salesman walked away briskly.

CHAPTER 23

The Cure for What Ails You

Mabel White had two recording sessions scheduled today, which most people in the music business would call a good thing. But Mabel was aware of the tentative quality of her singing voice, and that she was no longer young. Two gigs in a day was a lot to ask of a vocal artist pushing fifty. She was grateful for the work, but she had to take care of herself. It was time for honey and cayenne pepper.

Honey keeps forever, but cayenne isn't efficacious unless it's fresh, so Mabel stopped at one of Nashville's smallish grocery stores on her way to Music Row. A&H Grocery kept its spice section well stocked, and they never ran low on cayenne. Mabel wasn't the only local singer to swear by this herbal remedy. She bought two of the smallest metal boxes of McCormick's cayenne—one to keep at home and one for her manager's office at RCA. She also bought six fresh lemons. She had plenty of honey.

It was a bright, cold day in Tennessee. Winter might be coming a little early this year—not a good thing for the professional singer. Mabel was from Mississippi, but except for a couple of years out in West Texas, she'd lived in the Nashville area most of her life. The traffic was getting worse every year, as both the music industry and the tourist trade grew, but she still loved the city. The winters she could do without, but somehow, she always got through.

Her first job today was scheduled for straight-up noon in the big building, Studio A. She was singing backup for a new Sonny James recording, along with Tanya and Sheila, two studio singers she had worked with many times. Mabel wanted a little extra time to go over the charts, so she came in to the studio a few minutes past eleven. It also gave her a chance to brew up her cayenne–honey–lemon cure, then warm up her voice.

She parked her car and walked through the big front entrance toting a paper grocery sack with the lemons and spices and was quickly waved in through the inner doors by the security guard. In the hallway, there was a big coffee machine that had two pots of black coffee sitting on burners, plus another pot with hot water for tea.

Mabel continued down the hall to the office of her manager, Fred Hawkins. He was on the phone, but he waved and smiled as she came in. She opened a cabinet where she kept a jar of honey and an oversized mug (*Historic Graceland*, with a picture of the house on one side and Elvis on the other) and spooned a couple of big dollops into the cup along with a half teaspoon of the bright red powder, then walked back up the hall to pour a big cup of hot water. From a drawer under the coffee bar she took a small paring knife, cut one lemon in half, and squeezed as much juice as she could manage into the steaming mug. The aroma of lemon and cayenne filled the room.

She returned to Fred's office, where he reached across his desk to hand her a folder.

"Two weeks is fine," he was saying into the phone. "I just can't guarantee Sonny will be available in December. I'll have to talk to him. But I can tell you right now that January is wide open."

Mabel sat on the couch, opened the folder, and began to sip the sweet, spicy, warm liquid, letting it slide down her throat slowly. It was old Doc Parker, the legendary Memphis blues man, who had taught her the cayenne pepper trick. He swore by the stuff and had continued to sing professionally well into his eighties. Mabel tilted her head back and let the sharp taste of pepper combine with the honey and lemon to open her sinuses. She made little "Ah . . . ah . . . ah" sounds with her vocal cords. She would never do this in public, but Fred was used to it.

She pored over the sheet music, hearing the notes in her head. This one was not too challenging, which was good, because she knew the second gig later this evening, with a British band called Stargazer, could be tougher, with lots of vocal power and multiple takes.

Fred finished his phone call and turned around in his chair to face her. "Everything going well today, Mabel?" he asked. "Are you recovered after that ordeal last week?"

He was referring to a particularly long, brutal session with the Kinks that had lasted from 6:00 p.m. to nearly dawn, with take after take of high, challenging vocals.

"I can do a gig like that about once a month," laughed Mabel. "When I was twenty-five, we'd pull six hard sessions in week."

"And then go out drinking afterward," said Fred, laughing. "Yeah, I remember."

Mabel returned to her sheet music, and Fred sorted through his mail, opening the interesting-sounding ones with a letter knife.

An assistant, a thin young man with horn rim glasses, stuck his head into the office.

"Mr. Hawkins, I'm supposed to remind you to call Mike Waters over at Polydor."

"Yes. Thanks, Karl," said Fred. "I better do that now before it gets too late over in London."

He looked at his watch, then picked up the phone.

"Karen, I'm going to need the Watts line," he said. "Yeah, that's fine. I can wait." He held the receiver next to his ear and poked through his stack of mail. He looked up. "Oh, Mabel, I forgot to tell you. Allen called this morning."

Mabel looked up. "Allen called? Did he sound okay?"

"He sounded fine, I guess," said Fred. "He was looking for you and asked if I had your home number."

"You didn't give it to him, right?"

"Of course I didn't. I told him you had moved a couple of times and I didn't have it anymore. I did say that I'd tell you he called."

"All right," said Mabel. "Thanks. I hope everything is okay."

"He sounded clear and sober to me," said Fred. "We had a good little talk for a couple of minutes. He's still recording out there at his little place in West Texas. He has some project he's pretty excited about, a band from Oklahoma."

"Well, that's good to hear," said Mabel. "Staying busy is the best thing that can happen to him. It's when he has nothing to do . . ." She trailed off. Fred knew what she meant. They both had a history with Allen Wallace.

It was 1958 when she had met and fallen for Allen. He was doing a project for Royal Studios in Memphis, recording a girl group called Lois and the Dreams. Mabel was never a full-fledged member of the Dreams, but she recorded and toured with them for more than two years, singing backup and subbing lead if one of the main girls got sick. Allen, a skinny white guy with a crewcut and a radiant smile, had flirted aggressively. He bought her an ermine coat and diamond earrings, told her she was the best female singer in the south, and took her to England on business trips with him twice. He convinced her that all she needed was the right band and the right producer to make her into the star he knew her to be.

A producer who really cares about an artist is a treasure to be kept. However, Mabel and Allen, as a couple, made less than no sense. It wasn't just that he was a white man twenty years her senior. More than a few eyebrows were raised, even in a forward-looking city like Memphis. But, as she soon learned, Allen was married—unhappily—and had a daughter back in Texas. Mabel was divorced and childless, raised in the Jim Crow south. Maybe she was attracted to Allen because her own father had abandoned the family when she was ten, and Allen was the opposite of Jimmy White in every way imaginable. Was Allen Wallace the father she never really had? Or just different from every other man she had known?

Either way, for whatever reason, when Allen Wallace proposed, Mabel said yes.

Allen's first wife didn't make things easy. She refused to give him a divorce without major concessions. They ended up before a judge, where Allen lost the house, the car, and half ownership of the studio. Being forced to buy back his ex-wife's share of the business, which he had built and personally managed, had galled him badly. But when the judge found out the woman Allen had an affair with—and intended to marry—was a Black R&B singer, he made no attempt to hide his disgust. As a final cruel blow to Allen's dignity, the judge awarded Sylvia Wallace full custody of their daughter, Grace, and imposed a hefty child-support obligation.

Allen had been a boisterous drinker for years, but as everyone who knew him could attest, he had the sort of rugged constitution that could shrug off heavy doses of alcohol and still allow him to arrive at the studio fresh and full of creative energy. After the humiliating divorce, Allen went off the deep end, combining whisky with antianxiety medication in a self-destructive quest for oblivion.

No, that wasn't true. Allen's disintegration didn't start with the messy divorce. He'd handled it remarkably well, considering. It really began when, six months into their marriage, Mabel left him and went back to Tennessee.

It wasn't anyone's fault, least of all Allen's. Living in a dusty, backward West Texas town in 1959 was just too much for Mabel. She tried to make a go of it, but she couldn't be seen in public with Allen anywhere in Duro without being the target of unsubtle stares and stage whispers of disapproval. He took her to a movie once at one of the newer downtown theaters, where a manager told Allen he could sit wherever he liked, but his "lady friend" would have to sit in the balcony.

School segregation had ended officially, but a legal end to segregation in everyday life was still five years away.

Mabel would probably have left sooner, but a short time after they were married, Allen suffered a horrific accident that severely damaged the tendons of his right arm. It would have been just too cruel to abandon him at that time.

It was during an allowed visit with his five-year-old daughter. He sat in the living room of the house he used to own, arguing with Sylvia about visitation arrangements, while Grace rocked furiously on her rocking horse in the porch room on the other side of a sliding glass door.

Allen was yelling "You can't use our daughter as a weapon against me!" watching Grace rock harder and harder, when the child suddenly pitched so far back she lost her balance, and the painted wooden rocking horse pitched over backward with Grace screaming. Allen leaped to the rescue—and crashed full-force into the crystal-clear glass door, which shattered from the impact.

The child was unhurt, but when she saw her father sitting dazed on the floor in a pile of glass shards, blood pouring down his shirtsleeve, she had run into her room and hid under the covers. That was the last time he saw her.

Allen had surgery the next day to reattach some of the severed tendons and, while still recovering in the hospital, learned that Sylvia had told the police he had come over intoxicated and screamed at her in front of their daughter before stumbling into a glass door. Very soon after that, the judge revoked his visitation privileges entirely.

A couple of months later, Mabel gave up and fled back to Nashville. The major studios in Tennessee would no longer hire Allen Wallace, so he had no choice but to stay in Duro and try to make a go of it with World Famous Best Studios. For six months, he rarely drew a sober breath. But eventually, he pulled himself together.

Mabel was tired. The Stargazer gig over at Columbia Studios was typically demanding. The British band had no good reason to record at Columbia, except for the mystique of playing in the same room where Bob Dylan had recorded *Nashville Skyline*. This time, Mabel was the only backup singer, and they insisted she do a variety of styles, all near the top of her natural vocal range. It was stressful and exhausting, but Mabel prided herself on her resilience. When she finally pulled out of the parking lot, it was 11:30 p.m. Well, it could have been worse.

She stopped by an all-night takeout burger joint to grab the first food she'd had since morning, then headed home. She'd be expected back at RCA by noon tomorrow.

What was up with Allen? She had remained fond of him for the past decade, though they rarely spoke. When he did call, the ostensible reason was usually to talk shop, to get her technical input on vocal recording, but she suspected he was just lonely. A few times when he called, especially late at night, he was obviously drunk, and she would tell him politely but firmly that she couldn't talk to him until he sobered up. Then the last time she moved and got a new phone number, she didn't share it with him. That was almost two years ago.

Had it really been that long? She had just needed a break. She had never meant to cut him off.

When Mabel got inside her apartment, it was a few minutes past midnight. It was possible Allen was still up and working. She hesitated, then dialed the number for the studio. At least if he got long-winded, the long-distance rates were cheaper.

He picked up on the first ring.

"Best," he said. That's how he always answered the studio phone.

"Allen, it's Mabel."

There was an inbreath on the other end.

He's collecting himself. If he's drunk, he doesn't want to sound drunk.

"Mabes, light of my world, how have you been?" He sounded a little hoarse, but he wasn't slurring.

"I've been very well, Allen. Working days and working nights. Drinking my cayenne tea. Sleeping occasionally."

He chuckled. "Fortunately, I don't have to sing these days. Been fighting a little head cold lately. I need to try the cayenne tea method myself."

"I swear by it," said Mabel.

She could hear him speaking to someone else. "Give me a couple of minutes," he was saying. Then he came back on. "I've been thinking about you, Mabes. We got a killer new sixteen-track machine, and I was remembering all the sweet tracks we used to record back in the day, with you and Ron and with Max Klinger on the upright. All on four tracks. I love the new machines, but sixteen tracks can make you lazy."

"Are you working on a project?" asked Mabel. "I didn't mean to bother you."

"Oh, that's fine," said Allen. "I can talk a few minutes. And yes, I do have a project. A good one. You remember JJ Johns?"

Mabel paused. "Was he with the Jordanaires?"

"No, no. You're thinking of JJ Hart. This is JJ Johns, who used to sing with the Blue Zephyrs."

Mabel drew a blank. "Uh . . . yeah . . . sure . . . JJ Johns. Is it a solo project?"

"Well, solo with a lot of side musicians. That brings me to why I called Fred this morning. We need a backup vocalist. High and clean. We'll be doing some tracks this weekend with full band and an orchestra. I have a line on a couple of young women, but . . . I was wondering . . . is it possible you could fly down and help me? You would be perfect for this project."

"This weekend?"

"They're booked Wednesday through Saturday," said Allen. "But if you can't make it 'til Saturday, we could work around you."

"Um . . . wow . . ."

"I realize this is sudden, and I'll understand if you can't do it. But I was listening to the demo last night, and it suddenly occurred to me—Mabel could do this part in her sleep. Probably in one take. It has that soaring style you do so well, high but not too high."

"Oh . . . gee, Baby," said Mabel. "I'm sorry. This weekend is just not good for me. I'm booked solid the next two weeks—weekdays, Saturdays, and Sundays. I could maybe do it after that."

There was a pause, then she heard Allen speaking to someone but couldn't quite understand it. "Okay," he said. "I know this was too quick. But the song will be long in the can in two weeks. I wish you could do it."

"I really wish I could, too."

Again, Allen was quiet.

"Well . . . I have to get back to work," he said. "I'm really happy you called. It's been too long."

"Way too long for me, too," Mabel said. Allen was silent. She didn't want to end the call on that note. "Are you really doing alright, Allen?"

"Yes, yes," said Allen. "I've seldom been better. Work keeps me going. I've had some good projects and . . . well . . . I just miss you, Mabes. Sometimes, I think maybe I'm . . . coming unstuck. Like the glue is all worn out, and pieces of me are falling off." He chuckled.

"Oh, Baby. I wish there was something I could say. You were always the guy I counted on to keep everything together."

"I'm really okay," said Allen. "Let's talk again soon. I really have to go now. It's going to be pedal to the floor for the next week, 'til we get this thing finished."

"I still love you, Baby," said Mabel.

"I love you too, girl. Always will. I have to go now. Bye."

"Bye, Allen. Good luck with the session."

After she hung up the phone, Mabel sat quietly for several minutes. She had never heard Allen say anything negative about himself before. After a while, she stood up to get ready for bed, though she was jazzed up from her busy day. The conversation stuck with her as she undressed and brushed her teeth.

Unstuck? For all his faults, Allen was not a complainer. *Unstuck* was probably Allen's term for something worse. What's wrong?

Mabel read a magazine for a few minutes, then turned off the light, lay quietly, and tried to settle her mind. Still, she couldn't sleep. Too many memories.

CHAPTER 24

The King's Glossolalia

Grover almost yelled at Martha, then stopped himself. They weren't late. Martha wasn't taking any longer to get ready than she usually did. She never objected to attending church. In fact, she loved it, especially on Wednesday evenings, when the service was looser and the music livelier.

You can't take your anger out on the little ones, he thought. *Be generous and forgiving.*

That was easy to do with Martha and Peter, but a tough call with Rebekah. He couldn't forgive her unless he could understand her, and he couldn't do that until he talked to her. Which he couldn't do until she returned from Fort Worth Thursday night.

"Come along, now!" he hollered out the car window. Grover waited, as usual, for his family to meet his schedule. *I bet Holly will forget to lock the door*, he thought, then immediately chastised himself. *Don't criticize her until she does something that merits it. What's wrong with me?*

He knew what was wrong. After a solid day of stewing, he had decided to see for himself what Rebekah was getting into. So on Tuesday, during his lunch break, he called a local radio station to ask a very simple question. They put him through to the DJ, who was playing songs off the Top Twenty Countdown. They probably assumed he had a request.

"KDUR," said the DJ.

"Uh, hi. This is Grover Paulson. I'm a . . . big fan of the station."

"That's good to hear. How can I help you, Mr. Paulson?"

"I heard a rumor that a big rock star is in town making a record at . . . one of the local music studios, but I don't know which one. I was wondering if you have heard anything about that."

"Big rock star making a record in Duro? Can't say I have. Do you know the guy's name?"

"No," said Grover. "But one of my kids said he was recording at a tiny little studio way out south of town."

"Well, that would have to be Best Studios," said the DJ. "The only other studio I know about on the south side is Countrywide, and they focus on country music."

"Best Studios? Who is in charge over there?"

"His name is . . . Wait a minute. It will come to me . . . Hey, can you hold for a minute? I have to go on the air."

Grover waited. After two minutes, the DJ came back on.

"Hey, you still there? The studio owner's name is Allen Wallace. I didn't remember, but my station manager did. The guy hasn't been in the news in a while. Made a couple of minor hit records a few years ago, but that's all I know."

"Do you know the address?" asked Grover.

"No, but it's in the phone book, I'm sure. The actual name is World Famous Best Studios. Sort of like Mom's Famous Pies. It's not really famous, but . . . hey."

"Thanks, I'll call them," said Grover.

"If you find anything interesting, let us know," said the DJ. "That's the kind of thing I like to share with the listeners."

Grover did find Best Studios in the Duro phone directory, but he didn't call. He told his manager at Rochester Motors he needed to knock off early, then drove home briefly to pick up his hunting scope. He owned a pair of binoculars, but the scope was better and more powerful.

He drove south on Sherman Street for miles until he found the studio. He had a hard time believing somebody would put a business so far out of town. He did find it, however, a nondescript metal and cinderblock building with two cars parked behind. He pulled off to a mostly empty side street so he could watch the parking lot from a distance.

For most of an hour, nothing happened. Should he just walk up to the door and knock? Who would he ask for? He reached the point where he had to either drive away defeated or get out of the car and start a confrontation. But then the metal door on the back loading dock opened, and a man came out.

Grover put the scope up to his eye and focused, holding it steady against the door frame. The man in the crosshairs did look like a rough character, but not as bad as Grover had imagined. He had somewhat long hair neatly trimmed over his ears and round granny glasses, but his appearance didn't inspire contempt. Certainly, he was someone he would never allow Rebekah to consort with, but he didn't look dangerous. A small relief.

Then the other man came out. Grover bristled. *Oh, Lord, there he is!* It was the hippie his daughter was making a film about. Hair cascading down over his collar, sideburns that almost met in the middle of his chin, sunglasses, a leather jacket with tassels hanging along the sleeves.

I can almost smell him from here, thought Grover.

The two men stood beside one of the cars, a station wagon, talking for several minutes, and Grover watched them, his ears ringing. Finally, the hippie came around to the passenger side, waiting for the door to be unlocked, and Grover got a good, long look.

Here was the world at its very worst, the reason that good Christians like the Paulsons rejected the world and why God would surely punish America. Grover kept watching until the hippie climbed into the car. He quickly turned the scope to the car's license plate, with its motto: *OKLAHOMA IS OK.*

He kept the car in the crosshairs until it disappeared up Highway 341.

During worship Wednesday night, Grover tried to let go of his anger as long as he stood in the house of the Lord. But his mind kept drifting back to the greasy, hairy stranger who touched his first-born child. Grover had to keep dragging his attention back to the service.

He hadn't mentioned anything to Holly. Besides, she was even more remote than usual this evening, barely mouthing the words to the hymns and staring straight ahead during the Bible messages. Something was wrong. If he hadn't been so worked up and angry, he might have asked what was bothering her, but today, there were more important things on his mind. When Holly was in a mood, it was best to let her work it out. She would come around.

His immediate options were few. He could have taken a day off, driven to Fort Worth, and confronted Rebekah at her college. That would accomplish nothing and further alienate his daughter. There was already too much distance between them. No, the right answer was to stay calm, wait until Thursday evening when she got home, and take her aside with a fatherly firmness to ask her, calmly, *JUST WHAT WERE YOU THINKING?* He didn't want to make a scene at home, in front of the youngsters, but he might have to.

The most important thing was not to blast off like a rocket but to confront her with the facts and give her time to speak, to explain her actions. Maybe it wasn't nearly as bad as it looked, though Grover could hardly imagine how. Okay, most likely Rebekah was just caught up in the excitement of the film project and hadn't thought it through. The whole thing was that boy Dan's idea, anyway. Rebekah had wanted to do a film about a local crime. That wasn't a great idea, either, but at least that wouldn't have her carousing around town with hippies and low characters.

Oh, Lord, what if they give her drugs? The thought made him shiver. Grover had drilled the worldly evil of liquor and drugs into the brains of his children since they could speak, but it was well known that hippies often slipped drugs into the drinks of young people to hook them.

This whole film nonsense had to stop. Immediately. Rebekah would be really upset and fight him tooth and nail. But Grover had to stand firm.

The last hymn came to a rousing crescendo, and final prayer began. This was an uncontrolled, raucous occasion of pure worship and praise, which might take anywhere from five minutes to half an hour. If anyone was going to receive the Holy Spirit and speak in an unknown tongue, this was when it would happen.

Pastor Davies shouted in a singsong rhythm: "Praise him, all ye little children! All ye little children. We are all your children. Praise him!"

There were shouts of "Amen!"

Old Mr. Sawyer, a portly bald man with badly fitting false teeth—he was one who frequently got the Holy Spirit—began speaking in an unknown tongue, tilting his head back as if he were addressing the ceiling. Who knows how it would have sounded if he had good teeth, but it didn't really matter, not in this case.

What he was saying sounded like this: "Ah la pah la nah la nah la!"

The preacher continued to shout. "All little children. We're little children in His eyes."

"Ah la nah nah nah pah la!"

"Praise him, all ye little children!"

"Pah la DAH! Pah la DAH! Ah la NAH!"

The rhythm quickened, and some members of the fellowship began a steady clap. The drummer, who had been waiting for this sort of moment, began to thump his kick drum along with the claps, and then everyone was on the same beat.

"Ah la NAH! Pah la NAH!"

Holly, who was sitting between Grover and Peter in the second row, suddenly stood up and moved toward the aisle, almost tripping over Grover. He looked up, startled. Holly's eyes were wide and strange, and she was breathing fast. She stumbled into the aisle and turned toward the front. The preacher was standing off to the side of the stage at that moment, but Holly walked straight toward the center of the back wall, with its heavy wooden cross made of thick timbers, stepping up onto the stage and around one of the guitarists, who quickly pulled the audio cable out of her way.

As she reached the cross, she suddenly dropped to her knees and let out a piercing scream that was so unexpected that everybody stopped, including the bespirited one with bad teeth.

"They're coming for the children!" she shouted, out of breath. "The world! The world wants to take away the children! To make them wicked!"

Everyone, including Pastor Davies, was too taken aback to respond. Holly kept it up. It was unusual to hear a person with the Spirit speak English, unless they were translating for someone speaking an unknown tongue, which happened occasionally.

"The children . . . The world wants to make them wicked—sinful! Wash them in sin! Wicked world! Wicked world! Wicked world!" Holly's head swayed back and forth.

Grover had had enough. He stepped up onto the stage and tried to raise Holly to her feet, but she stayed face down, knees tucked under her body, moaning rhythmically with sounds one might make during sexual ecstasy.

"Ahh! Ahh! Ahh!"

Grover got a firm grip under both armpits and lifted her to her feet. That seemed to break the spell. She stopped moaning and allowed her husband to turn her around and walk her back down off the stage and down the aisle. Rather than return to the seats, he kept going for the back door. He turned to look at her face and saw anguish and tears.

"It's okay, love," he said quietly. Peter and Martha were confused but followed their father out of the church.

The preacher said "Praise him!" one more time, and the service effectively ended. The congregation was stunned and motionless, but when the bass player unplugged his instrument and starting wrapping the audio cable, they all gathered their things, talking quietly among themselves. There would be gossip among the Pentecostals.

As Grover walked Holly toward the car, she seemed to return to herself.

"Oh, wow," she said quietly. "I guess I made a spectacle."

Grover reached to open the passenger door for her, but she opened it herself and got in. Martha and Peter clambered into the back.

"Are you feeling okay, Mommy?" asked Martha.

"Yes, sweetie. I'm fine. I was caught up for minute, but now I'm fine."

"Your mother had the Holy Spirit," said Grover.

"That's right," said Holly. "The Holy Spirit."

Grover started the car and pulled out of the parking lot. No one spoke as they drove back to Bluebonnet Lane.

After a few minutes, Holly said, "I really can't talk to you right now."

"It's all right, dear. You don't need to talk," said Grover.

"I'm sorry. I didn't mean you," said Holly.

CHAPTER 25

Trouble at the Border

The school bus idled in front of Duro High, grumbling and puffing acrid fumes. The district's fleet of yellowhounds dated from the early '60s, and some of them were barely operational. This old beast was one of the better ones, so it was cleared for out-of-town functions. It was a reliable and smelly old clunker.

It was five-thirty Wednesday, after school. The Duro High Speech team was bound for Abilene and the UIL Fall Speech Tournament. They would spend one night at a Motel Six, compete in the event Thursday, then return that evening.

David Bellamy watched the members of the speech team climb aboard. Glenn Metcalf, one of the coaches, was helping chaperone for this trip (and getting paid overtime). He stood with his crewcut and clipboard, checking off names one by one as the students climbed the steps with their backpacks, pillows, and plastic bags filled with snacks.

Metcalf had a growly, penetrating voice honed on the football field.

"Listen up!" he bellowed. "Once you are on the bus, *don't get off.* I have to get an accurate count, or we can't leave. Keep it moving! Let's go!"

Bellamy kept a careful watch on the students, trying to spot contraband. One of the juniors had a guitar case, and Bellamy made him open it for inspection. He searched the case thoroughly, then picked up the guitar and shook it gently. Last year, one of the more brazen seniors had smuggled a pint of vodka inside a guitar. The students who were in on the subterfuge managed to conceal their late-night treat until the last bed check, when Bellamy had found one boy in a pathetic state, moaning, head resting on the toilet seat, flecks of vomit on the toilet, the floor, and his knit shirt. Another boy was not much better off, lying disheveled on the bed, one shoe off.

Bellamy and the other chaperone kept the incident to themselves, but from then on, vigilance on out-of-town trips was strict, and students violating the rules would be reported to the administration and banned from extracurricular events for the semester. Two violations meant suspension. Since then, there had been no major incidents. Wine and spirits still found their way onto school trips, he was sure, but at least the students were more discreet.

The bus was loaded and ready to go, with all students aboard except Chase McFall, who had gone home for some forgotten thing. As they waited, bus engine rumbling, Bellamy and the coach debated about how long they should wait before they gave up and left without her.

Just as they had decided to give her ten more minutes, Chase arrived, driven by her friend Beverly. She hopped out of the car carrying two suitcases (for one overnight trip) and climbed onto the bus, plopping herself down in the front-most seat, right next to where Bellamy would sit. She jammed her suitcases onto the empty second row seats.

Chase had a major disappointment when her duet acting partner, Andrew, flunked chemistry on his first report card of the semester. Following a school district rule, Andrew was banned from school trips and UIL events. "The Sand Man Wakes" would have to wait for a future competition.

Though the one-act play had never really come together, Chase had worked really hard, and Bellamy felt sorry for her. He had persuaded her to give extemporaneous speaking a try. In this event, a student had five minutes to speak persuasively on a contemporary topic, such as "Vietnam War protesters: loyal or disloyal?" or "Should police be required to knock?" It sounded stressful, but it was easy to win because everybody was terrible at it.

The driver looked over at Bellamy, who nodded. The driver pulled the door handle, checked the side mirrors, and dropped the engine into gear. The 1962 Blue Bird All American Model FE exhaled with a great whoosh, then pulled out of the school parking lot, engine roaring between gear shifts as they headed for the highway.

Bellamy stood up and faced the twenty-two students.

"All right! This trip is going to take us about three-and-a-half hours. Mr. Sullivan tells me we will be stopping exactly once, somewhere on the other side of Big Spring. When we stop, you will have fifteen minutes to do whatever you need to do."

There were titters from the students.

He continued: "My strong suggestion: Do *not* purchase an extra-large soda. Because if you do, by the time we get to Abilene, you will be ready to pop like an overfilled water bed. If you come up to me then and tell me"—He squinched up his face and spoke falsetto—"'Mister Bellamy, Mister Bellamy, I need to go . . . *so . . . bad*,' then guess what? We're all going to *make fun* of you! And if you have an accident, I'll make you *mop*." The kids laughed. Bellamy sat down beside Chase.

The bench seats were small and hard, and the very cute seventeen-year-old girl sat on the window side. She pushed her leg up against his. He smiled at her.

"Why can't the school give us regular buses?" she asked. "If this was Continental Trailways, I could just curl up and go to sleep 'til it was over."

"I'm all for traveling in comfort, too," said the teacher. "But we're not one of the rich school districts. This way, it makes us all tougher. By the time we get to the tournament, we can fight *giants*."

Chase laughed. "Feeling like I want to die won't make me tough. But I'm going to try to sleep some anyway."

The trip was not too bad. It wasn't a cold day, but it was gusty, and desert dust seeped into the drafty bus. The kids did the usual cutting up and grab-assing, told jokes and sang songs.

On the outskirts of Big Spring, the bus pulled into a truck stop and novelty store, and the students piled out to pee and shop for useless things. They bought candy in all forms, chips, cookies, and, of course, twenty-four-ounce soft drinks. One kid bought a bottle of disappearing ink and walked around splattering drops of the blue liquid on the others, to his own amusement and no one else's. Another came out with a trick baseball cap that squirted water, and walked up and down the aisle blasting students randomly until Bellamy told him to stop or his purchase would be confiscated.

Chase just got off the bus and stretched a little, then returned to her seat. She had brought a small blue pillow and tried to find a comfortable position leaning against the rattling bus window. Mr. Metcalf checked off the names one more time, and the bus roared back onto highway.

Dusk was settling in. Bellamy sat in his seat, listening to conversation, laughter, the crunching of snacks. Chase squirmed against the window, shifting and repositioning the little pillow. Finally, she gave up and sat up straight.

"Mr. Bellamy, do you mind if I lean against you and try to sleep?"

He grinned at her. "If you promise not to drool," he said.

She put her head against his shoulder and leaned into him. He felt her warmth and weight. After a few minutes, her breathing slowed and her mouth dropped open. He wished he could put his arm around her.

Oh, my God. She smells so good, he thought, then stopped himself. Under other circumstances, he could have let himself enjoy the innocent physical contact. But it brought back too many bad, bad memories. *Don't go back there.*

On school bus trips, one chaperone always sat in front and the other all the way in the back, bracketing the students and preventing mischief. These days, Bellamy made a point of being the one up front. This had not always been true.

Chase breathed slower and deeper, and her head snuggled into his shoulder. Despite himself, he thought about that one school trip, a year and a half ago. The UIL speech tournament in El Paso.

It was in the spring. He had sat in the very back, the last seat, with Helen Orlena. There had been only fifteen or sixteen kids on the outing that year, because it happened to conflict with the Duro–San Angelo basketball game. Except for the crosstown rivalry with Pelham High, it was the biggest game of the year.

The road trip to El Paso was a six-hour ordeal. As the bus rolled down the desert highway, and most of the kids had settled down from their initial adrenaline, Bellamy and Helen sat together and talked quietly. There were several rows of empty seats in front of them, so no one overheard.

After the sun set and the desert transitioned from deep blue to dark gray to inky black, Helen sat very close to Bellamy, and he didn't push her away. The only light in the bus came from small safety lights on the floor and the occasional moving glare from passing trucks.

Helen told him of her deep disappointment at not getting the part she wanted in the all-school musical and that she was sorry she had made such a scene. She thanked Bellamy for letting her attend this trip. She talked about how she had spent her life being the weird girl and how few real friends she had. She lamented the growing distance from her mother, who was settling into a divorcée's life of genteel alcoholism, spending most of her days at the country club. She also spoke of conflicted feelings about her boyfriend, Nicky, who not only wanted to spend all his spare time with her but had lately been hinting that he considered her his future bride. The one thing she was sure of, she said, was that she would never marry. But if she ever told Nicky, he would be crushed.

For his part, Bellamy had listened attentively and then told her things he had never dreamed of confiding in a student. There was his bitter disappointment at not making the 1964 Olympic team for long-distance running, despite landing on the alternates list. He lamented a too-early marriage, right out of high school, which had ended when his wife miscarried and then fell into inconsolable clinical depression and moved back in with her parents. He talked of his dream of going back to school for a master's degree and a shot at a dignified teaching position in college.

Much later, as the bus rattled west, he put his arm around her and held her very close. He told her he had feelings for her that he didn't fully understand, that were probably wrong, but at that time, at that moment, he was happy and wanted to kiss her. No one was looking. She did not say yes or no. But when he leaned over and put his lips against her cheek and kissed her softly, she didn't resist.

For the rest of the long bus ride, he just held her. Neither of them spoke. Bellamy imagined how things could be. Yes, he was ten years older than Helen. Okay, twelve years. But what difference did that make, ultimately? His own father had been fourteen years older than his mother (though it was a second marriage for Dad). In the old days, especially in the rural areas, it was understood that men would be significantly older than their brides. Men, after all, were expected to establish themselves, make the farm profitable, or get a stable career, like mechanic, grocer, or high school teacher. Helen would be eighteen in less than two years. He could wait, if he had to.

The speech tournament itself wasn't a major UIL event, but there was a barely tolerated tradition that made it worthwhile for the students. After the tournament ended on Saturday afternoon and awards were presented, the students were allowed to cross the international bridge into Ciudad Juarez, unaccompanied, with a promise that they would stay together in groups and return by 8:00 p.m. and the late-night bus ride back to Duro.

Most kids took advantage of the opportunity, walking in gaggles of three to five, and there had never been any real problems. At least one teacher walked across the bridge, too, to keep a benign eye on things. A few undeclared switchblade knives found their way back through the port of entry, along with sarapes and souvenirs, but within recent memory, no one had ever gotten into serious trouble.

There were usually two or three students who stayed behind, so one teacher would remain with them at the hotel, just a couple of blocks from the bridge. Bellamy volunteered to be the one to stay. There were only two students not going to Juarez. A sophomore boy, who had come down with a wicked case of the trots, just wanted to stay in bed, dreading the long bus ride to come. Then there was Helen, who begged off, saying she was just too tired.

Bellamy hadn't seen much of Helen during the day, but he noticed she had struck up a friendship with a boy from another school. He saw them talking in the hallway between rounds, and they sat together in the auditorium during awards. Helen placed third in poetry reading. The boy was a thin, dark-eyed senior with an aquiline nose and thick brown hair that landed just exactly at the top of his ears and substantial sideburns that ended at the corners of his mouth—exactly compliant with his school's dress code, in other words.

Midafternoon, the hotel lobby was quiet. Bellamy had sat in a vinyl hotel chair, thinking about Helen. He knew her room number. The three girls she'd shared the room with had all walked across the bridge. He needed to speak to her, to see her. Since yesterday evening, they'd had no opportunity to talk, to clarify where things stood. After a few minutes, he thought, *Well, this is probably my only chance to see her alone.*

She was staying on the second floor. He decided to knock quietly but not to press it if she didn't answer. She might be asleep. He reached the door, raised his fist to rap gently, but then noticed something: The door was slightly ajar, just a half inch. These old hotel doors often wouldn't latch if you didn't give them a shove. He gave the door a slight push, and it opened. He listened.

He'd heard muted splashing, soft voices, then a giggle. He pushed the door all the way open and stepped in. The room was unlit, but light came through the bathroom door. He recognized Helen's voice, laughing and happy. He pulled the door shut behind him.

"You'll get soap in your eyes," she was saying. "I don't care if it says *No more tears.*"

There was a boy's laugh. "It says *Lather, rinse, repeat,*" he said. "I think the instructions are pretty clear. I have to repeat. Can't go against the rules."

Helen's giggles came again. "Well, you are on your own, mister," she said. "I'm getting out. I wonder if anybody has a hair dryer."

There was splashing, the unmistakable sound of someone climbing out of a filled bathtub.

"Here, let me help with that," said the boy's voice. "You're so wasted you're gonna keel over." More splashes. "All the towels are wet. You and your friends didn't leave us even one."

"We'll have to run around outside 'til we're dry," said Helen. The she appeared at the bathroom door. She was naked except for one towel around her waist, pale skin flushed and glistening wet. She worked at her hair awkwardly with a hand towel.

She's high on something.

Helen didn't see Bellamy until she was several feet into the room. She saw him and froze. "Oh . . . uh . . ." She crossed her arms in front of her chest.

The boy, towel around his own waist, came out of the bathroom. "Hey, I'm hungry. Do ludes go with Mexican food?" he was saying. "I don't have to leave until—" He saw Bellamy, and his jaw dropped. "Oh, shit. Hi," he said. "Uh . . . We were just—"

"Get dressed, and get out," said Bellamy.

"Okay, but we were—"

"Get out!"

The boy fumbled, pulling on pants, neglecting his underwear, struggling with a T-shirt, putting on shoes, not bothering to tie them. He spotted his underwear by the bathroom door, swooped to pick them up and nearly fell over, then walked quickly past Bellamy and out the door.

He muttered "Sorry" as he exited.

Helen hurried to get dressed but was struggling with the buttons. Bellamy made no attempt to avert his eyes. She didn't look at him.

"What were you doing?" he demanded.

"Taking a bath, *obviously*," she said.

"With a boy from another school."

"Oh, am I supposed to stick with the Duro boys?" she asked. She didn't hide her sarcasm.

"You know what I meant," said Bellamy. "This is not appropriate. Not at all. And I'm in charge on this trip. I'm responsible for you—for your safety. You know, if I report this, I will get as much blame as you."

She glared at him as she sat on the end of the bed fastening her bra. "I have no response to that," she said.

He took a deep breath. "Okay, listen, Helen. I know you're on some kind of drug. I'm not stupid. Please finish getting dressed. The others should be back pretty soon. Get down to the lobby as soon as you can. Pack your suitcase, and bring it down. Can you do that? We'll talk some more."

He left the room and went downstairs. He had waited for fifteen minutes, sitting on a plastic-covered bench in the lobby next to an antique milk pail stuffed with artificial ferns. He had hoped to grab a little dinner in the hotel café, but he waited for Helen. It was after seven o'clock when she finally appeared in the lobby, in no hurry. She walked out of the elevator with her small suitcase, plopped down in a chair twenty feet from him, then sat looking at him, expressionless.

"Please come sit over here," he said.

She hesitated, then stood up and came over to stand in front of him, defiant.

He had been practicing a thoughtful lecture, but he just sat looking at her.

"Don't you want to sit down?"

"No, thank you." She stood there, short, delicate, beautiful, impassive.

"Helen, I'm not angry," he said. "I'm just concerned about your judgement."

"There is nothing to be mad about," said Helen. "Mark is a sweet boy. He's from Midland. We just took a bath. Nothing more."

"I think you need to consider appearances. What would your mother think?"

"I guess we'll never know."

It was odd, Bellamy sitting in a hotel chair, looking up at Helen. He stood up, stepped to a couple of feet from her, not too close. She looked at him with a steady gaze, not smiling, not scared, just waiting for him to make the next move. He waited several long seconds, the reached over and touched her shoulder.

"Helen, I know you're thinking that what we did on the bus last night was strange—."

She pulled back from him. "I don't want to think about it."

"But it's there," said Bellamy. "It will be the elephant in the room until we talk about it. I'm not ashamed of what happened. We did cross a line, but it wasn't awful. I know it was partly my fault. What we did . . ."

"I didn't do anything," said Helen. "I just sat there, and you did it."

"It was *both* of us, but . . . I think you and I fit really well together. We're alike. I'm twelve years older than you, but I feel a real . . . connection between us. Really, I wish we lived in a different universe. If I were your age or a little older—"

At that moment, two boys from the speech team came into the lobby, returning from Mexico, laughing and talking. One of them wore a preposterously wide sombrero. Helen turned away and went back to pick up her suitcase.

"Please, Helen," he said quietly. "I really wish circumstances were different."

She turned back to him. "Mr. Bellamy, if you were not the teacher, even if you were my age, or Nicky's age, I still wouldn't have you as a boyfriend."

"Uh . . . I know you think . . ."

"And we are *not* alike," she said. "Not even a little bit. I am absolutely nothing like you. I plan to *do* something with my life."

"You realize I can report you," said Bellamy. "I'm betting if we searched your luggage, we'd find drugs, isn't that right? I could report you."

Helen had glared at him. "The 'drugs,' as you call them, are prescribed. My mom's psychiatrist gave them to me."

"Your mom gave you Quaalude?"

"It's called methaqualone, and it is for my anxiety attacks. It's from a doctor."

"But you gave some to a boy you just met?"

"Just one."

"Why?"

"Because he asked me *nicely*."

THAT WAS ALMOST THE LAST TIME they spoke, that April, a year and a half ago. The next Monday, he'd reported her for violation of school policy but didn't mention the drugs. There was a teacher–administrator conference in the principal's office. Helen's parents were both called in. They weren't shocked, just annoyed. Helen had made no attempt to defend herself and mentioned nothing about Bellamy. She was suspended from school for three days and banned from school trips for the remainder of the semester.

There were no more out-of-town events scheduled anyway.

CHAPTER 26

The Ley of the Pluton

Nicky didn't like taking days off. When he had nothing to do, he was prone to brooding, not a good place to be. But working twelve-hour shifts six days a week was exhausting, and he needed the rest.

This week, his day off was Wednesday. He made himself stay in bed an extra hour, then he got up and drove to the EAT café for his weekly treat of eggs and patty sausages. It was a sunny day with a clear sky, breezy but not cold. The kind of day where, years ago, he might have called a couple of friends and headed out to Lake Lenorah, where his dad owned a cabin and a small motorboat, to fish, drink beer, and get rowdy. Sometimes, he had taken Helen out there. She had loved the place, though it was hard to coax her into the boat. Mostly, she'd sat on the porch and watched the water. She liked the lake even on overcast winter days, when the water was cold and steel gray.

Nicky couldn't go there anymore. Neither could his dad. Recently, the cabin had been put on the market.

Nicky took his time over breakfast, paid the check, and drove back to his apartment. As he pulled into the lot, it occurred to him that he hadn't checked the mailbox in a couple of days. Not that there was much chance of interesting mail, but he didn't want the box to fill up with advertising and grocery store flyers.

He located the mailbox key on his key ring, turned the stubborn lock, and opened the metal door. To his surprise, there was a package, not very large but bulky enough to fill most of the small mailbox. He quickly checked and discarded the rest of the mail—all junk—and inspected the package. The return label said *A. Dunbar* and listed an address in Lubbock. The name was familiar, and then he remembered that conversation at the lodge, one of the more interesting ones he'd ever had.

When he got the package inside and opened it, there was a book—or something like a book. It looked homemade, Xeroxed and bound with thin metal rings. The text was typewritten, with occasional hand corrections. The sheets weren't just photocopies but copies of copies, with small wrinkles and bits of dust reproduced from earlier copies. The cover was made of cheaply printed cardboard. The title was *Understanding Earth Energy*, and under that was a longer subtitle: *Ley Lines, Monuments, and Spiritual Geology of North America*. The authors were Douglas Pyle and James Holland. Taped to the cover was a handwritten note:

Nick –

Here is the book I was telling you about. Please take care of it so I can get it back one of these days. The manuscript was never published, and there are only a few copies. One of the authors is the son of the original monument designer. I think you will find the whole book interesting. The part about the Pyle Monument starts on page 40. We will discuss next time I'm in Duro.

– Fraternally, Alex Dunbar

Nicky wasn't sure when he'd get around to reading the whole book, but he was flattered that Alex Dunbar had singled him out. Few lodge members had displayed more than polite interest in Dunbar's talk, but to Nicky, it was fascinating. Since he was first introduced to the monument as a child, he had believed it to be magical. Now he knew there was more to it than legend and superstition. It wasn't magic after all. It was science.

After the meeting, Dunbar had spent some time explaining to Nicky his theory that the first Freemason monument, the small one, had been built in the right place, but a subsequent survey decades later erroneously concluded it was off by a significant distance.

Nicky flipped through the yellowed pages. In addition to all the paragraphs in typewriter font, there were many illustrations and maps. These were blurry and hard to make out, with lots of penciled-in notes. Most of the maps were of geological features at various places on the continent, with some highways and towns included for reference. He turned to page 40, which was a full-page map with several hand-drawn arrows and notations. There was another note from Dunbar:

Read what he says about the Wiberg rock and ley lines. The monument is in the wrong location!

The right-hand page was all text, with the heading "The Wiberg Pluton, Ferris County, TX." The author wrote in geologist's jargon, but the message was clear. The monument was near, but not actually on, the intersection of three major energy lines. The writer did not hedge his position.

*Geological studies of the region have shown that the Wiberg Pluton, an extrusion of Precambrian schist, gneiss, and granite, extends from an unknown depth of several miles up through the surrounding Cretaceous and Quaternary formations. The Central Basin Platform subplate is extraordinarily stable and has not moved with respect to the rest of the North American plate in many millions of years. The existence of natural ley lines emanating from the exposed part of the pluton suggests that the focus of Earth energy has stayed with the rock even as the continent has drifted west, which astrocartographers at the turn of the century apparently understood. This fact could explain the discrepancy between the pluton and the 1937 survey. It is possibly the most underappreciated center of Earth energy in the US.**

The asterisk referenced a footnote that took up the bottom quarter of the paper:

**According to historians, local Jumano Indians believed that the rock, which they called "Nuktimi," was the place where their ancestors had emerged from the underworld. The site was often used for shamanic rituals, in which medicine men would ask the spirits to save a severely ill or dying person or, in some cases, to return a deceased member of the tribe from the world of the dead. C. A. Browder, in his book* Grandpa's Lore of the Pecos, *recounts the legend of two early explorers, one of whom was stricken suddenly by a heart attack and died. His distraught partner thought it too late in the day to dig a grave, and so he laid the dead body upon the top of Wiberg rock for the night. The man was astonished the next morning when the partner walked into camp, complaining only that he'd had a bad night's sleep (Browder 1952).*

Nicky studied the map. He did not remember ever seeing a large rock jutting out of the ground, though he had visited the Pyle Monument with his family many times as a child. On Sundays when there was good weather, the family would sometimes pack a picnic lunch and drive out to the Imperial sand dunes, which was in many ways the equal of the Sand Hills State Park, thirty miles to the north. There was no admission charge, since the dunes were on private land, but nobody ever objected. As a young boy, he'd enjoyed climbing on the monument, which was adjacent to a vast stretch of perfectly flat desert. Dad said it had been a lake thousands of years ago. He also said there was a powerful energy force coming from the structure, and Nicky imagined that he felt it, especially if he stood on top of the center obelisk, warm wind rustling his clothes. From there, he could see the salt flats extending for miles to the east.

But had he been in the wrong place all along? He looked hard at the map and tried to determine the rock's location relative to the monument. The scale on the map was one inch to 1,000 feet, which would place the rock a little over a thousand feet to the southeast. The most useful thing was that someone had penciled in a compass direction, 144°, on the ley line that ran near the monument.

Nicky looked up at the clock. If he found a compass somewhere, he could drive out to the monument, get his bearings, and follow the trackway while counting paces. Even if the ley line was not visible, he could stay on course and, hopefully, find the rock.

He wondered where he could buy a compass that had degree marks instead of just the usual N, NW, W, and so on. Did he have time to drive out there? Could he let himself feel hope again?

Days were getting shorter in late October, but there was still a good hour of daylight left when Nicky pulled the Javelin off the highway next to the historical marker. He had skipped lunch, and his stomach grumbled. He should have grabbed a candy bar or a bag of chips before he drove out here, but there was nothing to be done, and time was critical.

He did bring a flashlight, in case he needed to stay past dark, and he'd stopped by the Boy Scout Shop on his way out of town to buy a good compass. The store was still in the same old building on Eighth Street, where it had been since he was a kid. An old man in a faded khaki uniform had given him a quick refresher on using this kind of compass: Don't try to keep a constant direction by walking with your eyes glued to the compass, he said. You'll just trip and fall on your face in a prickly pear. Instead, get your compass pointed right, then use the built-in sights to line up some object in the distance that lies in the path you want to travel. That way, if you have to walk around obstacles, you can stay headed in the right direction. When you get to your target point, do another sighting, and keep going.

He got out of the car and walked out to the monument. It was in a disgraceful condition. There was more trash around it than the last time he was out here, over a year ago. When he was a kid, the lodge had always maintained it, clearing away debris and weeds, even keeping the brass plaque polished. Now, tumbleweeds, shredded plastic bags, and yellowed newsprint were scattered around the base, and sand drifts partially covered one corner. On the lowest level, there were remnants of a campfire that somebody had made months ago.

If he'd had more time, Nicky would have tried to tidy up the monument himself, at least picking up the trash, but he had to keep moving while there was enough light to see. He stepped up onto the lowest tier, then hoisted himself up to the second and third tiers so he could reach the top of the obelisk. He reached up on top and felt around.

The ring was gone. It had been a nagging fear, and now it had happened.

What else had he expected? He had never retrieved the ring after the bad thing happened. Why? He couldn't say, except that at the time the diamond engagement ring was the last thing on his mind.

Nicky climbed down off the monument and pulled the compass out of his pocket. It was a little tricky to work, but he lined up the arrow on magnetic north, then rotated the base so that the sights lined up with the 144° mark. Holding the compass up to his eye, he searched for a landmark.

There was not a lot going on out here, certainly no distinct rock or tree to use as a point of reference. The best he could do was a mesquite bush with a blue plastic bag caught in its thorns near the top. He walked toward it.

The old scouter was right. It was really hard to walk a straight line out here, with thick clumps of prickly pear, thistle, yucca with its deadly-sharp spines, and the ubiquitous mesquite. But he kept the flapping blue plastic bag in sight and kept walking. He wished he'd worn his work boots instead of flimsy tennis shoes.

When he arrived at the target mesquite bush, he didn't have to do another sighting. He saw the pluton, about 400 feet distant, its dome of gray and reddish-brown rock weathered smooth. Funny that he'd never seen it before or even heard of it.

As he walked through the desert landscape, he devised a plan. The closer he got to the rock, the more sense it made. The thought was both thrilling and terrifying.

CHAPTER 27

Sweet Notes from a Makeshift Orchestra

At about eleven o'clock Wednesday morning, Harold began to believe. He should have had faith that everything would come together. It had happened before—a slow train wreck of a project slowly untangling its own wreckage, smoothing out, synching up, finding alignment with the universe just as all hope appeared to be slipping away.

The first clue that it was going to be a good day, a lucky, artistically successful day, was when he arrived at the studio a few minutes past nine to find a college-age woman, Spanish features, faded jeans, and a white cotton cowgirl shirt, sitting on the loading dock at Best Studios, waiting for him.

Harold was by himself. JJ had said he needed a couple more hours at the hotel, alone, to put the polish on the guitar solo that would follow the second verse. Harold said he'd pick JJ up before noon, official start time for the first rehearsal.

Harold parked the car and stepped out. Was this one of the classical musicians, arriving early? The woman hopped off the loading dock and came up to him.

"Good morning," said Harold.

"Hi," the woman said. "I'm Claire Kaine. Are you Allen?"

"No, no. I'm Harold. Harold Prensky."

"Oh . . . good," she said. "You're the one who ran the ad in the *Post*. Are you still looking for classical musicians?"

"Yes, indeed," said Harold. "Would you happen to be one of those?"

"I play cello with the Duro Symphony," she said. "If you still need cellos, I'm definitely interested."

"Yes, oh yes!" said Harold. "I have only one cello signed up. A guy from Lubbock named Garrett Miller. Do you know him?"

"Nope. Don't know many musicians outside of Duro. I went to music school in Boston, but my husband got a job with Mercy Oil, and so here I am. I've been with the Duro Symphony about a year."

"Are you good at learning charts?"

"Yes."

"Okay," said Harold. "Do you have a cello with you?"

"Yes."

"Well, bring it inside. You can look over the music and see if it's something you want to do. Rehearsal doesn't start 'til noon, but you can get a jump on everybody else."

"How many others are there?" Claire asked.

"Umm . . . if you count the drummer, who isn't coming 'til tomorrow, and the bass player, plus the seven classical musicians and JJ Johns, the lead singer, plus you, that's . . . eleven in the studio when we get full strength. Actually, twelve if you count me; I have a piano part. Big crew. But we have a large room to work in."

Harold went up the stairs and unlocked the metal door while Claire retrieved her cello from her car.

Allen Wallace wasn't in yet, which surprised Harold. The owner had been eager to get going on the project and said he'd be in early to help set up. Harold went through the studio, unlocking doors as he went, then opened the double doors to the big studio, flipped on the lights, and stepped inside. Everything was ready as it could be. Folding chairs were set up in a semicircle, with stands ready for freshly copied sheets of music. They would need one more chair. Harold fetched one from the storage closet.

Claire took out her cello, tuned it, and began warming up. The soft, rich sounds of cello scale runs soon filled the warehouse. *She's good*, thought Harold. *Our luck is changing.*

"Hey, you found another cello!" It was Allen Wallace. He stepped into the big room, rubbing his wrist.

"Yep, she just kind of dropped out of the sky," said Harold. "I think she's going to fit right in."

He looked at Wallace. His eyes were puffy, and he was pale. Or maybe it was just the fluorescent lights in the warehouse.

"Are you okay?" Harold asked.

"Oh, yeah," said Wallace. "Just a little under the weather today. I'll be fine." He turned around and headed back into the control room. He seemed a bit feeble to Harold.

Oh man, please don't let him be drinking this early.

Over the next hour, one by one and two by two, classical musicians arrived. A bass guitar player from Tulsa had flown in the day before and showed up in a cab. He held the obvious moniker of Lizard, because his last name was Izzard. Harold had worked with him many times.

In all, there were four violinists, two men and two women; two violists, both men; and, finally, Garrett Miller the other cellist. Miller, who had cast doubts about how many string players would show up, had managed to persuade most of them. He had driven straight from Lubbock that morning.

While the musicians got acquainted and looked over the charts, Harold drove back to the Golden Sunset to retrieve JJ.

He expected his star to be packed up and ready to go, but when he got to JJ's room, he could hear guitar notes coming from inside. Whatever he was playing, it wasn't "Earth Is Crying." Harold banged on the door.

"Hey, pop star! Let's record!"

JJ opened the door. He was a little disheveled, but then JJ was often that way. His acoustic guitar was on the bed, along with sheets of paper.

"I'll be ready in three shakes," he said. "Let me hit the head and pack up the guitars. Is your orchestra ready to go?"

"They seem that way," said Harold. "And you won't believe it. A sweet lady was waiting at the door with a cello. A brave member of the Duro Symphony, risking the wrath of the conductor. We got the whole setup now."

"Great. How about kettle drums?"

"Okay, no kettles," said Harold. "But we have everybody else. I just hope we can get the song in good shape by tomorrow night."

JJ went to the bathroom, washed his hands, gathered his papers and one guitar, and toted everything to the car. Harold carried the Telecaster in its heavy case.

"Did you get some sleep last night?" asked Harold. "I know how you are when you get close to recording day."

JJ stowed the instruments in the back and climbed into the front seat.

"I didn't sleep just a heck of a lot, but I had a good reason. I wrote a new song."

"Really?" laughed Harold. "You couldn't just practice the one we are actually recording?"

"I have 'Earth' nailed tight," said JJ. "Oh, and by the way, if we can find the time, I really would like to lay down a demo of my new song."

"We have to focus on priorities, my friend."

"I promise you'll love it," said JJ. "We need a B side anyway."

"I'll see if we can get to it, but it might not be today. We have to get our A side first."

Three hours into rehearsal, the song was coming along. The string musicians got their parts quickly. Even without a drummer, they were listening to each other and staying together. They followed Harold's directions and didn't second-guess decisions. It really made a difference working with serious professionals. Harold had known some of the other kind in his day.

The master plan was to rehearse the orchestra the first day, then incorporate JJ's part and give them a feel for how the whole song was structured. Thursday would be devoted to bringing in the drums, bass guitar, and Harold's Rhodes piano and tweaking the strings. Maybe, if they got lucky, Harold could even locate a timpani player and some kettle drums.

Friday, the mics would be set up, and if all went well, they could get a good recording of all the basic tracks by the end of the session. Finally, Saturday would be devoted to vocals, with two female singers flying in from Memphis to lay down their voices on top of JJ's. This allowed time, hopefully, for fixing any flaws and punching in small corrections. The orchestra would come in Saturday only if they were needed.

By Saturday night, if the music gods smiled, the sixteen-track master tape of "Earth Is Crying" would be in the can.

Harold rehearsed the band much of the afternoon. Allen Wallace stayed out of the way, contributing a suggestion now and again but letting the producer run his gig. At five o'clock, Harold called a one-hour break so the band could rest and grab something to eat. The musicians left the premises, driving away in multiple cars, searching for something edible in Duro.

Harold and JJ conferred with Wallace in the control room.

"I've been thinking," Harold said. "I don't want to jinx us or anything, but this mess is turning into a real song. I want to start setting up the microphones."

"That's fine by me," said Wallace. "The tune is sweet. We could record it now, if we had everybody here."

"We still can't do anything final until Brendan the drummer gets here in the morning," said JJ.

"Well, let's assume he gets here when he is supposed to," said Harold. "Brendan Bibb is a pro. I'm betting he can fit in without breaking a sweat. Then, just maybe, we can do some real recording tomorrow. We'd be a day ahead of schedule."

With the studio cleared of people, Allen Wallace was in his element. He brought in microphones—delicate, expensive ribbon mics for the subtle sounds of the guitar and strings and rugged cardioid mics for the electric piano, the drums, and JJ's vocals.

Wallace subscribed to a school of sound engineering that was increasingly rare. He believed the room should be considered one of the instruments. In recent years, younger producers had gravitated toward a dry recording style, producing tracks with nothing but the raw sound of the instrument or voice. The theory was that all the atmosphere, the reverb, echo, presence—the room, essentially—could be constructed artificially later, using various filters. Wallace believed in doing most of the work up front, moving microphones, amplifiers, and sound baffles around, listening closely and listening some more until the sound was as near perfect as possible. It took a lot of time and skill, but the results spoke for themselves. With some of the great recordings of the '50s and '60s, an experienced producer could name the studio in which they were created, just by listening.

Wallace ran the cables out into the big room, then started rearranging some of the chairs. In particular, he focused on the corner in which JJ Johns would be singing. After he had set up mics for his voice and guitar, he called JJ into the room.

"I need you to sit and play a couple of verses," said Wallace. "We'll see if we've got too much bleed between the mics."

JJ sat down and strummed the opening chords to "Earth Is Crying," while Wallace went back into the control room to cue up a tape. After a minute, JJ stopped playing.

"Hey," he said. "Do you mind if I play a completely different song?"

"Doesn't matter to me," Wallace called from the other room. "As long as it's guitar and voice."

JJ fetched a few loose sheets of paper from his guitar case, grabbed one of the music stands, and repositioned himself. On Wallace's direction, he sang,

"Toothpaste, la la la, bug spray, la la la" a couple of inches from the vocal mic and strummed chords while Wallace went in and out of the studio, moving the mics by a few inches and changing their angles until he was happy.

"Okay, let's do this," said Wallace.

"Let me know when you're rolling," said JJ.

Wallace put on headphones, ran a couple of minutes' worth of two-inch tape through the sixteen-track, which was standard recording protocol, pointed his finger at the ceiling for a few seconds, started the reels turning again, and pointed at JJ through the glass.

"'Blue-Eyed Becky,' take one," JJ said.

CHAPTER 28

Nicky Wants a Do-Over

Tony Pomeroy was worried about Nicky. His son had sounded odd on the phone, talkative and a little bit out of breath. Tony asked him more than once if he'd had a few beers, which Nicky firmly denied. It wasn't that he sounded upset—the opposite, in some ways. He'd seemed almost giddy, though maybe a little confused. He said he had important news that he needed to discuss in private, and they should meet for dinner somewhere they wouldn't see anybody they knew. It would have to be about eight o'clock, so he'd have time to shower and change after work.

They picked Bobo's Sichuan Palace, out on the Goldwater Highway. It had been there, lurking outside the city limits, for a couple of years now, and everybody wondered how it stayed in business. There were a dozen tables inside, though no more than two or three were ever occupied. Their take-out business was acceptable, however, and slowly growing. It didn't hurt that they were the only Chinese place in the county.

It was a little past eight when Tony arrived. Nicky's Javelin was in the parking lot.

When he got inside the restaurant, Tony found that the only dine-in customer was his son, sitting at a table by the window, chatting with the waitress. A couple of people waited for takeout.

Nicky looked up at Tony and grinned. "I haven't ordered yet," he said. "I could have gotten you something to drink, but I didn't know what you wanted."

Tony sat down at the table. "Well, since I'm here, I should get the house specialty, right? That green drink I had last time. What was it—dragon something?" He looked up at the waitress.

"You mean celestial dragon?" she asked.

"That's it," said Tony. "Please provide a celestial dragon."

Nicky ordered a beer. The waitress handed Tony a menu and departed to fetch the drinks.

Tony leaned over. "It's really just a mai tai with something green in it," he said. "Probably food coloring. I just like it."

Nicky studied his menu, so Tony picked up his own. Tonight, he'd go with the moo goo gai pan. *I wish Chinese food had bigger chunks of meat in it,* he thought. But the dish was salty and tasty and would hit the spot, especially with a cool beverage.

Nicky closed the menu. "Chow mein," he said. "Don't know why I even bother to look. I always get the chow mein."

"We are creatures of habit," said Tony.

The beer and the sweet green drink arrived, and they ordered the dinner. When the waitress walked away, Nicky reached under the table and pulled out a flat cardboard packing box from which he removed the old battered copy of *Understanding Earth Energy.*

"I want to show you this before the food gets here," he said. "Mr. Dunbar would be pretty upset with me if I got soy sauce on his book. I know it looks like it's in pretty bad shape, but this book is very old and rare. There are only a few copies in the world."

Tony tilted his head and eyed the volume curiously. "What is it?"

"They keep this book in the library at the lodge in Lubbock," said Nicky. "It's about energy lines and ley lines. You know how Mr. Dunbar was saying the monument should be moved, that it's in the wrong spot? This book explains why."

"I hope he doesn't think we're going to actually move that giant thing," said Tony. "Besides, the surveyors back in the '30s worked really hard to get the location exactly right."

"I know they *thought* they got it right," said Nicky. "But those guys seventy years ago knew things that modern scientists don't."

"Like what?"

Nicky opened the book to the blurry map on page 40. "See this? They put the Pyle Monument where they did because the numbers sounded . . . I don't know . . . *magical.* Look at this inscription: *Latitude 31°31'31" and longitude 103°10'3".* But the author claims that's not right, because energy lines don't follow strict positions on any map. They are like magnetic fields. They are mostly straight, but there are also little curves and twists in the lines. They align with important features on the

Earth, not just some made-up numbers. I mean, the north pole and the magnetic north pole are hundreds of miles apart."

"Well, I guess that makes sense," said Tony. "Latitude and longitude come from dividing the world by 360 and then drawing lines on a globe. Still, somebody thought the location with all the ones and threes was important."

Nicky turned a page in the old book. "Right here, he says that the point where the major energy lines cross would be pretty close to where the monument is now, except for that giant rock. He calls it the Wiberg Pluton. The rock draws the energy to itself."

"I guess that's interesting," said Tony. "But nobody wants to spend the money it would take to move the Pyle Monument. It's just not going to happen."

"The monument doesn't matter!" said Nicky. "Nobody has to move it. The important thing is the place and the rock. When I was a little kid, you used to tell me that the monument had special energy."

"Mostly, that was just me telling a fun story," said Tony. "But I always believed it was possible. I remember how I'd put you on top of the center stone, and you'd raise your arms in the air and shout that you were feeling the energy. It was pretty hilarious."

"Until mom yelled at me to get down," laughed Nicky.

"Yeah, she hated when I put you up there," said Tony. "She was always so damn protective."

Their food arrived. Tony slathered soy sauce over the plate of sweet chicken strips, mushrooms, and bamboo shoots. It was good, and he was hungry. He made a game attempt to use the provided chopsticks but quickly gave up and dug in with a fork.

Nicky took a couple of bites but seemed distracted. He set down his own fork.

"Dad, the book says the place where the ley lines cross . . . He calls it the vortex. Let's see . . ." Nicky carefully flipped back a couple of pages in the old book. "Here it is. He says, *Considering that the Wiberg rock marks the most important and powerful focus of Earth energy in the contiguous US, its significance has been all but forgotten, even among antiquities scholars and astrocartographers.*"

"I was always told it was important," said Tony. "But, frankly, I don't know what that really means. Important for what, exactly? Historically important, sure. I'll buy that. We have to remember our traditions. But these days, who even thinks about these 'Earth energy' places?"

"Dad, I found it," said Nicky.

"Found what?"

"The rock. The pluton. I drove out there. I started at the monument and just walked the direction the map said, and I found it, yesterday. It's about a quarter of a mile away."

"Really?" said Tony. "How do you know that was really it and not just some big rock?"

Nicky sat up straight in his chair. "I have zero doubt that was really the place. And not just because it's the only big, smooth rock out there. I *stood* on it. I *felt* it. It is *real!"* Nicky was unconsciously raising his voice. The waitress came over to them.

"Are you gentlemen doing all right?" she asked. "Can I get you refills?"

"I'm doing good," said Nicky.

"I could use another dragon," said Tony. The waitress went away.

Nicky spoke quieter. "I'm serious, Dad. It's all true. I stood up on that rock, and I felt it. Like all the energy in the world was pouring up from my feet and out the top of my head. My scalp was all . . . tingly."

"Like . . . static electricity?"

"More than electricity. It's exactly like the book says. It has life energy. In two minutes, I felt like I was ready to run ten miles. If you went out there, you'd believe it, too."

"Okay," said Tony. "I'll take your word for it, though I'd like to see that for myself. My question is, what are you going to do about it? Get enough energy to move the monument yourself?"

Nicky didn't even crack a smile. He stared straight at his father. "I don't *care* about the monument. Leave it where it is. What matters is the . . . vortex. I want to take Helen out there."

Tony's second celestial dragon arrived. He took a slow sip to collect himself.

"Nick, listen. What you're suggesting is not possible. Helen is gone. Nothing is going to bring her back. Not all the energy in the Earth."

"I used to think that, too," said Nicky. "But I have to try. It's the only way all this can be over."

A young man in oilfield coveralls came into the restaurant to pick up a call-in order. Nicky resumed eating his dinner thoughtfully. Tony took a couple of big gulps of celestial dragon. When the new customer got his takeout and left the restaurant, Tony spoke again, quietly.

"I want you to remember," he said. "You and I made a deal with each other two years ago. We were never even going to talk about it ever again, for any reason. Not with other people and not with each other. It wasn't your fault."

"It was my fault. And I need to make it right. I want Helen to go out to the pluton with me," said Nicky.

"That's crazy, and you know it," said Tony. "It's over. Nobody knows where she is."

"But we do," said Nicky.

Tony closed his eyes, biting his lower lip. When he spoke, it was just above a whisper.

"We can't talk about this, son," he said. "I don't understand why you want to bring it all up again. It was a terrible time, but you've moved on."

"No," said Nicky. "I haven't. Turns out I couldn't."

CHAPTER 29

JJ in the Crosshairs

They had the studio booked until midnight, but there was no point in continuing the Thursday session. The string musicians knew their parts well, as did the bass guitar. The mix sounded good, the guitar was blending in where it should, and the electric piano fit within the sonic range of the song. The song was ready to record, except for a little wrinkle: no damn drummer.

Brendan Bibb, the drummer from Nashville, was still in Nashville. After a long session the night before, Brendan overslept Thursday morning and missed his flight. The only other flight that day didn't arrive at the Midland airport until 11:30 p.m., with a long stopover in Dallas. Bibb figured he might as well catch the early-morning flight Friday, which landed at nine-thirty in the morning. He did not bother to call Best Studios with this news until mid-morning Thursday, well after Harold was on his way to pick him up at the airport, where the drummer wasn't waiting, almost thirty miles away.

This delayed the second rehearsal over two hours. The upside to the setback was that documentarists Dan and Becky were able to get all their camera and field-recording equipment set up and had time to engage in a long, rambling interview with Allen Wallace, wherein the old recording engineer regaled them with stories from the Golden Age of the American music industry. Some of these tales were mostly true, some highly exaggerated, and others were complete whoppers, but they would all make good cinema. Dan used up four of his precious eleven-minute reels on just Allen. It dawned on him just how badly he was blowing through his stock of Kodak panchromatic film, and he determined from then on to limit individual interviews to one reel maximum.

As promised, Dan and Becky stayed out of everybody's way. Claire, the Duro Symphony cellist, was afraid to have her face appear on camera, but nobody else minded. They got some shots of the orchestra warming up and some of JJ strumming his guitar while Wallace fine-tuned the room.

Eventually, Harold called from the airport, saying Bibb was a no-show, and Wallace broke it to him: They were drummerless until tomorrow. The drum kit Harold had rented from K&R Music sat useless in the corner.

JJ was upbeat, however, and used the occasion to explain his vision of "Earth Is Crying" to the skeptical string players. Though he was a notorious mumbler, JJ found his voice when explaining his art. Spotting an opportunity for an opening scene, Dan set up the camera and microphone, and they filmed the singer doing an abridged version of his speech, followed by shots of some of the orchestra looking thoughtful and nodding. They then did short interviews with one of the more articulate violists and with Lizard the bass player, who spoke little and made no sense when he did.

When Harold returned from his futile mission, he put the band through four solid hours of rehearsal, tweaking and adjusting the parts between run-throughs until he was sure they could play the parts in their sleep. He even conducted while playing his Rhodes piano, a neat trick, but Harold knew how to lead a band with just the sway of his head. For a rhythm section, Wallace thumped the piano case. On the very last run-through, Harold allowed Dan to film around and among them with his Bolex. Even with the distraction, they still played the song perfectly.

Harold cut them loose at six o'clock. "Recording session is tomorrow at noon. Get lots of rest. Tomorrow, there will be a drummer."

DAN PARK loaded the exposed reels of film into a plastic bag, sealed it with tape, and placed it inside a rugged canvas bag originally designed for .50-caliber machine gun ammunition. The Bolex was placed carefully in its case, a hard-sided suitcase with the scars of untold adventures etched into its sides.

"Becky, we need to get going," he called. "I'm supposed to be forty miles from here thirty minutes from now." He headed out the back door lugging the two bags.

"I'll hurry," said Becky, rolling the cord for the field microphone.

Now or never, thought JJ.

"Hey, I . . . We can give you a ride home," he said.

"Okay . . . Yeah, if it's no trouble," said Becky.

"None whatsoever," said JJ.

Dan came back into the studio for the heavy tripod.

"Danfour, you are released," Becky said. "These gentlemen will take me home."

"Okay, great," he said. "That will help a lot. See you tomorrow. I'll pick you up by nine o'clock, or earlier if I can manage it." He hurried out the door.

Becky stepped into the office to speak to Allen Wallace. JJ went back into the big studio, where Harold was carefully winding microphone cables.

"Hey, my buddy, my pal," said JJ, "Best friend a guy could ever have—"

"What do you want, JJ?" asked Harold. He had a feeling where this was going.

"My bestest, goodest, most true of friends," said JJ.

"What?"

"You think I could . . . uh . . . use the car tonight?"

Harold chuckled. "I think what you meant to say is 'Daddy, can I borrow the car tonight?'"

"You'd have a friend for life."

Harold looked around. "You want to take the sound girl out, don't you? Have you even asked her?"

"I couldn't exactly ask if I didn't have a car," said JJ.

"Well, as long as you get me back to the hotel. I can go downstairs for dinner. You'll owe me one."

"I'll owe you two!" said JJ.

"Well, be careful," said Harold. "She's super Christian. She'll have you going to a Baptist church before long."

"Worth the risk," said JJ.

Allen Wallace would stay late and lock up after, as always. JJ, Harold, and Becky climbed into the front seat of the station wagon. This time, JJ drove, and Becky sat in the middle.

"What shall we do for dinner?" asked JJ. That was Harold's cue.

"Hey, if it's all the same to you, I'll pass. I have some phone calls I need to make, and I'm not really hungry. Just drop me at the hotel. You guys can go grab dinner."

JJ flashed an innocent grin at Becky. "Would that be okay? Just you and me?"

"Sure," said Becky. "If your intentions are pure."

"As Ivory soap," said JJ and started the car.

ONE BLOCK AWAY, Grover Paulson had watched with alarm as Dan Park left the studio and drove away without Becky.

That's enough, he thought. The last straw. *I'm going in. She's coming with me.*

He would have to go inside the metal building, locate Rebekah, and force her to come with him. Okay, he couldn't use force, but he would do everything in his power to get her to see reason. Put a stop to this ungodly nonsense. He was still her father and master of the house.

Grover had been watching Best Studios for some time. Several cars were in the parking lot when he arrived. As dusk approached, he was surprised at the number of people who came out of the building one by one and two by two. They were normal-looking people, some young and some middle-aged, many carrying musical instruments. The studio must be wrapping it up for the day. But where was Rebekah? He sat in the car for several minutes, watching and debating whether he should just go in and grab her. *Young lady, you're coming with me, now!*

When her friend Dan—whom Grover had charged with watching out for her—suddenly departed on his own, that made up his mind.

He reached for the ignition key to start his car but hesitated. He pictured himself standing on the loading dock, banging on that heavy security door like a fool. He made himself wait, but no one else came out.

"Ah, to heck with it!" said Grover. He was going in. He started the car, but then the back door of the studio opened, and Rebekah came out. With the hippie. And that other creep.

Grover raised the scope to his eyes and put the hippie in the crosshairs. There was no way in this world he would allow his eldest daughter to consort with *that*. For a fleeting moment, he wished the scope was attached to its rifle.

The three of them got into the station wagon, and Grover noted that she was now sitting *between* the two lowlifes. He put the car in gear but waited. He would hang back at least a block, follow the Oklahoma station wagon, and see where it went. If it was anywhere except his own house, he would barge in and break up the situation, whatever that might be. It would embarrass Becky, make her angry. She might not speak to him for a while, but it had to be done. His mission on this Earth was to guard his family from the world, and this was the world at its very worst.

The station wagon left the studio parking lot and headed north toward Duro. Grover followed, staying about a block away. As they approached the railroad crossing just before the freeway underpass, the crossing signals began flashing red, and the gate arms started down.

Grover slowed. With the station wagon waiting at the crossing, he couldn't pull up right behind them. He'd have to stop a good distance back to avoid being spotted.

But the station wagon didn't stop. To Grover's horror, the driver sped up and bounced over the tracks just ahead of the descending gate arms. Grover dropped the gearshift into first and floored the accelerator. Of course, he didn't make it. He had to slam on the brakes just as the train reached the railroad crossing at full speed, four enormous diesel-electric engines pulling a string of box cars and tanker cars that appeared to stretch off to the horizon. He was stuck.

"Damn it!" Grover cursed, something he did not do often.

CHAPTER 30

No Out-of-Body Experience Necessary

Allen Wallace had dinner at Ben's Guadalajara, his favorite Mexican place. It was busy for a Thursday night. The owner, Ben Aragon, spotted Allen sitting by himself and came over to chat. The eating establishments that recognized Allen Wallace were fewer every year, but he could count on Ben.

The owner greeted him warmly. "Hola! Cómo estás, Señor Wallace?"

"Me siento muy bien. Gracias, mi amigo." Allen's accent was terrible, but Ben never teased him.

Allen ordered pork enchiladas with a fishbowl, a glass of beer with a fishbowl shape that held about twenty ounces. It quenched and complemented the heat of Ben's secret red sauce.

When he had finished eating, the waitress cleared the table, but Allen lingered. He turned down the offer of a second fishbowl and sat in his corner sipping water, listening to the Spanish music. As a sound engineer for thirty years, he was attracted to less-familiar forms and found their style and structure interesting. Tonight, the stereo played a lot of *norteña*, a Mexican variant of the South American *cumbia* style, itself a descendent of African dance music. Allen loved the interplay between bass guitar and snare drum and the tight vocal harmonies.

It might be fun to record some songs in Spanish. Maybe expand the client base.

The fishbowl was a lot of beer, but it made him feel good. He'd only resumed drinking beer a few months ago. Allen had denied himself the pleasure of beer with his enchiladas for too long. Five years stone-cold sober, and what had it gotten him? Just a lot of late-night TV and long walks around the neighborhood. Thinking too much, sleeping poorly.

Allen realized he'd forgotten his second pill. He was supposed to take it on an empty stomach, but it was too late now. He washed down the Equanil with a swallow of water, popped his hat on his head, walked to the counter, and paid the check. He picked up a few coffee beans from a bowl by the register and popped them into his mouth. It was a Mexican folk remedy for chili mouth. He didn't know why it worked. Allen walked out to his car sucking on the coffee beans and picking around his front teeth with a cinnamon-flavored toothpick. He was tired, in the did-a-good-day's-work sense.

He sat in his car with the engine running for a couple of minutes, searching for something interesting on the radio. *Good luck these days. Nothing but chewy candy for the tasteless.* Then he found a Roberta Flack song and let the station play as he pulled out the parking lot. So what if the song was from a hit movie? It was still good, and Roberta had more ability than ninety percent of the no-talents out there. Allen drove west on Twenty-Second Street, listening.

Then that god-awful, insipid "Candy Man" song started, and he switched the radio off.

Should he go home? Tomorrow he was going for something that had eluded him for years—a hit song. The sensible thing to do was get a full night's sleep. But it was still early. He could go home and search for something good on one of Duro's two TV stations. Or he could play some of his old records, stroll down memory lane until he was ready for bed. Neither sounded appealing.

Allen passed the J&H Package store and thought how nice a small glass of bourbon and rocks sounded. He had finally finished the gift bottle of scotch he kept in his desk. He never cared for scotch, but he still held a fondness for bourbon. It had been several years.

Ah, hell. Why not? He stopped and bought a fifth of Evan Williams Kentucky Straight Bourbon.

As he came out of the store with the paper bag under his arm, he had a fleeting thought: *What are you doing? Are you starting again? Don't be a fool.*

He paused a moment and listened to the night sounds of Duro: the traffic, a car door slamming, far-off country music from a radio. He hadn't bought whiskey for himself in a long time, but . . . he deserved this. Just a drink or two. Hell, that bottle of scotch had lasted six months. He wouldn't repeat that foolishness of a few nights ago. Tomorrow was his most important recording date in years. He would take it easy with the liquor, his oldest friend and sneakiest enemy.

At this moment, what he wanted more than anything else was to hear Mabel sing, and there was only one place he could do that. He headed back to the studio.

"Let's find a truck stop," said JJ. He and Becky had been driving around for a while. They were both hungry.

"There are a lot of places to eat around here," said Becky. "What's special about a truck stop?"

"Hey, I've been on the road since I was sixteen," said JJ. "One thing you learn is where to find the best food. Truck stop cafes have to be good and cheap, or the truckers won't show. I'm the voice of experience. Trust my judgment on this."

Becky snorted. "I'm more likely to trust the judgment of somebody who doesn't *try and beat the trains*."

"I said I was *sorry*! I just couldn't stand the thought of sitting there watching five thousand rail cars go by. I just get too . . . I don't know . . ."

"Impatient," said Becky. "Yep, let's die in a pile of twisted metal, but at least we won't be bored. Makes sense." She tapped him on the shoulder. "But, I forgive you. Just . . . *never again*."

"Never again," said JJ, raising his right hand. Despite their little spat about his driving, JJ was having a good night. Instead of moping in a small hotel room, smothered in doubts about tomorrow's gig, he was out with a beautiful bundle of energy, a cute girl who talked about everything in the world *except* music. It was rejuvenating.

Truck stops are always on main highways, where anybody can find them, even a stranger to the city. JJ drove to Highway 80 and turned east.

They landed at a place called The City Limit Cafe, in a building that hadn't been updated since Eisenhower. Seven big rigs and a dozen cars were parked outside. The room was busy and loud. JJ was delighted to find that it had a working jukebox, and every booth had one of those tabletop sub-controllers—the Wall-o-Matic. A quarter bought three songs. JJ flipped through the selections and chose three country swing tunes, fed in a quarter, and punched in the numbers.

"This is great," he said. "I missed a normal childhood. My family never went to diners. I started touring with my brother's band in 1959."

"Didn't you go to high school?" asked Becky.

"Only a couple of years. I dropped out. It's not something I'm proud of. I still try to learn interesting stuff when I have time. I love to read, especially about science. Also, technology."

The waitress brought them menus. The choices were mostly burger variations and club sandwiches. Becky read the lunch/dinner side of the laminated menu, then turned it over.

"Breakfast is on the back," she said. "It says they serve it twenty-four hours. I may go for that. It's usually good and cheaper."

"Why do you care?" asked JJ. "I'm paying. Get anything you want. Go crazy."

"Oh, are we on a date?" Becky giggled.

"I certainly thought so," said JJ. "It sounds like a date to me. I'm having dinner with a beautiful girl."

"Oh, stop it."

"Hell—I mean, heck—I could even throw in a movie, if you like."

"I'd rather just talk," said Becky and returned to her menu. Even though JJ said there were no limits, she ordered an omelet. "Oh, by the way," she said. "You can say 'hell' if you want."

JJ got the cheeseburger, which the City Limit rendered marvelously well, and onion rings, which were just okay. Becky ate her omelet with refined manners, holding her fork just right, one hand in her lap. This made JJ a bit self-conscious. He knew he was a slob and could still hear his mom's voice telling him not to lean over his food. He sat up straight, spread out a napkin, and tried to keep bits of onion and lettuce from landing in his lap.

Oh, my lord, I like this girl. JJ Johns was smitten, he had to admit it. He loved her voice and her face, loved the way she looked up at him radiantly. She maintained steady eye contact except when she was thinking how to reply to a question. At those moments, she would look off to the right.

They talked long after they had both finished eating. JJ thought it might be nice to go to a bar or lounge but doubted Becky would be up for that. Anyway, it was satisfying to just talk to her. Her earnestness made him want to be honest.

He told her about the loneliness he had felt much of his life, hoping he didn't sound pathetic. He described his life on the road and how he never felt at home anywhere, even at his house in Tulsa, where he stayed only a few months out of the year.

One of JJ's song selections came up on the jukebox, "Please Don't Talk about Me When I'm Gone" by the immortal Bob Wills.

"If I was born twenty years earlier, that's the kind of music I'd play," said JJ. "Notice how many of these old western swing tunes are about broken hearts and faded love. Probably because the songwriters were all on the road, like me."

"Didn't you ever have a girlfriend?" asked Becky.

"Yeah, sure, I suppose," said JJ. "There was never anyone I felt like I would want to settle down with. I think my relationship record is six months. I'm traveling eight months out of the year. I haven't even dated in a long time. There are always girls, of course. Everywhere I go."

"Groupies. That's what you call them, right?"

"When I was touring with the Zephyrs, we called them 'road ladies.' They're pretty much all over the place. Some of the guys would take them along on the bus, which was annoying. Even on a really big bus, it's close quarters, and nerves get . . . frayed. It's hard enough with six guys. Personally, I hated when girls went on tour with us. I brought a girl along with me a couple of times, and it always ended as badly as possible. One girl a few years ago nearly landed me in jail. Turned out she had a quarter ounce of cocaine in her purse, and nobody knew about it 'til the Alabama troopers were turning the bus inside out. It almost killed the tour."

"Were there a lot of drugs?" asked Becky. "That's what the pastors were always telling us when I was a kid—rock and roll equals drugs and Satan."

"Drugs were all over the place. There was a strict no-hard-drugs policy at my record label, but, still, they found their way into the band. I was never a druggie, personally. I smoked grass sometimes, but it fucked up . . . messed up my singing voice. I drank a lot of beer. It made the time pass." JJ looked around the room. "Hey, Becky, should we go somewhere else?"

"I'm fine, but we can leave if you want."

A group of three truckers was sitting behind them, drinking coffee and smoking. One of them got up and came over to JJ and Becky's table. The trucker plopped a dollar bill down on the table right in front of JJ.

"Haircut," he said. "It's on me." He returned to his table as the other truckers chuckled.

"Wow. That was rude," said Becky, quietly.

"I'm used to it," said JJ. "It was worse in the old days. I remember in '66, we were working in Nashville for the first time. I went out looking for a convenience store, and three guys jumped me, chased me all the way back to the hotel. In *Nashville*."

"I don't understand people," said Becky. "I'm afraid my father is like that. Long hair on guys makes him insane. He'll be rude to a total stranger in public. He also hates the hippie look on girls, like floppy hats and beads. He thinks God is going to bring the Apocalypse down on America because guys have long hair."

"Hah!" said JJ. "What does he think about Jesus? Long-haired dude if there ever was one."

"But don't say that to my father," said Becky. "Really. He has a personal friend in Jesus. He'd go off like a bomb."

"I guess we aren't going to have a meet-the-dad moment, are we?"

"Well . . . not soon. Maybe some time."

"Let's *do* go somewhere else," said JJ. They stood up. JJ was going to leave the trucker's dollar on the table but changed his mind and pulled out a five-dollar bill of his own for a tip. He put the dollar in his shirt pocket, walked over to the register, and paid. On their way out, they passed the table with the three truckers. JJ plopped the dollar on the table in front of the haircut fan.

"Mouthwash," he said.

As they walked to the car, JJ glanced back to make sure they weren't being followed.

"You're a hoot," said Becky. "But you shouldn't provoke people. Could mess up our date if you get chased all over again."

"Yeah, I know," said JJ. "Couldn't resist." They reached the station wagon, and JJ opened the passenger door for her. "So . . . it's officially a date, then."

"I suppose it is," said Becky, settling into the bench seat and scooting over to the middle. "Technically, it's my first. I never went on dates as a teenager. My parents wouldn't even consider it. I did have a boyfriend for a while, from church. His name was Rich Bailey. But what we usually did was a lot cruder than a date. He'd buy me a coke sometimes. That's about it."

JJ started the car. "What did you do that was so crude?"

"Well, to be honest, we would usually just sneak into the back of his dad's car and have sex." She looked over at JJ. "You can close your mouth now. Are you shocked?"

"Uh . . . no.... But, wow . . . just, wow." JJ grinned at her. "But you're all . . . religious. I mean, wow."

"I was raised in church, but I wasn't a nun. We were Pentecostals. We sang and shouted and spoke in tongues. It's a very emotional religion. Sex just seemed to fit right in. I know I wasn't the only teenager doing it. One day, when I was thirteen, I had a . . . I don't know . . . spiritual experience, and decided that what they were teaching us about sex was just stupid. Sex is part of life and love. I know it's not all that simple. I was lucky, because a lady at Sunday school took several of us young girls aside one day and told us straight up about birth control and rubbers and everything. She didn't even mention it to our parents. I wouldn't have gotten that in a public school."

"You're not worried that God will get mad at you?"

"I think God is another word for life and love. It's not some angry old man looking down from the sky, telling you how to behave. It's about people caring for each other."

"Wow. Sweetest Becky, I think you could start your own religion. And I'd join."

They drove around Thursday-night Duro for a while. JJ knew he should get some sleep, but he was happier than he'd been in a very long time. He could spend all night with Becky Paulson, if she'd let him. Sleep be damned, he'd still make the best recording of his life tomorrow. But it was Becky who suggested they should rest up for the big day.

"I do need to get home," she said. "I didn't tell my parents what time I was coming in, but they'll worry. It's almost eleven. Danfour is picking me up at nine in the morning."

"Could we go one more place?" asked JJ. "I have an idea. Just for half an hour, tops. I want to show you something."

"Okay," said Becky. "Let's not be crazy late, though. I've been worried about my mom lately. I don't want to make things worse for her."

"Your mom? Has she been sick?

"No, not exactly. She's just been . . . I don't know the word . . . removed lately. Like she's somewhere else. And she talks to herself a lot. I mean, she's always talked to herself, but now it's more often. She says nothing's wrong, but something is bothering her."

"I won't keep you too long," said JJ.

He drove to the Golden Sunset Hotel and took her inside the lobby. He smiled at the woman behind the desk. She regarded them suspiciously, as always, but didn't say anything.

"This is where Harold and I have been staying, and most of our orchestra, too," said JJ. "I discovered something cool. You can go up on the roof. There's a pool and a deck, with chairs."

"What? You don't want to swim, do you? It's about fifty degrees tonight."

"It's a heated pool, but I don't want to go swimming. I just want to show you something beautiful."

They took the elevator to the roof. They had it to themselves, a pleasant discovery. The pool was lit by underwater lights, which cast green shimmers against the tile and concrete.

"Look at this," he said. He took her to the four-foot-high brick wall that lined the roof's edge. Down below, in all directions, the lights of Duro twinkled. Far off to the west, there was the red glow of oilfield flares, and to the east, a group of large buildings completely covered in lights. It made JJ think of the Emerald City. Someone had explained it was actually a cement plant. "Isn't that great?"

"That *is* beautiful," said Becky. "Really. I've never seen Duro from this high up." She shivered and hugged herself. "It's cold up here, though."

JJ wrapped her in bear hug, and they stood for several minutes, saying nothing, listening to each other breathe. Then JJ surprised both of them by kissing her deeply on the mouth.

"Thank you," Becky said. "That was a first for me. Not even Rich Bailey kissed like that."

After a while, they put two pool chairs side by side and sat together. JJ found a large towel that had dried on a chaise lounge and draped it around them. They kissed some more. Despite the city lights, stars were thick.

JJ wanted it to last. "Tell me about that thing that happened to you," he said. "Your spiritual experience."

"It happened in church when I was a teenager," said Becky. "It was like speaking in tongues, I guess, except I didn't babble. There was the usual music blasting away, with everybody rocking and clapping and singing. I was not even paying much attention, and then something really strange happened. It's hard to describe. I . . . went outside myself."

"Outside yourself?" said JJ. "Like an out-of-body experience?"

"Sort of. I suddenly wasn't me anymore but a thing outside of me, seeing me as a separate person. Time slowed way down. It almost stopped. And while I was outside of myself, I could see how everything—I mean *everything*—was just part of this huge electric cloud of . . . of life, I suppose. It wasn't like I started thinking my religion was wrong, just that it was tiny . . . a miniscule part of a thing that goes on and on forever."

"Were you scared?"

"Scared to death at first," said Becky. "But when I didn't go back inside myself, I just let go and let it happen. I thought I was dead, but I wasn't scared anymore."

"You were how old? Thirteen?"

"Yeah," said Becky. "After some time, it stopped, and I was back inside my body. That was the only time, but I never forgot it. It changed everything about how I see the world. I decided right then I wasn't going to stay in Duro and get married, have kids, go to church, and be a good Christian. I knew the answer wasn't here. I had to get out."

"It's good that you did," said JJ. "You're not like me. You got your education and went away to college. I bet you're the first woman in your family to do that."

"Well, you'd lose that bet," said Becky. "My mother went to college. She is brilliant, in her own way. She studied science, astrophysics."

"That's great. I'm sorry. I assumed she was an unschooled country girl. Did she get a degree?"

"No, unfortunately," said Becky. "I wish she had. There was a tragedy in the family, so she had to quit school and go help my grandmother, who was living alone."

"Did something happen to her dad?"

"No.... Well, yes, but that was years earlier," said Becky. "My grandfather ran off when she was a kid. Apparently, he was a bum and drank a lot. Somebody said he died in Alaska, but I don't really know."

"It's tough growing up without a dad," said JJ. "My dad and me were like matches and gasoline, but at least he was around."

"It wasn't as bad as it sounds, at least not when my mother was a kid. Grandmother's brother moved in with them—my great-uncle Jim. He never married, so it wasn't weird. So she had a father figure growing up. He died before I was born, but she says he was a genius. He was an astronomer and worked part of the year at that big telescope in Alpine."

"So that was why she studied . . . What was it? Astrophysics?"

"I'm sure that was why she got interested in it. Unfortunately, Uncle Jim died in an accident. My grandmother was so broken up that my mom dropped out of college to be with her."

"That's awful," said JJ. "And she never went back?"

"She met my dad, and that was that. I sometimes think she regrets it. I've seen her go out in the middle of the night and just look up at the stars. She's probably thinking about what could have been."

"I'm sorry I brought up a painful subject."

"It isn't painful to me," said Becky. "I used to think about it a lot, though. After my spiritual experience, I could put it all into perspective."

They sat in silence. Most sounds from the street didn't reach this high. Becky nested her head against JJ's collar bone.

"That's a pretty incredible story," said JJ. "I think I know what you're talking about. It sounds like something that I did a few years ago. It was a drug thing, but it changed me forever."

"What happened?"

"It's embarrassing, but I did something very dumb. A guy I knew, a guy who sold T-shirts for the band, came up with this stuff called Electric Blue—just a tiny little pill with crossed lines on it—and asked if I wanted to try it with him. Of course, I said 'sure,' because I'm an idiot."

"Was it a bad drug?" asked Becky.

"It was exactly as advertised, but we both assumed it was a two-way hit, and it was actually a four-way. Four full doses in a pill the size of an aspirin. Who knew? I took half a pill."

"So you . . . overdosed?"

"Double-dosed, full-bore, launched into orbit, everything out of control," said JJ. "It was just like you were saying: I wasn't part of myself anymore. I lost the sense of being *me*. I was something else, seeing myself from the outside. It was really terrifying. Not a good experience at all."

"But it didn't hurt you in the long run, right? You seem okay now."

"The whole episode just made me think my life was small and stupid, and I wasn't going anywhere. Really shoved it in my face. I was just a blubbering idiot who'd sing the same pointless songs until I died."

"I'm really sorry that happened to you," said Becky.

"It was alright after a while, but I was never the same. A week later, I told the band I was quitting. That was crazy, because we were doing great, playing shows in large venues. But I just couldn't do it anymore, and I left after that tour."

They sat quietly a few more minutes. Becky pulled the towel off her shoulders and stood up.

"I really need to go home now," she said. "I loved tonight. I loved being with you. But there's this film I have to shoot tomorrow, about some washed-up rock star trying to make a comeback."

"Wouldn't want to keep you from that," said JJ.

They drove back across Duro. The traffic lights had gone into after-midnight mode, blinking yellow. JJ drove with one arm around Becky, the other on the wheel, leaning back.

This is it, man. She's the one. I hope she thinks so, too. Please, please.

When they arrived at the Paulson house, Becky intended to give JJ a little peck on the lips and get out, because it was very, very late. But they ended up in a lingering wet kiss. Finally, she broke away and hopped out of the car.

"See you in the morning," she said.

"Bye."

What a night, thought JJ. *I did not expect that! And what a girl!*

He turned the car around in the Paulson driveway. He didn't notice Grover, seething in the shadows between the mailbox and a weeping willow.

CHAPTER 31

The Keeper

In a ritual performed by muscle memory, Allen Wallace threaded tape onto the old four-track console. It was the only way he could do it, because his double vision was giving him fits again. His eyes had been less and less reliable as he grew older, and there were nights when he could only drive home if he kept one eye covered, especially if he'd had a drink or two.

But the old ears were still sharp. Allen had always protected his hearing and insisted his artists do the same. It wasn't difficult. Keep the volume prudent, know where to stand during a show. Do master painters stare at the sun? Why would sound artists punish their ears with brutal, badly mixed sound? But he knew many musicians, engineers, producers, and promoters who'd done exactly that and spent their declining years in a hollow world of hearing aids, confusing echoes, and muddy noise. Not Allen. His hearing had never been tested, but he was pretty sure he still had the ears of a thirty-year-old.

He also took care of his recordings. His most precious tapes were stored in the echo chamber, which stayed below sixty degrees year-round, like a cave for fine-vintage wines. Clients might complain about the deep freeze that was World Famous Best Studios, but Harold's tapes from twenty years ago still sounded pure as a mountain rain, clear as the day they were laid down.

Tonight, he played one of those. *Barry Ward and Junior Walter—7-11-59* was the note on the box, in Allen's own handwriting. He ran the tape forward at double speed for a few seconds until he found the cue and punched the *ON* button. The soft and assured notes from Ward's piano came through as true as the moment they were first played. Allen shut his eyes and leaned back to find the sweet spot. After a few seconds, he covered his right eye to remedy the double vision, found the master gain slider with his left hand, and backed off the volume just a smidgeon. Perfect. He closed his eyes again.

What a beautiful track! And Junior's bass so clear and fat. Bass information was the first thing to go on an old tape, but not Allen's tapes, not as long as he was in charge of care and storage. He listened to all ten minutes of the recording. If the song had ever made it to vinyl, the record company engineers would have faded the song out at three and a half minutes or sooner. It was often said about blues and jazz that some of the best stuff came after the fade. At the end of the recording, the piano stopped, and Ward's resonant voice spoke to him from 1959.

"I think that was a keeper, Allen."

Indeed, it was, but only Allen would keep it. He rewound the tape, carefully returned it to its box, and reached for his glass of whiskey. He misjudged the distance and knocked the two fingers of bourbon onto the floor. *Damn. What a slobbering fool!* At least the glass didn't break.

"Wallace, you are DRUNK AGAIN!" he shouted to the publicity photos on the wall. He went into the washroom and retrieved half a dozen paper towels from the dispenser. On the way out, he bumped his shoulder painfully against the door frame.

Ouch! Shit! Collect yourself, man.

He cleaned up the spill, washed his hands, returned the tape box to the echo chamber, then selected three more tapes from the shelf. Two were mixdowns of gospel songs from the early '60s, field recordings from an AME church choir, and one was his favorite Rockin' Rick Watson tape, an unreleased version of the Nat King Cole song "Send for Me." He set the boxes on the edge of the console, then paused. He was forgetting something. What?

My pill. I forgot to take my medicine. Or did I?

Allen went back into the office and opened the middle desk drawer, taking out the bottle of Equanil. He shook it. There were six pills left. He must have skipped one. He opened the bottle, tossed one pill into his mouth, swallowing it dry, and set the pill bottle down. He closed the drawer a little too hard, and it banged.

"Sorry," he said to Mabel's photo.

Allen threaded up the tape, carefully poured another two fingers of bourbon, settled back into the producer's chair, and shut his eyes.

Rick sang as smooth and confident as always, but what Allen loved about this particular recording was Mabel on backup. It was the only time she'd sung behind

Rick. The part was unusually low-pitched for her, but her perfect understated clarity in the chorus brought soft tears to Allen's eyes.

Don't you fret, my pretty pet

I'm gonna treat you right

The song ended, and Allen wiped his eyes with a crumpled paper towel. "Oh, baby, my darling, light of my world, my sweet Mabes, I miss you so," said Allen. He raised the volume a little bit.

Maybe I should call her. How late is it? He looked up at the wall clock. *Three-fifteen! Holy moly!* He was losing his sense of time. He'd only listened to five—no, six old recordings, and—wait. It couldn't be that late. He glanced up at the clock again, but it had become two clocks. He rubbed his eyes.

Jesus, Jesus. You have things to do tomorrow, Allen. It's a recording day, and the clients are paying. Better call it a night.

Just a few more songs.

Nicky missed his turn in the dark. There was no excuse. He'd driven this way many times but never at night. He was a long, unmeasured time into his solitary journey when the Notrees Carbon Black Plant loomed out of the dark, an enormous brooding hulk lit by only a few vapor security lights. The plant had been closed for a few years, but the surrounding land was still darkened from the clouds of soot that had once belched out of its two eighty-foot stacks. Carbon black was an aptly named petroleum product used in manufacturing car and truck tires, and the plant had once been the county's biggest employer. Its output was so toxic to people and property it had been built far away from everything. Nicky knew he was many miles past the exit he should have been watching for, State Highway 652.

Man, what an idiot! Well, he had not only the darkness to blame but also his own distraction, the thoughts and plans weaving in his mind. No wonder he hadn't seen the small highway sign.

Should he go back? Nicky pulled the Javelin over in front of the rusted steel gate at the plant's entrance. He turned on the car's dome light and took out the worn and badly folded Texas road map from the glove box. Even in the yellow light, he could barely make out the tiny words and lines on the map.

He was at least ten miles past the turnoff. However, the map showed a state ranch road that veered off to the south. He was pretty sure he hadn't passed it. If he found the ranch road, then a few miles farther there was a county road. Not too far down that road, there was an unnamed section road, which, if the map was accurate, would take him back to Highway 652 a couple of miles south of his goal. It would be hard to spot the road markers in the dark, but the bootleg route would save him many miles. He put the Javelin in gear and drove on, watching carefully.

Within half a mile, he spotted the small sign: *RR 4412*. He turned left.

There had been very few vehicles besides Nicky's on the state highway, but on this ranch road, narrow and poorly maintained, there was no one. Rusty, unrepaired barbed wire fence lined both sides of the road, though there was no evidence of cattle, no pens or tanks or windmills. Twice, he caught a glimpse of something moving quickly just out of the beams, perhaps the white flash from the tail of a deer bounding away. A few miles farther, he saw yellow eyes glowing through the mesquite, probably a small coyote or kit fox.

He watched the miles on the odometer, and when he thought he should be getting close, Nicky slowed down and watched for the sign. He found the turnoff for the county road and turned left. It was paved, but there was no divider line. In a couple of miles, he came to a dilapidated sign, peppered in small-caliber bullet holes.

Bledsoe Motel, 10 Mi Ahead, Clean Rooms, Good Rates

The Bledsoe, in Awtry, had been out of business for twenty-five years. Nothing decayed out here, at least not in one lifetime. The sign would be there until someone took it down, or it was shot to fragments.

A short distance past the ghost sign, he found the section road, which was marked by a single pole and reflector. Just past the reflector was a break in the fence and a cattle guard. Nicky turned right and bumped across the guard and onto the gravel road.

Maintenance on these old roads was sporadic, at best. Nicky watched carefully for potholes that could make his low-slung muscle car bottom out. He kept his speed below twenty miles per hour, stirring up a cloud of fine dust behind him, lit red by the taillights.

This was not a hospitable place. The plants that grew out here were small and rugged, gradually giving way to desert-scrub grassland interspersed with tarbush and ocotillo and thick clusters of opuntia prickly pear. It was said that the seeds of some of these plants had first arrived in the sixteenth century, stowaways hiding in the bags of fodder that Spanish explorers brought for their horses.

The road was rough, pitted, and corrugated but perfectly straight. Gradually, it smoothed out, not from better maintenance but from disuse and a lack of erosion. He passed some low, dark hills. At the far reach of his high beams, white salty patches appeared on the desert floor. The road, which had pointed almost due south, gradually curved to the east. Soon, off to his right, a ghostly stretch of flat white landscape appeared, barely lit by a rising gibbous moon.

Nicky knew its name: La Sal del Rey, the Salt of the King. It was the remnant of an enormous shallow lake left behind by ice age floods. The lake had glistened here for centuries, at first supporting herds of large animals, including bison, giant ground sloths, mammoths, several species of deer, and innumerable birds. As the climate warmed and dried, the evaporating lake gradually shrank and grew saltier. All but the hardiest animals disappeared, and a fine layer of sand blew in from the plateaus to the east, burying the salt deposits in many places. These days, there was only standing water here and there after rare desert rains.

Unexpectedly, the road ended at another fence opening and cattle guard, and he found himself emerging onto Highway 652.

Which way now? To the right, according to the map. He turned and picked up speed, but not too much, watching for the only landmark he knew. After less than a mile, he spotted the historical marker and pulled off the road. He stopped the engine and turned off the headlights. The darkness was near total, and it was quiet as death.

In the glove box, there was a small, cheap flashlight. It hadn't occurred to him to check its batteries. When he clicked the button, the light was yellow and feeble, but it was a light. It would have to do. He opened the doors, casting a bright swath from the dome light across the parking area. He shut the door and stood still for several minutes, allowing his eyes to adjust.

Outside, the moonlight was starting to reveal the dim landscape. Overhead, the stars were shockingly dense. The Pyle Monument was close by, but Nick couldn't see it, even with the flashlight. However, he knew where it was. He picked his way down the disused path, playing the light at his feet to avoid stones and cactus. He spotted the step pyramid from the way its angular shape cancelled out the stars. He shined the flashlight, but the beam would barely register on the gray stone and concrete. Moving carefully, he stepped up onto the lowest tier and walked around to the back side of the monument. Well, technically there was no back side, but the side away from the road. The structure's base was aligned so that its corners pointed precisely north, east, south, and west.

He stood at the east corner and looked out across the desert, its ghostly white patches of salt dimly lit by growing moonlight. Far, far to the northeast, there was a wash of light in the sky, and along the horizon a twinkling string that were the suburbs of Duro. It was funny to think that, as far as he'd driven that night, he could still see his hometown. And just past one end of the light string was a single point of white light, a solitary building standing somewhere on the other side of the salt flat, miles away, precisely east of where he stood. If he walked straight toward it, he thought, he would eventually reach that building, whatever it was, and could knock on the door to see who, if anyone, lived there.

But his goal was much closer: fifty paces straight east from the corner, right at the shore of the ancient lake, the nearest place where the ground was relatively soft. Nicky would never find it in the dark. His task was impossible until daylight.

It occurred to him that he would not be at work today. He hadn't told anyone. He couldn't call in and say he wasn't coming, couldn't make some excuse or pretend to be sick. He just wouldn't show up. The foreman would try phoning his apartment, then grumble and load up the shorthanded crew, drive off to the field for a day's work without him. Nick Pomeroy a no-show? That was unheard of. Well, there was nothing he could do.

Nick returned to his car to await the morning. He would not be sleeping.

CHAPTER 32

No More Rehearsals

The Mercury was there again, the fourth morning in a row. This time, it wasn't parked across the street. It sat in the parking lot, just a few feet from his car. He would have to walk right by it. It *was* the police. He was almost certain.

He'd tried to imagine they were stalking someone else. After all, the Crown apartments had eight units. That young man who lived downstairs in the corner apartment came home really late most nights. Who knows what sketchy pastime he was in to? Really, those cops could be watching anyone.

But who was he kidding? The same car had been parked across the street from Duro High School yesterday, when classes let out.

David Bellamy looked at his watch. Ten past seven. There was a faculty meeting at 7:30. He had to get to school.

He looked closely into the bathroom mirror. Bellamy was obsessive about a clean, precise shave, and he'd been distracted lately. Nothing he hated quite as much as a rogue bit of stubble on his face or, for that matter, a hair out of place on his head. Leaning close, he spotted a quarter-inch-wide scruffy place near the jawline. Licking his index finger, he rubbed it on a bar of soap, then applied the slick emulsion to the bristly area. He drew the safety razor carefully three times across his skin, then rinsed his whole face and toweled it dry.

He'd messed up his hair a little bit in the process, so he added a little more Brylcreem and recombed.

Can't wait any longer. He picked up his keys and briefcase, then remembered the pile of graded papers he'd taken home last night. These, he gathered up and placed in the briefcase, took a deep breath, put his shoulders back, and headed out the door.

There were two men in the Mercury, but he thought maybe the driver was not the same one as yesterday. Should he approach them? Ignore them? Either way, he had to walk past them. Since he was running late, he certainly didn't have time for .conversation.

Bellamy walked briskly toward his car. The Mercury's driver-side window rolled down as he approached.

"Good morning, David," said the driver.

Bellamy refused to show fear. He stopped and turned his head, as if noticing them for the first time.

"Can I help you?" he said. "I'm not sure we've met."

"We haven't," said the man. He was middle-aged, with graying hair, short but just long enough to show a hint of curl. "I'm Bob Lamborn. I'm helping the Duro police wrap up some old cases. I believe you do know Sergeant Correa."

Bellamy leaned over so he could see into the Mercury. "Oh, yes," he said. "You're the guy I talked to last year. What can I do for you gentlemen? I'm due at school in about fifteen minutes."

"We're just hoping you can help us," said Lamborn.

"Is this still about the Helen Orlena disappearance, or is there something new?" asked Bellamy.

"Yes, it's the same old case," said Lamborn. "We're trying to close the door on this one, and I hope you can clarify a few things for us."

Bellamy glared. "I talked to you fellows twice last year, for at least six hours," he said. "I couldn't be any help then, when it was fresh. I certainly can't remember anything new."

"Perhaps not," said Lamborn, "But there are some things we'd like to go over with you anyway, when you have time."

"Well, it will have to be after school," said Bellamy.

"That's fine," said Lamborn. "We can talk later. Here's my card." He handed Bellamy a plain business card. "Give me a call when you get out of school this afternoon."

"I'll be pretty busy today," said Bellamy. "Can it wait 'til Monday?"

"Today would be better. Call me." Lamborn rolled up the window.

Bellamy had trouble with the car door lock, which had been sticking lately. He put his briefcase on top of the car so he could use both hands. Pushing gently on the car door with his left hand to take pressure off the latch, he turned the key firmly, and the door opened. He looked back. The cops were still there, waiting for him to leave. He slid into the driver's seat, put the key in the ignition, held the pedal to the floor, and cranked the engine. The carburetor was prone to flooding, but he'd developed the trick of holding it wide open until the moment the engine caught.

The engine started with a roar. He let it idle a few seconds to warm up, then revved it a couple of times. Usually, he'd let it go a minute or so, but he didn't want to wait. He put the car in drive and started forward—and the engine immediately died. He stepped on the brakes. There was a scraping sound above his head, and suddenly, his briefcase, which he had forgotten on the roof of the car, slid across his windshield and banged down onto the hood with a startling crash.

Idiot, idiot, idiot! He wondered what those cops were thinking. He stepped out and retrieved the briefcase, slammed the door, and started the car again. *I bet they're saying, "There goes a guilty man."* If they were talking about how he felt, they were right. Guilt had been his companion for some time now. He'd been living in the intermission between two acts of an unbelievable play.

IN THE SUMMER OF 1970, Helen had seemed happier. After school was out, she auditioned for a lead role in *The Glass Menagerie* at the local community theater and got the part. Bellamy had gone to see the play on its last night, Saturday. The production was pretty good. The lead male actor was a little too old for the role and overacted to compensate. But Helen was great, with exactly the right mix of shy and mysterious to fit the part of the iconoclast daughter Laura.

After the performance, Bellamy had waited in his car until the parking lot was mostly cleared. He had three roses. As the cast and crew were leaving the Duro Playhouse, he spotted Helen coming out the back entrance with a female friend. She was holding a bouquet given her by the other cast members.

It was a moment he'd rehearsed in his mind. He got out of his car carrying the three long stems. She was all smiles as she walked with her friend, talking and laughing, but when she spotted Bellamy, the smile dropped. He moved in quickly.

"These are for the star," he said, giving his sincerest smile. "I see somebody else had the same idea, but this is my contribution."

She took the roses. "Thank you," she said.

"There's nothing I love more than seeing one of my students do something great outside of school," he said. "Helen, I think you and I ended the semester on a sour note, but I want to make sure bygones are all bygone. You were just great tonight."

"There's no hard feelings," said Helen. Turning to her friend, she said, "This is my drama teacher from last year, Mr. Bellamy."

"I'm Sue," said the girl. "I go to Pelham."

"It's a pleasure," said Bellamy, taking her hand gently. "Your friend here absolutely nailed the sweetest role in my favorite Tennessee Williams play. One of the best versions I've seen, truthfully. I had to come tell her."

"Thanks, really," said Helen. She allowed a shallow smile. "It's fun to do, but it was hard to keep up the energy for twelve performances."

"Well, Stanislavski would be proud. You inhabited the soul of Laura Wingfield. I think you have really found your voice in this play. I hope this is the beginning of a real stage career. You signed up for that theater workshop in Fort Worth, right?"

"Uh . . . yes. Yes, I did. It starts in a few days."

"That's just wonderful," said Bellamy. "I know the theater department at CenTex. You'll get a lot out of the program, if you apply yourself."

"Yeah . . . I'm sure I will," said Helen. "Hey, Sue and I need to get going. There's a strike party for the cast and stage crew at the director's house. But thanks for coming out, really, and for the flowers."

She and her friend turned and walked away.

"I'll see you," said Bellamy. "Is Nicky going with you tonight?"

"Nicky and I aren't together anymore," said Helen, over her shoulder.

"Sorry to hear that," said Bellamy. "Have a great night anyway."

"It's okay. Thanks."

He watched her depart. He'd never seen her more beautiful. Her friend Sue was pretty darn nice looking, too, but Helen glowed. Well, he'd planted the seed. Maybe she'd forgive him for their misunderstanding.

It was a good thing that the big jock was out of the picture. She deserved better. Bellamy had known about the breakup even before he asked, from one of his students. He just wanted to make sure.

The next Monday afternoon, after his summer school classes let out at noon, Bellamy sorted through some old notes in his desk and came up with the name of a college friend, Jean Griffin. He and Jean had acted on stage together in college, and a few years ago, he heard she was named head of the Drama Department at CenTex. She would be the person in charge of the theater workshop.

He found the number for the department and reached Jean on the first try.

It took her a minute to recall who he was.

"David? Oh, yes! Yes, David, I *do* remember you," she said. "You're teaching in high school now? That's great. I hope you're steering a lot of young talent our way."

"Always have and always will," said Bellamy. "In fact, I wanted to give you a heads-up about one of my students. She's one of the good ones, and she will be at your workshop next week. A delicate creature in some ways, tons of untapped talent."

"Excellent! That's the kind of student the workshop was made for. What's her name?"

"Helen Orlena. I'm hoping you'll keep pushing her to find her best self. She doesn't have much confidence."

"They seldom do at this age," said Jean. "The name sounds familiar. Hang on a moment." There was paper shuffling, and the sound of a drawer closing. She came back on the line. "Um . . . actually, David, it looks like she isn't attending. I don't see her name."

Bellamy hesitated. "I'm . . . pretty sure she is. Didn't she get in as an alternate?"

More shuffling. "Let me see. Yes, but she's on the decline list. I have her application here. She was an alternate. We sent her a letter telling her there was an opening, and she returned it signed, so we included her. But . . . um . . . there's a note from one of the teaching assistants: *H. Orlena called, cited commitments, asked to be withdrawn.* That was it. We gave her spot to another kid."

Bellamy was stunned. Helen had lied to him. What was happening? She had talked about the workshop for months and was crushed when she didn't make the first cut. Then she got accepted. Why would she change her mind? There had to be more to the story. Probably had something to do with that dumb boyfriend of hers.

CHAPTER 33

The Rock v. the World

It had been a long night for Grover, waiting up late for Rebekah to come home from doing who knows what with the hippie bum.

When she finally did come home, he hadn't yelled at first. He'd simply said "Your film project is over now. If Dan wants to finish it, that's his business. But you will no longer participate."

Holly, who had waited up with him much of the night, said nothing, not even a *Listen to your father, young lady*. She'd just sat with her hands folded in her lap.

Rebekah had simply said, "I'm sorry I didn't call, Father. I had a lot to discuss with Mr. Johns. We can talk about it in a couple of days when everything is finished."

That had been too much defiance for Grover. "It's finished *now*!" he'd yelled. "And so is college! Now, go to your room!" It was the same tone he'd used when she was eleven years old.

Becky had retreated into her childhood bedroom without further comment. Grover had paced the kitchen and fumed, then finally said, "Let's go to bed, Dear."

Grover and Holly retired to their bedroom, but of course Grover couldn't sleep. He relished his role as king of the household but hated being dictator. The Bible had nothing good to say about them: "The Lord has broken the staff of the wicked, the scepter of the tyrants." That was in Isaiah. But as father and husband, he was the ruler over his own house, his wife, and his children, no matter their age.

Tired as he was, he stewed. Finally, as he resolved to put the matter out of his mind until morning and drifted toward sleep, Holly had gotten out of bed.

"I need to check the stove," she'd muttered. That woke him up. Did Holly always have to do that? He got mad about Rebekah all over again and didn't get back to sleep for a long time.

In the morning, when she came out at breakfast, Rebekah, who had never held a grudge in her life, was effervescent and cheerful.

"Good morning," she said. "Is there any coffee left?"

"Of course," said Holly. "I'll get you a cup. Milk, right?"

"I can get it, Mother," said Becky. She poured herself a cup from the Presto percolator, which swished as steam vented out the top.

Grover nursed the last of his second cup. He had to get the situation settled and wasn't sure where to start.

"Rebekah, I apologize for last night," he said finally. "I had no business yelling. I don't put up with that kind of behavior in my salesmen, and I don't like it in myself. I'm really sorry."

"It's okay, Father," she said. "I'm sorry I didn't call. The film is really eating up my time. It won't happen again."

"Very good," said Grover.

Martha's voice came from the other room. "Mother! I can't find my Big Chief tablet. It's not here!"

"It's in the drawer of your desk!" called Holly.

Martha walked into the kitchen. "No it's not! I've looked *everywhere*." She hovered on the verge of tears.

"Let's look together," said Holly. "School starts in half an hour. You need to finish getting dressed. Now, hurry." She rose from the kitchen table and followed her youngest daughter out of the room.

Becky peeled a banana and popped a slice of bread into the toaster.

"I hope you understand I'm not being a monster," said Grover. "I just care about you and about the rest of my family. It's the job that the Lord gave me, and I take it deadly seriously."

"Of course, Father," said Becky. "You're a great provider. You're the rock we all depend on."

"I didn't mean what I said about college. That's something you've put a lot into, and I want you to see it through."

"I knew you were just mad," said Becky.

"I'm glad we understand each other," said Grover. "It's just this . . . film . . . and those men . . . especially *that* man. You know why I can't let it continue. I'm protecting you."

The toast popped up, and Becky slathered it in margarine. She remained standing at the kitchen counter, crunching the toast, taking small bites of banana, sipping her coffee.

"Come sit down," said Grover. "Even at breakfast, we sit together in this family."

"I need to watch for Danfour," said Becky. "He'll be here in a minute."

"Well, when he comes, we'll tell him why you won't be helping with his film anymore. If you want, I'll explain that it was my decision. He'll understand."

Becky drained the last of her coffee. She didn't sit down, didn't seem all that interested in what Grover had to say. Her thoughts were somewhere else. There was the sound of a car engine, and she glanced out the window.

"Here he is," said Becky. She set her cup in the sink, tossed the banana peel and toast remnants in the trash, and headed for the front door.

"Wait!" yelled Grover. "I said it was over. You go out there and tell him you can no longer participate!"

Becky paused at the door. "This has nothing to do with you, Father," she said. She headed out the door, Grover close behind. Dan was in the car, idling by the curb.

"Wait!" said Grover. "Let me speak to him!"

"I'm leaving!" said Becky. "I'll see you tonight." She opened the car door and climbed in, pulling the door shut just as Grover reached for it. He got his hand on the handle, but Dan's car drove away, almost pulling Grover off his feet.

Grover's chest throbbed. Never had he seen such disrespect. He struggled to process it.

"Grover, let her go." It was Holly. She had come out of the house and stood behind him. "She is her own person now. She's lost to us. She's part of the world."

"She is NOT OF THE WORLD!" screamed Grover. "She is MY CHILD!"

"Grover, the neighbors will see you," said Holly. "Settle down. Come inside, and finish your breakfast."

More defiance, this time from his helpmate. Grover watched Dan's car disappear around the corner. He breathed hard. He had a sudden notion to jump into his own car and pursue, maybe try to drive them off the road, like in an old police-chase movie.

He had to collect himself. *Okay, stop,* he thought. *You're being ridiculous. She's right. It's time to settle down. Breathe.* He stood for a few moments, fuming with helplessness, then went back inside. Holly followed silently.

Well, he had been right the first time. Not only would he have to stop Rebekah's participation in this film, but college had to end as well. Now. Starting today. It was the worst decision of his life, letting the world take his firstborn. She was coming back home.

"I have to get ready for school," said Holly. "Rachel will be here soon. I think you should go to work. You've been missing a lot lately." She disappeared toward the back of the house.

Grover looked at his watch. Holly was right again. He had missed significant time at work this week. His colleagues had noticed, and probably his boss. Today, they planned to reprice the cars for the big end-of-year sale, when the '73 models would start arriving. Whatever he did, what decisions he made, whatever choices he would force on Rebekah would have to wait for his lunch break.

Grover returned to the bedroom, put on a blood-red tie, and left for the dealership. At the end of the street, he came to a complete stop and signaled before turning, though there was no one behind him.

CHAPTER 34

Sweet Repose

Air molecules hummed against JJ's eardrums, and he heard the thud of his own heartbeat. Harold had switched off the air blowers so that a cold silence descended at World Famous Best Studios. On the floor, Allen Wallace looked peaceful, comfortable even. Harold knelt over him.

"I don't want to touch him," said JJ.

"I know. I get it," said Harold. "But I need your help. Please do this. Just touch his neck right here, gently, below his ear. Use your middle two fingers."

"Can't we just call an ambulance?"

"The man is *dead,* JJ. I'm almost a hundred percent sure. I just need somebody to back me up. My hands are too shaky."

JJ knelt down and placed his middle and ring fingers against the cool skin of Allen Wallace's neck, on the left side.

"Use just a little pressure," said Harold. "There's this artery that runs beside the throat. Don't remember what it's called. They taught us in the army. It's the biggest pulse on the body. Feel around for it."

JJ shifted his position, paused, then moved his fingers an inch to the right. He held his breath.

"Nothing." He looked up at Harold. "Now what do we do? Call somebody?"

"Help me roll him over," said Harold. "I want to listen to his chest."

They had found Wallace face down, next to the open door of the echo chamber. A couple of feet away, there were three tape reels in boxes. They were stacked neatly on the floor, as if he had carefully set them down before lying on the floor.

"Here, let me show you how to do this," said Harold. He pulled Wallace's right arm up so it was straight out from his body above his head. Then he took his right foot up and crossed it over the left ankle. Harold reached under his left shoulder while JJ put both his hands under Wallace's left thigh.

"On three," said Harold. "One . . . two . . . three." They rolled the man's thin body easily.

"I think I heard him breathe," said JJ.

"I'm pretty sure it was just air coming out of his body," said Harold. "Now, be completely quiet. I need to listen." Harold knelt down and put his head in the middle of Wallace's chest.

JJ's heart thumped as he held his breath.

Harold raised himself up again, put his hand on Wallace's forehead, and pulled up an eyelid with his thumb. The eye stared straight ahead. Harold closed it again and stood up. "That's it. He's dead."

"I think we should let somebody else decide that," said JJ.

"His heart has stopped. He's cool to the touch," said Harold. "There's nothing anybody can do for him."

"Ah, Jesus, Jesus," said JJ. "We can't just leave him here."

Harold rubbed his neck, dusted off the knees of his pants, and sighed. "Let's not get crazy." He looked at up at the studio clock. 8:40 a.m. "In about three hours, we're going to have ten people showing up and crowding into this little place."

"Twelve," said JJ. "There's Becky and that cameraman."

"Oh, God, I forgot about them," said Harold.

"That's why we need to take care of this," said JJ. "Call an ambulance. Get them to take him away."

Harold reached down and picked up the tape boxes from the floor. Not knowing what else to do, he carried them into the control room and placed them on a stack of five other tape boxes. Two tape reels were lying naked in front of the soundboard, leader tape hanging loose. Another tape was threaded onto the four-track recorder.

"He was listening to old tapes last night," said Harold. He examined an empty box. *H. Green and M. White, 7-18-62.*

"Poor old guy," said JJ. "I wonder what he was doing by the echo chamber?"

"That's where he kept his most important recordings," said Harold. "Because it's so cold and dry in there."

A water glass sat on the desk beside the console. JJ picked it up and sniffed. "Booze," he said, and set it back down.

In the trash can beside the chair they found a dozen wadded-up paper towels and a fifth of Kentucky whiskey. Two inches of liquor remained in the bottom. On the desk in the office, they found Allen's porkpie hat and a prescription bottle marked *Equanil 500*. There were four pills left.

Harold sat down in Wallace's office chair and folded his hands.

"So?" said JJ. "What now?"

Harold looked up at the office clock. "We can't call anybody," he said. "Not yet."

"We have to get him *out of here*."

"Wait," said Harold. "Think about it. As soon as we bring in the cops and the ambulance, this studio shuts down. Closed. That's it. Gig is over. Everybody goes home, and you and me will probably go downtown for questioning. The one thing that definitely *won't* happen is a recording session."

"But . . . we can't leave him lying there."

"You're right. We can't."

Harold walked back into the little studio. Allen Wallace lay with one arm up as if he were waiting to ask a question.

"Okay, let's think a minute," said Harold. "Here's what happened. You and I came in this morning, and we didn't see Wallace. We didn't think anything was weird, because he said he might stay home today, because he felt sick."

"He did?"

"No, of course not, but he *could* have said that. So when we got here this morning, we didn't think anything was weird. Everybody shows up, we record the song in as few takes as possible. I'll be the engineer. Then everybody leaves."

"Can you handle the sixteen-track by yourself?"

"I hope so. We don't have a choice."

"Oh man," sighed JJ. He looked around the room. "So . . . what do we . . . *do* with him?"

Harold stooped and peered inside the echo chamber, which was lit by one yellow light bulb in a protective cage. He looked at the body on the floor, then back to the low door. "We can put him in there."

"We're gonna *hide his body*?"

"No . . . no, we're going to find his body later on today. In the echo chamber. After the session's finished and everybody leaves."

"We won't get away with it," said JJ. "The cops won't believe he just happened to be in there when he collapsed."

"Why not? That's where he kept his old tapes." Harold stuck his head inside the small room again. "We put him there, by the back wall. Face down just like we found him. Take a couple of those old tapes, and put them on the floor."

"I don't like this," said JJ. "It's just not right."

"We have no choice," said Harold. "Not if we want 'Earth Is Crying' to happen. But . . . hey, it's your record. You wrote the song, you're the singer. Seriously, my friend, if you want to call the cops and say goodbye to the song, I'll go along with it. We'll pay everybody off, go back home, and try again another day. I really will leave it up to you. But think about it, man. We're *ten feet* from the goal line. This is probably the last song that will ever be recorded at Best Studios. This place won't continue without Allen Wallace. He was sole owner. His relatives will probably just sell the gear and close it down. The building will get turned into a liquor store."

"Oh, man, don't make me decide," said JJ. He forced himself to look at Allen Wallace's body, so sad and skinny on the floor. The scars on his wrist stood out plainly against his crepey skin. JJ stooped down and looked inside the echo chamber. "All right," he said. "I guess . . . if we could ask Allen, I think I know what he'd say."

"Yep," said Harold. "He'd say, 'Record the song.' You know he would. It'll be part of his legacy."

Harold took him by the wrists, and JJ got his feet. Grunting and tugging, they dragged the sad form of Allen Wallace, owner and engineer of World Famous Best Studios, into the cold room and rolled him over face down. Harold retrieved the old tapes from the control room, including the one that was wound onto the machine, put the boxes back onto the low shelf in the echo chamber, and put one of the boxes on the floor near Wallace's head. For good measure, he opened it and tossed the lid close by and pulled the reel partway out of the box, as if Wallace had dropped it there as he was stricken. Harold went back into the office and retrieved Allen's porkpie hat, which he placed on the floor next to body. Finally, he flipped off the light and closed the door.

The two stood there, and their gazes met.

"I think we're fuckin' crazy," said JJ.

"Yep," said Harold.

"Do you have to get the drummer at the airport?"

"He's supposed to take a cab. I'll reimburse him. Right now, we need to make sure all the channels work and the mics are set up right. I was counting on Allen to do that. We just have to wing it."

"At least we have a couple of hours before—"

A sudden tapping on the outside metal door made them both jump.

"What!?" said Harold. "Nobody is supposed to be here yet."

"What do we do?"

"Answer it, of course." Harold took a deep breath to collect himself, looked around the room to see if they had missed anything, and walked back through the office to the outer room with its dusty filing cabinets and derelict tape recorder. He opened the door.

It was Dan Park, standing there with the bulky camera case in one hand and a tripod under his arm.

"Y'all ready for us?" asked Dan. Behind him stood Becky Paulson, carrying the field recorder. She smiled brightly.

"Come on in," said Harold. "Watch musical history being made."

CHAPTER 35

The World v. Holly Paulson

School had not yet begun. As soon as little Rachel arrived every morning, Holly liked to put the three children through simple exercises to stimulate their circulation and start the day in energetic moods.

"All stand!" she said. The three children stood, along with Lucille, the teaching assistant. Peter stood up, favoring his bad foot but standing straight.

"Hands up, reach toward God," Holly said. They all reached. Together, they sang:

"Reach up for the hand

Reach up for the hand

Reach up for the hand of God"

"Bend over, knees straight!" Holly called, and they bent down. Peter had trouble with this one, but he tried.

"Push the Devil right down

Push the Devil right down

Push the Devil right down in the sod"

They sang all six verses, variously reaching, pushing, twisting, and stretching, until the song ended, and they sat.

"Get out your tablets," said Holly. "Time for writing practice."

The doorbell rang. Without being prompted, Lucille hopped up and left the room to send away whatever salesman or neighbor was disturbing their school day.

Holly picked up a piece of chalk and wrote on the board in circular cursive:

My cat eats meat and she's light on her feet.

"Okay, write this sentence five times. Think about flowing the letters together, *e* with *a* and *e* with *e*."

Lucille came back into the room. "Mrs. Paulson, there's some men from the school district. There's a policeman, too."

"I wanna see!" said Peter.

"Stay seated and work on your sentences," said Holly. "I'll find out what they want."

It was Claud Vanderberg, the truancy officer, in his dark gray suit. Behind him stood the assistant superintendent Jim Fellows and a uniformed police officer.

"Good morning, Mrs. Paulson," said Vanderberg.

"What can I do for you gentlemen?" asked Holly. "I don't need to remind you that we are running a Christian school here, and you are interrupting our day."

Jim Fellows spoke. "Mrs. Paulson, we don't want to interrupt anything, but I believe you can guess why we're here."

"Am I under arrest?"

"No, ma'am," said Fellows. "Of course not. But we are here to offer you a clear choice. Come with us, right now, to the school district office so you can enroll your children in school, starting today. The folks down there will help you with the process, make it as simple as possible."

"Or what?" Holly glared.

"Or we will have to do what we don't want to do," said Vanderberg. "We'll have officer Ramos place you under arrest for violating state truancy law. It's your decision. May we please come in?"

Holly wasn't about to budge from the doorway.

Ask them if they have a warrant, said James.

"I suppose you have a warrant?"

"Yes, ma'am," said Vanderberg. "Signed by a judge yesterday. But I can tell you truthfully that if you voluntarily comply, starting immediately, there won't be any criminal charges."

"How about the children? Are you going to arrest them, too?"

Fellows took a step forward. "Mrs. Paulson, nobody is getting arrested if you'll just agree to come with us and follow the law. You can bring the children with you or leave them here if there is some responsible adult who can take care of them. But you need to go with us to the district office. Now."

Let them in, but stall them.

Holly stepped aside and motioned for them to come in.

"Please wait in the living room. I have to wrap some things up first. I need to call Rachel's mother and explain that the police are closing down a Christian school. It will take a few minutes."

"Take as much time as you need, ma'am," said Fellows, "but the sooner we take care of this, the better."

The two school officials and the police officer came into the living room but did not sit. Holly hurried back to the classroom and shut the door behind her.

"What's going on, Mrs. Paulson?" asked Lucille. "Is everything all right?"

"It's too hard to explain in a hurry," said Holly, "but I'm going to need your total cooperation. Those men out there want to arrest me for running a religious school."

"Oh, Lord!" said Lucille. "They can't do that!"

"They can, and they will," said Holly. "The world works according to its own laws, not God's. Now, listen carefully. I need you to stay in here with Rachel. I'm going to take Peter and Martha away from here until we can straighten this situation out."

"Anything you need me to do?" asked Lucille. "Should I call Rachel's mom?"

"Yes, but wait 'til we're gone." Holly carefully opened the side door that led from the classroom to the carport side of the house. She could see a white FCISD vehicle parked in front of the house and behind that, a police car. No one would see her. But where could she go? Grover had the family's only car. How far could they get on foot?

Go to your neighbor, Jean. Ask to borrow her car. Say one of the kids needs to go to the doctor.

Holly crept out the side door and, staying far from the street, slipped next door. Jean was the closest thing Holly had to a friend on the block. The woman had provided medicine for Peter's burned foot, a kindness Holly had deeply appreciated.

Holly rang the doorbell and tried to collect herself. Jean answered the door in a blessedly short time.

"Oh, Holly. Hi." She looked at her neighbor, puzzled. "Are you okay?"

"Yes, but . . . uh, it's Peter," said Holly. "Jean, I need the most enormous favor a person could ask. I need to borrow your car, if you can possibly do it. I have to get my son to the doctor. Grover can't get away, so it's just me."

"Well . . . yeah. Sure. What's wrong with Peter?"

"It's his foot again," said Holly, "I thought it was getting better, but this morning, it's completely inflamed. I'm really afraid it's infected. He's in so much pain."

"Oh, my goodness! Yes! Of course. Do you want me to drive you?"

"I can drive," said Holly. "I'll be very careful with your car. Who knows how long it will take. It's just . . . he's in so much pain."

"I'll get the keys," said Jean.

Holly shifted her weight from one foot to another, glancing back over her shoulder, expecting to see the policeman behind her at any moment.

Jean appeared with a key fob and handed it to Holly through the screen door. "You're sure I can't drive you?"

"No, it would be best if I did this by myself. But thank you! Oh, thank you so much. You don't know how much this means to me. I'll get him and be right back."

Holly walked as quickly as she could back to the classroom.

"Peter, Martha, come with me, immediately."

"Where are we going, mother?" asked Martha.

"We have to take a little ride in Miss Jean's car. I can't tell you why just yet. Now, come along quickly, and don't fuss. Rachel, you stay here with Miss Lucille. School is cancelled for today. Your mother will come get you in a few minutes."

Holly put her purse over her shoulder and, holding both her children's hands, she walked them next door, through the yard, and to the neighbor's carport, where her Ford station wagon was parked. Jean came out of her house.

"Peter, you'll be all right," she said. "Holly, call me from the doctor's office if you get a chance. Let me know what they say. I'm worried."

"It'll be okay, I'm sure," said Holly. She opened the rear door and got the two children situated in the backseat. "Put on your seat belts."

Holly looked back toward her own house. No one was coming out. She tried to put the key in the ignition, but it was the wrong one, and she fumbled. She found the correct key and started the car. Fortunately, it was an automatic transmission. Grover had promised to teach her to drive a clutch someday but had never gotten around to it.

The children should crouch down in the back.

"Okay, both of you lie down sideways."

"Why?" asked Peter.

"No questions! Do what I say!" said Holly. "It will be for just a minute." She pulled the gear shift down to the R position and pushed on the pedal. The car lurched back, startling her, so she hit the brakes. Jean was standing in her front yard, concerned. Holly gave her a little guilty smile and took her foot of the brake, letting the car idle back out of the driveway.

"Where we going?" asked Peter.

"Away," said Holly. "Just away. Away from the world."

"Is Father coming?"

"Not on this trip. Now sit still and be quiet." She put the car into gear and pulled away slowly down Bluebonnet. As she passed her house, no one was coming out, no one was following her, not yet.

Get as far away as possible. Don't drive too fast, or you'll get pulled over.

"Please, don't talk to me right now," said Holly. "I can do this."

"We didn't say anything," said Martha.

CHAPTER 36

Bellamy and the Case of the Haunted Stage

"Are you okay, David?" It was Suzanne, the Spanish teacher.

Bellamy turned around. "Huh? Yeah.... Hello, Suzy. Yeah, I'm fine."

"I was just wondering if you're feeling all right," said Suzanne. "You were staring off into space."

"Just lost in thought," said Bellamy.

They were in the teacher's lounge. He had found a table where he could spread out and read the latest batch of class essays. He had given the assignment the first of the week, received the essays two days ago, and still hadn't finished grading them. For the life of him, he could not focus.

Suzanne fed a quarter into the soft drink machine, and a can of Fanta clattered down. She plopped down on one of the couches.

"It's really none of my business," she said, "but you haven't seemed yourself lately."

"I know," said Bellamy. "I've had a lot on my mind."

"Anything you'd like to talk about? I'm a good listener."

"Thanks, but it's nothing special." Bellamy put a big *B–* on the front page of one essay and picked up another from the stack. "I've been teaching seven years at Duro, including every summer semester. That's too soon to burn out. But lately, it's been a struggle to keep my mind on the job. And here it is only October."

Suzanne chuckled. "This is my third year at the high school level, and I have a hard time imagining doing it for seven years or ten years. Maybe you could take next summer off. Do something different for a couple of months or just take a long vacation."

"I've thought about that," said Bellamy. "I may or may not teach this summer. Just have to decide how important the money is."

"Do you remember my predecessor, Margie White?" asked Suzanne. "She taught Spanish for twenty-five years before I got here. She was retired only two years before she passed away. She was in this old building's DNA. That's how teaching used to be."

Bellamy laughed. "I'm not sure I want to stay so long I become part of the building. Sort of like Hill House." He switched to a Mid-Atlantic accent. "'We who walk here, walk alone.'"

"Yeah. It's funny," said Suzanne. "There've always been these legends about how the school is haunted, but I've never heard anybody claim that Margie White's ghost is wandering the halls. If any old spirits were going to hang around Duro High School, Margie would be one of them."

Bellamy tried to read the next essay. This one was from that sweet and eager girl Chase McFall. For all her flaws, she tried hard on every assignment and deserved his full attention. He read the essay to the end, then scribbled a few notes, partly criticism, partly encouragement. The assignment had been to write 1,000 words about some famous speech in history and what made it great. Chase had chosen William Jennings Bryan's "Cross of Gold" speech, and though she didn't really seem to understand the financial issues involved, she gave it a good try. He hesitated, then wrote an *A–* on the first page.

He picked up another paper and attempted to read it. A couple of paragraphs in, he put his red pencil down and rubbed his eyes.

"Suzy, let me ask you a really dumb question. Do you really think there's anything to those stories about the school being haunted?"

"Seriously?"

"Yes.... Well, half serious," said Bellamy. "There are always legends and rumors about any old school. It's just that some of my students completely believe it—not like it's some fun old school story but believe it is actually, literally haunted by the spirits of former students. One of my students won't go into the auditorium by herself, even in the middle of the day. It's crazy."

"The kids all say the hauntedness—whatever you call it—is centered around the stage," said Suzanne. "And I'll tell you this: Some strange things do happen up there, stuff getting knocked over when nobody is nearby. I've heard that from teachers. And you remember, a light exploded above the stage last year."

"Yeah, but that wasn't caused by ghosts. The janitor said some condensation dripped onto the hot light from an air duct."

"That's probably true," said Suzanne, "but you can't convince the students it was just a water drip. One of my kids said she and her friend heard a voice that sounded like a girl in pain coming from the back of the stage, but when they looked, there was nobody there. I don't know what to say about that."

"Sounds like somebody's getting a little too much into the legend, if you ask me," said Bellamy. "Once the stories start circulating, they feed on themselves. But it is strange how many of the students believe it."

Bellamy tried to read a few more essays, and it was like jogging through mud. The assignment was for speech class, not English lit, but it seemed like the kids weren't even trying to get the spelling and grammar right. He graded three more papers. On the last page of the third one, he wrote *Your penmanship and spelling badly detract from your main point.* On the first page, he put a big red *C+*. That's all he could stand for now. He'd pick this up later when he was less distracted.

Really? When will that be?

David Bellamy felt he had been holding his breath for two years. His early-morning encounter with the police just confirmed what he'd always thought: People blamed him for what happened to Helen. What he'd actually done or not done wouldn't matter if they've all made up their minds.

What should he do about the police? Talk to them? There was no getting out of it. Detective Lamborn had said they were trying to close the door on the Helen Orlena case. Other people might have found comfort in the idea that the whole thing was wrapping up, that just a few little details would be filled in. Rubber bands snapped around a loose deck of cards, snapshots tucked away in tidy boxes, knickknacks sorted. Then the door could be closed for good. But at what cost for Bellamy?

He wasn't stupid. Nor was he ready to sit under the lights and tell his side of the story. For one thing, the story was just too complicated to tell without explaining a lot of other things.

His last class of the day was finished, and the kids had all cleared out, eager for the weekend. He puttered at his desk, thinking there must be something he could do. He still had a dozen essays to grade but couldn't bear the thought. Maybe he would go home, change, and go out for a run. Though daylight saving time was still in effect, he couldn't count on enough evening light for one of his long, long runs, the kind that produced waves of endorphins to overpower the memories. Anyway, the Mercury might be waiting for him at this very moment, outside the school, ready to intercept him and take him where he was not yet willing to go. But he couldn't stay here all night.

He packed up his briefcase and headed for the north exit and the teacher's parking lot. In the back hall, he passed an unlabeled door. It was a side entrance to the auditorium, leading to a short hallway that ended in stairs up to the main stage. He hesitated, then tugged at the door. It was unlocked.

The little hallway was pitch black, but he could see diffuse gray light coming from the stage. He stepped forward carefully and mounted the steps. Still carrying his briefcase, he walked out onto stage center. The only light in the main part of the auditorium came from three red-glowing EXIT signs. High above the stage, accessible only from the catwalks, were four small windows, which dimly illuminated the stage even when it was full daylight outside. The wings were dark.

Something crunched under his shoes. He bent down and looked close. There was broken glass on the stage, just off center. Did another lightbulb explode? Bellamy looked straight up toward the small windows, which were spray-painted white. Too-bright light came from one of them. A pane was broken.

Bellamy set the briefcase down at his feet, stood on the stage, and tried to clear his mind. Helen wasn't here. Why would she be? Nevertheless, Bellamy closed his eyes and imagined her voice, her pretty sing-song voice with exaggerated spikes and dips in pitch, an accent hard to place, just not from around here.

Salutations, Mr. Bellamy!

Will they start casting next week?

I need this part so badly!

I have no response to that!

An actor has to own a role. I could own it.

Yes, I could come with you, but I won't. I have my own life!

And

Please . . . Please, don't . . .

Bellamy shook his head sharply and spoke out loud: "No! I will not go there!"

In the corner of his eye, he thought he saw something move. He turned his head reflexively. Nothing there.

"If I could do it over again, I would," said Bellamy. "I wouldn't have followed you. But you lied to me about where you were going."

A tiny click behind him, and he turned quickly to look. There was nothing. Perhaps it was just the restless sounds of an old building.

"If you hadn't lied, I wouldn't have followed you," he said. "If you had just been honest, I would have accepted it. I could have helped you."

He held his breath and listened. Nothing. But then there was a louder click, like a switch, and the school air system shut off. He had not noticed the sound, which was part of the background noise to every school day. But now that it was absent, he realized it had been there all along. Of course, they always turned off the ventilation system at the end of the week, every Friday.

"Are you here?" Nothing. With no other sounds to mask them, he could faintly hear distant echoes outside the auditorium, footsteps, shutting doors, muffled voices.

"Can you forgive me?" Silence.

What an idiot I am! If somebody saw me standing here on the stage talking to a dead girl, they'd send me to the state hospital.

"Oh well, then. I tried. I really did." Nothing. Bellamy stood in silence. The only sound was his own heartbeat. "For what it's worth . . . I forgive *you*."

He picked up his briefcase and turned to leave. Something moved; he was sure of it. Then he saw it in the dark, a mass of gray material like a wadded-up rag, on the stage a few feet away. He walked around it and crouched down.

It was a bird. A gray speckled pigeon. That explained the broken glass. The pigeon had struck one of the high windows with such force it had gone through and fallen all the way down to the stage.

Was it dead or just stunned? It didn't look very much like a bird—more like a ball of feathers with wings strangely askew. Its head was cocked sideways, and the eyes were shut. Bellamy stooped close to examine it. It was almost as if the bird had taken its own life. He couldn't just leave it here. Better let the janitor know, so he could remove the dead bird and sweep up the broken glass. Bellamy reached out and gently touched the soft down feathers of the breast.

The pigeon bit him, hard, on the skin between his thumb and index finger. With an involuntary yell, he jumped up. He stared at the crippled, fluttering bird, then looked at his wounded hand. Despite the dim light, Bellamy saw blood.

CHAPTER 37

Prensky's Law

Harold and JJ wanted to avoid telling lies, if possible. Their official story was that Allen Wallace was feeling tired and ill, would not be in the studio today, and had given Harold full proxy to run the session. Unfortunately, they had to lie right out of the gate.

The first words out of Dan Park's mouth, after "Good morning," were "Is Mr. Wallace here? I have a couple more questions for him, just to clarify some things."

"No," Harold said quickly. "He went home. Poor old guy's wiped out. Been pushing himself way too hard. I'll be running everything today."

"His car is still here," Dan pointed out.

Harold and JJ exchanged glances. *Holy shit! The white Ford is still in the parking lot!* They'd forgotten.

"I took him home," Harold improvised. "He was not in great shape to drive."

"Oh," said Dan. "I was hoping for a few more quick interview shots, to fill some gaps."

"I'm sure he'll be back tomorrow . . . or Sunday," said Harold. "If he's feeling better."

Harold should have driven the Galaxie somewhere—anywhere—and parked it a few blocks away. Or driven it back to his house and left it. But then, they had to pretend they didn't know Allen Wallace was cold and dead in the echo chamber. The more they tried to cover it up, the more it would look like they had let him die deliberately. Or killed him.

Over the next hour, the classical musicians arrived in small groups and tuned their instruments. Lizard the bass player set up quickly, then got out a paperback with a strange mandala design on the cover—the book was called *Be Here Now*—and quietly read to himself. It was close to noon when Brendan Bibb the drummer arrived by cab from the airport. He immediately pronounced the rented drum kit "a piece of crap" and began the interminable ritual of tuning the drumheads. Endless thumping, twisting the drum key, then thumping again. It was a process that could induce madness.

An hour into the usual thirty-minute process of tuning the drums, Bibb took a bathroom break. The little improvised orchestra waited. The musicians chatted among themselves and stepped outside frequently to smoke, stretch their legs, and warm up. They were all on the clock. If overtime was called for, everybody benefitted except the man paying the bill.

"Let's call it Prensky's Law," Harold told JJ. "Any session involving three or more musicians means that one of them makes you go overtime."

Harold had worked with Bibb before but had somehow forgotten the man's most exasperating trait: He was a perfectionist beyond the limits of reason. Plus, the more you pushed—Harold knew not to push hard—the more stubbornly meticulous he became.

"How's it coming there, Brendan?" asked Harold, when the drummer returned. "Are we getting close?"

"You can't hurry good sound, man." *Thump thump thump thump . . . twist twist.*

Dan the cameraman had filmed everything but an actual performance. He sat inside the control room reading a philosophy textbook—catching up on schoolwork.

Becky lounged on the couch in Allen Wallace's office, wishing JJ would talk to her. Something was off kilter with him. He had greeted her warmly when they arrived, but something was on his mind, and he said very little. She wasn't sure what to expect from him, but in her own case, she had spent a mostly sleepless night, excited and afraid, glowing from their night together, thinking about him and imagining being with him. Even her father's juvenile tirade hadn't spoiled her elation.

Was she kidding herself? JJ had been with dozens of girls, if not hundreds. Maybe he just wasn't capable of a relationship outside the superficial world of a pop star. But then . . . She caught him looking at her, and his expression was . . . What was it? Pleading? Like somebody in trouble, hoping to be saved. Then he saw her looking at him, and his face lit up into a big smile that she thought was a bit forced, as if a paparazzi had unexpectedly pointed a camera at him. Then he looked down at his notes.

What was going on? While they waited for Bibb to declare himself happy with the drumhead tension, why couldn't JJ just come and sit beside her, talk a little bit?

Everything was ready. The microphones had been set up by Allen Wallace, and Harold wasn't touching them. He was horrified when one of the violists bumped a delicate ribbon mic, almost knocking it over. All Harold could do was put it back in place and hope it wasn't damaged.

Everyone waited.

Thump thump thump thump THUMP! Twist twist twist. Thump. Thump-ta-THUMP. Twist twist.

Finally, Bibb said he was satisfied. "That's the best I can do with this junk."

Harold guided the band through one and a half run-throughs. During the first attempt, Bibb suddenly stopped playing in the middle of the second chorus, pushed his stool back, and bent over to adjust the tension on his kick drum. Harold stopped the band, and they waited some more. On the second try, they made it all the way through the song.

JJ thought the strings sounded too Hollywood and said so.

"What do you want us to do different?" asked a violinist.

"Sound less Hollywood," said JJ.

"Uh . . . okay."

Finally, at 1:15 pm, October 20, 1972, they were ready to record "Earth Is Crying."

JJ was ready. The musicians were rehearsed and ready. The drummer knew what he was supposed to do. Dan Park had an eleven-minute reel of film loaded into his Bolex, and Becky sat with headphones on, holding the boom mic, ready to record live sound.

Harold was more than ready. He took the office phone off the hook so there would be no distractions. He unwrapped a brand-new Ampex two-inch tape reel and threaded it onto the sixteen-track recorder. He let the tape run two minutes and stopped it, setting the counter to double-zero. Then he threw the kill switch on the air conditioner.

He had the musicians play one by one for a few seconds, to double-check the levels. There was too much sonic information from the bass guitar, so Harold backed off the input. He wasn't completely happy with the resonance of the floor tom-tom, but he wasn't about to risk another delay.

"All right, ladies and gentlemen!" Harold announced. "We're going to go straight through in one take. Everybody knows what to do. For an intro, I want two snicks from the high-hat, then JJ will start—"

BAM BAM BAM! Someone was banging hard on the metal outside door.

"Jesus Christ and Mary!" said Harold. "Everybody, stand by. I'll handle this."

He strode through the outer room and pulled open the heavy security door. There was a short-haired man wearing a short-sleeved shirt and a red tie.

"I'm here for Rebekah Paulson," he said.

"Who?"

"Rebekah . . . Paulson. I'm her father. I'm here to take her with me."

"Uh . . . look, sir, we're in the middle of a recording session."

"Fine," said Grover. "You just keep going with your little session. I'm taking Rebekah out of this place."

Becky came as far as the outer room but wouldn't approach the door.

"Father, I'm working on my project, and I'm going to do it. This doesn't concern you."

Grover stepped closer, but the producer wouldn't get out of his way.

"Man, this is a professional recording session," said Harold. "The meter is running. Whatever you want to say, it can wait 'til later. Now, please go away and let us work."

"I'm not here to get in your way," said Grover. "I'm here to take my daughter away from this filth and from—" He spotted JJ coming up behind Becky. "Away from that." He stabbed his finger in JJ's direction.

Harold needed this like he needed a heart attack. He turned to Becky. "Maybe you could just talk to him outside?"

"No!" shouted JJ. "This girl is going to stay and do her job, and you're going to take your ass out of here!"

Grover shoved his way past Harold and grabbed Becky by the wrist. She screamed and pulled. JJ lunged and tried to grab Grover by his necktie, but Becky yelled "STOP IT!" and pushed herself between the two of them. Grover let go of his daughter's arm and stepped back, shocked by hippie aggression and Becky's defiance.

"Father, just go away!" she said. "I'm not your little kid. Go home. Or go back to the dealership. Let these people work. Let *me* work!"

From inside the studio, Garrett Miller called out, "Should I call the police?"

"NO!" yelled Harold and JJ in unison.

"You heard the lady," said JJ. "She's not yours. And you'll take your ass out of here or I'll *kick* it out of here!"

"I could take you and six more like you, you piece of trash!" Grover yelled. "Rebekah, come home with me now—or don't come home at all!" Once more, he grabbed Becky by the wrist, but JJ pushed forward and threw his weight into Grover, and they both stumbled through the door out onto the metal landing, where they struggled.

"Stop! Stop! STOP!" Harold yelled. "Man, we don't need this. Just take your bullshit outside! JJ, let him GO!"

Grover and JJ separated momentarily, both breathing hard. Harold took JJ by the arm and tried to lead him back inside, but he pulled away sharply and stood glaring at Grover on the landing. Grover collected himself and took a step back, eyes locked on JJ.

"So that's what it comes down to," said Grover. "My daughter has made her choice. Filth and disgusting so-called music. And drugs. And sex. That's what it comes down to. You probably think you've got your very own Christian virgin now."

JJ stepped closer and pointed his index finger at Grover's chest. "Virgin? Hah! You don't even know your own kid!"

Grover lunged and grabbed JJ by the hair, pulling him forward, and threw an off-balance punch that caught him on the ear. JJ ducked his head and started throwing body punches.

"STOP, NOW! Both of you!" yelled Harold. The two men broke apart, and Grover pushed JJ back with a hard shove. JJ raised both fists, but Harold stepped between. Grover paused, then turned without another word and clanged down the metal steps.

"You *better* run, motherfucker!" yelled JJ.

Grover turned at the bottom of the steps and glared up at JJ, then stalked to his car.

They watched as he started the engine and drove away. For a moment, Harold feared he might do something crazy like ram his car into the building, but Grover simply left, driving normally.

"JJ, that was pointless!" said Harold. "He was *leaving*."

"I know," said JJ. "I shouldn't have said that. But he was being such an asshole." He looked around behind him. "Becky? Where did she go?"

The two men went back inside, where Harold shut the security door and threw the deadbolt.

"Becky?"

Several of the musicians had left their chairs and were congregating in the office.

"Where's Becky?" asked JJ.

"She's crying in the bathroom," said the female cellist.

Harold herded everyone back into the large studio. "Let's get set up again, folks. I'm really sorry. Nothing like that has ever happened in my career. It's okay now. It's over. Let's record."

Gradually, the musicians resumed their places and picked up their instruments. JJ fretted in the office, waiting.

"Come on, man," said Harold. "We have work to do. You're a professional."

"I need to talk to her, man," said JJ.

"She'll come out when she's ready," said Harold. "Go get your guitar."

The bathroom door opened, and Becky emerged. Her eyes were red, and she had a wad of toilet paper in her hand.

"I'm sorry," she said. "It was my fault. I know what happens when somebody defies him. He's really not a bad man. He just thinks . . . there are two worlds, good and evil, his world and everybody else's. I'm really sorry. I should just leave now."

JJ wrapped his arms around her.

"No, no. Don't leave. Please, please, don't leave. It wasn't your fault. It was me. I lost my temper. I didn't mean to get so mad. I'm the one who's sorry."

Becky let JJ hug her for several seconds, then she just said, "You should do your song now."

"You're not going to leave, are you? Please don't leave."

"No. I guess not. Somebody needs to record the live sound."

JJ went back to his chair, picked up his guitar, and nodded at Harold, who resumed his seat in the control room.

"All right, folks," said Harold. "We had a little distraction, but let's refocus. From the top, I need two snicks from the high hat, then JJ will start. All quiet, we are now . . . recording." He punched the start button, and the reels turned.

"'Earth Is Crying,' take one," he said, and pointed at the drummer.

Grover did not exceed the speed limit. He obeyed all of Caesar's traffic laws. He came to a complete stop at each stop sign. He would follow the laws of the world until . . .

He was driving home to get a gun. He would not lose his precious daughter to the world without a fight. Momentarily, he considered calling the police to report that a girl was being held against her will at a warehouse on the south side. Drugs were probably involved. But that would be cowardly. He'd take care of this himself.

Grover owned two rifles and a small-caliber target pistol. As he drove, he considered the advantages of each. The pistol was smaller, easier to conceal, and less lethal, making accidental murder less likely. There was also the Remington .243 deer rifle, which allowed him the option of hanging back two hundred yards and nailing the creep through the lungs as he emerged from the building—if it came down to that. But the scope, which he had removed for surveillance of the music studio, would have to be reattached and would certainly need resighting.

Before he got home, he had decided upon his weapon of choice. He would use the .30-caliber M1 carbine, a light and rapid-firing military rifle made for the Korean war, wrapped in oily cloth and stored in a warehouse until Grover bought it at a government sale ten years ago. He'd gotten it because a man who owed him money had given him several boxes of military-grade ammunition as repayment. He bought the gun to match the ammunition.

Because Grover had served among the support troops in the army, the carbine was the only rifle Grover had been trained to handle. Simple, reliable, and half the weight of the standard-issue infantry rifle, the carbine wasn't much use for hunting anything larger than small doe, but it was fast and accurate and packed a ferocious punch at close range. A day at the range, pumping .30 caliber slugs into hay bales, was a great way to blow off steam.

Grover's ears rang. He shook his head to try and clear them. He never went to doctors, but a doctor friend once told him he might have hypertension, based on his ruddy complexion and high-strung personality. Ringing in the ears was a bad sign, he said. Cut back on the salt. Try to relax.

To calm himself down, Grover went through the mental checklist of field-stripping the M1. The gunnery sergeant at Camp Wolters who had trained Grover and his fellow draftees had drilled the routine into them so relentlessly that he remembered it perfectly even twenty-five years later. He went through the breakdown and reassembly sequence in his head to give himself something to focus on and not let any pesky inner angels try to talk him out of what he had to do.

Step one, release tension on the screw holding the barrel band. Place your thumb on the bottom of the bayonet lug, and lift the hand guard off the gun. Lift out the receiver. Take out the trigger housing pin. Pull back on the trigger assembly, and remove it from the receiver. Remove the recoil spring guide, and remove its spring (don't let it get away!). Remove the slide. Remove the bolt.

He would have to be quick. Park his car out of sight of road, load the clip into the carbine, and wait by the landing. No one would see him behind the steel building. As soon as anyone opened the door for any reason, Grover would force his way in with the M1 and grab Becky.

I don't want to kill anybody, but so help me God, if either one of those hippie bums even moves, especially that JJ, he's going to hell with a steel-jacketed slug through the chest.

No, he was lying to himself. He *did* want to kill somebody. He relished the thought. He'd be arrested and probably go to jail, but he had to do it. How could a jury of Christians convict him?

Settle down now. Reassembly: Put the bolt back into the receiver. Reattach the slide. Put the spring back into the hole (don't lose it!). Replace the—

Grover turned onto Bluebonnet Lane and slowed down, puzzled. Something was wrong. There were two police cars, one parked right in front of his house. An officer was standing in the neighbor's yard, talking to a woman he had seen but didn't know. He pulled into his driveway.

As he got out of his car, an officer approached. "Excuse me. Mr. Paulson?"

"Yes, sir. What's the problem?"

"We've been trying to reach you at your work. Mrs. Paulson has taken a neighbor's car, and she hasn't returned."

"What?" said Grover. "Why would she take a car?"

"We don't know exactly," said the officer. "She told this lady she needed to take her son to a doctor."

"That makes no sense," said Grover. "Peter was hurt a few weeks ago, but he's healed now. He doesn't need a doctor."

"That's what the young woman who works for Mrs. Paulson told us. We believe your wife fled to avoid being served with a warrant. She took the two children with her. Your neighbor said she was acting strangely. We put out a citywide bulletin with a description of her and the car, but she hasn't been spotted."

"You came to serve a warrant?" said Grover. "I know nothing about this."

"An officer told her she would have to register the kids in a public school or face charges, and that's when she fled. We were hoping you'd have some idea where she went."

"Oh, Lord Jesus!" said Grover. "No, I don't know where she'd go."

"Obviously, we're concerned about her and the safety of the children," said the officer. "If you have an idea where she might be, we need to know."

"Holly wouldn't go anywhere without talking to me. A warrant? This is crazy."

"Do you think she's been behaving strangely?" asked the officer.

"No," said Grover. "She's been talking to herself a lot, but she always has. She would not have just run away with the kids. It's impossible, absolutely impossible."

"Why do you think it's impossible?"

"Because I would have seen it coming," said Grover. "And I did not see it coming."

CHAPTER 38

A Break Is Imminent

Harold ran three full takes of "Earth Is Crying." The band was tepid and hesitant. The strings were uncertain, and JJ Johns didn't have his usual charge-into-the-fray vocal chops. His guitar was dragging the tempo, and he muffed a couple of lyrics. On the fourth take, they played a little better, but JJ's voice broke during the second chorus. He stopped singing and unstrapped his guitar.

"I can't do it, man," he said. "My playing is bad, and my voice is shit. I need a few minutes."

"Everybody take ten," said Harold.

Some of the musicians sat where they were, and a few got up and stretched. Brandon Bibb pulled out a drum key and started tweaking one of the small toms.

JJ headed for the back door.

"The clock is running," said Harold. "I don't need to remind you."

"I know. I'm sorry," said JJ. "I just gotta feel the breeze for second."

He walked out into the sunlight and down the steps to the parking lot. There was not a cloud in the sky, but the air was cool. JJ walked. Maybe he'd do a couple of laps around the building.

You're a professional, he thought. *This is exactly the kind of shit you hate when other people do it. Pull yourself together.*

Instead of pacing around the studio, JJ walked straight across the graded parking lot to the edge of the crushed caliche, where it met the desert. He hesitated a moment, then stepped out onto the white, salty hardpan. He continued in a straight line, watching the horizon. What was out there? How many miles would he have to walk to get anywhere at all? At about fifty feet, he stopped. He closed his eyes.

A couple of years ago, a friend had talked him into a one-day class on transcendental meditation. JJ never had the patience to stick with it, but he always liked the breathing part. He stood erect with his head back and breathed deeply. A slight puff of breeze ruffled his hair, and his scalp tingled.

In breath: one, two, three, four, five. Out breath: one, two, three, four, five.

He opened his eyes again. The air was so clear he could see for miles, and the longer he stood, the sharper his vision seemed. The oxygen filled his lungs and joined his blood to surge through his brain and body. It felt for a moment like he might rise up like a hot air balloon and glide over the landscape.

"Are you okay?"

It was Becky. She had followed him out. He hadn't heard her footsteps.

"I'm fine," he said. "I really am. Come here. Stand in front of me and look that way."

She complied, and he wrapped his arms around her.

"Look out there," he said. "Do you see it?" He pointed toward the horizon.

"See what?"

"Way over there. That gray, flat-top hill. I saw something glimmering. It must be . . . What? Ten, twenty miles away. I feel like I could run all the way to it."

Becky looked but saw nothing unusual. Then, for a split second, there was a tiny glint of reflected light. Then it was gone.

"Well, don't take off across the desert yet," she said. "You have a dozen people waiting for you inside."

JJ laughed, turned her around, and kissed her cheek. "I'm almost ready," he said.

"Are you still mad about what my father did? That upset everybody."

"No. It's weird, but I'm over that now. Just standing still out here and breathing clean air did it, I suppose." He took one more deep breath, throwing his shoulders back, and exhaled through his mouth. "Let's go back inside," he said.

On take five, JJ's guitar rang like a crystal bell, and his voice soared. The rest of the band wasn't quite back in the pocket, but on the sixth take, it all came together, and they had a candidate for finalist, minus background vocals and keys.

"Damn, JJ!" said Harold. "I think you found your sound, my friend."

He sensed there was still a better version out there and pressed on. After take seven, he called a five-minute break and warmed up the Fender Rhodes piano. The original plan to overdub the keys was scrapped. The piano part was too integral to leave out. There was already a microphone standing ready and a track assigned to it.

Dan Park had used up all his 16mm film, so Harold commandeered him for the engineer's spot and gave him a quick lesson on the MM-1000. When the band regrouped, Harold and his keyboard were out among the troops. Becky came into the studio and sat a few feet from JJ.

Dan put on the headphones, hit the *START* button, and pointed at the drummer. That effort was very good, with minor imperfections, but on the ninth take, they nailed it. The strings played with authority, the cymbals crashed dramatically but not too loud, the electric piano filled out the middle register, and JJ sang like a tormented angel. Harold noticed that JJ kept his eyes on Becky.

Harold called for one more take "for luck," but it wasn't any better. He asked everyone to crowd into the control room to listen. Most of them squeezed in, but a few stood outside the door. Harold turned up the monitors and played the best couple of takes. They all agreed number nine was the keeper.

Harold pronounced the gig complete and thanked the members of his ragtag orchestra one by one. He wrote checks to the bass player, the drummer, the rogue Duro cellist, and to Garrett Miller, who would take care of the Lubbock people from his end. Dan Park packed up the camera, film, tape recorder, and tape; promised to keep everyone informed on the progress of the film; and drove away to see his family in McCauly. The others drifted out one or two at a time.

Within half an hour, everyone was gone but Harold, JJ, Becky, and Lizard the bass player, who had packed up his gear but wasn't in a hurry to leave. JJ sat with Becky on the office couch, drained. Harold rewound the tape, labeled it, and boxed it. As he was turning off all the equipment, he noticed that Lizard had come into the office and was just standing there.

"Good gig, man," said Harold. "I'll keep you on my first-call list."

"Thanks," said Lizard. Then lowering his voice, he said, "Hey, I need to talk to you for a second."

"Okay, shoot," said Harold.

"Can you come in here?" said Lizard, and stepped back into the dimly lit studio. Harold followed.

"What's up?"

Lizard leaned close and gestured with his thumb. "There's a dead dude in that room back there."

Harold closed his eyes and sighed. "Ah, man."

"I know, I know," said Lizard. "I could hardly believe it myself. I was looking for the john, so I opened that little door, and I turned on the light, and there he was. I thought he was just passed out, but then I poked him, and I'm like, 'Wow, that dude is stone cold dead.' I thought I better tell you guys."

Harold lowered his voice. "Yeah. Yeah, I know. That's Allen Wallace. He died of a heart attack last night. I found him this morning."

"You didn't . . . like . . . *call* anybody?"

"Nothing we could do for him. He was dead. He doesn't have a family. If I did call the cops, they would have shut down our gig. One thing Wallace always told me: 'The gig must go on.' It's what he would have wanted."

"You're gonna just leave him there?"

"No, no. We'll call some people."

"Yeah," said Lizard. "Somebody needs to take care of that guy."

"You're right," said Harold. "He was a good man and a great sound engineer. We'll take care of him. And . . . uh . . . if you could just keep this to yourself, I'd appreciate it. Just for now."

"JJ doesn't know?"

"JJ knows, but that little lady out there doesn't."

"Oh." Lizard nodded. "Well, I guess the dude can't get any deader. If anybody asks, I'll be that fat German guy on *Hogan's Heroes*. 'I know *nothink*.' All right, I'm out of here. Call me if you need overdubs. I'll check you back in Tulsa."

"Thanks, man."

Harold set the building's thermostat as low as it would go and turned off the lights.

The recording session was over for the day. No one called the authorities about the corpse in the echo chamber. They couldn't. The song wasn't finished. They'd have to come back to the studio tomorrow. Harold called Nashville to try and cancel the Saturday session with the two backup singers, but he couldn't get ahold of either one. They would be at the Midland airport in the morning. Allen Wallace would just have to stay put.

However, a good—if incomplete—version of "Earth Is Crying" was in the can.

JJ drove the car. Becky rode in the middle, leaning against him. They dropped Harold in front of the Golden Sunset Hotel, just as they had done the night before, and the two of them went to dinner.

They had no plans for the evening, but as far as JJ was concerned, the farther they got from World Famous Best Studios, the better. At least for now.

"Should we try and find some place a little bit nice to eat?" asked JJ. "You know the city. Where do you want to go?"

"I'm not dressed for anything fancy," said Becky.

"Neither am I, but I feel like celebrating. It's done. By this time tomorrow, we'll have the song."

"Are you happy with it?" asked Becky.

"Well, yeah. Of course."

"I was just asking, because you seem on edge. Is everything okay?

"Everything is definitely okay," said JJ. "I feel bad about the fight I had with your dad. I hope you don't think I'm like that all the time. I was just afraid . . . that you'd leave, and I wouldn't see you again. So I kind of blew up at him."

"He was being a jerk," said Becky. "He's not like that either. I guess he's afraid of the same thing—losing his little girl. He can't really accept that I'm grown and will leave home for good."

They were driving Harold's station wagon down Seventh Street. JJ spotted a small steak restaurant in a low-slung building.

"We could go there. Anyplace is good if I'm with you."

"Oh, stop it," said Becky. "I'll tell you what I want. There's a cafeteria called Fonde's up on North Lee. It has perfectly acceptable food, but a dessert selection you wouldn't believe. I want some key lime pie."

"All right, Fonde's it is," said JJ.

"Just one word of warning," said Becky. "There's something there you might find upsetting."

"All right. I'm intrigued. What would I find upsetting?"

"Bennie the organist."

JJ looked over at Becky. "You mean, it has one of those old geezers who plays showtunes on a Hammond?"

"He's not that old, just . . . so enthusiastic it brings tears to your eyes. He plays the hits of yesterday and today."

JJ laughed. "I'm sure I can handle Bennie the organist. Hell, if he's any good, I'll drag him over to the studio, and we'll lay down some tracks."

"Well, I gave you fair warning," said Becky.

"I'll be sure and make some requests. I wonder if he knows 'Step Outside Our Love' by some weird group named the Blue Zephyrs?"

"I can *guarantee* he knows it," said Becky.

"I can't wait. Let's go."

BENNIE DID, IN FACT, know "Step Outside Our Love" and played it at a peppy pace in the key of C. After they'd gone through the food line, JJ insisted they sit close to the organ. JJ sang along, to the delight of Bennie and the bewilderment of most of the elderly Friday night crowd. JJ then challenged him with other hits, famous and more obscure, and Bennie knew them all.

Becky had salad and macaroni with cheese and pimentos, to save room for key lime. JJ picked chicken-fried steak with extra white gravy and soft, pale broccoli. For dessert, he ate chocolate meringue and made a show of licking his little plate while Bennie played the theme from *Shaft*.

After they had finished eating, and a small woman with a hair net had cleared the table, JJ reached over and took Becky's hand.

"Where shall we go?" he asked. "I have an idea what I'd like to do, but I'll take any suggestions."

"I have an idea, too," said Becky, "But I want to hear your idea first."

"No, no, ladies first."

"I defer to you, as a man," said Becky.

"I insist."

Becky took his other hand and leaned across the table. "Okay, then. I want to go someplace where I can kiss you as much as I want and you can kiss me back and nobody will bother us the rest of the night."

"Becky, sweet Becky who has taken my heart away, I accept your proposal."

"Suggestion."

"Your suggestion. By some incredible, once-in-a-hundred-years coincidence, that is exactly what I was going to suggest."

They sat holding hands for a couple of minutes. Bennie played "I Found That Girl" by the Jackson Five.

In her periphery, Becky could see that somebody a few tables away was looking at them. She glanced over. It was Nolan Batts, the newspaper reporter. He was dressed in a stylish vest and mod cabbie hat and sat with a thirtyish woman who seemed less interested in him than he was in her. He waved at Becky, and she waved back. Batts leaned over and said something to his date, then scooted back his chair and walked over to their table.

"Hello, Mr. Batts," said Becky. "This is my friend JJ." Nolan gave JJ a perfunctory handshake, then turned his full attention to Becky.

"I was hoping I'd see you at some point," said Batts. "It's regarding that conversation you and I had a couple of weeks ago."

"About the Helen Orlena case?"

"That's it," said Batts. "There have been some developments, if you're still interested."

"I had to drop the film idea for now," said Becky, "But I'm always curious."

"This is *not* for attribution, as they say," said Batts, "but I have some hard intelligence from one of my contacts in Duro PD." He leaned close to Becky's ear and said something quietly, but the music from Bennie's tonewheel drowned it out.

"I'm sorry, what?" said Becky.

"I said there's a break in the case," said Betts, louder. "I have it on good authority that an arrest is imminent."

"Arrest?" said JJ. "Who's getting arrested?"

Batts held up is hand. "Can't tell you. This is strictly on the q.t., but it's going to happen."

"When?" asked Becky.

"Imminently," said Batts. "That's all I can say. Hey, it's good to see you again. I need to get back to my lady. It was nice to meet you, Jay." He returned to his seat and cast a sly look back at Becky.

"Is this that murder case you were telling me about?" asked JJ. "Back before you settled for me instead?"

"That's the one," said Becky.

When they rose to leave, JJ looked for a tip jar near the organ, but there wasn't one.

Late in the night, Becky got up to wash herself. The light was dim in the hotel room, but JJ could see her by a narrow shaft of light coming from a small gap in the blackout curtains.

She is so beautiful.

The soft curve of her buttocks, her sleek pale form as she walked, her narrow and somewhat boyish hips, her round and high breasts, the way her sandy blonde hair fell in soft curls on her shoulders. No makeup and no beauty products for her hair, just an earthy loveliness. He could imagine her as a strong, sexual pioneer woman. Blue-eyed Becky.

JJ got an idea. Her rose from the hotel bed and retrieved his guitar from its case. He sat on the bed with his back against the headboard, under the generic picture of a ranch house, windmill, and a small herd of grazing horses. He strummed his guitar to check the tuning, then lowered the low E string to a low D, which worked better for what he had planned.

Becky emerged from the bathroom carrying a towel but making no efforts at modesty. She grinned when she saw him sitting cross-legged on the bed, naked, holding his guitar.

"Are you going to play for me?" she asked.

"Yes, I am. A new song, in fact."

"That's exciting," said Becky. "When did you write this one?"

"Day before yesterday," said JJ. "Now, sit down."

Becky plopped herself down in front from him on the queen-sized bed. "Okay, let's hear it," she said.

JJ strummed an open chord, then put his hand way up on the seventh fret and started playing. It was "Blue-Eyed Becky," of course. He played and sang to her, dropping his voice lower than she had heard him sing before, intoning slow and mournful notes, then letting his voice rise teasingly in the chorus.

"I fell asleep to the lonely blues
But woke up to the happy news
That Blue-Eyed Becky's Tulsa-bound"

JJ stopped after the second chorus. "So . . . what do you think?"

"Did you really write that for me?" asked Becky.

"I did."

"Do you swear?" Becky said. "Because I'm sensitive about these things. When I was twelve, this boy I liked at church gave me a card with a beautiful poem on it for Valentine's Day. He said he wrote it for me, and I totally believed him. Then I found out he swiped the poem from some poet named Bret Harte. Not only that, but he gave the same poem to two other girls and swore he wrote it for them."

"Wow, that's ballsy," laughed JJ. "You got to give the guy points for audaciousness. And he did it because he wanted to impress you, even if he was keeping his options open. But you can trust me, there is no other Becky. The song is for you and only you."

"Well, I like it," said Becky, and leaned forward to kiss JJ on the cheek. She then turned around and sat beside him with her back against the headboard. "Well, I hope you don't ever put it on a record, even though it's a great song. I don't want the other Beckys, Bekkas, and Rebekahs of the world fantasizing that the song is for them."

"Honesty time," said JJ. "I already recorded it. At least a demo. And, no, I do not promise not to put it on an album. I don't want love standing in the way of a gold record. But the song will always be yours."

Becky put her arm around his shoulders. "So you love me, Jerome Johnson?"

"I do love you, Rebekah Paulson, and I plan to keep loving you."

JJ strummed a minor chord, then played more songs for her. Not romantic ballads but slow, quiet versions of '60s pop songs: "Johnny Angel," "Let Me In," "I Will Follow Him." After a while, she began to breathe deeply and evenly. He stopped playing and ever so carefully got up to put away the guitar. He slipped back into bed, gently eased her body over beside him, and covered them both with the blankets. She stirred but didn't wake. He looked at the hotel clock: 3:40 a.m. He'd better get some sleep, because he expected that Harold would be pounding on the door by eight o'clock. He snuggled into the spoon position and put a hand on her breast.

Honesty time? What would she think of him when she found out what they had done with that poor man? Despite the intoxication of new love, JJ's thoughts kept returning to Allen Wallace, who, at that moment, lay in the cold echo chamber, alone, unattended, and unmourned.

CHAPTER 39

An Even Louder Surveillance

David Bellamy's typical Saturday, when the weather was bearable, involved rising before dawn, eating a light, high-fiber breakfast, stretching for ten minutes on the living room floor, then putting on his track shoes and going for a long run. When it was too cold or windy, he opted for a mile swim at the YMCA, but he always preferred running. Usually, he ran at least ten miles—and more often fifteen. Today, he didn't do any of that, except the high-fiber part. Outside, the Mercury would be waiting for him.

He'd known this day was coming since the last time they'd interviewed him, a year and four months ago. *We're going to want to talk to you again,* Sergeant Correa had said, though he didn't say when that might be. They asked him to provide a blood sample, and he had done so, but it unnerved him. From that day, Bellamy rehearsed what he would say when they found her. And every morning, he opened the paper and read the local news section, then the state section, and finally the police blotter, which carried the minutia of local crime. *(A Ferris County man was charged with indecent exposure and public intoxication Friday.)* There was not one word about Helen Orlena. Nothing.

Helen's family reported her missing. A few weeks later, her car was found in the small town of Stanton, parked at a flea market named Traders' Paradise, where it had sat unnoticed. Though it had a fine layer of dust from the parking lot, it appeared to have been washed at one point and was spotlessly clean on the inside. The case was now considered a murder investigation. After a few weeks, there was nothing more. Bellamy was baffled. He waited for the call, but none ever came. What did the cops know that they weren't saying?

It would be a nice relief to go for a long run this morning. The weather was mild and clear, with little wind. But all he could think about was how they'd probably pick him up on the road, and he'd end up being questioned downtown in nothing but shorts and running shoes. If he didn't budge from his apartment, maybe they'd get bored and leave him alone. After all, they hadn't bothered him after school yesterday.

As it turned out, they didn't get bored. There was a knock on the door, struck with the force of someone who wanted his attention, right now. Bellamy made sure his hair looked presentable, then opened the door. There were two uniformed cops.

"Are you David Bellamy?" asked one.

"Yes, sir."

"We need you to come with us, please."

"Am I under arrest?"

"No sir, not if you come with us voluntarily."

Delaying tactics would be pointless, and he didn't want to leave in handcuffs.

"Okay," he said.

HAROLD BANGED ON THE DOOR of JJ's room before eight o'clock. When there was no immediate response, he knocked again. A bleary JJ Johns cracked open the door a few inches.

Ah hah! So he did spend the night with the church girl.

"It'll take me a little bit, man," said JJ. "I had a late night."

"I'll bet you did," said Harold. "Go ahead and take your time. I thought I'd drive to the airport to pick up Lynne and Shelly."

"Lynne and . . .?"

"The singers," said Harold. "Their flight from Nashville gets in at 9:30. I'll just pick them up and then come back for you. Get a little more rest, and have some breakfast. I should be back here a little after ten-thirty."

"All right," said JJ. He shut the door.

JJ felt like he had run a marathon. It took him some time to wake up, but a shower put some life back into him. Three minutes into it, the bathroom door opened, the shower curtain was pulled aside, and Becky stepped into the shower tub with him. Delighted, he planted a deep kiss on her mouth as warm water ran down over both of them.

"Are you going to wash your hair?" asked Becky.

"I don't know," said JJ. "I could. I don't wash it very often, because it gets all fly-away."

"It needs washing," said Becky. "Let me wash it for you." They both sat down in the tub, Becky behind him. As warm water slowly rose in the tub, Becky lathered his long hair, working the shampoo in from the top down, rinsed it out, then washed it again. She worked in most of the small bottle of hotel conditioner, then rinsed it a final time.

"You're getting split ends," she said. "You should trim it back a couple of inches."

"It's also falling out in front," said JJ. "Split ends are the least of my worries."

"You have great hair. Most guys with long hair don't bother to keep it nice. You should. You're a star."

After a lazy breakfast at the Golden Sunset's restaurant, they both returned to the room and waited. JJ wondered if he should check out of the hotel but figured that was Harold's call.

It was nearly eleven when the producer returned from the airport. When they got out to the car, there was only one passenger, a tall young Black woman with an Afro.

"This is Shelly Dewalter," said Harold. "Shelly, this is JJ Johns and . . . his friend Becky."

"Hello," said Shelly.

"Hi," said Becky.

"Hi," said JJ. "Where's . . .?"

"Lynne didn't make the flight, apparently," said Harold. "Who knows why?"

"She's having man problems at the moment," said Shelly. "But she usually doesn't miss gigs, even when they're out of town."

"We'll have to make do," said Harold.

"Let's get on it," said Shelly. "I'm flying out of here tonight."

Harold managed to put the back seat of the station wagon up, something he hadn't even tried since the previous decade. It was sticky and stubborn, but with JJ pushing from the other side, they got it snapped into position. Bits of paper, foil, and ancient dried fast foot clung to the seat. Harold brushed off the seat with his hand, and JJ and Becky slid in for the short ride across Duro.

When they arrived at the studio, Becky saw that Allen Wallace's car still sat where they had left it the day before.

"Has anybody checked on him?" asked Becky.

"Who?" said Shelly.

"Mr. Wallace. The owner of the studio."

"I've heard of him," said Shelly, "but we've never met. Will he be here today?"

"He's sick at home," said Harold. "I doubt we'll be seeing him."

"Somebody should go by his house and check," said Becky. "He doesn't have a family. We should at least call his house."

JJ and Harold didn't say anything. Harold unlocked the steel door, and they all went inside the dark, quiet studio.

"Je-SUS, it's cold in here," said Shelly.

"I'm sorry. I'll turn off the air," said Harold. "We need it off so we can record."

"I'm glad I brought a jacket," said Shelly. "I thought I was getting a warm-weather break from Nashville. This place is a tomb."

Harold switched on the equipment in the control room, cued up the tape, then set up a standing microphone out in the middle of the big room. Without the large, awkward band, the space seemed enormous.

"Let's listen to the song," said Harold. They all gathered in front of the small monitors. Just as Harold started to hit *PLAY*, the office phone rang. JJ and Harold looked at each other.

"Maybe we shouldn't answer that," said JJ.

"I don't know," said Harold.

"Are you kidding? Answer it!" said Becky. "It might be Mr. Wallace."

Harold hesitated, then went into the office quickly and picked up the phone.

"Best Studios," he said. He listened. "What's the name again? Murphy?… Uh, tomorrow? I'm not sure. Hey, listen, I'm just helping out today. Mr. Wallace is . . . under the weather.… Yes, I'm saying he's not in today.… I don't know.… No, really, Mr. Murphy. I just can't say.… I know, but you'll have to take it up with him when he gets well.… Okay, but please call first.… Yeah, sure." He hung up.

Harold returned to the control room. "Weird," he said. "That was a guy from a group called the Jingleaires. I think that's what he said. He told me they were supposed to record a thirty-second radio commercial. I don't know anything about it."

He turned to the console. "All right, Miss Shelly, you have the charts, but it should be clear when you come in. Second verse background, chorus, also background, then start tearing it up in the third verse and the bridge. Of course, where we really want you to shine is the final chorus."

He played the song, and the singer followed along on her sheet music.

"I can do this," said Shelly when the song ended. "Let's do a couple of warmup takes. Maybe we'll get something you can use."

"You know," said Harold, "since we don't have the second voice, maybe you could do the higher part on another track."

Shelly looked over the charts again. "This is outside my range," she said. "Lynne has the high voice. I could try, but I don't want to disappoint you."

Harold offered her a set of headphones, and she took her place close to the microphone. After a moment, she said, "Wait a second," and raised the microphone stand a few inches. "I sing better when I'm looking up," she said. Harold returned to the control room.

The phone in the office rang again.

"I'll handle it," said JJ and jumped up.

"Just tell them we're closed for the weekend," said Harold, "then take the damn phone off the hook."

JJ went into the office and closed the door behind him. In a few moments, he came back out.

"Becky!" he said. "It's for you. It's your dad."

Harold stayed behind to record Shelly Dewalter while JJ drove Becky home.

"It makes no sense!" said Becky. "Why did she have to take Peter and Martha?"

"Maybe she just couldn't be separated from them," said JJ. "She wouldn't hurt them, would she?"

"Not in a million years," said Becky. "She doted on both of them, especially Peter. She'd throw herself in front of a bus to save those kids. That's why it makes no sense that she'd just leave with them. Of course, she was afraid of what might happen to them in public school, but how far does she think she'll get just running away?"

"Maybe she went to a hotel, just to give herself time to think."

"But she doesn't have any money, except the grocery allowance my dad gives her. It's just crazy."

"I guess your dad is pretty upset," said JJ.

"I've never heard him like that in my life. I'm afraid he's falling apart, like he did yesterday at the studio, but worse."

"Sounds like it's the idea of losing his kids that makes him crazy," said JJ. "I suppose that's why he got so pissed off at me, because he thought I was taking you away."

"It's more than that," said Becky. "It's the idea that if he loses control of anything, it becomes part of the world, and then it's gone, destroyed."

"But . . . *everything* is part of the world, including him."

"He doesn't see it that way," said Becky. "To him, everything and everyone is on one side or the other. They're either with God, waiting for the rapture, or they're part of the world, which is run by the Devil. He's drilled that into me since I can remember."

Becky clenched her fist and chewed at her knuckle. "Oh please, oh please! Don't let her hurt them . . . or hurt herself."

They turned down Bluebonnet Lane. One police car was in front of the Paulson house. JJ pulled the station wagon up behind it.

"You can just drop me off," said Becky.

"I'd like to come in for a second, if it's okay," said JJ.

"Are you sure? I really don't want . . . anything to happen."

"No, it'll be okay," said JJ. "I just need to come in for a split second."

Inside, in the living room, Grover sat leaning forward on the big couch, while a rotund, bald cop sat in a dining chair across from him.

"I understand, sir," said the officer, "but we still need to treat it as a stolen car."

"It's not stolen," said Grover. "She borrowed it. She never stole anything in her life."

"Yes, sir, but if we put it on the stolen car registry, it will go out to the state police as well as the county, and we'll have more eyes looking for it."

Grover looked up as Becky came in. He stood up and came toward her.

"Rebekah!" he said. "Why didn't I see it? I should have known something was wrong. I just didn't see it."

Becky hugged her father. "I didn't see it coming, either, father. I'm sure she's just . . . upset and confused, and she'll be back soon. I know she will."

"It's been twenty-four hours," said Grover. "Nobody's seen her. The police are checking all the motels, but they haven't found the car. It just isn't like her to do something without talking to me about it. I don't get it. I just don't get it."

Grover spotted JJ standing by the door. Becky clenched her teeth, waiting for an eruption. But, instead, her father's tone was subdued.

"Do you want something?"

"I just wanted to . . . say I'm really sorry about what happened yesterday," said JJ. "That's all. I was an ass- . . . I mean, I was a jerk, and I don't like . . . being that way. I just needed to come in and say that."

"Okay, then, you've said it," said Grover. "Now please leave. Let me be with my daughter."

"Yeah, of course," said JJ. "I really hope everything turns out with your wife and the kids. I'll go now. Becky, call me at the studio later, okay?"

"Okay."

Becky exhaled. JJ Johns, the only long-haired man who had ever been in the Paulson house, left quietly.

The police officer stood up and folded his notebook. "Mr. Paulson, we'll keep you apprised of anything we find out. Meanwhile, if you hear from her or from anybody who knows anything, call us right away."

"Yeah, of course I will."

"Also, if you can think of any relatives or friends she might contact, you could call them and let them know she's missing."

"She's not close to her relatives," said Grover. "And she has no friends."

When the officer was gone, Becky sat beside her father. They were alone together for the first time in months. In his face, Becky saw doubt and confusion, alien things that did not belong. Grover stared at the wall, where there was a cheap frame print of *Christ Entering Jerusalem*. The cyan ink had faded, leaving a sickly yellow cast over the scene of Jesus on a donkey, with happy multitudes placing palm fronds in his path.

Grover put his face in his hands for a moment, then folded them under his chin and closed his eyes in a posture of prayer.

"Lord, if you were trying to get my attention, you have it," he said, his voice breaking. "I see it now. It was my fault. Please tell me what to do. I'm listening."

Becky put an arm around his shoulders. "Father, it wasn't your fault. Stop thinking that."

"But it was," he said. "You just don't know. I brought this on. I was selfish and vain. If I had just paid attention, opened my eyes, I could have seen what was happening to her. This is punishment."

"God is not punishing you!" said Becky. "This is not even about you. Neither of us saw it, because Mother kept it all to herself."

"No, you're wrong," said Grover. "It was me. Your mother carried a huge burden all by herself, because I was busy thinking horrible thoughts. Sinful thoughts."

"It wasn't like that . . ."

He turned to face her. His eyes were bloodshot. "You really don't know, Rebekah. I was going to do something terrible. I wanted to commit murder. I was going to do it. He knew. It turns out there are consequences."

CHAPTER 40

Too Many Holes

By the time JJ got back to Best Studios, Harold and Shelly the backup singer were listening to vocal takes in the control room.

"JJ, you have a great song," said Shelly. "I confess I had my doubts when I read the charts. So many rock songs are using orchestras these days it's getting to be a gimmick. But this one works. I really like it."

"Thanks," said JJ. "So, Harold, are you happy?"

"Happy as I ever am. At some point, we just have to declare victory and have a parade."

"I could do the first chorus better," said Shelly. "Let me have another shot at it."

"All right," said Harold. "I thought it sounded great, but we can do it again. Just the chorus?"

"Let's just do the whole thing," said Shelly. "You have the tracks, right?"

"Plenty," said Harold.

He rewound the tape while the singer took her place in the studio. After one false start where Shelly accidentally bumped the microphone, they ran a full take. She listened to the whole song one more time in the control room, then said she was satisfied.

"Well, folks, I think we're done," said Harold.

"If we just had the timpani," said JJ. "That was the plan from the beginning."

"That's just not in the cards," said Harold. "If you insist, we can try to add the kettle drums later when we get back home. We always have options."

JJ sat quietly, thinking.

"Your song is *done*, man," said Harold. "And it's a good song. In a few weeks, you're gonna hear it on the radio. Right now, it's time to . . . take care of some things that need taking care of. You know . . . so we can go back to Oklahoma . . . *soon.*"

"You're right," said JJ. "We need to wrap up the . . . uh . . . loose ends. And take Miss Shelly back to the airport."

"She says she has a friend who can take her," said Harold.

"You do?" asked JJ. "You know somebody in Duro?"

"Dr. Louis P. Creech," said Shelly. "He was my mentor when I first started singing gospel. He's mostly retired, but he has a little church in Odessa. I called him, and he's coming in a little while to pick me up for a late lunch. He'll get me back to the airport. He knows Allen Wallace, too."

"All right," said JJ. "Too bad Mr. Wallace couldn't be here."

"So are we done?" asked Harold. "It's your decision, man. If you say 'Earth Is Crying' is now a song, then it's a song. Personally, I think it is. But I have to hear it from you."

"Me too," said Shelly. "Though I don't get a vote."

JJ stood and walked to the door of the big studio, as if he were listening for something. Suddenly, he shouted "Boom BAH!" and listened to the resonance.

"You want to record a guide for the kettles, don't you," said Harold.

JJ turned around. "Yeah. I do. I need some idea what they'll sound like. Set me up. I can do it in one." He donned the headphones. Harold ran the tape back to the bridge, started playback, hit RECORD, and pointed at JJ.

As the sound of string instruments swelled in his head, JJ took a deep breath.

Boom-BAH! Boom bah, boom bah BOOM!

When the final chorus came up, he did it again.

Boom boom BOOM bah-BOOM!

Harold ran the tape back while JJ returned to the control room. "Let me hear it," he said.

"Dry?"

"No, give it some echo."

HAROLD WROTE A CHECK to Shelly Dewalter, and she left with her old friend the singing preacher, a tall and imposing man wearing a bow tie. Dr. Creech was disappointed that Allen Wallace wasn't at the studio.

With the backup singer gone, JJ and Harold had to face reality. They sat in the studio office, talking quietly, as if the man in the other room might overhear.

"We gotta make the call," said JJ. "The longer we wait, the worse it gets."

"They'll put us in jail," said Harold.

"Why? We didn't kill him."

"We didn't report it. That man's been dead since Thursday night. As soon as the cops see him, they'll know we knew about it."

"They might suspect we knew," said JJ, "but how could they prove it? We can just do what we planned all along. We'll say we didn't hear from him for a day, then suddenly we had to go into the echo chamber for some reason and . . . there he was."

"His car is going to be a problem," said Harold. "And now we can't move it. Everybody has seen it sitting there for two days."

"Well, we can't tell them the truth," said JJ. "We just have to stick with our story. We found him in there on the floor."

"If they start questioning anybody in the band, we're screwed," said Harold. "We told everybody we drove him home. And then there's Lizard. What if they ask *him*."

JJ shook his head. "We have to face the music on this one, man. Even if they bring charges, it wasn't murder. How bad could it be?"

"Man, we're long-haired hippie strangers in this town," said Harold. "You may think you're famous, but I guarantee that won't win you any friends in redneck land. They'll throw everything in the book at us. I mean like abuse of a corpse or covering up a crime or whatever. It could be really, really bad. We'll have to get lawyers. And they'll seize your tape, man. We might not get out of here for six months."

JJ leaned back on the couch and shut his eyes. "Maybe we *should* call a lawyer. Today. Ask him what we should do. Do you know any lawyers in Tulsa?"

"Just a couple of copyright guys," said Harold.

Harold got up from his chair and left the office. After a moment, JJ followed. Harold turned on the light in the little studio, then opened the door to the echo chamber.

"At least he doesn't smell," said Harold.

"Thank God for Texas air conditioning."

Allen Wallace lay exactly where they had left him. Lizard had picked up the tape from the floor and put it back on the shelf.

"I have an idea," said Harold. "Help me find his keys."

AFTER MUCH DISCUSSION and persuasion and realizing how few choices they really had, the musician and the producer agreed on a plan. They would take Allen Wallace home, put him in his own bed. Then, at least, their lie might hold water.

The lie went like this: Thursday morning, Wallace had complained of feeling ill. He was too unwell to drive, so Harold had given him a ride home. On Friday, Harold had spoken to Wallace on the phone, who said he wanted to rest the entire weekend. They had spent the whole day recording. Saturday, they did some follow-up recording, tried to call Wallace during the day, but he didn't answer. Weren't they concerned? Of course, they were, but they were so caught up in the creative musical process, they didn't think about checking on him. Yep, that's how it went.

Sunday morning, they would drive to his house and knock on his door and call the police for a welfare check when he didn't answer. Tragically, he would be discovered in his bed, passed away.

Would it work? The story had more holes than a county road in Oklahoma, but it was all they had.

JJ was sitting in the control room, with a red kaftan wrapped around his shoulders. With the thermostat back to its lowest setting, the colorful knitted decoration was the closest thing to a blanket he could find.

"I need to go outside and warm up," said JJ.

"We can't go outside!" said Harold. "Not while it's daylight. We can't be seen lurking around the premises. Remember, we're supposed to be in here recording all day. Be patient. We have to wait 'til it gets dark."

"Man, it's just so . . . damn . . . cold," said JJ. He glanced at his watch. 5:30 pm. "What time do you suppose the sun sets around here?"

"It will be dark by seven," said Harold. "Then we can move him."

Harold puttered around the large studio, putting microphones away in their protective cases, and wrapping up cables. He tried to understand Wallace's organizing system for the cables, which he had carefully categorized by length and gauge and hung on the control room wall. Setting the studio in order was the least he could do for the legendary recording engineer.

The kaftan-wrapped pop singer had nothing to do but huddle for warmth and blow on his hands. He wished Becky would call. There had been no word from her. The phone had rung only once, and that had been a wrong number. After a few more shivering minutes, JJ got up.

"I'm going outside," he said. "I can't take it."

"Man, I wish you wouldn't," said Harold.

"Jesus, man! I'll stay behind the building." He tossed the kaftan onto the couch and walked briskly through the outer room to the security door.

Stepping out into the warm desert air was a huge relief. The late-afternoon sun hung low in the sky, intense and red. It was quiet, except for the hum of the air conditioners. JJ stood on the concrete landing with his eyes tightly shut and let the sun bathe his face and the heat soak into his hypothermic body.

Much better! Maybe just a quick walk around the parking lot to—

JJ noticed something odd. A white sedan was parked on the south side of the building. Where did *that* come from?

"Excuse me, sir!" A woman's voice startled him. JJ squinted into the bright sun. A woman was standing at the bottom of the steps.

"Huh? Yes?"

"Hi, I'm looking for Allen Wallace. Is he here?"

"Hi . . . uh, no. No, he's not."

It was a middle-aged Black woman, wearing jeans and a light suede jacket.

"I've been trying to reach Mr. Wallace for two days," she said. "Are you sure he's not here? Isn't that his car over there?"

"Uh . . . yeah," stuttered JJ. "But he's not here. He was feeling sick, so I . . . I mean my friend . . . took him home."

"I went by his house," said the woman. "I rang the bell and knocked, and I tried to look in the windows. It's locked up tight. I don't think he's there."

"Well . . . I'm not sure then . . ."

"Can I come up?" she asked.

"Yeah, sure," said JJ.

When she reached the landing, she offered her hand. "I'm Mabel White. I'm . . . a friend of Allen's." JJ stepped aside to let Mabel through the door. "Are you working for Mr. Wallace?" she asked.

"I'm JJ Johns. We've been recording the past couple of days."

Mabel went through the outer room to the office, JJ following close behind.

"I tried calling a lot yesterday, but the phone was busy," said Mabel. "And he didn't answer his home phone. I got really worried, so I caught a flight this morning." She shivered. "My lord! It's cold in here."

"We were recording yesterday," said JJ, "so we kept the phone off the hook."

Harold came into the office carrying a roll of audio cables in each hand. His eyes popped open wide.

"This is . . . Mabel," said JJ.

"Uh . . . hi. I'm Harold Prensky. Are you his wife?"

"Ex-wife, yes. Please, if you know where he is, I need to speak to him. It's important. I'm really, really worried. He sounded so strange when I spoke to him the other night. He asked me to come out and sing backup on a project, and I told him I couldn't do it."

"We recorded a backup vocalist this morning," said Harold.

"He asked me, and I wish I'd said yes," said Mabel, "but I told him I couldn't do it. Then I changed my mind and tried to call him back but . . . Please, I just need to see him."

"I understand," said Harold, "but he hasn't come around since—"

"I called the Duro police," said Mabel. "They said if I can't find him or anybody who's seen him, then call them and they'd send an officer to his house with a locksmith. I was really hoping he was here. Do you know where he is?"

"Not really," said Harold. "Well . . . it's kind of complicated."

"Yes," said JJ.

Mabel looked from one to the other.

Harold sighed. "Mabel, you'd better sit down."

"What's going on?" she said.

"Please sit down," said Harold.

His head was turned to the side, had stiffened into that position. When they rolled him over, at Mabel's insistence, his head now pointed the other direction, and one arm stayed raised.

"You left him on the floor," said Mabel.

"We put him in the coldest room in the building," said Harold. "We couldn't think of another plan."

"Another plan might have been to call the authorities," said Mabel. "Instead, you just drag him into a dark room and go about your business."

"Yes," said Harold. "I know that sounds awful. But the song was ready to record, the musicians were here, the equipment was set up. There was nothing we could do to help him."

Mabel was kneeling on the floor next to what had been Allen Wallace. She stroked his head with its short gray hair. "Oh, Allen. You were alone your whole life. And you died alone. Why didn't I say yes? I wanted to sing on your record, I really did. I was such an idiot." After a few moments, she looked up at the two men standing over her. "So . . . *now* are you going to call somebody?"

"It's already been two days," said JJ. "I mean, it's Saturday night. Maybe we should at least wait until tomorrow. That way, when everything comes down, it will at least come down in daylight."

"What are you *talking* about?" said Mabel.

Harold spoke quietly. "He means that when we tell them what happened, we will likely get arrested for knowing he was dead and failing to report it. It would be better to have a very long day than a very long night."

Mabel looked back down at the thin, sad figure of her former companion. "It's just not right," she said. "I can't think of a worse way to treat a great man." She started to stand up stiffly, and JJ gave a hand to help her. "Thank you," she said.

They all went back into Allen Wallace's office, not bothering to close the door to the echo chamber. Mabel sat on the couch, back straight and knees together, hands folded in her lap.

"Maybe we should lock this place up and go get some coffee," offered JJ. "You can tell us about his life. I'd really like to hear about him. I didn't know him."

Mabel looked up. "He was a man who was never really happy," she said. "Except when he made records. That was the one time I saw real joy in his eyes, when he got a really great take. Everybody knew when that happened, because then he lit up like a child at Christmas. I wish I could have seen it one more time." She put her head down and gasped. Then she began to sob.

Harold found a box of tissues in the desk and offered her one. She dabbed her eyes. "I could have come," she said. "All I had was a stupid throwaway gig I could have easily skipped. It was really sweet of him to ask me to come sing. Maybe he wanted to try and get us back together. I guess I'll never know. As soon as I told him no, I regretted it. Why did I do that?"

JJ sat in one of the office chairs, and Harold stood by, waiting. Mabel got another tissue and blew her nose.

"Would you like to sing on the record?" asked Harold. "There are a couple of spare tracks, and there's a part we couldn't get anybody to sing. I think that's the one Allen intended for you."

Mabel looked up curiously, dabbing her eyes. "Do you have the charts?"

"Sure." Harold fumbled around in his briefcase and produced several sheets of staff paper. "'Vocal 2 B,'" he said, and handed her the sheet music. Mabel wiped her eyes and looked over the pages for a couple of minutes. Then she hummed the tune quietly under her breath.

"I could do this," she said.

"Pitch not too high for you?"

"No . . . no, it's good. It's just about perfect," said Mabel.

"Let's listen to the song, then," said Harold.

CHAPTER 41

The Salt of the King

Elsa Patel drove her pickup truck out Highway 652 while her son Carlo sulked in the passenger seat.

"You said it was close to a bridge?" asked Elsa.

"A couple of miles past," said Carlo. "There's this marker on the side of the road."

"What kind of marker?"

"You know, the kind that says, *Boring historic stuff happened here a long time ago*. A metal sign."

Carlo was still peeved about the brow-beating that had forced him to give up his diamond ring. Ever since he found it sitting on top of that concrete post out in the desert, he had fantasized about bigger, faster dirt bikes. If he had managed to take the ring to a jewelry store in Duro or Odessa, then maybe he could have sold it for cash, and nobody in Autry would have been the wiser.

His mom wouldn't have found out if it wasn't for Ken and his big mouth. Ken just *had* to tell his little sister about the mysterious ring his friend had found, who told their mother, who called Carlo's mother, leading to the confrontation and a reluctant forking-over. Everybody acted like he'd stolen it. He hated that. Whatever happened to finders keepers? There were rules in the world, and that was one of the most basic.

Elsa was understandably suspicious. Expensive rings don't just get left out in the middle of nowhere. She insisted that Carlo show her where'd he'd found it, so on Saturday, Elsa drove out east of town to see for herself.

After many miles, they crossed a bridge over a deep dry wash. There wasn't much of anything out here, much less a historical marker or a monument.

"Are you sure it's this far?" asked Elsa.

"Yeah," said Carlo. "We rode a long way."

Elsa wondered if her son might be giving her the runaround to avoid losing his treasure. She drove on.

Up ahead, on the left side of the road, a blue car was parked. As they got closer, Carlo pointed.

"It's right up there. That's the marker I told you about."

The car, a big coupe with a long nose and smooth sloping back, was parked about forty feet from the state historical marker. Nobody was visible inside the car. Elsa pulled the truck over on the opposite side of the highway, and they both got out.

"It's out there," said Carlo. "See? That thing with the big post sticking up? The ring was on top of that."

"The very top?"

"Yep."

Elsa was hesitant to walk out there in her good shoes. There was no paved trail, though a faint path through the weeds and rocks suggested there may have been a regular trail at one time, and there were recent footprints in the dirt. Who did the blue sports car belong to? She didn't see anyone around.

"You want to go look at it?" asked Carlo.

"I suppose," said Elsa. She was curious about the odd structure. She read the marker. "Masons," she said. "That's the people your grandpa wouldn't do business with."

"Why not?"

"Because he was Catholic."

"Were they a different religion?"

"No, he just said they didn't like Catholics." Elsa studied the monument the best she could from this distance. "How did you get up there?"

"It wasn't hard," said Carlo. "Ken gave me a boost. The ring was up on the top."

"Okay, let's go see."

Carlo led the way and his mother followed, watching her step and picking her way around rocks and clustered prickly pears. When they reached the lower tier, Carlo stepped up, scrambled up to the second level and then the third. Elsa stayed on the lowest platform.

"I can't get up there in my shoes," called Elsa. "It smells bad out here. I think there's a dead animal."

Carlo, up on top, walked around to the other side of the central obelisk, then quickly returned.

"Mom! There's something weird on that side! I think it's a dead person." He jumped back down from the two higher levels to rejoin Elsa.

"Oh come on!" said Elsa. "What are you talking about?" She walked across the lower level, then rounded the corner and stopped.

It reminded her of a couple of Halloweens back, when she had helped the elementary school with its spook house. Her contribution was making a scary lady. They had taken one of her mother's out-of-date dresses and a cheap blond wig and made the scary lady out of paper-mâché and tempera paint. It was like that, except much, much worse—a grotesque parody of a human being.

"Is it real?" asked Carlo.

"I don't know," said Elsa. She tried to look but not look. There was the side of a head, with brown hair that looked like it had been brushed, and the side of a face with tight, shrunken skin clinging in radiating lines. There was hand and lower arm sticking out from the sleeve of a dress, thin finger bones visible all the way up to the wrist. A fly crawled across the hand.

"Mom, there's somebody coming."

Elsa looked back toward the highway, where her pickup and the blue car were parked. She didn't see anybody.

"No, way over there," said Carlo. He pointed out into the desert.

Carlo was right. Someone was out there, walking carefully, stepping around and over small obstacles. It was a man, about 500 feet away, approaching.

"Oh, lordy! Let's get out of here!"

The two of them hurried, Elsa disregarding the welfare of her shoes. She glanced over her shoulder toward the distant stranger. He had stopped. Was he looking their way? As they neared the pickup, Elsa glanced over at the shiny blue Javelin. She had a sudden thought: What if he came after them in that fast car? Her foot struck a rock, painfully, and she lost her shoe.

"OW!" she yelled.

Carlo had reached the truck. "Come on, Mom!"

Hopping on one foot, she replaced the damaged shoe and kept going, heart pounding in her chest. Another look back. The man out in the desert was walking, walking, moving toward them.

Carlo hopped into the passenger seat. Elsa climbed in and started the truck, which always took at least five agonizing seconds of grinding to catch. As the engine sputtered and roared, Elsa gunned the throttle and threw it into gear,

U-turned, and headed back toward Autry. The old truck accelerated with painful reluctance. She watched the highway and the blue car in the rearview mirror, waiting for it to move, to start coming after them. But it never did, and it soon disappeared behind a low rise.

The old GM pickup truck would only go sixty-three miles an hour flat out on a level road. She kept it at sixty-three.

It had taken Nicky Pomeroy most of the day to undo what had been done two years ago. After the desert sun rose, he'd had no trouble finding the spot. He had walked straight east, counting off fifty paces from the corner of the monument, but when he got there, he could still easily see the location. The turned soil was a different color from the undisturbed part, even after all this time.

He had picked the location because it was as close as he could get to the monument where the ground was still soft enough to dig and there were no jagged chunks of caliche stone. It was the shore of the lake whose waters had shimmered here thousands of years ago, and the soil was soft windblown dirt mixed with fine salt.

He'd dug very, very carefully, keeping the blade of the shovel almost parallel to the ground. Slowly, slowly, removing an inch of soil at a time, he worked patiently, rested, then worked some more, until he saw the cloth of her dress. Then, after resting again, he knelt on the ground and used his hands, carefully scooping away the loose dirt. His stomach throbbed with hunger, and his throat was parched, but he'd brought neither food nor water. There was nothing to do but keep going. It took a long, long time.

She was on her side, knees pulled up to a right angle. When enough soil had been removed to allow him purchase, he reached under her shoulder and carefully lifted her from her resting place.

Nicky had done his best to get the powdery salt off Helen's dress and out of her hair. She was locked in a permanent sitting posture, which made her easier to carry. He left her propped up on the lower tier of the monument and walked out to the pluton to prepare the ceremony.

"Everything's ready. Let's go," said Nicky. "I'm sorry you had to wait so long."

He picked her up carefully from where she sat on the old monument. Unlike the first time he carried her, she weighed almost nothing, like a bundle of dry sticks.

He'd spotted a couple of people near the monument, a woman and a kid, saw them get into an old pickup truck, and heard it roar away. Had they seen Helen? Someone might come along any time and ask what he was up to. It would be dusk soon, and then no one would see him from the road or from the monument.

He bore her with loving care. It was a long way to the rock, but the track was straight and distinct. Nicky had walked it several times. His shoes flattened the small desert flowers that had sprung up in a recent shower.

"You probably don't know this," he said. "But we are at one of the most important places on Earth." His footfalls made a steady rhythm. "Yeah, and the funny thing is that almost nobody in Texas even knows about it. *Almost* nobody."

He paused a moment to look back. The monument's spire was catching the last of the sunlight. He pressed on.

"Anyway, as I was saying, almost nobody knows about the place. It's called the Wiberg Pluton. It's a fancy name for a very simple thing. A pluton is a huge rock that sits where a volcano erupted millions of years ago. Ninety-nine percent of it is below ground. What nobody seems to remember—or maybe they never knew—is that these sorts of giant underground mountains are like antennas. They focus the energy lines that flow around the world."

She didn't seem interested, but he kept trying. There was something he needed to confess.

"So, I mentioned that almost nobody knows this," said Nicky. "But my friend Mr. Dunbar does. He's an expert on this sort of thing—one of the smartest people I've ever met. He is the official historian of the Grand Lodge in Lubbock. He has spent years writing about vortexes and the energy lines that connect them. He goes around to different lodges and other groups trying to make people appreciate this amazing thing that's right under their noses."

Nicky yawned broadly as he walked. He couldn't help it. He was so tired. Hungry, thirsty, and exhausted.

"So here's the funny part," he said. "It turns out, the Pyle Monument is not where the energy collects. They put the marker in the wrong location. They should have built it on the pluton. That's where we're going."

She probably didn't care, but at least she was listening.

"What I'm getting at is I have a confession to make. It's something really bad." He hated to say it, but he had to. "I lost your ring."

If she was surprised or angry, she didn't let it show.

"After you . . . told me you didn't want it, I blew my top and said some very mean things, and I'm really, really sorry. But I tried to make it good. I took the ring out to the monument and left it there, to absorb energy, and then figured we'd try again when things settled down between us. What I'm saying is my heart was in the right place, but it turns out the ring wasn't. There's not as much Earth energy around that monument, not nearly as much. And so I went back to find your ring, but it was gone. I don't know what happened to it. It was a really dumb thing to do."

As bad as he felt about losing the most expensive thing he'd ever bought with his own money, the ring was irrelevant now, and he knew it. Nicky didn't need her forgiveness. It was his folly to bear.

Off to the west, the brilliant sun softened into an intense red at the horizon, and, just as he reached the rock, it touched the rim of the world. He thought this was a good omen.

"Here we are," he said.

Nicky solemnly mounted the shallow rocky slope and set Helen down gently as close to the center of the smooth rocky dome as he could. By placing her in a small dip, he was able to prop her upright.

He had brought three objects to the desert with him. One was the precious copy of *Understanding Earth Energy*. It was not a sacred text, but Nicky felt it was the key to everything, and he wanted it there. The second was a small branch from a mimosa tree, one of two that grew in front of the Masonic lodge. Finally, there was the letter Helen had left him before she drowned herself. It was her last communication with him. He had read it a hundred times, and still didn't understand what she was trying to tell him.

My Dearest Nicky,

Today, I found out some news that will change everything for me, and between us. I drove out here to your lake house because I wanted to talk to you face to face, but you are not here, and perhaps that was meant to be. I will leave this letter and depart, alone, to take care of all responsibilities by myself.

I feel bad and evil that I rejected your offer so cruelly, and I don't blame you for the way you acted. I trust that someday you will think back and realize I spared you from a big mistake. I must now continue my journey alone. I hope your future is a good one and you find happiness.

I'm sorry that I had to take this drastic step.

He still choked and teared up every time he read it. So much about it bothered him. Why hadn't she signed it? Helen had a looping, florid signature that she used every chance she got. And the last line was so odd. It didn't fit with the rest of the note. At one moment, she was talking about the future, and the next saying she was ending her life. He tried to picture her writing it, deciding she would go on with her life, then changing her mind and ending it. The thought tore his heart out.

The morning he had driven out to the lake house and found Helen in the water, bobbing against the rocks by the jetty, was the worst moment of his life. And then he had made it much worse by lifting her out of the water, carrying her, heavy and dripping, to the house and drying her off. Concealing the note. No one saw his crime.

He had found and destroyed the brochures that had revealed the awfulness of what he had done. He still remembered their titles:

10 Myths about Motherhood.

The Importance of Good Nutrition: You're Eating for Two Now!

What to Expect When You're Expecting.

And another, very official looking:

Adoption in the State of Texas.

He had behaved like a murderer because he *was* one, twice over. He had killed not just Helen but his own unborn child.

Nicky had so many chances in those first few hours to set things right and face what was coming. Instead, he had called the one remaining person in the world he trusted—not for advice but to ask for help with a horrible task. Dragging his father into the plot was deeply unfair. But the plain fact was it took two people to do what was necessary. Tony Pomeroy had his own choice to make and decided to help his only son. He'd driven out to the lake and willingly made himself complicit.

If Nick had only known the truth about the Pyle Monument back when it would have mattered. Instead, he had interred her in salt, on an ancient shore. In the wrong place.

But . . . now was there still a chance to make it right?

Nicky took the mimosa branch and laid it gently in front of her. From his pocket, he took a sheet of folded paper, where he had written words copied from one of his father's books. The evening light was growing dim, but he could still see well enough to read. He spoke haltingly but loud and clear, as if he were addressing an audience.

"This evergreen . . . is an emblem of our enduring faith in the immortality of the soul. By it, we are reminded that we have an imperishable part within us, which shall survive all earthly existence and which will never, never die. Through the loving goodness of our Supreme Grand Master, we may confidently hope that, like this evergreen, our souls will hereafter flourish in eternal spring."

Nicky folded the note, sat down beside Helen on the smooth rock, still warm from the late autumn sun, and waited. It was dead quiet. Only the lightest breezes wafted across the desert, and even those died down to nothing after it became very late. There was no moon yet, but the stars were out. The desert air grew chill. Nicky had no jacket but didn't feel cold. He no longer felt hunger or thirst. He waited.

No sight visible to the human race matches the desert stars. One of Nicky's high school science teachers had tried hard to interest his students in astronomy and the awesome gift of the night sky. Few of the kids listened attentively, but Nicky did. One Saturday night in September, the teacher took a group of six boys and one girl out to the sand hills for an astronomical field trip. He brought his six-inch reflector telescope, but they didn't use it much. Mostly, they just looked up while the science teacher talked. He could name many of the stars—Antares, Vega, Arcturus—and pointed out the late-summer constellations, both the major ones and the lesser-known—Cepheus, Boötes, Hercules. But the real lesson of the night was the Milky Way. In summer, he said, Earth faces the center of the galaxy, called the galactic core. And as he talked, the core rose into the southeastern sky, like a rumpled curtain of light.

Paradoxically, the very center of the galaxy is relatively dark, the teacher said, because interstellar dust blocks out much of the visible light. But around the edges of the core shines the luminous foam of a billion suns.

Most people who lived in cities had never seen it, but Nicky had, and at this great intersection of Earth energy, he waited with his true love for the core to rise and work its power. This time of year, late fall, it would not rise until long after midnight.

"Are you cold?" he asked.

She didn't answer. It was just as well. He had nothing to cover her.

They waited together. In this place of power and deep magic, small talk was uncalled for, so they sat quietly.

When she is ready to speak, she will.

The night was timeless, but when it was very, very late, the core rose over a distant low mesa, even more vivid and intense than he had remembered. It was followed sometime later by the moon.

There came a single howl, starting high and climbing higher, ending in sharp yips that carried far in the dry air. It started again, pitched low and mournful, and as it rose again, it was joined by another voice, this one from a different direction but just as far away. Coyotes, spaced miles apart, were announcing their place in this desolate world.

For five minutes, the coyotes sang, then they stopped. Nicky waited. In the east, the stars faded, and the dark sky gradually turned to gray, then deep blue.

"I fucked it all up, didn't I?" said Nicky.

Yes, you did, said Helen. *But you weren't the only one.*

"Is there a chance you would have ever come back to me?"

No, Nicky. It was time for me to move on.

"I wanted to keep you."

I wasn't yours to keep.

"You were going to have my baby."

It wasn't yours, said Helen.

"Why did you die?"

I wanted to live, said Helen, *and to be a mother. Someone else took me.*

They didn't talk any more. Gradually, imperceptibly, night gave way to predawn. Nicky didn't want to look at her, but as dawn approached, he turned to face Helen.

She wasn't there. There was only a useless, horrible, shrunken thing that was no longer Helen. He turned his head away and wept.

Go away, Nicky, said Helen. *You don't belong here.*

She wasn't being cruel. She was telling him the truth.

Leave me here. Go away now.

CHAPTER 42

Memory Serves

"I could go for a candy bar," said Sergeant Correa. "Can I get anybody something from the machine?"

"No thanks," said Detective Lamborn.

"How about you, David?"

Bellamy had been distracted by a television on the wall out in the public area, which he could see through the glass window. He couldn't hear the sound, but the show was familiar. What was the name of the show? He looked back at the sergeant.

"What? . . . Oh . . . yes, please," said Bellamy. "A Mars bar, if they have it. I think I have a quarter." He dug into his front pocket.

"It's my treat," said Correa. "Mars bar. Got it." He left. For a brief moment, while the door was open, the sound of the TV show was audible. There was canned studio laughter. He recognized the actor, Rich Little. It was a comedy set in San Francisco, which he could tell from the frequent establishing shots: the Golden Gate Bridge, Coit Tower, rows of Victorian houses on a steep slope. But what was the name of the show?

The police were in no hurry. Didn't these men have families and lives? Past one o'clock in the morning, and the pace of the interview was as casual as ever. The questions were relentless, slow paced, and repetitive. They had been at it off and on for hours, with odd fifteen-minute breaks where they left him alone in the room with nothing to read or do. They had brought him a deli sandwich and a cup of coffee about seven o'clock, then returned to the questions, often the same ones they'd asked before. Sometimes, when Bellamy thought he had answered a question completely, with nothing more to say, the two officers would just sit quietly, leaving a conversational gap they clearly expected Bellamy to fill.

A few minutes before, Bellamy had let something slip, but it did not elicit any reaction from Correa or Lamborn. They were talking about Helen Orlena, and the detective had said, "It was my understanding the young lady was prone to personal drama, not just on stage. Would you say that's accurate?"

"Of course," said Bellamy. "She was like a lot of teenagers. Everything was about her and how the world affected her."

No response. So Bellamy kept talking.

"For instance, most people, when they disagree with you, they'd say, 'You're wrong,' or even 'That's nuts.' Helen would say something like, 'That is the most outrageous statement that has ever been uttered.' She was all drama."

No response. Waiting.

"Even the note she left was melodramatic."

Waiting.

"If memory serves."

Correa wrote something down, then asked some unrelated questions about his experiences as a high school teacher, which led to further digressions and long pauses. Something about their response bothered Bellamy. Had he said something wrong? Now that he thought about it, he wasn't sure the news had reported the contents of Helen's note.

Correa took a very long time. Bellamy kept glancing up at the TV, where that old, discontinued show was playing. Didn't television stations sign off for the night anymore? They used to end the broadcast day with an American eagle superimposed over a flying flag while the national anthem played. Pretty soon, TV would be twenty-four hours a day. No morning sign-on and no test pattern. The world was becoming nonstop.

When Correa returned and the door opened for a second, Bellamy suddenly remembered. The show was *Love on a Rooftop*. The comedy had only played a season or two, but Bellamy had liked it. It was funny how his subconscious brain was still trying to find the answer to a pointless question even after he quit thinking about it.

The Mars bar plopped on the table in front of him. Bellamy unwrapped it and took a bite.

"Sorry that took so long," said Sergeant Correa. "I got sidetracked. Let's get back to something you said earlier. You describe the note the young girl left as being . . . what was the word you used?"

"Melodramatic."

"That's it," said Correa. "What about it did you find melodramatic?"

"Ummm . . . I don't remember now. Something about 'The world will be a better place without me,' or something similar. It's been a long time."

Long pause. Correa jotted some notes, while the older detective slouched, resting his chin in his hand. The sergeant finished his Milky Way and crumbled up the wrapper. He paused for a few seconds before leaning forward and looking straight into Bellamy's eyes.

"David, where is Helen Orlena?"

"I wouldn't know."

Lamborn spoke for the first time in several minutes. "Why wouldn't you know?"

"Because I wasn't there when she killed herself."

"So in your view, she's dead," said Lamborn. "Why do you think she committed suicide instead of being abducted and murdered? Or just leaving town on a bus and not telling anyone?"

"Because she left a note."

"Then why was her car found clean in Stanton?" said Correa.

"I don't know. Maybe somebody stole the car *after* she drowned. I've always assumed it was completely unrelated. I don't know."

"And you think a thief might have stolen her car, washed it, then left it in a small-town parking lot?"

"I have no idea."

"And why do you say she drowned?" asked Lamborn. "There isn't a body of water within fifty miles of Stanton."

"I meant . . . died. I didn't mean to say drowned."

Correa wrote some more, then sat quietly. It occurred to Bellamy that maybe he had said too much. Finally, the sergeant stood up and stretched, then shook his head and yawned. It was the first sign of fatigue he had shown. "Whoa! Long day," he said. "We've made some progress today. I think we can continue this discussion later. What do you think, Bob?"

"Yeah, we should call it a night," said Lamborn.

The two officers gathered their notes and papers. Bellamy rubbed his face and twisted his head to try and pop his neck, something he always did before a long run. He hoped he could manage a good night's sleep. Maybe he could still go running in the morning or take a swim at least.

"Oh, I have just one thing I'm confused about," said Correa. "You know when I mentioned the car being cleaned, I didn't just mean it had been washed and vacuumed. That was in the newspapers. When I was grabbing the candy bars, I went back and double-checked the case notes to make sure. There was only one piece of paper found inside the car."

"I know. I read that too," said Bellamy.

"It was not a suicide note."

"It . . . maybe I'm mistaken . . . but I'm pretty sure the newspaper said there was a suicide note, written by Helen."

"David, there was no note in the car, suicide or otherwise," said Correa. "The news stories said nothing about that."

"Well, I suppose . . . I could be thinking about something else. I'm so tired. I can't even think straight."

"Here's another fact that never got mentioned in the news," said Correa. "The car may have been cleaned, but it's impossible to get the interior of a car completely clean. Tests have gotten very, very sensitive. We found small remnants of blood on the carpet. Two different blood types. One of them matched Helen Orlena."

"I suppose the other one matched me," said Bellamy. "I have B-positive blood. It's not uncommon. I was completely willing to let you have a sample when you asked. I cooperated from the beginning."

"David, where is Helen Orlena?"

"I don't know!" Bellamy said. The two detectives waited. Bellamy looked at the polished tabletop, where the overhead lights reflected in parallel rows. A minute of silence, then another minute. Bellamy sighed. "I don't know where she is now, but I know where she was."

Wake up!

Holly smelled gas and sat up suddenly, disoriented. Have to check the stove!

But where was she? She had been lying on her right side. She was in a car, parked somewhere. What had happened? Then she remembered. This was Jean's car, which Holly had taken and never returned. Holly felt bad about that, but it was the least of her sins.

Wake up, now. It's almost morning.

The sky was cloudless, blue-gray. The stars had mostly faded, but a brilliant Venus shone over the lake, reflecting in the water.

"I don't know this place," she said. She had arrived after dark the night before, after the road stopped, here between two small, empty houses.

You're at the lake. You need to get moving soon.

Someone stirred in the back seat. It was Peter. "Mother, when are we gonna go home?" He yawned.

"We'll be going home soon," said Holly. "Now lie back down and sleep."

"I need to tinkle," said Peter.

"Just hold it. We'll be going home in a little while."

"But I need to tinkle real bad," whined Peter.

"Then get out of the car and go."

"Where's the bathroom?"

"There's no bathroom," said Holly. "Just go tinkle right there, by that tree. Nobody will see you."

Peter hesitated, then opened the back door and climbed out. Holly could see his outline as he stumbled over to a row of trees and stood facing one of them.

"I smelled stove gas," said Holly.

No. There is no gas. You dreamed it.

Holly rolled the window down and sniffed. There was only the smell of lake water, hardwood trees, and the sour odor of decaying plant matter. A soft morning breeze blew off the water, pleasant and cool. Holly shut her eyes and let the breeze tickle her face.

Peter returned to the station wagon and opened the door, which squeaked. He got back onto the broad bench seat and pulled the door shut with a *THUNK*. Martha sat up, rubbing her face.

"Mother, what day is it?" she asked.

"It's Sunday."

"Are we going to church?"

"Not today," said Holly. "Today, we're going home."

Lake Lenorah supplied drinking water to the eastern third of Duro, as well as smaller communities in the surrounding counties. The lake was created by damming the Upper Colorado River in 1952. Over the next few years, impounded water gradually flooded a series of dry valleys until the lake resembled a squid, with tendrils extending north, west, and southwest. Each of these had dozens of smaller coves and horseshoes, so that the devious shoreline eventually extended over 200 miles.

The principal purpose of the lake was agricultural and drinking water, but regular yearly infusions of walleye, catfish, bluegill, and largemouth bass fingerlings had spawned recreational fishing and boating. Several small vacation resorts grew on the larger arms of the squid, with cabins, docks, and boat ramps. In colder years, when lakes to the north froze over, clamorous flocks of mallards arrived, and Lenorah became a hunting resort. This fall, with a hard winter predicted, there was hope of a good duck season.

Just south of the dam were two recreational areas. The larger one, uncreatively named Lakeshore, was more accessible from the highway. It had several rustic cabins for rent, along with two public boat ramps. The smaller, called Thomas Village, was private and sat more secluded on the other side of a sandy peninsula. It featured larger, better accommodated cabins and private docks.

Tony Pomeroy had bought one of these in 1962. He didn't make it out very often these days. The house was closed up tight, and his Blue Star outboard fiberglass boat sat high and dry on a trailer, protected by a canvas cover. It was between this house and the next one farther down the shore that Holly had parked Jean's purloined Ford.

From this vantage point, the road that hugged the south side of the lake was clearly visible. As the sky grew lighter, the sound of chirping rose as birds became active. There were migrants—such as warblers and flycatchers—and regular residents—herons and egrets, hawks and vultures, and smaller songbirds like swifts and finches.

Holly needed to stretch. She opened the car door and turned to place her feet on the ground. She was barefoot, and the gravel hurt her feet. The shoes were in the car somewhere, down on the floor or under the seat, but she couldn't find them quickly.

It's all right. It's just a little gravel.

She stood up, moved her shoulders around to loosen them up, and walked toward the water's edge. Closer to the lake, the shoreline was sandier and easier on her feet. Near the shore, there was a grooved concrete road that went straight to the edge of the water and disappeared beneath it. A road into water. Right where the road began, there was a sign.

PRIVATE BOAT RAMP
VISITORS USE PUBLIC RAMP

Holly walked down the incline until her feet touched the water. It was not as cold as she thought it might be. She waded farther, and the water splashed her ankles. She pulled up the bottom of her cotton dress to keep it dry and took a few more steps. The water was reassuring.

The birdsongs grew as sunrise approached, blending into a cacophony of chirps. The breeze off the water stroked her hair. She closed her eyes and imagined the lake filled with hope, love, and forgiveness. With approaching daylight, she could appreciate how large this place was and how far the shore extended. To her left was a long spit of land, a jetty that extended a hundred feet out into the water, and to her right was a series of wooden docks, each one associated with a small house. Some of these docks were double, one farther from the lake and sitting high on the mud flats, connected by a wooden walkway to a second dock that sat on piers in the water. What an odd arrangement.

The water level has fallen. The lake was deeper once.

Of course. That made sense.

Something far away on the other side of the lake caught her attention: headlights from a car, coming toward the water, then turning as it reached the lakeside road. A second car followed that one and also turned, revealing a third pair of headlights bringing up the rear. That one was different, with a row of red lights glowing across the top. Emergency lights of some sort.

It's a police car.

Her heartrate quickened. Were they coming here, for her and her children? She stood for a moment tracking the three cars with her eyes. She held her breath as the two sedans and one police car disappeared behind the jetty. A few moments later, the first car emerged. They weren't stopping on the other side. They were coming here.

Get back to the car.

They had come from Duro in two cars, two officers and a civilian employee in the first and Detective Lamborn, Sergeant Correa, Deputy Karyn Crowsie, and David Bellamy in the second car. They had been joined by two deputies from Scurry county in a third vehicle.

Bellamy was still feeling a sort of high, the giddiness that overwhelms someone who has been relieved of a heavy weight. When a burden is carried for a very long time, a man forgets the heft on his shoulders. When it's lifted, his body almost floats.

He had been read his rights, said he understood them. He agreed to take the officers to the place he had left Helen Orlena. They had called Deputy Crowsie at home, woken her up, and asked her to join them on a trip out to Lake Lenorah, and she had agreed. Crowsie was quiet, friendly, a good listener, and not judgmental. It was an uncanny personal trait of Crowsie's that suspects often opened up to her, even those who usually clammed up and dug in their heels talking to cops.

"David, have you ever been out to the lake before?" asked Deputy Crowsie.

"Of course," he said. "Many times over the years. I never went to the private part of the lake, the part past the stone archway."

"But you did that day?"

"That's where Helen went," said Bellamy. "I was following her."

"Do you know why she picked this place?"

"No."

The cars had turned onto the lakeside road and were traveling southeast. The horizon glowed brighter, with hints of red in the gray sky.

"You have to understand. I didn't kill her," said Bellamy. "I tried to save her."

CHAPTER 43

The Purge

I never meant to follow her. I was going to the hardware store, I think. When I was coming back, I spotted Helen on East County Road, going north, like she was headed out of town, and I decided to follow her.

What time was that?

I'm not sure. Middle of the afternoon. It was a spur-of-the-moment decision, completely unplanned. But I wanted to see where she was going. She had lied to me about the theater workshop in Fort Worth. I wondered what in the world she was up to.

I was going to follow her only a few miles, see what highway she took. But when she got to the north side of town, she turned onto the Odessa Highway, so I kept going. When you're trying to follow somebody in a car without being seen, you always leave a car or two between them and you. It's harder than it sounds. Plus, Helen drove fast. A couple of times I thought I had lost her. Sometimes I had to race, pass cars dangerously, exactly like those drivers I hate. When I'd see her car—it was small Ford—I'd have to hang back and hope other some car would pass me so I could keep following without being spotted.

When we got to Odessa, she drove almost all the way through town and then turned into this parking lot. It was just a plain building. When she went inside, I drove up close to the door so I could read the sign. It was *Planned Parenthood of Texas*. That sort of made sense. I was thinking maybe she drove all the way to another town for birth control pills, so she wouldn't run into somebody she knew. I could understand, even if I didn't approve. Don't get me wrong, I'm not against birth control in principle. But, my God, this girl was sixteen! Shouldn't there be laws about that? Adults and parents need to be involved in those decisions.

So, I parked across the street and waited for her to come out. She was in there a really long time. Lord, it was hot! I had to keep starting my car so I could run the AC. The darn thing never worked very well anyway and was getting worse. So I'm just sitting there cooking. My clothes were soaked. Eventually, Helen came out again.

How long was she inside the building?

I don't know. At least an hour. When she finally came out, I almost missed it. I was looking the other direction, and she just walked out of the building really fast and jumped into her car. It was hard to tell from that distance, but it looked like she was holding something in her hand, like a stack of papers.

She started the car and was out of the parking lot before I could do anything. By the time I got my car started, she was gone. I had to drive like a maniac, but I finally caught up to her at the big highway, Highway 80. She turned left.

Which direction was that?

East. For a while I thought maybe she was going to Fort Worth after all. By then I was ready to give up and drive back home, because the sun was setting, and I was down to a quarter tank of gas. I was planning to turn around when I reached Midland, but then she turned on that highway that goes up to the lake.

Highway 302?

I'm pretty sure that's right. I started to worry that she was going to do something stupid, so I just kept following her. By that time, I had already wasted most of my day, so I figured in for a dime, in for a dollar.

When she drove under the arch—we'll see it in a minute—I parked by the side of the road near this rocky peninsula that sticks out into the water. It's a manmade thing, I suppose so the rich people won't have to look at the regular people. I knew the road didn't go any farther, so she'd have to stop. Sure enough, that's where she was going. She parked in front of one of the lake houses on the other side of this rocky peninsula that sticks out into the water.

She got out of her car and went to the door. I guess she was knocking, but it didn't look like anybody was home. After a while she got back in her car and drove. I thought she was leaving, so I scooted down in my front seat so she wouldn't see me. When she didn't drive past, I looked and saw she had just driven a couple hundred feet and parked right beside the lake, next to that peninsula.

She sat there in her car for quite a while, doing something. The sun was in my eyes, and I was at least a hundred feet away, but I think that's when she was writing the note.

The suicide note?

It was her "goodbye, cruel world" note, I guess. I didn't know that at the time, of course. Then I saw her tilting her head back, at least twice, which looked strange. I could see she was drinking something from a paper cup and swigging it. I think it was her drink from that drive-through in Snyder.

She went to a fast-food place?

Yeah. I don't think I mentioned that. She'd stopped at a burger place beside the highway in Snyder. It looked like she just bought a soft drink at the window. Anyway, when she got to the lake, she just sat there in the front seat, and she put something in her mouth, then took a drink, two or three times. Then she just sat there. I expected she'd get out of the car at some point, but she just sat in her car a long time, at least half an hour. By that time, the sun had set, and it was getting dark.

When she finally did get out, something was wrong with her. She stumbled like she was drunk. It finally dawned on me what had happened. She had been taking those pills, probably several of them. If I had stopped her at that point, she'd be alive today. I tried, but it was too late. I got out of my car and called to her, and she started to run away, out onto those rocks in the lake. I don't even think she knew it was me, just that somebody was trying to stop her. But it was rough, and she was tripping and falling down.

Do you think she planned to jump into the water?

I don't know. That might have been what she was intending, but she collapsed before she did it. When I got to her, she was totally out of it, crying and saying stuff that made no sense. There was this thick spit coming out of her mouth.

Why didn't you go find a phone, call somebody?

I probably should have, but all I could think was that she had taken pills and needed to throw up, to get rid of whatever it was. So I tried to make it happen. To make her throw it up.

How?

I slapped her on the back, but nothing came up, and she was fighting me, hitting at me. So I turned her on her side and put my finger down her throat. I thought it would work. She gagged, but all that was coming out was this thick, white saliva. She bit me, hard, just a reflex, I'm sure, but it drew blood. I kept trying, though, and slapping her on the back some more. She said a few words, but she was not making sense. Then I think she stopped breathing. At the end, I tried mouth-to-mouth. It was awful.

When did you stop?

When it was clear that she was dead. She wasn't moving or breathing, and blood was coming out of her mouth.

Blood?

I . . . maybe . . . probably caused some . . . tearing with my fingers when I was trying to get her to throw up. In the end, there was a lot of blood. It was horrible, horrible. The worst day of my life. There was nothing I could do.

You could have called someone.

Yes. Yes, I should have done that. But it was too late. She was already dead.

CHAPTER 44

Catchy by Design

JJ had not risen before seven o'clock in the morning—at least not voluntarily—in over a decade. The only sunrises he ever saw followed all-nighters. Today, however, both he and Harold were up well before dawn for coffee at EAT. Neither one of them were hungry, but Harold made himself eat a two-egg breakfast with grits. JJ settled for one of Harold's triangles of white toast and coffee.

The plan for this final day at World Famous Best Studios was to meet Mabel White at the studio at eight, do a little housekeeping, then call the police.

They checked out of the Golden Sunset. It wasn't the sort of establishment one might feel wistful about, this sad old hotel with weekly rates, but it was where JJ had fallen in love, and he'd grown fond of the place.

They drove through the empty Sunday-morning streets of Duro.

"We can't push our luck on this," Harold said. "We don't have to tell the whole story unless they press us. But as soon as they figure out the guy has been dead for three days, then we'll be expected to give some answers."

"We can just say we didn't find him," said JJ. "We were—I don't know—so caught up in recording we just didn't bother to look in the echo chamber."

"They'll know we were lying," said Harold. "And that will make it look like we had something to do with it or at least that we didn't give a shit about him. It's going to look really, really bad. I can see the headlines: Oklahoma Hippies Make Pop Record with Dead Body in Next Room."

"Well, it would give us some publicity for when we release the song."

"Not the good kind," said Harold.

"You know what they say," said JJ. "There's no such thing as bad . . ."

"Yes there is."

Harold parked behind the building in the same spot he had used for the past week.

"Two things we need to make sure are out of that building," said JJ. "The master tape and your piano."

"I'd rather leave the Rhodes in the studio for now," said Harold. "If we get arrested, I don't want it sitting in my car for days."

That was a thought JJ had not allowed himself to dwell upon: jail. Harold was right. It really might happen. They also might get charged with a crime, go to trial, and end up in a much worse place than county jail. That darkened what little positive mood JJ had managed to find.

"Well, we still have to figure out what to do with the tape," said JJ. "We can't risk having the cops take it. We might never see it again."

"I don't want to leave it in the car," said Harold. "If it weren't Sunday, we could ship it back to Tulsa."

"We could ask Mabel to keep it for us," said JJ. "She's part of the project now. I'll bet she'd do that."

At that moment, a dark blue Lincoln pulled around the corner of the building. It wasn't Mabel's rental car, but she was in the front passenger seat. A Black man in a suit was driving. The car stopped, and the two of them sat talking for a moment. JJ and Harold couldn't hear what they were saying, but Mabel gestured in their direction a couple of times. Who was this guy? A plain-clothes cop, maybe?

The man shut off the engine to the Lincoln, and the two got out.

There were no formal introductions. Mabel simply said, "This is Mr. McLeslie, a lawyer. He's a friend of Dr. Creech."

"Hello," said Harold. "Did Mabel tell you about . . . the situation?"

"She did," said the lawyer, unsmiling. "I want to make it clear that I'm not working for Miss White, and I'm not working for you. At least not at this time. What I'm going to say isn't legal advice, but I am going to tell you what someone might do in this circumstance. What you decide is up to you."

"Okay," said Harold. "What would you do?"

"I wouldn't do anything. I'm not involved. But I can suggest what a person might do, hypothetically. First, let me make sure I understand. The man we're talking about is inside the building right now?"

"That's right."

"He died sometime Thursday?"

"Or early Friday morning," said Harold.

"And it was a natural death," said the lawyer. "He didn't leave a note or anything?"

"No," said Harold.

"Definitely not suicide, then?"

"Definitely not," said Harold. "There were pills and booze, but I'm sure it was accidental. He was excited about the project and wanted to get started."

"Well, then since you believe the death wasn't suspicious, you might—I mean, a person might just call the city coroner's office and report that a person has died of natural causes. They'll send somebody out. Now they might decide to call the police, but they also might just file a death report and take the body to the morgue. Of course, they'll want to notify family and so forth."

"He had no contact with his family," said Harold. "He never talked to his first ex-wife, as far as I know. He told me he was an only child. I presume his parents are dead."

"Well, there's me," said Mabel. "I'm the other ex-wife. Allen and I were definitely in contact. We talked on the phone. We were still friends."

"That could make things easier," said McLeslie. "You'd be the closest thing he has to next of kin. Anyway, that's all I have to say. You folks will have to decide."

"Do you want to come inside and see the body?" asked Harold.

"No, thank you. If it's all the same to you, I'll be on my way. Let me give you my card. Could you make sure Miss White gets back to her hotel?"

"Of course."

"Then have a good day. I am sorry for your loss."

McLeslie handed each of them a business card, and, as quickly as he'd appeared, he drove away.

Harold unlocked the studio. They all went inside but didn't venture farther than Allen Wallace's office. Harold found a Duro phone directory and called the county coroner.

While Harold was on the phone, Mabel walked around the office, examining the rows of publicity photos. JJ followed. Of all the names and faces, the only one JJ had heard of was a minor Tejano star named Daniel Alvarado, a.k.a. Danny Gibson. At the bottom of the picture, he had inscribed *To Allen, who taught me everything I know—Danny.* Many other nonfamous artists had written similar grateful messages. *Allen, you're the best of the best* and *To a friend and a dang good producer* and just *THANK YOU!!!!—Bobby.*

"Everybody who worked with him loved him," said Mabel. "It breaks my heart that he died alone. If I had just come out sooner."

"The last thing he did was listen to recordings of you," said JJ. He wasn't sure that was a kind thing to say, but Mabel didn't react. She just walked from photo to photo, pausing at each one. "A sweet, sweet man," she said.

Harold hung up the phone. "Get this. When I called the coroner's office, the number goes to an answering service. The lady said she'd call the coroner . . . when he gets back from church."

"We might be here a while," said JJ. "Welcome to the small city."

A now-familiar sound came from the metal door in back, an insistent knock.

"Well, we know who that isn't," said Harold. "I'll get rid of them." He went through the outer room and opened the door. There were three well-dressed middle-aged white people, two men and a woman.

"Hi, I'm Seth Osborne," said a tall, wide man with a droopy mustache.

"Okay," said Harold. "I'm sorry, but the studio is closed right now."

"We're the Jingleaires," said Osborne.

"Okay."

"We have a date to record this morning. Is Allen Wallace here? I set this up two weeks ago."

"It's Sunday morning," said Harold. "He's not here right now. I'm really sorry. You'll have to schedule this for later."

"Wait a damn minute," said Osborne. "This was all arranged. I told Allen Wallace that Sunday morning was the only time I could get everybody together, and he said that was no problem. His exact words were 'Sunday morning would be perfect. The other group will be done by then.' Now, where is he? I wrote him a check for the deposit, and here we are."

"I'm really sorry," said Harold. "Allen is sick. I was the engineer on the last project, and we're just wrapping a few things up."

The Jingleaires conferred. The woman said, "Seth, we told Rochester we'd have it to the station by Monday. It's supposed to start airing this week."

JJ had come up behind Harold. "What are you recording? Just a vocal spot?"

"Yes, a thirty-second commercial for Rochester Chevrolet," said Osborne. "I figured we'd be in and out in half an hour. It couldn't be simpler."

"But . . . it's just that Allen Wallace really isn't here right now," said Harold. "He's not coming in today. It's not my fault. I know nothing about your gig."

"This is awful," said Osborne.

"Really unprofessional," said the other man. "I've recorded six commercials at this studio, and there's never been the slightest problem. Seth, who can we call? This is damned ridiculous."

"William, your mouth!" said the woman.

"Sorry. But this is really stupid. I've never seen such unprofessionalism in a studio."

JJ whispered to Harold, "We could just record them and get them out of here."

"I suppose," whispered Harold. "But this is getting worse all the time."

JJ addressed the Jingleaires. "Just a four-track vocal spot? Thirty seconds?"

"Thirty seconds including the voice-over," said Osborne. "And we usually record two-track."

"All right, come on in," said Harold. "Let's get it done."

The Jingleaires filed in.

"Damn, you keep it cold in here!"

"William!"

Harold set them up in the little studio with two boom microphones at a forty-five-degree angle. While the singers warmed up their voices, he plugged the cables into the board and turned on the MM-1000. Mabel came in and sat in the control room, bewildered about what was unfolding.

"JJ, find a blank tape," said Harold.

JJ took a new, unopened two-inch tape off the shelf and peeled off the cellophane. Osborne saw what they were doing and called out from the little studio.

"Are you recording this on that monster machine?" asked Osborne. "I told Wallace I was fine with the two-track."

"The sixteen-track is what I know how to use," said Harold.

"I don't want to pay for that giant reel of tape. Not for a damn thirty-second radio spot."

"Seth, your mouth!" said the woman.

"The tape is complementary," said Harold. "Take what you can get."

After a couple of run-throughs, Harold set the sound levels and indicated he was ready. The singers put on headphones and crowded close to the microphones. Harold punched START and pointed. Osborne began with a spoken part:

"Come on down to Rochester Chevrolet of Duro. We'll make you a deal that'll have you singing . . . in your brand-new Chevrolet!"

They sang:

"We're Rochester, come see us today
At Rochester Chevrolet
It's like coming home. It's like coming home
Because we treat you like faaaam-ly
Rochester Chevro-laaaaaaaaay!"

Then Osborne intoned:

"Rochester Chevrolet of Duro, South Lincoln at East County Road."

He looked up at Harold, who realized the spot was done and punched the STOP button.

"Okay, what's our time?" asked Osborne.

"Uh . . . let's see," said Harold, and ran the tape back. "Okay . . . uh . . . Do you have a watch with a second hand? I forgot to set the timer on the recorder."

"Yes," said Osborne. "Jesus, you guys are unprofessional!"

"Seth!"

They listened to the spot while Osborne timed it.

"Twenty-six seconds," he said. "We need it to be twenty-eight. Let's do it again."

They did it again. It timed at twenty-nine seconds. A third take brought it in at the required time, but Osborne wasn't happy with his voice-over. On the fourth try, he said he was satisfied.

"I didn't like that one," said Harold. JJ and Mabel gave him an alarmed look.

Harold pointed at the woman singer. "Uh . . . you. What's your name?"

"Claudia."

"Miss Claudia, you need to get closer," said Harold. "Your voice isn't coming through very well."

"I've had a cold," she said. "My voice is weak. I know."

"Let's run it again, and this time, lean in, especially on that last 'Chevrolet.'"

They tried it again twice, but Claudia coughed in the middle of the first one and was still too quiet on the second.

"I'm sorry," she said. "I can do this."

"I can help," said Mabel. "It's a pretty easy song."

"Whatever," said Osborne. "I can't pay you."

"I'll do it for free," said Mabel. Harold found another pair of headphones, and Mabel stood beside Claudia. This time, everything seemed to work. The paired female voices came through strong, but the timing was a little long, and Harold still wasn't happy with the vocals.

"You need a mid-range male voice," said Harold. "Both you men are baritones." He turned around. "JJ, get a pair of phones and get in there. We're going to get this right."

"I can't pay you either," said Osborne.

"This is getting damn crazy," said William.

"William, please!" said Claudia.

Finally, with five voices, the Jingleaires recorded their radio spot. Osborne listened and said it was good enough.

"Excellent!" said Harold. "Now, I don't want to hurry you, but we have something we need to take care of, so if you folks could just—"

"I need my tape," said Osborne.

"Of course," said Harold. He rewound the two-inch master.

"No, I need a quarter-inch mix. Not the two-inch."

"Just take the big tape, please," said Harold. "It's on the house."

"The radio stations can only use quarter-inch tape," said Osborne. "You have to give me a mix master."

"Jesus Christ!" said Harold.

"Please, sir," said Claudia. "That's unnecessary."

"Sorry."

Harold and JJ lugged Allen Wallace's old quarter-inch recorder out of his office and struggled to connect it to the stereo out on the soundboard while the Jingleaires went outside to get warm. For lack of a better idea, they used the tape JJ had brought down from Tulsa to play for Allen Wallace. It took a few tries, but they finally did get a respectable mix. Harold put the tape in its box, took out a marker pen and crossed out JJ Johns—"Earth Is Crying" Demo and wrote Jingleaires—10-22-72—Rochester spot.

"I can't believe we did that," said JJ. He laughed. "If that thing goes national, I'm suing for royalties."

"Well, as my mama used to say, if you're going to do something, do it right," said Harold. "But it's kind of funny. Sad and funny. Your song is no longer the last one recorded at Best Studios."

"That's fine with me," said JJ. "I don't think I want to be the last one."

"Excuse me, sir?" It was Claudia the Jingleaire.

"Yes?"

"There are some policemen outside."

CHAPTER 45

Water Is a Living Thing

Wait until they leave. They aren't interested in you.

"One of the officers keeps looking this way," said Holly.

They are here for another reason. Pay no attention to them.

"Mother, I'm hungry," said Peter from the back seat. "Can we go to that same waffle place?"

"No, I'm afraid not," said Holly. "It's too far away. Anyway, I'm out of money."

"But I'm *hungry*!"

"Have patience and faith, just like the pastor says. It will all be fine."

Bellamy sat at the water's edge on a log that had been sawed in half lengthwise and planed down to a flat bench.

"No dead person has turned up in this lake in the past two years," said Detective Lamborn. "Did you weight the body?"

"What?"

"Did you tie something heavy to her, like rocks or cinder block?"

"Of course not," said Bellamy. "I wanted her to be found."

"And you're confident this is where it was."

"Absolutely."

A couple of the officers and Sergeant Correa poked among the rocks and tree stumps on the shoreline where the jetty met the mud beach, but it was obvious that a human body would have been discovered long ago.

It was turning out to be a comfortably cool Sunday morning in October. Visitors were arriving at the public part of the shoreline, and a few boats appeared on the water, motoring slowly, fishing lines cast. It was a bit chilly for waterskiing, but skiers would be out on the lake by afternoon. No one stirred in Thompson Village.

A station wagon had been there when Bellamy and the cops had first arrived, parked a hundred feet inshore from the second boat ramp. It was Sergeant Correa who noticed there was someone in it. He wondered if it was a homeless person sleeping in their car, but the car looked too nice for a liveaboard. Someone sat in the driver's seat, a woman. He considered strolling over and asking what she was up to, but they had other things to do.

The sun was up, and the air warmed. Bellamy had shown the police where he had spotted Helen Orlena, two summers ago, and followed her. He pointed out where she had fallen, the sandy shore on which he had tried to resuscitate her, where he had finally accepted reality.

Lamborn sat on the log bench with him.

"David, you said you saw a note. Where did you find it?"

"In the front seat of her car. Just sitting there, not folded. There was also a ballpoint pen and a magazine of some sort. I guess she used it as a lap board to write the note. The keys were in the ignition."

"And you're sure it was a suicide note?"

"I am sure. It didn't expressly say she was planning to kill herself, but there was a lot of . . . dramatic despair, I guess you'd say. Hopelessness. The last line said something like *That's why I've decided to take this drastic step*. Something like that."

"Do you remember the first line?"

"Yes. It was just *Dear Nicky* or *My dearest Nicky*. That was her boyfriend's name."

"We know," said Lamborn. "We've talked to him."

"He could tell you more about what was going on between them. The suicide note was written to him, but it was also general, about how the world had treated her so badly."

Deputy Crowsie and a male deputy came around from behind the other side of the jetty.

"Detective, there's no trace over there either," said Crowsie. "It's pretty clean. No hidden places where a body might have caught."

The other deputy, who was from this county, said, "We've spoken to the sheriff. He says if we need to drag this part of the lake, we'll have to notify the state Parks and Wildlife people, so they can close it off."

"It probably won't come to that," said Lamborn. He stood up and took a few steps along the shoreline, keeping his black shoes out of the muddy patches. He too had noticed the station wagon with its mysterious occupant. From here, it looked like the woman might be watching them.

A moment later, one of the car's back doors opened, and a child got out, a little girl in a dress. Then the driver also emerged. She wore a long dress that reminded Lamborn of the Mennonite women who worked in the fields of the Texas Panhandle.

"Right over there," he heard her say. "Hurry up."

The little girl disappeared behind a thick stand of manicured bushes that extended from one of the cabins. "Be careful with your dress. Keep it high," said the woman. When the girl reemerged, Lamborn heard the woman say, "Hurry up! Get back in!"

Lamborn took out his notebook and pen. He adjusted his glasses and squinted. From here, he could just make out the car's license plate. He wrote down the tag number, tore off the piece of paper, and beckoned to one of the deputies.

"Yes, sir?"

"Get on the radio and run this plate, please. See if it's on the stolen list."

He turned his gaze away from the car and back to the lake, where a morning breeze was rippling the water. In a couple of minutes, the deputy returned. Yes, the car was on the hot list, reported stolen in Duro two days earlier.

"Okay. Let's go talk to her," said Lamborn. He and two of the deputies trudged up the sand and gravel slope toward the station wagon.

ROLL DOWN THE WINDOWS! All of them! Hurry!

Holly leaned over and cranked the handle on the passage-side window.

"Peter! Martha!" she said. "Roll your windows down! Just turn the handle and keep turning."

"What's wrong, Mother?" asked Peter.

"The world is coming for us, dear."

"Is it those men?" asked Martha.

"Yes, dear."

Start the car. Quickly.

Holly cranked the motor and gave it a little too much gas, so that it started with a roar. The two uniformed officers started trotting in her direction, hands on their holstered guns.

"Hold it right there!" one shouted.

They're coming. Drive straight at them!

"But I might hit them!"

They'll get out of the way. Straight at them. Do it! NOW!

Holly put the transmission in drive and stomped on the accelerator. The station wagon lurched forward and slid sideways as the wheels spun on the hard-packed sand, then found purchase and accelerated. The two officers and an older man scattered. The car missed one of the deputies by just a couple of feet. Holly heard him yell "STOP!" as she drove past.

The car was going thirty miles an hour as it reached the boat ramp and plunged down the slope. When the front of the car struck the lake, a cascade of water burst up and rolled over the hood. Holly was thrown hard against the steering wheel.

You did it! Brave girl.

"There are children in the vehicle!" shouted Lamborn. As he ran down the boat ramp, a wake of lake water washed up over his black shoes.

A Scurry County deputy, a young man of twenty-five, kicked off his shoes, tossed his hat, and unbuckled his holster belt, letting it and his pistol drop to the sand. He plunged forward into the water, which quickly rose above his waist. He used his hands to paddle forward, then began a slow crawl stroke toward the car, which was sinking about fifty feet from shore.

On the right side of the car, a little girl's head appeared above the surface.

"MOTHER! MOTHER!" She emerged partially from of the car, clinging to the top with both hands. Water had reached the level of the roof.

The deputy who had gone into the water took a deep breath and disappeared below the surface on the left side. A few seconds later, he emerged, sputtering. He hyperventilated for a couple of seconds, then dove back under. A portly Duro deputy waded out into the water but didn't try to swim.

Beside the sinking car, the first deputy's head popped up again, then a pair of small arms appeared. When the young boy's head cleared the surface, he coughed violently then reached for the deputy, flailing.

"Don't grab me!" shouted the deputy. "Turn around and let me pull you. Be still!"

The boy did as he was told, and the deputy got him around his neck and under one armpit, then swam an ungainly sidestroke toward shore.

"My mother's in the car!" screamed the boy. "Help my mother!"

On the right side of the car, the little girl was all the way out of the window, trying to crawl onto the roof, which was now several inches below water. The rear end of the station wagon came up and broke the surface, and the girl slid off the roof, screaming. By now, Deputy Crowsie was in the cold water, swimming toward her.

"FLOAT!" she yelled. "Don't fight! Just let yourself float! I'm coming!"

Crowsie reached the panicking girl and got her by the collar of her dress. The girl turned around and embraced the deputy. Crowsie was a good swimmer, but with a little girl clinging to her in a panic, it was impossible to get a rescue grip. She used a technique she had learned in lifeguard training: She took a deep breath and submerged a couple of feet under water, and the little girl dropped her grip. Crowsie popped back up the surface and shouted a command.

"TURN AROUND! I'm going to get you!"

The little girl's face was wide with terror, but she obeyed, and Crowsie was able to get her around the chest. They were still far from shore and drifting farther, but the deputy hung on, doing her best to keep moving. She heard a shout.

"Wait for the boat!" It was Detective Lamborn. He had gotten the attention of a lone fisherman in a small outboard skiff, which was now motoring toward Crowsie.

The first deputy, who was dragging the young boy, searched for the mucky lake bottom with his feet, and found it. He dug in and slogged forward until he was able to pass off the child to the fat deputy standing in waist-deep water. He then turned around and slogged back toward the car, where only the rear window and taillights were above water, bobbing in the small waves sixty feet away.

"MOTHER!" screamed the boy. He tried to splash his way back into the lake, but Lamborn restrained him, holding him tight and pinning his arms while he struggled.

With a great belch of air, the car sank, water washing over it.

David Bellamy had been watching from shore, dumbfounded. It suddenly occurred to him that he was the best swimmer there. He kicked off his shoes, tossed his wallet onto the sand, splashed down the ramp in his stocking feet, then dove in an arc into the water, a perfect competitive start. He swam in a rapid freestyle, quickly passing the deputy. When he reached the car, barely visible under the dark water, he sucked in a deep breath and dove.

He located the driver's side window. Reaching blind into the car, he got a handful of fabric, which he gripped and pulled with all his might. The cloth gave way. He let go, swam to the surface, took five quick breaths, and dove back down. Reaching as far as he could through the window, he grabbed what he quickly realized was a handful of long hair. Planting his feet on the car door and steadying himself with his left hand, he pulled the hair until he had extracted the woman's head and upper body from the car window, then reached farther in and got a hand under her right shoulder. Utterly out of breath, he paddled hard with his free hand and was just able to break the surface if he tilted his head back. He spit out a mouthful of lake water, took a deep gulp of air, and hung on, pulling the woman up with him.

When he got her head above water, Bellamy tried to roll her onto her back so he could give her an immediate rescue breath, like they taught in Red Cross swimming. Just get some air into her. But she suddenly convulsed and vomited a copious amount of water, sucked in a ragged breath, coughed out more water, and starting panting hard.

Bellamy looked around. The first deputy was still on his way, slowly swimming out to him. The little fishing boat was on the other side about forty feet away as the owner struggled to take the shrieking, dripping little girl out of Crowsie's arms and over the gunwales without capsizing his boat.

Bellamy worked to turn the woman around, but she was badly tangled in her long, saturated cotton dress. One bare arm was out, and the back was ripped from neck to waist. As she regained consciousness, she flailed wildly. Bellamy fought to keep his own head above water and get behind her. The heavy cloth was floating in a clump up around her neck. Bellamy pulled the torn side of the dress over her head, then with heroic effort, he extracted her right arm from its sleeve and pulled the soaked dress completely away. She was wearing a cotton slip underneath, which floated up under her armpits.

The young male deputy swam up, out of breath.

"Get her under the other arm!" shouted Bellamy. "We'll pull her." They both began swimming slowly to shore, trying to haul the woman along with them, on her back, her long hair floating in the water and tangled across her face. Her broken nose streamed blood.

She whipped her head around frantically, confused.

"JAMES!" she screamed. "JAMES, PLEASE HELP ME!" She tried to push her rescuers away.

"Be still!" shouted Bellamy, but the woman continued to wave her arms, throwing hands and elbows as she fought, and the two men struggled to keep their grip and stay afloat.

"STOP FIGHTING ME!" yelled Bellamy. "I need to hang on to you!"

"JAMES!" she screamed again. "Don't let them take my children!" She tried to push them away again. "JAMES!"

"I'll take you to him!" shouted Bellamy. "Your kids are safe! I'm trying to help! Let me save you!"

She stopped fighting. "Oh, James, I'm sorry," she muttered. "I tried. I tried so hard." She sobbed and muttered incomprehensible words, but she let them take her slowly to the shore.

CHAPTER 46

More than They're Letting On

Four cop cars and an ambulance surrounded World Famous Best Studio. Local kids on bicycles hovered nearby, hoping an interesting crime had taken place and a perpetrator would be led away.

They got their wish after a while, but it was disappointing. A policeman emerged from the front door escorting a trimly dressed Black woman in handcuffs. She looked straight ahead, defiant. He took her to one of the police cars, opened a back door, and guided her in so she wouldn't bump her head. He got into the front seat of the car but didn't drive away.

Well, that wasn't very exciting. The kids pedaled away to find something more fun to do.

Inside, Harold and JJ sat in handcuffs on the couch in Allen Wallace's office. Seth and Claudia of the Jingleaires sat in chairs. They were not cuffed. Out in the control room, a policeman was taking a statement from Jingleaire William. They were interviewing them separately one at a time so they couldn't conspire to get their stories straight.

Harold and JJ were resigned and quiet, but chief Jingleaire Seth Osborne was quite agitated. If this kept up, he would miss church and work, which were the same thing.

"I—I mean, we—my group knew nothing about this," said Osborne. "We had a confirmed appointment with Allen Wallace to record a radio commercial this morning. This gentleman"—he indicated Harold—"told me Wallace was sick at home, so we let him do the recording. We would never have continued if we'd known what was going on."

"Sir, you'll get your chance to make a statement," said a young rookie policeman, the kind most likely to be stuck with a Sunday shift.

"I realize . . . I don't want to sound selfish here," said Osborne. "I realize a man is dead, and that's not a small thing. I get it. But we had absolutely nothing to do with it, and I have a job that starts in exactly forty-five minutes over at Broadmore Baptist Church. I am the choir director. I'm expected and needed there. At the very least, I have to call and explain what's up so somebody can fill in for me."

"I understand your situation, sir," said the young cop. "You'll have to be patient."

Fortunately, one of the other officers was a sporadic attendee at Broadmore and recognized Osborne as the guy in purple robes who conducted the church's fifty-voice choir. He conferred with the sergeant on duty, who came in to talk to the Jingleaires.

"Okay, sir," he said, "if you can make a brief statement for us, we will let you folks go. Though we may need to speak with you later." Claudia had already completed her statement, and William was finishing his.

"Thank you, thank you!" said Osborne. In a couple of minutes, he followed an officer into the control room and spoke quickly while a cop took a few notes. He then returned to the office.

"Okay, William, Claudia, let's go," he said.

"Don't forget your tape," said Harold.

"Of course. It's this one right here, right?" He picked up the quarter-inch tape in its box.

"Wait," said an officer. "You're not supposed to take anything. The sergeant said we're locking everything down."

"It's their radio commercial," said Harold. "We recorded it this morning. It's why they're here."

"It's scheduled to go on air day after tomorrow," said Osbourne.

"Okay . . . I suppose," said the officer.

The other Jingleaires stood up.

"Don't forget your multitrack master," said Harold.

"I don't I need it," said Osborne.

"It's yours. You should take it," said Harold. "In case the radio station doesn't like the mix, you can do it again."

"Okay, okay. Whatever. Which one is it?" asked Osborne.

"Right there on corner of the desk," said Harold. "Take it."

Osborne put the small reel on top of the enormous one, and the Jingleaires left, taking their thirty-second spot with them.

The Rochester jingle would be on the radio at seven o'clock Tuesday morning and for countless mornings thereafter, burrowing into the brains of Duro residents for years and years to come. No one would ever know that the vocalists included Grammy-nominated pop star JJ Johns and world-class recording artist Mabel White.

The cops scurried around, bagging potential evidence, scribbling labels. Everything in the refrigerator was removed and examined for clues. In the desk, they discovered Allen's pill bottle with its remaining tranquilizers and the mostly empty bottle of Evan Williams Kentucky Straight. Another young cop had the thankless task of sorting through the trash cans, separating, bagging, and labeling everything, including food wrappers and snot-stained tissues. They took Allen's porkpie hat and sealed it in a plastic evidence bag.

The men from the Coroner's office manhandled the great sliding door in back, then hoisted a portable gurney up and into the building. With many awkward twists and turns, they got the gurney, partially folded, into the little studio, where they lifted the rigid body through the low echo chamber door and up onto the gurney. Then Allen Wallace, strapped down and discreetly covered, was rolled out of World Famous Best Studios for the last time. The air conditioners were turned off, and the doors left wide open, to allow the building to warm up for the comfort of investigators.

JJ had said barely a word during the long, intrusive evidence-gathering process, but when a sergeant passed through the room, he spoke up.

"Sir, can we make sure our tape is put someplace safe?"

He looked over at JJ as if noticing him for the first time.

"Your tape, you say? What would be on this tape?"

"My song," said JJ. "The one we've been recording the past three days."

"That's what you were doing while that poor man was dying in there?"

"He was already dead," said JJ. "Please, I just want to make sure the tape is safe."

"Right," said the sergeant. "Well, everything at the crime scene is going to be collected and labeled and stored downtown as evidence. Whenever the investigation is completely finished and officially closed, then you can take it up with the judge. You may or may not ever see your little tape again." He leaned down and grinned at JJ. "If I were you, I'd be worrying about a murder charge, not the top-forty countdown."

"Ah, Jesus."

JJ and Harold watched helplessly as stacks of tape boxes were removed and loaded into a police van. They were headed for the Duro PD property room, a cluttered warehouse, where Allen Wallace's life work would remain indefinitely at temperatures that sometimes reached a sweltering ninety degrees.

The sergeant informed the two men they were under arrest for failure to report a death and for tampering with evidence. He told Mabel White she would be charged for failure to report a crime. He considered her their most promising suspect, an ex-wife who quite possibly harbored ill intent toward the victim.

The police allowed JJ and Harold to load the heavy Rhodes piano and JJ's two guitars into Harold's car, which was then towed away.

Tulsa's favorite son JJ Johns and producer Harold Prensky spent a very long day at the Duro Police Department. Harold used his one phone call to contact the attorney Jeremiah McLeslie, who told him not to say anything and to wait for him (not that they had a choice). Since the lawyer was taken care of, JJ used his phone call to try and reach Becky, but no one answered at the house on Bluebonnet Lane. JJ and Harold were separated and kept apart to prevent them from coordinating their stories. The attorney spoke to each of them briefly, then they were taken in separate cars to the Ferris County jail for what would be a long, chilly night.

The police released Mabel that evening, without charges. She had been subjected to uninterrupted questioning much of the afternoon. But she never budged from her account of events, and efforts to intimidate or confuse her were unsuccessful. A police detective told her she might want to stick around town. She didn't.

JJ's neck was painfully stiff, and he wished he could brush his teeth and hair. He might have slept an hour in his cell, when you add up all the dozing minutes, but there had been no real rest. He was told that he and Harold would go before a judge at ten o'clock Monday morning. After a breakfast of powdered eggs and black coffee, they drove him the four blocks to the courthouse a little after nine. Harold arrived a few minutes later. When they entered the courtroom, they were discouraged to find themselves on the docket with several other unfortunates who had also run afoul of the law.

The judge was announced and entered the room a few minutes past 10:00. Their lawyer had told them they were third on the list, which didn't sound too bad. However, number two, a small fellow whose first language was not English (nor Spanish, apparently) took an inordinately long time. JJ rubbed his neck and yawned on the hard bench, waiting for his name to be called. Finally, it was their turn.

"Jerome Johnson and Harold Prensky!"

They rose together and stood in front of the judge, along with Jeremiah McLeslie in his crisp black suit. Harold had managed to look pretty good, considering, but JJ knew his own appearance—puffy eyes and long, tangled hair—was only one step up from the drunk-and-disorderlies waiting on the bench.

The judge took several minutes reading his notes. From time to time, he would look up at JJ and Harold with a scowl. Or maybe his face was always like that.

Finally, he spoke. "Mr. Prensky. Mr. Johnson. You are charged with failure to render aid and tampering with evidence. These are misdemeanors in the state of Texas, punishable by a fine not to exceed ten thousand dollars and/or confinement in the county jail for a period not to exceed one year. Do you understand?"

"Yes, your judge . . . your honor," said JJ. *Not good, man.*

"Yes, your honor," said Harold.

"How do you plead?"

"Not guilty," they said together.

"Very well. Mr. Prensky, Mr. Johnson, your attorney tells me you have waived the right to a jury trial. Therefore you are both instructed to appear in this court on January 15, 1973, at ten o'clock in the morning, with counsel. I am setting bail at five thousand dollars apiece." He leaned over his bench and looked down at them. "Do either of you have any questions?"

"No, your honor," said Harold.

"Actually, your honor, I do have something I need to bring up," said JJ. His lawyer looked at him sharply, but didn't say anything.

"Yes, Mr. Johnson?"

JJ cleared his throat. "Judge, Harold—I mean, Mr. Prensky—and I have just finished recording a new song, and the police seized the tape. The officer told me that a judge could tell them to give it back. Can you do that for us?"

"A new song, you say," said the judge. "Would this be the song you two were working on for three days while that poor man lay dead in the next room?"

"Yes, your honor," said JJ. "It's called 'Earth Is Crying,' and it's about how—"

The judge laughed out loud, which was so unexpected it stopped JJ in mid-sentence. The judge leaned back in his chair, shaking his head and grinning.

"Mr. Johnson, I've been a judge in this court for five years, and I've seen a lot, believe me. Do you know what the word *chutzpah* means?"

"Uh . . . no, sir."

"Okay, then, I'll give you an example. A man murders his mother and father, then asks the court for clemency based on the fact he is an orphan. That's chutzpah."

The judge chuckled at his own joke. JJ looked blank. The lawyer started to speak, but the judge cut him off.

"What you have just shown is classic chutzpah. You were dancing around in a studio, singing your little heart out making a be-bop record for *three days*! Knowing full well the owner of the studio had dropped dead right in the next room. You could have notified somebody, but you couldn't be bothered to stop the party long enough. And now you want your reward."

"But, your honor, we worked really hard—"

"Of course!" said the judge. "I'll *bet* that was hard. For one thing, you had to keep from tripping over a dead body. But . . . you asked a straight question, and I'll answer it. When you appear in this court next January and after your case is decided, you can fill out and submit a form requesting return of property. Who knows? Maybe I'll be in a musical mood that day. But if I were you . . ." The judge leaned forward again, glaring at JJ. "If I were you, I would let it go. It would be a sort of retribution, a small sacrifice. Consider yourself lucky to escape a charge of negligent homicide. That's a *felony,* my friend."

He picked up his gavel. "You know, Mr. Johnson, you're going to appear before me again in a couple of months, but someday you'll face a very different sort of judge, the one we all have to stand before. And then you'll have to explain to him why you lived such a free and easy life, caring about no one but yourself. Maybe the Lord will be more forgiving if you can find some humility."

The gavel came down.

HAROLD WROTE TWO CHECKS, five hundred dollars for the lawyer and a thousand to secure the bail bond. They were sprung by noon.

A courthouse clerk gave them a ride to the impound lot to retrieve Harold's station wagon. Blessedly, the car had been stored in the shade, and the musical instruments were undamaged.

"How was your night?" asked Harold as they drove out of the police lot. The two hadn't had a chance to speak in private since their arrest.

"I've had worse," said JJ.

"You ready to go back home?"

"I have to see Becky," said JJ. "And also, there's a little matter of my goddam tape. Maybe that lawyer can help." He turned to Harold. "Whatever that judge said, I'm *not* being selfish. We both put our hearts into that recording. I can't just let it go!"

"Relax, JJ," said Harold. "You're getting yourself worked up. It's okay."

"Yeah, I did something bad!" he said. "I let that poor old man lie there. And I'm sorry. But is this what I get? Is this the price I have to pay now? My song is gonna die in fucking police storage room? Is it like that judge said—a *sacrifice*? A sacrifice! I give up the first good song I've done in years, and I get my soul back? Is that how it works?"

JJ leaned out the car window and shouted up at the sky.

"I was WRONG!" he yelled. "I'm a bad person! I'm SORRY!"

"Settle down, man," said Harold. "You can go see your girlfriend. We'll swing by and grab the tape on the way."

"What? How do we manage that?"

"Easy," said Harold. "Step one, we get a phonebook and call Seth Osborne the Jingleaire. Step two, we get our tape back."

"You mean . . .?"

"You think I would give that guy eighteen hundred feet of two-inch professional tape for a rinky-dink car commercial?" said Harold. "I just grabbed a chance to slip your masterpiece out the back door—at some risk to myself, I might add. Now, let's go get it back before that idiot leaves it in the sun or his dog chews it up."

"Wow," said JJ. "Just . . . wow. You are a genius! My buddy, my pal, I don't know what I'd do without you."

JJ leaned back in the seat, exhausted but giddy, letting the wind from the passenger-side window whip his hair. He laughed out loud and grinned at Harold. "You know, I do love you," he said.

"Back at ya, rock star."

Grover's younger sister, Margaret, drove down from Denton Tuesday afternoon. She was a tax accountant, married but with no children of her own. She had always gotten along well with Holly, adored the kids, but her relationship with Grover had been strained over her decision to leave the true church and follow her husband into Presbyterianism. Though she hadn't spoken to her brother in over six months—the last time was when Grover called with a tax question—she volunteered to come back to Duro to help with the children. He took her up on the offer immediately.

Grover was shell-shocked, struggling to keep it together, to stay in business mode. There were so many things to do. After one night in Scurry County Medical Center for X-rays and general repair, Holly was taken to Big Spring State Hospital, a psychiatric facility, for evaluation. Grover knew she would have to be admitted and was willing to sign commitment papers, but in the end, Holly committed herself. Grover, who had rejected the world's medicine, put all his hope into it.

Rebekah didn't go back to the university right away. She contacted her professors to work out plans for completing courses and taking exams. She thought she might stay in Duro as long as four weeks, but Grover was adamant that she return to school as soon as possible to finish out the semester. She would have a long break at Christmas, just a few weeks away. She had to keep her grades up and graduate in the spring.

She was still trying to absorb something her father had told her. Rebekah grew up hearing stories about Mother's Uncle Jim, a brilliant man—some said a genius—a scientist who published academic papers about stars and planets. Mother had loved him deeply and depended on him. Becky had been told and always believed that Uncle Jim had died in a tragic accident, a gas explosion while he slept in his bed at the little house he rented in Alpine, near the observatory.

Becky thought about Uncle Jim when the police told them that Mother frequently heard a voice in her head, which she referred to as James.

"Do you think it was because of Uncle Jim?" Becky had asked her father. "It must have been awful for a young girl to lose somebody she loved that way, in such a horrible accident. Maybe she missed him so much that her mind just replaced him."

"I don't know," Grover had said. "It was awful. But it wasn't an accident."

"What do you mean?"

"Jim did it to himself. I don't know why."

"You mean he turned on the gas deliberately?" Becky asked.

"He did. And sealed all the doors and windows with tape. Made himself a cup of coffee, drank it, turned on the gas, and went to bed. He probably didn't intend to cause an explosion. They said a water heater set it off, after he was already dead from the gas."

Perhaps James was just a restless soul.

Peter and Martha handled the trauma in different ways. Peter talked—and talked and talked—about the events of late October with investigators, with his family, friends, church members, anyone who would listen. But Martha withdrew, responding little, spending the first few days huddled against her big sister on the couch. She had nightmares about drowning.

Aunt Margaret arrived and settled in, and Martha gravitated to her quickly. Grover relented on his no-television rule. The three females and Peter sat together in the evenings watching programs like *Here's Lucy* and *The Carol Burnett Show.* Peter wanted to see *Hawaii Five-O,* but Margaret nixed that, thinking it too violent.

Aunt Margaret enrolled the children at Tom Green Elementary and met with their teachers to plan for transition into public schooling. Preliminary testing showed they were both ahead of their age groups in reading and math. About government and the civil structures in America, they knew next to nothing. Peter, for instance, did not know that Texas had a governor. But he was bright and a fast learner.

With the kids in public school, Grover back at the dealership, and Aunt Margaret providing a stable center to the household, Becky finally caught her breath. She needed to make a decision. Well-meaning church members had kept them supplied with food, but soon that source would be exhausted. Would Father teach himself to cook? How long would Aunt Margaret be willing to stay? How long would Mother be in the hospital? Would she ever be a regular person again, or would they have to settle for something less?

Almost two weeks after the terrible Sunday, Dan called from Fort Worth to report that all the film footage was back from the lab. When would she be available to view the rushes? He offered to come to Duro Saturday to pick her up, save her the long bus ride, and she accepted.

Becky had spent much of her life determined to escape from her hometown and make her own life, liberated from family and church. Now she knew that, after graduation, she would have to come back.

CHAPTER 47

Take Me Back to Tulsa

The body of Helen Orlena was recovered from the desert, but no trace of Nicky Pomeroy was ever found. Searches by airplane, jeep, and horseback uncovered no clues, and nothing in his apartment or car suggested where he might have gone. After two weeks, the search was called off. Months later, a rancher found a Boy Scout compass sitting on a rock about half a mile from the pluton.

The county coroner's office tried to damp down hopes that anything could be learned from an autopsy of Helen's body. Sixteen months is a long time for a corpse to decay. However, the alkaline salts were remarkably preservative. Though thoroughly desiccated, the body was mostly intact. The examination and autopsy took several weeks, with help from the Texas State Forensics Lab. In his final report, the coroner concluded, with "fairly high confidence," that cause of death was drowning. The liver was found to contain "traces of narcotics" but not in amounts considered lethal. It was not possible to conclude whether or not she was pregnant.

David Bellamy hired a flamboyant attorney named Carson Hobbs, already well-known for defending a notorious upper-class murder suspect years earlier. Hobbs wanted to stop the case before it went to trial and spent weeks dribbling out information to reporters, including the interesting fact that the "suicide note" found near the body was in all probability written by two different people. An investigator with the Ferris County Sheriff's Office noted that the handwriting in the last line did not match the rest of the note in several crucial respects. Other facts of the case were troubling, not least that the person suspected of removing and burying the body was nowhere to be found.

Though Bellamy had confessed to putting Helen Orlena into the water, the grand jury did not find sufficient evidence to bring a murder charge. If the district attorney was contemplating other charges, he didn't say.

Bellamy, who was on paid leave from his teaching position, resigned. Two months later, he moved away. He told friends he was going to Georgia.

Allen Simons Wallace was buried in Falba Cemetery, Walker County, just north of Huntsville, next to his father, mother, and uncle. Falba was one of the earliest Anglo settlements in Texas, but all that remained of it was the graveyard. An anonymous donor paid for a stone monument. Along with Allen's name, birth, and death dates was a simple motto:

SING TO THE LORD A NEW SONG

A short distance away in the oldest section, beside the low wall near the entrance, was an obscured but still readable headstone:

HAMISH MALLOCH
1835–1912

Above that was carved the square and compass.

Dan and Becky's film about Allen Wallace and Best Studios didn't win first place at the Dwight Awards that spring. However, *Last of the Little Studios* was well received and notched a win for best cinematography. There had been some tough competition, but Dan was happy, since the camera work had been his. Later, fortune would strike from a different direction, and the film would get a second chance.

Eventually, Becky got to make a documentary about Helen Orlena. Over the next few years, there would be others, of varying quality, but Becky's was the first and best. The film wasn't really hers, of course. It was produced by KDUR TV, in Duro, Texas, and directed by a filmmaker from San Antonio. Becky had gone to work for the station right after graduation as a minimally paid intern, but her enthusiasm and instincts for telling a story soon landed her on the crew for *Salt Grave: The Mystery of Helen Orlena.* Subsequently, they offered her a full-time job as a junior newswriter, and she joined the lowly ranks of bona fide local journalists.

The film was shown on local TV over two nights in October, then picked up by the statewide media. In the spring of 1974, it won a Donaldson Award for local reporting. It was subsequently nominated for a Peabody, where it received an honorable mention. Rebekah Paulson was listed on the credits as an assistant, though she had written much of the script.

In January, Harold and JJ returned to Duro for a court appearance. Their attorney worked out a deal with the DA's Office: They both pled guilty to failure to report a death in a timely manner and paid a small fine. Harold vowed never to set foot in the city again. JJ wouldn't go that far. For him, it was a little more complicated.

"Earth Is Crying" demos circulated among A&R people throughout the winter and into the new year. Several labels expressed interest, but the first to bite was Loquis Records, a small label founded in the '50s for spoken-word records, now expanding its repertoire.

Retitled "World Anthem," the song was released as a single in February 1973 and got some modest airplay in California and the Southwest, before dropping out of the rotations. However, it had been noticed by a national planning committee, and in April, "World Anthem" was named Official Song of Earth Day 1973.

That was enough to put the song back on the radio nationwide, and "Anthem" reentered the charts with a bang. It climbed to number one on the Billboard Hot 100 by the second week of June, where it stayed three weeks. It would remain on the charts for the rest of the summer. Reviews were mixed (one writer described the song as "boiling treacle"), but a review by Aksel Christensen in *Rolling Stone* opened the doors to acceptance by the hip crowd.

> *JJ Johns's first solo single in over three years is both spare in conception and grand in execution. Working with former Blue Zephyrs producer Harold Prensky and recording with unknown side musicians in a second-tier studio, Johns deliberately shuns the expectations of Nashville and Hollywood to craft a song like no other. "World Anthem" is a rare gem, at once joyful and heart-breaking.... There are many surprising moments, but my favorite comes in the crescendo during the chorus. Where we might expect thundering drums, we hear only Johns's lone voice, exulting: BOOM-BAH, BOOM-BAH....*

The B side of the record, a pretty ballad called "Blue-Eyed Becky," made it to number twenty-two for one week in July. Becky didn't let anyone know the song was about her.

After working on the Helen Orlena documentary for KDUR, she had settled into life among the ubiquitous underpaid. She rented an apartment in Duro and drove a used Datsun she bought with her own savings (having declined the family discount at Rochester Chevrolet).

She visited her family at least weekly. Martha and Peter were making new friends and were thriving. Mother was home and had returned to something like her old self. Medication quieted the voices in her head, but Becky thought it had left her dull, like a damp sponge.

On a warm, windy Thursday morning in late June 1974, Becky arrived at the newsroom early, as usual. The serious workday began around 9:00 a.m. with the daily staff meeting, but she tried to be at her desk no later than 8:15 so she could get her bearings and go over current assignments.

In her company mail slot were the usual press releases, a few ad flyers, and a note from her boss, the news manager. It said, *Miss Thump Comp moved to second day (Saturday). Make plans to travel Sat morn.—Stewart.*

The Miss Thump Competition was a beauty contest for girls fifteen to eighteen held in Knox City, Texas, as part of that town's annual Seedless Watermelon Festival. Becky sighed. She had volunteered to work the story—it was, after all, a story—but now she had to give up much of her weekend.

Becky started to return to her desk, but she noticed there was a small envelope lying flat in the mail slot. On the outside, it just said "Becky Paulson," with no stamp or address.

She showed it to one of the mail boys. "Where did this come from?"

"A guy hand-delivered it last night."

"Who?"

He shrugged. "A guy."

Inside the envelope was an unsigned note: "Can you meet me noon Thursday for lunch? Same place."

She laughed at the presumptuous of it. Essentially, it was saying *You know who I am and what I'm talking about.*

Well, she did. About 11:45, she told Stewart that she was going to lunch a little early but would make it up, got her Datsun out of the parking garage, and drove downtown to Fonde's cafeteria. The wind buffeted her little underpowered car.

Fonde's had a good-size lunch crowd. As she entered the large dining area, Bennie the organist was bouncing away at "Sugar Sugar" by the Archies.

She found him in the same booth, sitting behind a slice of butterscotch merengue pie. His sunglasses and car keys were on the table.

"Jerome Johnson," she said. "Isn't this a surprise?"

"Rebekah Paulson," said JJ.

"I thought you left town forever."

"Well, now I'm back. I drove my own car."

Becky scooted into the booth and sat. "So, you left a note in my mailbox? Why didn't you just call?"

"I got in town late last night. I know you go to work early, so I just dropped it at your office. I was surprised at how many people were working there."

"It's a twenty-four-hour deal," said Becky. "I write for the evening broadcasts, so I get to work pretty much normal hours."

"So . . . do you want to grab lunch? I thought I'd go ahead and start with dessert while I was waiting for you. There's no rule, you know."

Becky leaned forward so she could be heard over the tonewheel organ. "Yeah, I'm pretty hungry. But first, I want to know something. Why did you come back?"

"To see you, of course," said JJ. "The last time we spoke we were both in a big hurry. There's some things I needed to tell you in person."

"Why?"

"Because I needed to. That's the short answer."

"That's not a real reason," said Becky. "What's the long answer? Why me?"

"The long answer is the selfish one," said JJ. He paused to take a bite of merengue. "You might think I'm blowing smoke here, but the idea of not making a comeback—of the song not putting me back on the charts—I could have handled that. I'll be a musician until they make me stop, no matter how much I complain about it. It's all I know how to do."

"It sounds like you were preparing to fail," said Becky. "The one thing that struck me the first time we met: It was your self-confidence. You were so sure you'd have a hit record. I think it kind of rubbed off on everybody, even those locals you hired. It certainly worked on me."

"Confidence is a trick you play on yourself," said JJ. "You can't even think about what you'll have to go through if you don't convince yourself your plan will work. Well, it did. The song's a hit, and now it's on an album. It was ninety percent luck and good timing, but here I am."

"So, why did you come back?"

"I was getting to that. I can stand the thought of failing. Almost all of us fall flat on our faces or spend a lifetime almost making it. I accept that. But I can't imagine not having somebody to be with when the plans all fall through . . . or when everything works out perfectly and the world goes crazy."

Becky watched his face. He was so much more appealing when he wasn't hiding behind the ever-present sunglasses. She smiled at him and reached for his hands with both of hers. He put down his fork and gripped her tightly.

"Now that we've finished recording the album, I have to go on tour," said JJ. "We're starting on the East Coast next month, then working our way across the Midwest to California. I'm doing what I swore I'd never do again, go back on the road. Years ago, it would have been exciting, but now I'm just getting a little sick feeling in my stomach. But it has to be done."

"Are you saying you want me to go away with you, JJ Johns?" she said. "Be your road lady?"

"God, no!" said JJ. "I wouldn't ask that of you, Becky. I know you have work and everything."

"Yeah. I do. And the everything part is even bigger than the work part right now."

JJ let go of one hand so he could take another bite of sweet pie. He chewed thoughtfully, never taking his gaze off Becky. Finally, he looked down at his plate. "Okay, enough stare-eyes," he said. "Let me toss out a crazy idea. Next February, we're taking the tour to—are you ready for this?—England. Then, it's on to France and Belgium, and finally—drum roll, please—Greece."

"Sounds amazing, but then I won't see you for a long, long time," said Becky. "I was hoping things would start to slow down for you."

"Come with me, Becky."

"You mean to England?"

"Yes, and all the other places, too," said JJ. "I can hardly stand the thought of another European tour. I haven't done this in five years. I'm not young anymore. I need a leveling influence."

Becky chuckled. "Leveling influence? All this time I thought it was my body."

JJ laughed. "That, too. But seriously, Becky. Please consider this."

"I want to," said Becky. "I really do. It's not just my family. I've had a real job for barely a year. And I'm trying to get better at it, get real assignments, be taken seriously. I can't just drop everything and go."

"I've thought about that," said JJ. "What if you go to work for the tour? I'm telling you, there are stupid amounts of money being thrown around by the gray suits. We can give you a real job. Be the official documentarist. Make a film about the European tour. It would be great. It's not going to last forever, but this is an opportunity."

"I'm not a camera person," said Becky. "I'm trying to make it as a writer."

"Then *write* about the tour," said JJ. "You could write—I don't know—dispatches from the field. I know people at *Billboard,* at *Rolling Stone,* they love those kinds of stories, and the readers eat it up."

Becky took his other hand. "Oh, JJ. I'm sorry. How many girls get that kind of offer? But . . . I'm so sorry. You know, if I could . . ."

"February is a long time away," said JJ. "Maybe you'll think about it?"

"I'll think about it. But I don't want you to get your hopes up."

"Okay," said JJ. "I understand." He let go of her hands and picked up a napkin to wipe his mouth. Then he discreetly dabbed his eyes. "Just let me know one simple thing: Becky, do I stand a chance with you?"

"Long answer or short answer?"

"The short answer would probably hurt less."

"Okay, then," said Becky. "The short answer is yes. You have more than a chance, JJ Johns."

"I guess that will have to do," said JJ.

"Do you want to hear the long answer?"

"Sure."

"The long answer is yeeeeeeeeeeeeeeeeeeeessss!" Becky beamed a wide smile, like Doris Day.

JJ burst out laughing. People at nearby tables looked over at them.

"Good enough for me," said JJ. "Of course, you have to tend to your TV career. And you need to look after your family and help your mom. But . . . then you'll probably marry some local Christian boy. . . ."

Becky leaned all the way across the table, took his face in her hands, and planted a long, wet kiss on his mouth. At least a dozen Fonde's diners watched with intense curiosity. When she finally pulled away, she gave him a quick peck on the forehead and plopped back in her seat.

"All true, yes, yes, and yes," she said. "But not that marriage part. I think the Christian boys are done with me. Hey, are you ready to eat?"

JJ sat back and looked around the room. "Yep. Let's get in line." They got up from the booth. JJ turned and pointed at Bennie the organist. Bennie winked at him, stopped playing "Rainy Days and Mondays" in mid-phrase, and launched into another spritely tune.

"I don't know that song," said Becky.

"It's 'Take Me Back to Tulsa,'" said JJ, grinning with all his teeth.

"You set that up with him," said Becky.

"Of course I did," said JJ. "It would have been better if you'd said yes. And if you had known the song." He put one arm around Becky's shoulders and guided her toward the food line. As they passed the chirping organ, Bennie grinned and nodded at them, playing with all the abandon a cafeteria would allow.

"I think I have a friend for life," said JJ.

EPILOGUE

At the Focus of the Leys

"We are ready, Colonel," said Finn.

Malloch returned from his reverie. The red marker flag snapped in the warm morning wind. They had driven the flagpole into soft ground as close as they could to the rock and anchored it with guy lines. The wagons were packed, the equipment stowed, and the men waited.

"I'll be only a few moments," said Malloch.

The men of the survey crew wondered why the colonel had them relocate the flag that morning. Just the day before, he had seemed so certain of its correct placement. But no one questioned the decision, and they followed his instructions without complaint. The colonel was a learned and sophisticated man, one who inspired trust in those who worked with him.

After they had moved the marker flag, and as they struck camp and loaded the wagons, the men watched Malloch curiously. He stood atop the smooth surface of the rock, turning his body this way and that, lost in some other place or time. If any of them found the behavior odd, they didn't say so.

Malloch was trying to see the future. And if he stood just right, at the place where energies met, he could almost do so. The hairs on the back of his neck rose, his old war wound throbbed, and he could hear the beating of his own heart. It was as if electricity were flowing from his feet to his scalp. Finn stood nearby, awaiting instructions.

"There could be a great public edifice here someday," said Malloch. "And it should face this way, northeast."

Finn understood, or thought he did. "The rock would certainly provide an unmovable foundation for a courthouse or city hall," he said.

"No," said Malloch. "I believe the stone should remain open to the sun and wind. Where we stand could be the center of a large square, and the town may grow around it." He pointed southwest. "They should construct the public building over there, facing in this direction." He turned his body ninety degrees. "On this side, perhaps, a library, and this way"—he turned again, so he faced east—"could be a lodge or temple. All streets should extend outward from the center point. There could be a great city, a planned city, right here."

Try as he might, Finn could not envision civilization in this blasted place. Without rain, a reliable water source, or good soil, how could that be? How could it become even a dusty way-stop, much less a city with streets, trolleys, shops, and schools, thousands of citizens?

On the other hand, great men of earlier times had stood in similar unpromising places and seen the future—Romulus on a barren hill over the Tiber River or King Theseus upon the rocky Acropolis. Nothing great ever began without someone first imagining it. To remain unbroken, the adamantine chain had first to be forged.

The men were eager to depart, to see their families, to sleep in soft beds, to celebrate their payday with food and drink. The mules stamped and snorted. However, no one would try to hurry the colonel, so they waited as he stared off into the distance.

Malloch's eyes were keen for a man in his eighth decade, and it seemed that the longer he stood on the rock, the sharper his vision became. Again, he turned himself all the way around, marveling at how far he could see, as if his old eyes were spyglasses.

Just as he had made up his mind to step down off the rock, something far away caught his attention. Something that simply could not be.

"Mr. Finn, do you see that?" he asked. He extended his arm and pointed northwest.

Finn turned to look where Malloch had indicated. He saw nothing remarkable. A landscape of loose pale stones, short and rugged plants that had adapted to the gypsum desert, century plants, mounds of low pink crinklemat, ringstem wildflowers. In the far distance was a glint of reflection, either salty lake water or a mirage from the hot desert air.

"I see nothing unusual, Colonel," said Finn.

"No, look there," said Malloch. "I see a person, walking. Right over there. I believe it is a woman. Look."

Finn squinted into the distance but saw nothing out of the ordinary.

"Mr. Finn, are my field glasses packed away?"

"Yes, Colonel, but I know where they are," said Finn. "I can find them quickly." Finn went to the lead wagon and stepped up onto the running boards, bending over to unlatch and open a wooden box. He retrieved a leather case, opened it, and removed the brass field glasses.

While he waited, Malloch gazed to the northwest. It *was* a woman. He could see her clearly, walking away from them, moving with a quick stride. Her long hair swayed, and her arms swung by her side. She was perhaps a thousand yards distant. Malloch did not want to take his eyes off her. Was she real or an apparition? How could anyone be out there? He looked down, rubbed his eyes, and looked again. Now he saw only the shimmer of rising air.

Finn stepped up onto the rock and handed Malloch the field glasses, which he quickly raised to his eyes and pointed exactly where he thought he had seen the woman. He adjusted the focus. There was nothing human out there and no animal either. A large red yucca plant, with leaves like sharp swords, was in his line of sight. He would not have mistaken that for a person. Or would he?

He scanned back and forth with the glasses, panning across the horizon. There was no one. He shook his head.

"I'm sorry, Mr. Finn," said Malloch. "I was wrong. It must be the sun." He handed the field glasses back to Finn, who raised them up to his own eyes for a few moments. Where the colonel had been looking, Finn saw only bone-colored desert and white patches of salt, with a few hardy desert plants adapted to the hot, dry soil. He spotted something moving a few degrees to the right, very far away. It was a whirlwind of dust skittering and dancing across the desert floor.

"Colonel, I believe what you saw was a dust devil," said Finn.

Malloch stared a few moments longer, as if his bare eyes might somehow see what the expensive field glasses could not. Then he stepped down off the rock and brushed the dust from his trousers. Some day, he might return to this place, but now it was time to leave.

"All right," he said. "I'm ready."

Afterword

Like my previous West Texas stories, this one is a yarn. By that, I mean you may find it entertaining (I hope), but you will not glean anything useful. In a novel packed with faux details, it's important to emphasize that. For instance, you will learn nothing whatsoever about Freemasonry. And, as I always disclaim, there is no city of Duro. More pertinent to this story, there is nothing significant about the location 31°31'31"N and 103°10'3"W. There is no Pyle Monument, no Wiberg Pluton, and no salt lake in that part of West Texas. There is a natural lake called La Sal del Rey in South Texas, about twenty miles north of McAllen. It's an important bird sanctuary but nothing like the place described in this book.

The idea that the Earth is divided into grids of magnetic and life energy—and that the points where these "ley lines" cross create vortexes of energy—is an ancient and busy subject and about which I am agnostic. A quick internet search reveals complex world maps, inspired by Buckminster Fuller's unified vector geometry, wherein the globe is divided into "great circles," pentagons, triangles, and vertices. It all sounds very scientific until you dive into the details, where madness lies. Suffice it to say that many people who have thought hard about these things believe a significant vortex lies out in West Texas. Most sources put it in Pecos or Reeves Counties, and more than a few place it right on the intersection of US 285 and Texas Highway 652 in Orla. This part of the state was completely ignored until the hydrofracking revolution resulted in the state's most annoying four-way stop sign, with oilfield service trucks sometimes backed up for miles just trying to get through it. So, in one sense, I suppose it is an energy vortex.

The seed for the Earth energy parts of the book was a family ancestor on my wife's side who, along with partners—all Huntsville Freemasons—purchased land in Reeves County, Texas, just after the turn of the century. No primary literature about the deal has survived—no letters, diaries, or legal documents. But we have good reason to believe they bought the land based on its location on the spectral Earth grid. It certainly had little else going for it until oil and gas changed the equation. Modern Freemasons seem to have lost interest in ley lines and vortexes, at least in the US.

Regional music recording in West Texas experienced something of a golden age in the late 1950s and into the '60s. Norman Petty's NorVaJak Studio in Clovis (which isn't quite in Texas but might as well be), along with other small-town recording studios such as High Fidelity House in Big Spring, Checkmate Studio in Amarillo, and the Palm Room in Lubbock, were able to compete with the big-city venues by offering lower costs and personal service. They realized that clock-watching is a creativity killer, so musicians were often charged by the song rather than the hour. Regular business schedules were ignored, and tape rolled long after the clubs closed and normal people were in bed. It was a legendary time, but it didn't last. By the mid '60s, most of the great talents like Roy Orbison, Buddy Knox, Jimmy Bowen, and others had been lured away (poached) by the big Memphis and Nashville labels with their A-list studios.

Among the last entries in that early wave was the Nebraska folk-rock duo Zager and Evans, who arrived in Odessa in 1968. With producer Tommy Allsup, formerly of Buddy Holly's touring band, they cobbled together an orchestra from members of the local symphony, gathered everybody at Allsup's Westex Studio, and recorded the world's least likely number one hit, "In the Year 2525 (Exordium & Terminus)." It's a great true story that went mostly unnoticed at the time. There were a few other notable projects at the same studio—the Lubbock trio The Flatlanders did some of their earliest recordings there—but the era was winding down. At the time I'm writing this, that little studio still exists, under different ownership.

Homeschooling is so common today that we often forget how unusual and controversial it once was. In the 1970s, homeschoolers were rebels and outliers, frequently colliding with local school districts. While the US Supreme Court has never specifically ruled on homeschooling per se, several historic cases removed any doubt that parents may educate their children as they see fit, while leaving the details up to the states. In Texas, since 1987, parents have been allowed to homeschool to their hearts' content, provided the curricula include reading, spelling, grammar, math, and "a study of good citizenship." One hopes that science and history find their way in as well.

This is the last of the "Duro" books, I am fairly certain. The settings for my newer projects have followed me south and east across the arid hills of Central Texas to the humid plains of the Gulf Coast. I've lived here for decades now, long enough to set down roots, and the people and places deserve their own stories.

I hope I'm up to it.

– Henry D. Terrell, August 2021

Henry D. Terrell was born and raised in West Texas. He is a retired business writer and editor who lives with his wife in Houston.

Other fiction titles by the author:

Desert Discord
Wait Till I Come Down
Headfirst Off the Caprock

Contact: Books@HenryDTerrell.com